THE LAST WICKED ROGUE

The League of Rogues - Book 9

LAUREN SMITH

This book is a work of fiction. Names, characters, places, and incidents are the product of the author's imagination or are used fictitiously. Any resemblance to actual events, locales, or persons, living or dead, is coincidental.

ISBN: 978-1-947206-50-2 (e-book edition)

ISBN: 978-1-947206-51-9 (print edition)

ISBN: 978-1-947206-52-6 (hardback)

For Cambridge,
the university which inspired the stories of the League of Rogues
and changed my life forever.

PROLOGUE

London, December 1821

The deafening crack of ice breaking was like a gunshot. It halted Charles Humphrey, the seventh Earl of Lonsdale, dead in his tracks. He'd been racing across the frozen Thames, twilight bleeding over the wintry landscape ahead of him, creating eerie shadows that led to the figure just beyond his reach.

"Stop!" Charles shouted. Pain and rage filled him to the point that nothing else existed within him. He was a beast driven with one purpose: to kill the man he pursued.

His own brother.

But the sound of breaking ice was all around him now, echoing across the Thames. The man ahead of him stopped, skidding briefly along the ice. Charles did the same, listening for another warning sound, but he could see no obvious cracks in the surface.

"Not another step, brother," the man warned, his voice firm and cold.

The rage that had momentarily been pushed aside by the threat of breaking ice now came roaring back. His fingers curled into fists.

"Brother? You dare call me that? You took *everything* from me. She was my world." The fury inside him fell like a black curtain over his vision. He dared not close his eyes. If he did he would see her, his love, dying in his arms, and it would weaken him. His anger was his only strength now.

"It's no less than you deserve. You took *my* world from me," his brother practically growled. "You and your father destroyed my life."

"He was your father too," Charles hissed. "He was trying to save you."

"He left me to save myself! You are a disgrace."

Charles's fury was just barely controlled. "I've never had a problem with the man I am, but you? You are a murderer. If we're listing sins, yours will come first." Charles took another step toward him.

"*Murderer?* How *dare* you—"

Crack! The ice broke, and his brother cried out and plunged into the icy depths below.

"No!" Charles rushed toward the hand sticking up from the break in the ice, and like a damned fool, he shot down into the water as well.

Darkness, ice, and cold enveloped him. He struggled as he saw another figure in the murky water. He reached for him, his fingers brushing the tip of the man's shoulder, but the current was too strong. They were going to die. Every nightmare he'd ever had since university was coming true. This was going to be the end.

At least then he would be with her, his darling wife.

The man ahead of him choked, his pale face contorting as he drew in a lungful of water.

He should have always known it would end like this. Death in the dark for both of them. Only this time, he'd killed his own brother and his wife, because the past wouldn't let go of him.

Perhaps he had been the villain of this story all along...

I

League Rule Number 1:

A house divided against itself cannot stand. Nor can our friendship. We must stand together, or divided, we fall.

Excerpt from the *Quizzing Glass Gazette*, December 11, 1821, the Lady Society column:

The Quizzing Glass Gazette *regrets to inform readers that there will be no Lady Society column this week. We trust her readers will understand and hope she will return to us in the near future. We know many of you have written to Lady Society regarding the fate of Charles Humphrey, the Earl of Lonsdale. We hope and pray that Lady Society returns with news regarding this particular bachelor.*

. . .

Dear Lady Society,

It is a national tragedy that your column has been suspended at this particular time as it is with great curiosity and much trepidation that I write to you in horror of what my dear husband witnessed last night while returning home to me from a business meeting near Lewis Street. While strolling along the roadside, my dashing husband happened upon a disheveled lady in a striking red gown who was, according to my stalwart husband, running away from—and this is most unnerving, Lady Society, but she was trying to escape Lord Lonsdale!

It pains me to say this, but I do believe the incident with the swans alluded to in your column is not the only rakish behavior of this rogue! Indeed, my charming husband insisted Lord Lonsdale was most pressed in the middle of the night, looking for this lady who was running about barging into sober men of consequence like my husband!

And indeed, Lady Society, that wasn't even the most unusual bit of information my husband relayed to me! He did recall seeing, after the lady disappeared and Lord Lonsdale was already on his own way (home, I presume, to make himself suitable for courting), a most dangerous-looking bloke who skulked after Lord Lonsdale rather menacingly. What a horror!

Obviously, the only solution is to get Lord Lonsdale wed as soon as possible! If you could work some of your magic, Lady Society, as you have with his friends and others before him, I do think Lord Lonsdale needs your help about now.

Also, if you could point him in the direction of my lovely second daughter. She is quite adept at the piano, and her needlework is impeccable—though do not bring up her French, for it is abysmal.

Yours,

A Desperate Society Mama

Charles leaned forward in his chair, two rows back from the front of the audience, listening to Miss Matilda Brower sing, plotting how he might find a way to have the pianoforte beside her mysteriously drop out the nearest window onto the street below.

As she warbled the notes to some atrocious melody, Charles could actually feel his mind atrophy from a lack of proper stimulation. There were a dozen other things he could be doing right now, a dozen other *women* he could be seducing, including that lovely young widow Mrs. Forsythe, who was eyeing him over her fan just one row behind and to the left.

He shot the naughty widow a wink, and her fan fluttered a little faster. But there was no way he could simply stand up and walk out of the room, not while Miss Brower was still performing her impression of someone strangling a cat with a set of bagpipes.

Bloody musicales.

There were easier, more merciful ways to kill a man than forcing him to sit through a performance by a number of young ladies who had not an ounce of talent between them. He clenched his fingers around the evening's program and stifled a groan. He needed to escape, but that would require a distraction.

One row in front of him, his close friend, Godric St. Laurent, the Duke of Essex, was nodding off. How the man managed to fall asleep during the high-pitched warbling, Charles couldn't begin to fathom.

Charles carefully picked up the cane propped against the chair beside his. The cane's owner, Cedric, Viscount Sheridan, was staring off into empty space and didn't notice its absence. With a gleeful grin, Charles positioned the cane under the seat of Godric's chair and gave it a hard *thwack!*

Godric leapt off his chair as though bitten by a viper. "*God's blood!*" The dreadful cat-strangling sounds died off abruptly as everyone turned to stare at him.

"Er...I...say...bloody good music." Godric cleared his throat and sat back down, smoothing his waistcoat, his face now ruddy. Charles snickered to himself, but it was loud enough in the sudden silence that he was heard. The auburn-haired beauty sitting next to Godric turned to glare at him, violet eyes blazing.

"Keep it up, Charles, and I shall make it my priority to get you married. If only to put a leash on your behavior."

The woman, Godric's wife, Emily, had never made a threat she did not carry out, which was a great feat for a nineteen-year-old duchess.

"Not likely, my lady," he snorted. "If I stopped being myself, then you would all be bored to tears in a fortnight."

Emily arched a brow in challenge, and then the dreadful caterwauling began again.

Well, he'd had quite enough of this. Distractions be damned. Charles ignored the shocked gasps of those around him as he hastily exited with a rakish grin at the startled Miss Brower. Once outside, he leaned back against the wall, his palms pressed against the blue satin wallpaper.

"My lord?" a footman inquired. Charles glanced at him.

"Fetch my hat and coat. Bring a coach around."

He had to get out of this bloody house, get away from all this nonsense with balls and parties. The social amusements he'd once enjoyed were losing their appeal by the day. His breath shortened as a wave of panic flared to life. This past year he'd watched his friends all marry and start having children. They were moving on, leaving their days of being young and reckless behind.

They're leaving me behind.

The thought of facing the rest of his life alone had never bothered him before. He'd always had his dear friends, the League of Rogues, at his side. In that bloom of youth, he'd never once considered that he would be the last bachelor standing. Now, with marriages and christenings filling up his days, the pace of his life had been dramatically disrupted. And one thing had become startling clear. He was alone.

A hollow ache of loneliness descended upon his shoulders. There was not much he could do about it of course, except find a young wife and sire heirs. But Charles had seen the outcomes of men choosing their partners poorly and had hoped to avoid that fate.

He'd also never experienced the dreaded sensation of being a fool in love. It had turned his friends from rogues whose behavior was tolerated only because of their wealth or standing into gentlemen almost overnight. That transformation terrified Charles but also intrigued him. He may not want to fall in love, but he damned well wouldn't marry unless he was. Better to be a besotted fool who loved one's wife than the alternative.

Emily could tease all she liked about getting him married, but it wouldn't happen, not with any woman he knew in London, and he knew them all.

He closed his eyes a moment, dispelling his anxiety before he headed to the front door and met the footman who'd retrieved his hat and coat.

He left the townhouse and headed for his waiting coach. His valet, Tom Linley, would normally be waiting for him, but he'd given Tom a much-needed evening off. Given Charles's strained relationship with his own brother, the boy had become something akin to family over the last year. Someone he could trust with anything. With the gap between him and his friends ever widening, Tom was fast becoming the *only* one he could trust.

He couldn't help but wonder what the lad did when he wasn't tasked with following him about. The boy's shyness precluded any notion that he would be visiting a house of ill-repute or a gambling hell. More likely, Tom had spent the day with little Katherine. With a baby sister to care for, much of his spare time no doubt centered around her.

"Where to, my lord?" the driver inquired.

Charles glanced about the wintry roads. There was only place he could go to clear his head.

"Lewis Street."

The driver's brows rose, but he didn't object. It was a rather dangerous part of London, and most men avoided it. Thieves, murderers, and all manner of evil-minded men dwelt in the tunnels below Lewis Street.

In the past, Charles would have headed to a pleasure haunt, the rest of his friends in tow, and they would have spent the evening drinking and carousing in the company of London's finest courtesans. But everything had changed. Now they wouldn't come with him even if they wanted to. The despair of that thought, of being abandoned by them, made his throat tight. A recklessness soon possessed him. He knew he shouldn't go to Lewis Street alone, but he didn't care.

He climbed into the coach, and it jerked into motion soon after he took his seat.

It was late, half past eleven when the coach stopped on Lewis Street.

"Shall I wait for you, sir?" the driver asked.

"Not with a den of thieves nearby." Charles knew that the rookeries near the tunnels were full of men who would slit a man's throat if they thought they could get a penny for it. He was sure that when he was done, he could walk a few streets away and hire another coach to get home.

"Very good, my lord." The driver flicked the reins, and the two dappled grays rushed away, leaving him alone.

He straightened his hat, and with a dark grin he ducked into the shadow of the nearest doorway. He rapped his knuckles on the ancient, weathered wood. A panel at eye level slid open, and a burly man with a thick beard and hard, dark eyes scanned him from head to toe. The panel slammed shut and the door opened, the burly man allowed Charles to brush past him. From the street, the building looked like a small warehouse, but it was in fact a portal to a massive underground world of tunnels that led to rooms where men could box and wager without rules or interference. Even the Bow Street Runners feared coming down here, and they only ever did so in force.

Charles had been coming here more and more of late, the wild atmosphere and chaos feeding something dark inside him that he couldn't explain. Every rage, every fear that built up inside him, he could turn loose here. And then, for a brief few days, he would feel free.

"Ring three is available," the doorman said as they

traveled deeper through the craggy walled tunnels, which were said to date back to the Tudors. The main cavern held three large boxing rings, two currently in use.

In the third, a tall brute with meaty fists roused the crowd as he called for a challenger to face him. He was a thick-necked man with hair cut almost to his scalp, and his thick lips were evidence of a face that had been taking hits for years.

Yes, that man would give him a good night's work.

Charles cupped a hand around his mouth. "Oi!" His shout carried across the crowd. The man in the ring paused, and the crowd quieted as they all faced him.

"Two hits and you're down," Charles announced as he removed his hat and coat, giving them to a scrawny lad who stared up at him with wide eyes.

"Tuppence if you hold on to these for me."

The boy nodded anxiously, and Charles patted his shoulder before he climbed up onto the platform of the ring.

"Two hits?" the man growled. "Bit cocksure, ain't cha?"

"Absolutely, old boy." Charles rolled up the clean white sleeves of his shirt, baring his forearms.

The man shrugged. "Yer funeral."

"And the stakes?" Charles asked as he took his stance. He didn't need money, but winning off these fools was intensely satisfying. He usually donated the winnings to a worthy cause, or on the rare occasion his doctor, who patched him up after the rougher fights.

The other man laughed harshly. "All right. Whoever wins can take that pretty bit of muslin over there home."

Charles frowned. "Pardon?"

The man jerked his head to a woman who was suddenly pulled into the open as two men dragged her to the front of the crowd. This was not normal, even down here.

The woman wore a deep-red dress and had the most beautiful blonde hair he'd ever seen, caught in a loose Grecian style with ribbons threaded through it. Her creamy skin had been marred where it looked as though she'd been struck, and she had the purest blue eyes he'd ever seen.

Despite the red dress and the torchlit tunnels of this hellish hole, she looked like an angel. A terrified one. She struggled, but the gag in her mouth muffled her cries. Rage burst inside Charles, and he faced his opponent. His body spiked with a renewed vigor for the fight. He wouldn't have wagered to win a willing woman, but to rescue an unwilling one? Absolutely.

"There are plenty of ladies on the streets. You had to go and take one that was not for sale?"

The brute nodded. "Much better to hear 'em scream. I like it when they fight."

"Well, that does it," Charles declared in a disgusted tone. "I was going to let you have it easy since I was bored, but now you've gone and upset me."

The man leered. "The fancy gent thinks he can take

me, eh?" The crowd around them roared with excitement, but Charles paid little attention. He instead focused on the man in front of him, the way he moved, the slightly uneven gait that forced him to favor his left leg, possibly an old injury. His breathing indicated he hadn't fully rested from his last fight. These were useful things to know.

Charles let go of every thought outside of the ring and gave himself over to the moment. The brute raised his hands and without warning lunged for Charles, swinging a meaty fist. He wanted to end this quickly rather than study his opponent. Foolish.

Charles danced back, letting the blow pass. His opponent stumbled forward, and Charles gave his arse a hearty kick as the man stumbled right by him. The men in the crowd cheered for Charles, and this only enraged the brute, as it was intended to.

They danced, a mongoose and a king cobra, rounding each other counterclockwise, Charles carefully avoiding each blow, forcing the man to favor his injured leg, letting the man tire himself out as he stumbled again and again.

"Too much...of a bleeding coward...to hit me," the man panted, wiping sweat from his eyes.

When the man came at him this time, Charles swung. Hard. His fist struck the man in the jaw, and he went down like a stone, landing in a heap in the wood ring. He didn't move except for the faint rise and fall of his back as he breathed.

Didn't even need a second blow, did I?

The crowds around the ring roared, and Charles waved them off as he climbed down the platform to free the woman. She was breathing hard, eyes wide. As he got closer, he noticed that there was something about her, like a half-remembered dream. He shot glares at the men still holding her, and their hands fell away. He expected the woman to melt into him and cover him with grateful kisses.

That didn't happen. Instead, she struck out, kneeing one man in the groin before she punched the second in the throat.

This angel could fight—an archangel without the flaming sword. He was about ready to applaud her efforts, but then she whirled on him next. He barely caught her fist before it landed, and he tugged her against him, using his body to still hers.

"Easy, love, I'm not going to hurt you. I won't let anyone here hurt you." He gazed down into her eyes, feeling strange, like those twin pools were drawing him in. "I..." He cleared his throat and she looked away, breaking the powerful spell.

"I'm going to release you now. Please believe me, I mean you no harm." He let go of her, and she withdrew from him. But she didn't go far because of the lingering group of men around the boxing ring.

"I need to leave." Her tone was breathy, reminding him of how girls often spoke during their first season in the *ton*, trying too hard to sound like they belonged. She tried to flee, but Charles caught one of her hands.

"Not that way. Please, allow me to play the gentleman and escort you safely from this place."

The woman looked away but reluctantly nodded, allowing him to lead her back the way he'd come. He curled his fingers around her slender hand and marveled at how wonderful it felt. No doubt this was all simply due to the exhilaration of having rescued someone, but he still intended to enjoy it.

He saw the boy he'd left his belongings with and waved him over, handing over the promised tuppence. He noticed the woman smile at the lad as he scampered off. Did his angel have a soft spot for children? He was much the same. The boys in the tunnels faced a hard and dangerous life. Every bit of coin mattered.

"You know the way out, sir?" she asked as they passed through the crowds, who were already waiting for the next match.

"I do." They walked in silence through the now empty system of tunnels, but he kept alert in case the brute had friends who did not believe in the spirit of fair play. It was not easy, however, given how distracting it was to simply hold this woman's hand.

Finally, they reached the steep incline that would return them to the surface, and a chill wind from the outside teased his nose. The gatekeeper was still at his post by the door to Lewis Street. He opened it without a word and allowed them to pass.

Charles blinked as they stepped out from under the eaves. Rain was misting down now, soft and icy. His angel had no cloak and wouldn't get far in this weather without catching a chill.

"I'll call a hackney to take you to wherever you wish," he said as he offered her his coat. She waved it away, and in doing so deftly freed her hand from his. The loss of contact filled him with a strange desperation. He didn't want her to leave, he wanted... What did he want? He wanted her, wanted to take her home, to warm her by a fire, to explore the mysteries gleaming in her eyes.

"Thank you for the rescue, but I really must go." She wiped a hand over her eyes, dashing the rain from her dark gold lashes, and hurried away.

"Wait!" He ran after her into the street. "You must at least tell me your name." He flashed her his most devastating smile, the one known to send flutters through any feminine heart within a hundred feet of him.

The melancholy expression she returned was like a punch to his gut. She seemed unaffected by him, or worse, unimpressed. She had just escaped a terrifying fate, he supposed, but still, it was not the reaction he'd expected.

She paused, the rain darkening her red gown into a deep berry color that clung to her skin. "My name..."

"My reward for your rescue," Charles said, redoubling

his efforts. "Though I could argue that was reward enough in itself."

He swallowed down the shame that was growing inside him. After what she had been through, she needed a white knight on a charger to protect her, not a damned rogue. Yet he could not stop himself. She had bewitched him.

At last she broke the silence. "Lily."

"Lily," he echoed. The name was soft, delicate, and feminine, much like the way she spoke. "May I come to call on you? When...when you are suitably recovered from your adventure, of course." The idea of letting this mysterious woman go didn't feel right. He feared that if he let her go it would be the biggest mistake of his life.

"I don't think that would be a good idea, my lord."

"How did you know I'm a lord?"

She smiled again. "Your opponent was right. You are too fancy of a gent." She let her words reflect the brute's accent, and it made Charles laugh.

"I suppose I am." He glanced down at the silver and gold embroidered waistcoat. "But I'd like very much to be *your* fancy gent."

Her smile, so oddly bittersweet, tore at his heart. For a moment he thought she would run away into the night, but instead she caught him by the shoulders and kissed him.

He was startled, just for a second, before he gripped her by the waist and took control. It was a moment of fire and light, like a jolt to his system. He was a master of seduction, had built his life upon creating perfect kisses, and yet at this moment he felt like a boy fumbling with his first maiden. It wasn't possible, yet here he was.

After a long moment their mouths broke apart, the rain still coming down in a light mist as she shivered against him. He rested his forehead against hers, their ragged breath matching in perfect rhythm. Every sense came alight as he struggled to burn this memory into his mind. Her body pressed to his, the blue of her eyes like sapphires, the velvet of her lips, and the rasp of her breath.

"There is your reward," she said.

"Please, let me escort you home," he begged. Charles feared that she would vanish if he let her go, that he had somehow lost his fight and this entire moment was but a dream as he lay knocked out on the floor. A woman like this could not be real.

She pushed away, glancing at something behind him, startled with fear. Charles turned to face the dark mews behind them, fists raised, ready to take on whatever might be coming after them from the Lewis Street tunnels.

But nothing was there, only darkness and rain.

He turned back and found the mews was empty. Lily was gone.

He glanced up at the skies, letting the icy rain coat his face. Perhaps it really had been a dream. How could a moment like that have been real? To find the perfect woman only to lose her the very same night.

2

Lily hurried up the steps to her small room. The drunken revelry of the gambling hell one floor below was now a distant roar. She slid her key into the lock, blinking rain out of her eyes as she continued to shiver. Her gown was soaked clear through and possibly ruined.

This tiny room was her only true place of refuge, with its small wooden bed frame tucked away in one corner and a dusty brick fireplace in the opposite. It would be damp tonight, and she'd have to use all of her blankets to warm up after she removed her gown.

Tonight had not gone as planned. So much had gone wrong, and she didn't want to think about it. She trudged over to the fireplace and retrieved the flint and kindling from a tin box on the dresser. Once a healthy flame was burning, she added a few logs until a steady blaze warmed the room. She rubbed her arms, desperate for warmth. Those brutes in the tunnel had ripped her cloak from her when they had grabbed her from Vauxhall Gardens.

Of course, that had been expected. Everything had been arranged so that she would be taken into the Lewis Street tunnels, where the head of a local gang of smugglers was known to favor willing victims inside the ring and unwilling victims in bed—not that she would have allowed anything to go that far. She could handle herself well enough. Once she had what she wanted, escape would be easy. Everything had been going according to plan...

And then *he* came along and ruined everything. How was she ever going to explain this?

"I trust you had a productive evening?" a cold voice asked from the shadows behind her.

Lily grabbed the poker and spun to face the man who had spoken. She had been sure the room was empty when she arrived. When she realized who it was, she relaxed. But only a little. Her master, Sir Hugo Waverly, was a cold-hearted bastard and did not tolerate failure.

She raised her chin and answered nonchalantly. "No more than was expected."

The last thing she wanted was for this man to see her afraid. Fear was a weakness, and he killed those who were foolish enough to show any.

Hugo chuckled. "And the mission? Was it a success?"

Lily frowned. "I learned a little from the ones who abducted me. They didn't seem to care what they said once we were in the tunnels. However, their leader lost the wager, and I wasn't about to leave with the victor."

"No, of course not. Well, even the best plans are subject to the whims of chance, I suppose."

That was unusually understanding of him. "Why are you here?" Lily sounded bold, unafraid, but everything about this man filled her with deep fear. He'd caused her so much pain over the last few years, playing the puppet master, jerking her marionette strings at his whim. He'd taught her how to fight, how to deceive, how to survive, and she'd become stronger for it, but it didn't erase the truth that he was in control of her life.

"You failed to send me your weekly report on Lonsdale's movements."

Lily flinched. Her primary duty was to watch the Earl of Lonsdale and report his movements back to her master. She'd always been prompt, never showing any hint of distaste at the work.

But over time something had shifted. She had glimpsed the real earl, Charles, the rogue with a heart of gold, the man who would jump into a fray to aid his companions, no matter the cost. That man had caused her to rethink her duty, yet she pressed on, because she had no alternative.

"I would have sent it on time if you hadn't summoned me for tonight's task."

"That sounds like an excuse," he countered, but seemed to let the matter drop. It burned at her how she was always at his beck and call—or, as he put it, "at the service of the nation." She could also tell when he knew there was more to be said than she was telling him. The silence gnawed at her, drawing out the truth.

"There was a complication," she said at last.

"Oh?" He didn't sound surprised, more like he already knew everything and was waiting for her to confirm it.

"Lonsdale was there tonight."

Her master growled and her body tensed, ready to brace herself for any blow he might deal. "What does he know?"

"Nothing. I believe it was an unfortunate coincidence." She kept her voice calm, even though she was stiff with fear. "We know he enjoys pugilism, including the unregulated matches. Lonsdale rescued me from those men in the boxing tunnels."

"Rescued?" he snorted.

"From his perspective. I eluded him once he escorted me out of the tunnels. But...I told him my name." She saw his eyes flare and quickly added, "Only my given name."

"That was foolish. I thought you were more careful than that. Still..." Her master stroked his chin, a gleam in his dark eyes. The last time she'd seen that look, she'd learned of his plans to have Audrey Sheridan, a young lady Charles was friends with, murdered in France. That plan hadn't played out as he'd intended, and Audrey had escaped with her life, but it didn't stop Lily from worrying now.

"Would you say he found you...enticing?"

Lily remained still. If she showed any emotion, he would only use it against her.

"He likes women, as you well know," Lily said coolly.

He scowled and grabbed her roughly by the arm, shoving her up against the wall. She bit back a cry of pain as her back collided with the wooden slats. For a moment she was younger, more naïve, her body pressed facedown on a bed, her throat raw from screams and tears soaking the bedclothes.

Would she ever be free of this man?

His face pressed up against hers, and she felt her heart pound in her chest. "Do not think yourself clever. I taught you all that you know." He stepped back, releasing her so that she dropped to her knees.

"He hungers for you, like any man would." She nearly curled into herself, trying to make herself less visible to the predator he was. But that Lily had died years before; the one who remained had learned the value of strength.

"I think we will use that to our advantage," he began.

"No. I have done your bidding on *every* matter. I will not—"

Smack!

Her master struck her hard across the face. "I have given you more than most women in your position could ever hope for, and you will continue to do my bidding until I have no further use for you. Do you understand?"

Lily raised a trembling hand to her lips where she

tasted blood. He paced the room a moment before settling back on his heels, his powerful frame a menacing presence in the tiny bedchamber.

He suddenly let out a mirthless laugh, hit by some dark inspiration. "Yes, of course. You will be my young innocent cousin from the country. Melanie is in Cornwall for Christmas, and she won't see you."

Lily nodded numbly. "What would you have me do?" she asked, surrendering to the inevitable. Whenever Hugo wanted something or someone, he got it. Resistance would be futile. Had this been any other man, she would've struck back, but not with him. He held a bond over her that could not be broken.

"Lord Merton is throwing a ball in a week's time. Since he's acquainted with Lonsdale and his ilk, I expect they will be invited. That may work to our favor." He retrieved his cane from against the wall and tapped it against the floorboards, a habit she recognized whenever he was plotting. Each thud of the metal tip vibrated within her like nails being pounded into a coffin.

"I will let it be known that my cousin is in town and she and I will be in attendance. Once there"—he pinned her with a look—"he will realize you're the Lily he rescued. Knowing your relation to me, he may seek to gain information about me through you. I suppose I could provide you with something useful to dangle as bait. Then, once he's completely infatuated with you, we strike." These last words were uttered with such delight that she nearly tossed her accounts. He was inhuman at times, the way he viewed everyone as chess pieces in his own twisted game.

He stroked his chin as his focus turned back to her. "We'll have to pretty you up, of course. New gowns, jewelry, and the like. Perhaps a reminder on the ways of seduction. I suspect you are out of practice."

Lily shivered, unable to control her fear. If her master thought he would be the one to teach her seduction, he was wrong. She would *never* let him touch her like that again. Spying for him was one thing, but he would never take anything else from her again.

"You forget. I know Lonsdale better than he knows himself." Just as she'd known that kissing him tonight would distract him, muddle his thoughts and give her a chance to flee.

But it had also been an intense, wonderful kiss. A dream she hadn't wanted to wake from. "I know his likes and his desires. There is nothing you or anyone else can teach me that I don't already know."

Something about her tone must have had an effect. He seemed flustered somehow, muttering as he faced the door. "I've been here too long. I should go."

Her shoulders slumped, and she let out the breath she'd been holding. But before she could relax, her master whipped back around.

"And you." He growled the words so darkly that blood

pounded in her ears. "You still have to return to your first duty."

Lily nodded. "Yes, sir."

He turned to the bed where she'd left a pile of valet clothes and a wig. "We cannot let him suspect anything is amiss. Can we, Mr. Linley?"

Without another word, Sir Hugo Waverly slammed the door behind him as he left.

3

Tom Linley.

It was the name she'd assumed over a year ago when she'd been sent to Berkley's club to gain Charles's trust. The thin, scrappy lad known as Tom Linley did not exist; she was Lily Linley, daughter of a country gentleman and mother to a little girl she had to pretend was her baby sister. And she would protect that child at any cost, even if she had to destroy a good man to do so. She had no choice.

As much as she wished she could refuse, she couldn't. Nor could she confess to Charles. He could not protect her, even if he wished to. He did not understand how much of his life and those of his friends Hugo had infiltrated. Even she did not know the full extent, just enough to realize there was no escape from him. She could not win his game; she could only hope to survive it.

Lily sagged against the wall once Hugo had left. Her legs buckled, and she fell to her knees. A sob escaped her, and the torrent of emotions she'd been holding back tore through her like a raging fire. When she had no tears left, she stood and began to strip out of her rain-soaked gown. She wore dresses that discreetly buttoned up the front, specially made so she could dress and undress without assistance.

The red satin gown hit the floor with a soft smack. Her skin was chilled, and she knelt by the fire in her damp underclothes. She rubbed her arms for warmth and retrieved a blanket from her bed, wrapping it around her as she huddled by the tiny hearth. The fire restored some life to her cold body. When she was warm enough to dress, she removed the wet underclothes and put on a fresh set of gentleman's smallclothes and picked up cloth to bind her breasts.

The wig beneath the cap she usually wore concealed her tightly bound and pinned hair, and the breeches showed off her lean figure. She'd always been tall for a woman, and her legs were leaner than those of most ladies. Binding her breasts made her chest appear more masculine—well, enough to pass for a young lad. But she took the ruse even further and retrieved a small pot of colored face cream and applied it to her cheekbones, sculpting a more bony look, making her appear far more boyish. A false moustache had been considered early on, but ultimately rejected. It presented too many opportunities for accidental discovery.

Hugo's people had spent months coaching her in the arts of deception and combat. She'd trained with some of England's finest spies and had learned about boxing, street fighting, and fencing, the principles of which could still be applied to improvised weapons such as sticks or pokers. She had also mastered the use of poisons and drugs. She could write messages in a dozen secret ways and use codes to deliver them.

Despite Hugo's proclamations to the contrary, her job was not a noble one. She no longer served her king or her country. She served Hugo's own need for revenge. To bring down the Earl of Lonsdale and his friends, the League of Rogues.

A wave of self-loathing struck her, but she soon fought it back. She retrieved a small silver star pin and nestled it in her cravat, her symbol to Hugo's other spies that she was one of them, and left. She had only one or two nights a week to be her *true* self, assuming that Hugo did not call upon her for other tasks like he had tonight.

She left her room above the gambling hell and walked through the city unafraid. She could travel unseen in the shadows and knew how to avoid the dangers of London's streets. When one worked for Hugo as long as she had, all other fears became trivial.

By the time she reached Charles's townhouse, she was

ready to collapse in her small bed in the attic. She entered the house through the alley door and came into the kitchens. The Lonsdale house cook, Mrs. Farrow, saw her and grinned.

"Tom! You're late tonight."

"Evening, Mrs. Farrow." She used Tom's slightly deeper tone, though not so deep as to sound forced. She reached for a plate of scones freshly removed from the ovens. The cook let her take one, having stated more than once that she was far too skinny for a young man of twenty.

"Is Katherine in bed yet?"

The Irish cook nodded. "Aye. The wee lamb went to sleep easily tonight. Go on up and get some rest yourself."

Lily enjoyed the scone as she climbed the three flights of stairs to her room above the main living quarters. Her little bedroom was at the end of the hall. Most servants shared rooms, but because of Katherine she'd been given a single room and a cradle made by Davis, one of the footmen, who had a natural talent for woodworking.

Davis had lost his wife the year before and was raising his own son, Oliver, who was four years old. He was one of Charles's unconventional staffing choices, but Lily loved that Charles had taken a wounded, married soldier into his home as a footman. She and Davis had spent many nights talking about the rearing of children alone. It helped beyond measure in that part of her life. She was alone and trapped in all other ways.

As Lily entered, she noticed someone had lit a fire in the small stove in a corner near the crib. She tiptoed over and peered down at the babe asleep beneath the hand-stitched blankets Lily had made herself.

Katherine was the only bright star in an endless night of deception. Katherine's father's sins were not her own. She was an innocent, and Lily would do anything to protect her. Lily loved her more than her own life.

The babe's golden hair was getting long now, curling into gleaming gold ringlets. Her third birthday wasn't far away. Lily would have to think of something special to do for her. Perhaps Mrs. Farrow could make her a sweet tea cake and there would be a few presents. A doll perhaps. Maybe Davis could build her a small rocking horse?

The sudden tinkle of a bell by her door made her jump. The bell was connected to Charles's room. He wasn't in bed yet? She cursed under her breath, but at least the bell hadn't woken the baby. Lily exited her chamber and headed down the stairs, then across the hall and entered Charles's bedchamber. He stood by his bed, facing a full-length mirror, a frown tugging his lips down.

"Tom, there you are. Sorry to disturb you on your night off, but I'm in a deuced black mood."

"Oh?" Lily studied his fine profile in the firelight, remembering how it had felt to kiss those perfect lips. Charles was quite simply the most handsome man she'd ever seen. There was no weak chin, no pale face, no watery eyes, and no temperamental nature like many of the young aristocrats she'd come across in the last few years while training with Hugo.

Charles was quite simply a god among men. His skin was always sun-kissed, his burnished gold hair always looked as though a lover had run her hands through it, and his features were carved to perfection. It was as though the heavens had thought it would be amusing to create the most beautiful man on earth and drop him in front of her.

Gaze upon this icon of beauty, and despair.

But there was so much more to him. Despite the occasional immaturity of his actions or black clouds that at times hung over him, there was a kindness in his words, a gentleness with his staff, a loyalty in his heart to his family and friends that could not be matched. He was the most wonderful man she'd ever met...

And one day she was going to help Hugo kill him.

Charles saw her and nodded toward his boots, which were set by the foot of the bed.

"Yes, I went boxing at Lewis Street. The usual—"

Lily froze as she bent to pick up the boots he'd discarded. He considered that evening usual?

"And I met the most enchanting woman. A true angel."

She was glad of the makeup she wore and the dim light of the candlelit chamber. They would conceal her blush.

"I rescued her. Somehow she got nabbed by a few brutes."

Lily wrinkled her nose. Those men had been incompetent. She'd practically had to throw herself at them to get caught.

"Rescued, you say? That was chivalrous of you, my

lord." She straightened, boots in her arms, and headed for the door, hoping that was all he needed.

His deep chuckle sent a shiver through her. "Well, I suppose. But it wasn't as though I could leave her there with them. There was something in her eyes. She was so afraid, so vulnerable. It made me feel...mad with a need to protect her."

Lily almost laughed. That look he'd seen had been one of disbelief and fear that he was going to ruin everything, which he had.

"Perhaps it was simple chivalry, but when I looked at her..." He shrugged, a wry smile enhancing his painfully good looks. For a moment she remembered that kiss...

His gray eyes were like mirrors to her soul whenever she met his gaze. He was tall, six foot two, with a boxer's form and an angel's face. A woman could get lost daydreaming about what it would be like to... Lily gave herself a little shake. Even if the circumstances had been different, she was done with men. They'd only ever hurt her or threatened her; they could not be trusted. Yet part of her longed to trust Charles.

"So a lovely lady has put you in a black mood?" Lily asked, keeping her back turned as she set his boots outside the bedroom door. A footman would collect them later to polish them for her since it was still technically her night off. "How unlike you. I believe only Audrey Sheridan ever had that effect before, whenever she roped you into one of her schemes."

"Well no, not like that...but yes. I mean...I don't know." Charles growled. "I wanted to escort her home, perhaps pay a call on her later, bring her flowers... Bloody hell, I don't even know what a gentleman ought to *do* with someone like her. But she vanished on me before I could—"

"Seduce her?" Lily offered, unable to keep the cheek out of her tone. Hearing Charles talk about her, the real her, was both exciting and frustrating. Was it possible to be jealous of oneself?

"You jest, but I'm certain I could have managed a decent seduction if she'd only given me time. As it was, we only shared one kiss." Charles tugged on his cravat and removed it, tossing the bit of white cloth onto his bed before he unbuttoned his waistcoat and slid it off.

"If you had just rescued her, then I suspect a seduction of any kind would not have been appropriate."

"So you say, but I'll have you know that *she* kissed *me*." He took his shirt out of his trousers and lifted it off his head.

"Out of gratitude, one would assume, not...seduction." Lily swallowed hard at the sight of his muscular chest, the way he looked strong and utterly perfect.

"True enough, but you should have heard the way she spoke. It had a breathy quality to it, the kind I only ever hear in the *ton* when a woman is in search of a suitor."

Lily thought back. Had she? True, she had used a

different tone to reduce the chances of being recognized, but...

"Lad, stop pouting and come help me," Charles muttered as he unfastened his trousers. Lily caught an all too tempting glimpse of the two muscled indentations that formed a V in his pelvis, and she had to fight the urge to bolt from the room.

Charles headed to the dressing room, where a large copper tub was steaming with hot water. "I've got a neck ache. Come rub it for me."

Oh Lord...

She had seen him bathe a number of times since she'd become his valet, and rather than become accustomed to the sight, it was getting harder and harder to ignore how it made her feel. He wasn't just an employer, and he also wasn't just a man. He was a rogue, a scoundrel, a charmer, a deeply loyal soul, someone who showed her time and again that he took care of those he loved, no matter who they were.

Every person who worked for Charles was well paid, but almost all of them would've worked for half their wage just to serve a man like him. He'd taken in those less fortunate and gave them their lives back, like Davis, who'd lost the use of one hand in service to the king's infantry. He'd even helped Davis acquire a specially crafted wooden hand that enabled him to perform the duties which required the use of two hands. The cook, Mrs. Farrow, had been trapped in a debtors' prison after her husband ran off with another woman and she couldn't pay his debts. Charles had bought her out, and then all he asked was if she could make a decent figgy pudding. In some way or another, Charles had rescued every soul under his roof, and he'd only asked for honest work in return.

And it was that trait which Hugo had exploited, allowing him to position her directly in his path.

Charles had learned her story and taken her in. He hadn't even batted an eye at the news that she had a little sister, providing for her as well. For a wicked rogue, he was quite an expert when it came to children, having carried the baby himself more than once and gotten her to sleep when she'd been fussy. And damned if that didn't make her body burn with forbidden hunger for him.

"Tom, quit woolgathering," Charles called from the bath. "I need you."

"C-coming." She cleared her throat and entered his dressing room. He was thankfully already undressed and in the large tub. She'd been so lost in thought she'd saved herself the embarrassment of seeing him remove his trousers. Whenever she was around him, she was drawn in by an undeniable animal magnetism she had to fight to hide.

He dipped his head beneath the water. His gold hair was dripping with water, which sluiced down his back. He shifted to rest his arms on the edges of the copper tub, muscles taut and firm like those of a marble statue.

Lily drew in a steadying breath as she lifted a wooden

stool and set it down at the end of the tub behind him. "Where do you need me, my lord?" she asked.

He reached up and touched where his neck met his shoulder. "Here." She tentatively touched him, rubbing lightly at the corded muscles of his neck.

"I'm not going to bite, lad. Push harder. I believe I strained myself during tonight's fight. That brute I took down was, well...quite brutish. I got him with one punch, but I swear his face was made of granite."

Lily dug her fingers deeper into his skin, pushing on the knot she could feel in his neck, and he let out a soft sigh.

"Better."

They remained quiet while she worked on the muscles of his neck. She used to hate such silence. Silence meant fear, it meant pain. But now...silence was soft, and sometimes even sweet. Like when Charles had brought her a slice of cake at Audrey Sheridan's wedding. They'd settled on the stairs, eating together without speaking. Strangely, she had wanted to cry because it felt so nice. He was a good man. A man she would have to betray. Her mouth filled with a bitter taste.

Do not think of the future. Think only of now.

"Thank you, Tom. That's enough. Now, off to bed with you. We've a luncheon at the Duke of Essex's home tomorrow, and I don't want to be late."

"Yes, my lord." Lily exited the bedchamber but paused just outside, listening to the water splash, and tried desperately not to picture him climbing out. She headed straight back up to her room in the attic, checked once more on Katherine, and collapsed on her bed.

Sleep came swiftly, stealing her away into dreams of what might have happened if she'd only let Charles kiss her a little longer in the alley. But she would never know the feel of his lips on hers again. Despite Hugo's plan for her to seduce Charles, she wasn't going to let him kiss her. She'd let him do anything else, but if his lips touched hers and he kissed her like she *mattered*, she feared she would break down and confess everything to him.

She was damned.

❧

CHARLES FINALLY SETTLED INTO HIS OWN BED. SLEEP came fitfully, plaguing him with dreams, dreams he feared would turn to nightmares. The past never let him go. It kept dragging him back under, over and over.

THE PICKEREL PUB WAS FULL OF YOUNG MEN FRESH FROM dinner after their classes. Charles, for the first time in weeks, had been able to have an ale with a classmate. Being so much younger, he'd found it hard to make friends.

Peter Maltby, a student two years older than him, roomed across the hall in Magdalene College. Peter had seen Charles eating alone at dinner and had come over to invite him for a drink at the little pub just outside the college's gates. They had quickly become good friends, and the pub had become a ritual of sorts for them.

Tonight, they'd bid good night to the elderly porter who manned the gates and settled themselves in a corner of the booth to drink and talk.

"Enjoying your lessons?" Peter asked, smiling broadly as he sipped his ale.

Charles nodded. "I'm not much for studying, but I suppose I'll make a habit of it the longer I'm here." He curled his hands around his ale, watching the gold liquid glint in the candlelight.

"You'll get it sorted soon enough. You're a Lonsdale, after all. Your father was a legend when he was here."

"What?" Charles blinked, startled by this. His father had never spoken of his time at Cambridge.

"You didn't know? He was quite the scholar, I hear," Peter proclaimed with a wink. "You'll be one too, I know it. Intelligence runs in the family. My family isn't much for schooling, but I'm proving to my father that we can improve our circumstances. I'm not a lord's son, as you know."

Charles listened intently as Peter spoke of his father, who was a banker at Drummonds, and how he'd grown up with a boy named Ashton, spending long summers getting into mischief while their fathers discussed investments. They'd ridden horses together with a boy named Cedric, a young man who was now a viscount.

"I should introduce you to Ash and Cedric. They're both here."

"I don't know," Charles said. He still felt unsure of himself in such situations. "I'm sure they're far too busy."

"Nonsense. You'd fit in with them splendidly. I imagine you'd like some of my other friends as well. Have you met the Duke of Essex, by any chance? He's rather funny, but don't get crossways with him—he's quite the pugilist."

"I'm no stranger to boxing," said Charles, trying to sound confident.

Peter smiled. "You don't have the build for it like he does. Not yet. And then there's the new Marquess of Rochester, Lucien. He'll find you a willing woman any night of the week. He's slept with nearly all the daughters of the professors. I suppose that's how he passes his classes," Peter mused with a chuckle.

"You'd think it would get him expelled."

Peter raised his glass. "Only if he ever gets caught."

A laugh escaped Charles as he pictured some young man sneaking into the beds of maidens, seducing information from them about their fathers' exams. Not a bad idea, though he couldn't do it. Most young ladies had laughed at him when he'd tried to court them before leaving for Cambridge. He'd quite given up on the whole endeavor as a bad idea. Women were unknowable.

"Dinner tomorrow?" asked Peter. "We could all meet in the great hall. I think the others would like to meet you."

Peter, it seemed, knew and liked everyone he met. Charles envied his free spirit and open heart. If only he could have a life like that, with friends like that. With Peter's help, he just might.

"I'd like that."

"Do you mind if I invite a friend to drink with us now?" Peter asked suddenly. "I saw him this morning and told him I'd be coming here. He's a good fellow—you'll like him. He's

had a rough time of late. Even rougher than you. I can't go into it, but he lost his father some time back, and it took him down a dark path. I thought maybe you could help each other."

"I don't mind," Charles said. He'd lost his own father only a few months ago. It might be nice to be around someone who understood that pain and loss.

"Excellent. He'll be here soon, I imagine. He is punctual, never late for anything. Mind you, he's a bit of a stiff at times, always focused on the rules. I try to encourage him to step out of bounds whenever possible."

Charles laughed. "I fear I'm always out of bounds." He hadn't felt like he'd fit in a long time, especially not here. He was smaller than the other young men, shorter and thinner...weaker. His mother had insisted he would grow into himself over time, but he didn't believe her.

"Ah, here he is!" Peter stood and waved at someone who'd just entered the pub.

Charles sat up eagerly, hoping that whoever this man was, he would be friends with him too.

When Peter eased back down into his seat, Charles saw who was walking his way and his heart came to a stop.

"Hugo Waverly, come and meet Charles Lonsdale..." Peter was still smiling, unaware that a rift was growing in the center of the pub, a rift that divided Charles from Hugo by miles of hatred and pain...

The pub vanished as the dream changed. Water rushed up around his body in the dark. Moonlight danced off the waves as he and Hugo splashed in the shallows of the river Cam, struggling against each other.

"Hugo! No!" Peter's voice was close. Where was he?

"Get out of here, Peter. This doesn't concern you!" Hugo snarled like a wild animal.

The cold water was up to Charles's neck, his bound hands and feet keeping him helpless. All he could do was flail desperately as Hugo dragged him farther into the river. The water closed over his head and he screamed, sucking it into his lungs...

CHARLES BOLTED UPRIGHT IN BED, SCREAMING. THE door burst open and Tom darted in.

"My lord! It's all right now. You're safe. Breathe." Tom set a lit candle by the bed and fetched a glass of water, putting it to Charles's lips. Charles tried to push the water away. It was the last thing he wanted to taste right now.

"Drink," Tom ordered firmly. Charles, body shaking, obeyed, gulping down the cool liquid. It did calm him a little, but he couldn't stop shaking, and his heart... Lord, it felt like his heart was going to punch right through his chest.

"Another dream," Tom muttered. He tried to fluff the pillows behind Charles's back. "I wish I could stop them for you, my lord. Shame you never dream about food. At least then I might know what it all means. Cabbage for bad tidings, chocolate for good fortune..."

"We were drinking ale," Charles said, trying to remember the pub and not what came after.

"Oh, that's always a sign of trouble," said Tom. "Now, if it had been wine, that would be a sign of good fortune—unless it was spilled, of course. That's bad."

Listening to Tom talk about dreams was oddly comforting, like he was helping to fight them off. Good lad.

"I'm sorry I woke you." Charles's voice was gravelly and it hurt to speak, but he felt he had to apologize. How many times had Tom run to him in the last year, helping him calm after each terrifying dream?

"No problem, sir. I was fetching water for myself when I heard you."

That was a lie. Charles knew most of the house could hear him scream. He'd told them all to stay away, to just ignore him, but Tom didn't listen. Tom always came down to check on him.

"I'm fine, Tom. Go on, back to bed with you." He waited until he was sure his valet had left before he lay back down, still shivering.

It was a long time before he let his eyes close again, and once he did, he could see the water rise up around him, drowning him and stealing Peter away in the icy darkness.

4

"It's far too cold for croquet!" Emily St. Laurent, the Duchess of Essex, shouted at her husband. She curled a gloved hand over her swollen belly, which might hold the future heir to the Essex title, as she watched her husband, Godric, and his half brother, Jonathan St. Laurent, struggle to press the wickets into the hard ground of the small lawn in their back garden.

"Nonsense, darling," Godric grunted. "Just needs a bit of *umph!*" He slipped on the icy grass and landed on his backside. His brother burst out laughing but also lost his balance and fell down beside him. Emily covered her mouth to stifle a laugh.

"Lord, what a pair." A light voice came from beside her. Audrey, Jonathan's new bride, was grinning beside Emily. The two had been friends for more than a year, and now they had the pleasure of being sisters by marriage.

"It's so wonderful to see how much Jonathan has changed since he settled down with you," Emily said more softly. She'd seen the young man suffer in silence as he had adjusted to life as the son of a duke. He'd lived his entire life before as a servant, and Emily had feared he would never feel like he belonged to the life he was entitled to.

"We have both changed," Audrey confessed. "Everything is so different now. I grew up my whole life surrounded by my brother and his bachelor friends. All that has changed...because of you."

Emily rubbed her hand over her stomach, feeling a flutter of movement within. Charles had once said she would be the ruin of the League of Rogues. Perhaps she had been. They may not be the rogues they once were, but their bonds to one another were still unbroken. In truth, all she had done was dared them to open their hearts to love. But Charles had feared that vulnerability, and still did.

"Audrey," Emily said. "We have to do something about Charles. He's growing more distant, and I am beginning to worry. I know he attends all the balls and dinners, but there is an emptiness to his gaze that frightens me. It's as though he's given up." She had once vowed to find someone who would love him and wished to keep that promise, even if it meant crossing every ocean and traversing every continent to do so.

"I've noticed as well," Audrey said. "I've been meaning to speak to you, because I know I can trust you."

Emily turned away from her husband and Jonathan, who had abandoned the croquet wickets and were carefully climbing to their feet. "Yes?"

"Well...it's about Tom."

"Tom?" Emily did not immediately understand who Audrey was speaking of.

"Charles's valet."

"Oh! Mr. Linley." She remembered now. Blond-haired, shy blue eyes that followed his master like a faithful spaniel. "What about him?"

"*Her*," Audrey whispered.

Emily blinked, not immediately processing Audrey's words.

"He...is a *she*."

Emily blinked again. "What? How can you be sure?"

"How long have I been Lady Society?" she asked. Though the secret was out, it was still contained within the League and their wives. "I have spent years observing people far closer than you can imagine. There are a number of tells, from her eyes to the way she looks at Charles."

"Looks of longing do not mean Tom is a girl. I've seen men who fancy Charles before. Perhaps you are mistaking it for open admiration."

Audrey shook her head. "No, there is more to it than you realize. She uses face paint to make her seem more masculine. I was trained in the art of disguise and recognize the techniques she's using."

"Audrey, I fear your time spent in those circles may have you seeing conspiracies everywhere."

"You don't have to believe me. Watch when Charles arrives. There will be signs. I promise you." Audrey was so earnest that Emily agreed.

"I will watch. But honestly, I think you are mistaken." She turned to her husband. "Godric, the others will be here soon, and your game, I fear, is a lost cause. Please come in and warm up."

Godric crossed the slick lawn and pulled his wife into an embrace, planting a slow kiss on her lips.

"Warm enough for you, darling?"

"Oh yes, quite so," she replied, smiling up at him.

"Good." He led her inside with Jonathan and Audrey following behind.

Godric's butler, Simpkins, met them in the hall. "Your Grace, your guests have arrived," the butler declared with a merry twinkle in his eyes. "As per your standing orders, I hid the best bottles of port, sherry, and scotch."

Godric smiled. "Thank you, Simpkins. Charles can't be trusted with the new carpets."

"A wise precaution." Simkins had yet to forgive Charles for the stains he'd left on the Arabian rug at the Essex country estate, or the Persian rug last spring. Or the bear-skin rug in the billiard room last month.

Emily led the way into the drawing room, now full of men and women talking excitedly. She noted Lucien, the Marquess of Rochester, and his wife, Horatia; Cedric,

Viscount Sheridan, and his wife, Anne; the baron, Ashton Lennox, and his wife, Rosalind; and then there was Charles, the Earl of Lonsdale, though he wasn't alone.

Tom Linley was once again his shadow. It was unusual to bring a valet into the drawing room of another man's house like this, but Charles tended to make an exception with the young man. It seemed out of place, and yet...

Was Audrey right? Was that tall, thin boy...not actually a boy?

Emily moved deeper into the room as she made her greetings, and when she faced Tom and Charles she offered him a warm smile.

"Charles, I've had the cook prepare a special luncheon for the staff. Would you allow me to steal your valet away so I might ask him something before he joins the others belowstairs?"

Charles's gray eyes glinted with mischief. "Trying to poach my best man for Godric? Tom's an excellent lad, but far too loyal to leave, no matter what you offer."

Tom's face paled, and Emily tried not to stare, lest anyone else in the room noticed her interest.

"No one is poaching anyone, Charles. Don't be silly."

Emily waited for Tom to follow her into the hall. She took a moment to watch the boy walk. There was a masculine gait there, to be sure, but there was also no mistaking the ever so slight sway of the hips.

Good Lord. Audrey could be right.

Perhaps Tom Linley was not Tom after all. But why the

deception? She had a young sister to look after. Was it simply easier to find work as a man? Life in the lower classes for an unmarried woman with a child was difficult, even dangerous.

"What can I help you with, Your Grace?" Linley asked, her eyes respectfully downcast.

"Help with? Oh...I completely forgot. It's nothing important, I assure you. Please, go and enjoy the luncheon with the rest of the staff." She watched the valet depart, and her curiosity only intensified.

That poor woman. Living a lie just to survive. It's not right. I'm sure I can help her. I must.

Lily finished the last bit of plum tart that Mrs. Fitzhugh had given her. She had taken her lunch with the rest of the Essex staff belowstairs and had a full belly. Given the size of the meals provided to the staff of the League houses, she couldn't begin to imagine how much the League themselves ate. Lord, she would become the size of an elephant if she ever dined with them as a lady.

"Mr. Linley?" Simpkins announced in the doorway of the staff dining room. "Your presence has been requested by Her Grace in the morning room. The gentlemen are playing billiards."

Lily went still. "Requested? Her Grace requested to speak with me?" That was twice in one day, and two times more than she wished to speak with any of the ladies upstairs. These were not ordinary women, and she had learned early on that she needed to avoid their watchful gazes to avoid detection.

"Yes. Go on now." Simpkins clapped his hands in a way only a butler could, and she knew she had to get upstairs quickly. She thanked the cook for her tart and rushed off. She found the morning room door and knocked.

"Come in."

Lily fixed her eyes on the floor as she entered. When she dared to glance up, she saw a parade of colorful skirts belonging to a number of young ladies as they moved about the room.

"Mr. Linley, please come in and sit down," the Duchess of Essex said.

"I believe I should stand, Your Grace," Lily answered, keeping her tone low as she faced the scrutiny of five grand ladies around her.

"Sit. Please, I insist." Lily moved to a chair about eight feet away from the others. She kept her eyes down, trying to figure out why she'd been called here.

One of the women spoke up. "We don't bite, you know."

"Nor will our gaze turn you into stone," added another.

Lily looked up, noting the expensive silks of their gowns, with lavish embroidery and beautiful embellishments that she once imagined wearing herself. When she looked upon the duchess, she was surprised by the warmth she found in the woman's violet eyes. Lily was older by two years, yet the duchess carried a mature, knowledgeable expression in her eyes that told Lily she was wise beyond her years. It made Lily nervous, because wise people could often see what others could not.

"So, you are not *Mr.* Linley, are you?" the duchess inquired, though it wasn't really spoken as a question.

Lily's heart froze. Not long ago, Audrey had said she knew the secret Lily was keeping. Lily hadn't been sure what she meant. It was certainly possible Audrey had seen through her disguise, yet it was equally possible she suspected something completely erroneous. Audrey was famous for her flights of fancy, after all.

"I am..." Lily whispered hoarsely. Linley was her surname—that had never been a lie.

"I mean to say that you are *Miss* Linley," the duchess clarified. The steely resolve in her eyes made Lily squirm.

"Please, you need not trouble yourself with denials. Your secret is quite safe with the ladies in this room," the duchess reassured her. "You see, our husbands have their League of Rogues, but we...we are the Society of Rebellious Ladies. Do you know what it is we do?"

Lily shook her head, too stunned to speak. It was all falling apart. There was no talking her way out of this. Hugo would kill her once he found out, and then Katherine would... Panic filled her, and she looked up from her chair, suddenly sick. She fled to the potted plant in the corner and retched into it.

"Heavens!" one of the women gasped. Lily, through her sick haze, heard the ladies gather around her. A cool hand touched the back of her neck, and she sank to her knees, her body tensing as she dry-heaved again.

"There, there." It was the voice of Anne Sheridan, the viscountess. "We didn't mean to upset you. We only wished to offer our aid. That's what we do."

Lily closed her eyes, moaning as she leaned against the tall potted plant. "I don't understand. What do you rebel against?"

"This is a man's world," said Audrey, "and heaven knows it is hard for us to survive within it. You are living proof. We rebel against that."

"If anything, you have already proven yourself to be one of us," added Emily. "It is no small or timid feat to do what you have done."

"Would you let us help you?" This came from Horatia, the Marchioness of Rochester.

Lily lifted her head and wiped her mouth with the sleeve of her coat. "Help me?"

"Yes. We wish to help you find a husband," said Audrey. "One who will take care of you and your little sister. Katherine is her name, isn't it?"

Someone to take care of her? These poor, naïve fools. They had no idea how impossible that was. Hugo had taken everything from her. Her only future was the one he allowed her to have.

"I can't," she said.

"Why not?"

"My life is more complicated than you realize," she said. It was the closest she could come to admitting the truth.

"I'm sure you've grown used to a certain amount of freedom disguised as a man, but you're living a lie," Horatia said. "And it can't possibly last. With the right husband, you could be just as free and far more secure. You could be yourself."

"We won't tell Charles, if that's what you're afraid of," Audrey said. "We will be clever about it. You can ask for certain nights off."

"He's quite lenient with his staff," added Emily. "I know he would allow it. Then you will be able to join us at our balls. We have already begun to craft a clever family history for you, one that will give you entrance to the *ton*."

"I have agreed to provide you a suitable dowry," Rosalind said. She was a Scottish banker, a rarity in itself, and Lily had always admired her for that. But the thought of these ladies helping her when Hugo had sent her to ruin their lives... The nausea returned with renewed vigor. She had to play her part though.

"I cannot be seen at a ball among the *ton*, not when I am a servant."

"But you aren't, are you? You speak and carry yourself as a lady, it's because you are, aren't you?"

Lily hesitated and then nodded. "I was not born a servant. My parents were gentry, my uncle a baron in

Cornwall. But after my parents died, I had to seek work since my father's estate had dwindled to nothing." It was the truth. There was no harm in sharing that.

"Then you're quite suited to a gentleman of the *ton* as a husband," Anne insisted.

"Please," Emily insisted. "It's not often we have a chance to help someone like this, and it would give us great joy."

Lily tried to think of a way to deny them, but she could not, not without raising further suspicions and having them uncover the truth.

And the worst part was that their aid might help make Hugo's plans easier. As soon as he learned of this, he would insist that she accept. He would find the irony too good to pass up, but he would insist on knowing about the offer first.

"May I have some time to think upon it?" Lily asked.

"Yes, certainly. Take your time, but I do hope you will consider it." Emily helped Lily to her feet. "Are you well enough to return downstairs?"

"Yes. Yes, Your Grace," Lily lied and left the room, thanking them for their discretion. Once outside, she could hear the men in the billiard room. The sound of their laughter was oddly comforting.

She tiptoed past the billiard room. The door was ajar, and she couldn't resist peering around the frame to watch. Lamps illuminated the billiard tables, and curtains were partially drawn to protect the paintings from the rays of an overeager late-morning sun. Godric leaned over the table, lips pursed, green eyes intent as he took a shot. The other men jeered playfully when he only sank one ball. Their easy camaraderie was a force of magic in itself.

How had these powerful and ambitious men, all so different from one another, become close friends? What had drawn them together? It was something she'd wanted to ask Charles a thousand times. Friendships were usually born out of wonderful moments, but whatever bound the League together was something dark and terrible, and it had to do with Hugo.

Yet Hugo was the one seeking revenge, not the League. Why? Had they done him some wrong in the past? Something unforgivable?

She saw Charles leaning against the frame of a tall window. The sunlight from the partially open curtains made his gold hair gleam in a halo. The golden strands were unrulier than they had been when she had first met him a year ago, yet it only added to his charm and sense of mischief.

When he was with these five men, the shadows in his eyes faded away. The night terrors that woke him in the middle of the night eased for a time. Lily knew his true fear, the one that grew daily. The fear that all this would end, that the wives and coming children would drive the League apart bit by bit until Charles was the only man left.

His deepest fear was losing everyone he loved, and she

knew with dreadful certainty that his fear would come true. Sooner or later, Hugo would set his final plan into motion. The League would fall, and Charles would be the last one standing.

Only then would Hugo kill Charles.

5

Something was afoot.

Charles took his turn at the billiard table, aiming and taking a shot. All of his friends were in the room with him, happy, laughing about something he couldn't begin to understand—married life. The rift was there, a widening gap between him and the rest of the League that made his stomach knot. How had it all happened so quickly? In the span of a year, he'd been cast out of their world as they all one by one settled down.

And they can't even see it...

He tried to banish the wave of despair sweeping through him before he spoke. "What's Em up to, eh?" he asked Godric.

Godric leaned against his cue stick. "Em? Nothing, so far as I know. Why?"

"She called on my lad Linley, and I wish to know why. Are you in need of a new valet?"

Godric snorted. "Certainly not. Jeremy does excellent work. Besides, I wouldn't dare take your friend away, not when it's clear he worships you."

Charles chuckled. "He doesn't *worship* me."

Godric and Cedric shared a look between them that made Charles's hackles rise.

"What?"

"Well..." Cedric blushed a little. "Are you certain he doesn't...have feelings for you?"

Charles laughed. "Don't be silly, Linley doesn't—"

Ashton cleared his throat, a stern expression on his face. "It's not impossible, you know. And if it were the case, perhaps you ought to find the lad a new employer, one less likely to break the boy's heart."

"Oh, come now. I wasn't much different at his age around you lot. Hero worship and all that." Charles refused to consider Linley's behavior to be anything else. Tom was his only faithful companion left, now that his friends had married themselves off.

Besides, they were wrong. Linley had a young lad's admiration for him, that was all. As he'd said, he'd been there himself long ago, admiring Ashton, Lucien, Godric, and even Cedric as heroic figures. They were older than him by only one or two years, but as a young man at university, those years had seemed like a lifetime.

As time went on and he grew closer to them, he realized they were men just like him. Fallible, lovable, but hardly the gods they had once seemed to be. And he was glad for the change. A man cannot be friends with a god.

That was how Tom saw him, no doubt. He had given the lad a better job, a better place to stay, and a better situation for his young sister. He'd also been witness to the kind of adventures Charles often found himself in. Hero worship was only natural from such a perspective. But it wasn't healthy.

An idea struck him. Perhaps he could spend more time with Tom, get him to spend time with Charles the man, not Charles the savior. Show him how to carouse, drink, gamble, perhaps even help him find a lady to spend the night with. That would help the lad find his own footing and stop looking to Charles like a baby duckling that had imprinted on a dog. Yes, that was an excellent idea.

"What if you let Emily do a bit of matchmaking for you? It would solve a few of your problems," Ashton pressed. "If Linley really admires you, seeing you settle down might make him do the same. Teach him to grow up a bit."

Charles bristled, not liking the idea that anyone, especially Emily, would matchmake for him. He slapped his cue stick down on the table. "I'm quite done with the four of you trying to be the boy's nanny. The lad is fine, and I'm not about to sack someone just because they admire me. And as for matchmaking, I'm resigned to living out my days as a bachelor, even if you all abandon me for it."

"Charles—" Cedric started to speak, but Charles refused to listen.

He left the billiard room and bellowed for Tom. The lad bolted out of the servants' quarters as if someone had fired a shot over his head.

"My lord?"

"We're leaving."

Tom's face clouded with worry. "We are?" Charles punched his shoulder the way he used to with his little brother, Graham—before things had changed between them. Now the two could barely be in a room together before it came to blows.

"I'm in the mood for some sport. How about we go home and practice a bit."

"Certainly, sir. Boxing?"

"I was thinking fencing. I have the sudden need to skewer something."

"I have no desire to be on the end of your skewer," Tom muttered.

Charles laughed as he and Tom left Godric's house. The brisk London air curled around them as they waited for their horses to be brought around.

Back at his home, Charles felt even more confident about his plan to show Tom how to live on the reckless side. Ashton and the others had done the same for him when he was younger. In that sense, he'd be passing on the tradition to the next generation.

Charles and Tom entered the leisure room and he

fetched two fencing foils. The blades were dulled with metal balls on the tips to prevent any actual harm.

"Catch, lad." He tossed a foil to his valet. The boy caught it and swished it in the air with dramatic flair.

"You know your way around a fencing foil, I see?"

Tom offered him a grin. "A little, sir." He then assumed the *en garde* stance. Charles removed his coat and rolled up his sleeves. He approached Tom and raised his own foil. He waved it slightly in a circle, trying to distract Tom. Tom frowned in concentration, and before Charles could react, the boy lunged. The attack caught him off guard, and he stumbled back a step, foil bent against his chest.

"A hit, sir," Tom said, trying to hide a smile.

"So, is that how you wish to play?" Charles recovered his footing and danced to the left, parrying the next blow from Tom's foil.

"The only way to play is to win, sir."

Charles grinned. "Quite right."

The next few exchanges were straight out of a textbook, as if each were studying the other to learn what they knew, so they could exploit a weakness later.

"Who taught you how to fight?" Charles asked between parries.

Tom countered Charles's next thrust, falling back a little. "My uncle, sir. He died before my parents, but they say he never lost a match."

Their foils and arms crossed as they crushed into each

other, each staring the other down only inches apart. There was a brief pause and a silent look between the two.

"Very well then," said Charles. "Let's see if you can do him proud."

And then they began to fight in earnest.

For almost half an hour, the two fought as though the devil were on their heels until they were both on the verge of collapse. Tom seemed to be enjoying himself immensely. Charles recognized the gleam in his eyes. He'd carried it himself whenever he'd entered a ring and wasn't quite sure he could defeat his opponent, but was dying to find out.

They had scored two hits apiece thus far, and neither wanted to give up a third. But he could see that Tom was growing tired, and it was only a matter of time before his guard would drop.

Tom was falling back now, strictly on the defensive. The fight had taken them close to a window, near a table and vase. As they passed it by, an errant swing from Tom tipped the vase over toward Charles, who, instinctively, tried to keep it from shattering on the ground by providing his foot as a cushion.

It worked. The vase gave his toes a nasty sting and clattered safely onto the wood, and Tom landed a third blow directly onto Charles's chest.

"That's three, sir," Tom panted heavily. "Sorry about the vase."

Charles started to catch his own breath. "An accident, was it?"

"I was getting tired, sir. I'm afraid I was a bit careless."

Or clever, thought Charles. "You got me. Well done, Tom. Well done indeed. Now show me a bit of mercy and let me fetch us some water."

Tom stepped back, setting the foil down, and he braced his hands on his hips, breathing hard. Charles pointed to a chair by the window facing the garden.

"Sit. I'll be back." When Tom didn't immediately move, Charles swatted his backside with his foil. "Now."

With a mutinous glare, Tom stomped over to the chair and plopped down. It was a relief to see Tom let go of his usual more rigid demeanor. Whoever had been his previous master had clearly damaged the boy's trust. It'd taken ages for Charles to convince Tom he wouldn't have his ears boxed just for making a simple mistake.

Charles left the leisure room and hurried to the kitchens, where he found Mrs. Farrow and the scullery maid preparing for dinner.

"My lord." The cook wiped her flour-covered hands on her apron.

"Please, don't let me interrupt. I simply wanted a pitcher of water and some glasses."

The scullery maid rushed to fetch the pitcher and blushed as she handed it to him. The cook gave him two water goblets.

"Thank you." He started to leave, but the cook cleared her throat, grabbing his attention.

"My lord...if I may..."

"Yes?" Charles noticed a blush on Mrs. Farrow's cheeks as she spoke.

"The staff, we been meaning to speak to you...about Mr. Linley's little sister."

"Katherine?"

The cook and her maid exchanged glances. "You see, sir, the baby isn't so much a baby anymore, and, well, we were thinking that she might need more looking after soon."

He cocked his head. "Looking after?"

"Yes. We, the staff, have been taking turns the last year during our work shifts to keep an eye on the baby, but it's time we had a little help. Could we hire someone to watch over her? It won't be long before she needs schooling. Mr. Linley I'm sure could do it, but he spends much of his time with you, and the little one misses him something fierce. I've had to put the lass to bed more than once, and she keeps calling for her mama."

Charles tried to ignore the rush of guilt he felt, knowing he kept Tom from his sister so often. He'd been keeping Tom away from the only family he had left, just to entertain him when he was indulging in a fit of the blue devils. How utterly selfish of him.

"Mrs. Farrow, you're quite right. And Katherine's not the only one. I've been meaning to do something for

Davis's situation as well. Now that his Mary is gone, God rest her soul, he's been needing help with young Oliver. I'll start the hunt for a nurse straightaway. She can help look after them both. And perhaps I'll hire one who can double as a governess, I know that's a bit unusual, but I believe in educating all children no matter their station."

The cook smiled in open relief. "Thank you, my lord. Davis and Tom will both appreciate it."

He nodded and ducked out of the kitchens, returning to the leisure room. Tom was lounging like a tomcat on the chair, one leg thrown over the arm. He bolted upright when Charles entered.

"Rest easy, Tom. You've earned it." Charles offered him a goblet and poured him a glass. Tom took it and drank quickly, looking away as though he was embarrassed about the situation. Oddly, Charles felt uncomfortable as well. He was used to being admired by women, but he'd never had anyone worship him as a hero before. It was unsettling. He was not a man one should try to be like. There were far better gentleman out there, like the Earl of Pembroke for one. James was a bloody saint compared to Charles.

"Tom, we need to talk."

"We do, sir?" Tom's eyes widened, and Charles couldn't bring himself to ask what he ought to. Men didn't simply go around discussing such delicate things like feelings. So he chose to broach the subject of Katherine instead.

"It has come to my attention that Katherine is in need

of a nurse. Given how much time you spend in my company, I've been remiss in providing for her, and I think—"

"Oh, no, sir. You don't need to provide for her. She's my sister. She's not your concern." Tom leapt from the chair, but Charles gripped his shoulder and forced him back down.

"Easy, boy, you're doing a damned fine job caring for her, but it's my fault you see so little of her. As of today, you will get more nights off to be with her. And I will be seeking out a nurse tomorrow to help with your sister and Davis's boy. Kat's growing older, and she needs looking after. Soon she'll be running about the gardens on her own, dirtying her pinafore and climbing trees. You can't be there every minute. She will need a proper governess in a few years."

Tom's eyes shimmered, and he wiped at his nose with his sleeve. The display of emotion from the usually closed-off young man made Charles feel like a villain. He hadn't meant to upset Tom, but he seemed to be doing a damned fine job of it.

"Buck up, lad. I told you, you're doing well. Far better than I did at your age."

Tom looked up at him with a hope and vulnerability that cut Charles to the core. It reminded him of himself when he'd been younger and had lost so much. "What do you mean?"

"My father died when I was eighteen. My brother,

Graham, was three years younger, and my sister was just a few years older than your Katherine. My mother was devastated by my father's death. For years I was holding my family together by a thread. Ella fell into my care, and I had no idea what to do with the girl." He hated to think of the past; there was so much pain there waiting for him.

Tom seemed more curious now. "What did you do?"

"I did what I could, and the first step was admitting that I was only human. I hired a nurse to help my mother and a governess for Ella, and she has turned out splendid."

"But I cannot afford—"

"Oh come now, Tom. Davis needs help as well, and I decided to treat Kat like my goddaughter when I took you on. I should take some responsibility for her."

More than once, he'd wondered if he hadn't crossed paths with Tom's mother at some point. The babe did favor him in looks in quite an eerie way. But Tom was so close-lipped about his past that Charles didn't even know the woman's name. He didn't even know she'd had an uncle until half an hour ago. Was it possible he had bedded the woman once and fathered a child he hadn't known about?

But if that were the case, what he didn't understand was why Tom's mother had not come forward. Most women did when the father was titled and well-off. Charles was willing to own up to the idea of being a father, but without knowing more about Tom's mother, it was hard to suggest the possibility.

Or perhaps he was letting his worries about being a lifelong bachelor get to him. Kat might have been his daughter—in another life, with a woman he loved. The thought teased him with dreams of what might have been, and it made him unusually somber.

"But why?" Tom asked. "Our children are not your responsibility, and you pay us well already."

"I had someone look after me when I needed it most. The least I can do is help someone else." Actually, there had been four someones to look after him that night Hugo tried to murder him. He shivered and buried the memory but not the gratitude he felt. Godric, Lucien, Cedric, and Ashton had saved him from more than just the river that night. They had saved his soul.

And he had repaid them by being boorish and rude, walking out on them today. He had behaved like a foolish, stubborn child.

"Are you all right, my lord?" Tom asked, his brows drawn together in concern. Lord, Tom really was so young. It would be good when manhood caught up with him and his shoulders filled out and his features hardened a little. Charles had been small once himself and knew the hardships one could face. The boy would run the risk of being bullied if he worked at any other house.

"I'm just woolgathering, Tom. Finish your water. I'll be out tonight, so you may have the night off. Tomorrow we shall interview some nursemaids for Kat and Oliver."

Tom climbed off the chair and finished his goblet

before he left. Charles threw himself into the chair Tom had vacated, and before he realized it, he was daydreaming about the blonde-haired angel he'd rescued from the tunnels, wishing he'd stolen another kiss beneath the rain before she'd vanished.

I have to find her again. I have to know who she is...

LILY CREPT INTO THE SERVANTS' QUARTERS AND FOUND Katherine sitting on Davis's lap. He was letting the baby play with a bit of blue ribbon, which she clearly found fascinating.

Lily smiled at the young man as she took her daughter from him. "Thank you, Davis."

"Anytime, Tom. I know his lordship keeps you busy, and I don't mind looking after her when time allows. After I lost Mary, it was damned hard to care for Oliver on my own. I don't know what I would have done if it hadn't been for Mrs. Farrow and the rest of the staff. We must help each other, right?" Davis tapped Katherine's nose with the tip of his finger. She squealed and clapped her chubby hands together. Davis laughed. Kat rested one of her hands on Davis's wooden hand, unbothered by the strangeness of it.

"You know I'm always happy to look after Oliver when time allows," said Lily.

"Thank you, the wee lad runs circles around Mrs.

Farrow now that he's older." Davis winced as he moved his wooden hand. His wrist often ached in the winter cold where it connected to his wooden hand. It made it difficult for certain tasks but he was still able to perform his duties. At least she might be able to help him there.

"If you bring me the boots you need to polish, I can do them for you," Lily offered. Davis was surprisingly capable with only one hand, but Lily was deeply indebted to the footman and wanted to make sure he knew how grateful she was. When Davis turned his back on her to stoke the fire, she buried her face in Kat's golden hair and breathed in her sweet baby scent. It didn't matter that Katherine came from a dark moment in her life; all that mattered was that Katherine was hers.

"Did Mrs. Farrow speak to his lordship about hiring someone to help with the children?" Davis asked. "We'd been discussing it earlier since I could use some help with Oliver."

Lily nodded and kissed the crown of Katherine's hair in a brotherly fashion. "He said he's going to interview nurses tomorrow. Please thank Mrs. Farrow for me." They both knew how unusual it was for a lord to hire a nurse for the children of servants, but that was how Charles was. His staff felt comfortable enough to ask for help and he gave it to them instantly.

She had been hurt at first when Charles had brought it up, but he was right. She had been barely there for Katherine of late, and the rest of the staff could not keep swapping duties to care for a child who wasn't theirs. As always, Charles surprised her with his open warmth and generosity. He was truly a good man. She swallowed down the rise of bile in her throat as she remembered where all this would lead someday.

Don't think of it as betraying him. You have to put your child first.

She closed her eyes, holding her daughter tight. Katherine was still now, as if she sensed Lily's distress but didn't understand. Her tiny hands grasped Lily's cheek, and she tilted her head up.

"Looks like she needs a nap," Davis mused. Lily tensed. She hadn't even realized he was still there. She'd gotten lost in her thoughts again, such a dangerous thing. She could not afford to let her guard down, not even for one second, especially around friends.

"I think you are right. I'll tuck her in her crib."

"She'll be too big for that before you know it," said Davis. "I'll have to build her a proper bed soon."

"Not too soon, I hope." Lily stood and started toward her room. As she heard Davis's footfalls fading away, the tension inside her began to recede. She set Katherine down on her bed.

"Mama," Katherine whispered.

"Yes, love, but you mustn't call me that. Remember?" She knelt in front of her daughter, trying to smile.

"Why?" the baby whispered. At only three she was intelligent. Too intelligent. She had her father's cunning, which filled Lily with a sense of dread, but she believed Katherine had her heart, one of love, not hate.

"It's a very important secret. You like it here, don't you?"

Katherine gave an exaggerated nod, making her curls bounce.

"Then we have to keep the secret. If anyone knows I'm your mama, then we will be sent away. No more ribbons." She toyed with the strip of blue silk still coiled in her child's hands. "No more biscuits from the kitchens, no more warm nights by the fire." Lily didn't want to frighten her, but Kat had to understand the importance of the secret.

Katherine's cornflower-blue eyes grew wide. "No more Unca Charles?"

"No more Uncle Charles," Lily agreed. "Remember, our secret is very important. You must call me Tom, not Mama."

"Toma!"

"No, silly. *Tom*."

She pulled the baby into her arms again, relishing the simple joy of just holding her. Spending most of her day away from Katherine was difficult, and the ache in her chest to cuddle her close and pretend she was her old self, Lily, was overpowering.

"Why don't we take a little nap?" She laid the child out on the bed and stretched out beside her. Katherine snuggled in close and fell asleep almost at once. Lily's muscles still ached from the vigorous fencing match, and she was relieved to have a moment's rest.

Charles would have beaten her if she hadn't knocked over that vase. She knew she shouldn't have done it, but she was expected to seize upon any advantage she found and exploit it. Charles, on the other hand, believed in fair play, even when fighting down in the Lewis Street tunnels. It was his weakness, one that Hugo knew all too well.

You have too big a heart, my lord, far too big of a heart. I'm so sorry.

6

Sir Hugo Waverly stood in the shadows of the gambling hell known as the Cockerel. His gaze roved over the mixture of peers and lower-class men gambling and whoring. Rumors of an underground boxing ring run by smugglers had surfaced earlier that morning, and Hugo wanted answers.

Smugglers were a fact of life, and one that he usually did not concern himself with, but this was different. What little was left of Samir Al Zahrani's slave trade had found new leadership and was said to be seeking out new recruits. It was important to sort them out before they found a toehold on the docks.

He'd given Lily the mission of discovering more about them, offering herself up as bait. His little pet had mentioned being dragged down to Lewis Street as a prize for fighters, but Hugo suspected the ultimate destination would have been a cargo ship headed for parts unknown. She'd failed to learn more, thanks to Lonsdale, but thinking over the Lewis Street situation did give him an idea.

"Sir?" Daniel Sheffield was at his side, only lately returned from a covert mission in France. Despite not achieving all of his aims, the mission for the Crown had proved successful. Seventeen expatriates causing unrest in London had been caught and quietly dealt with, several in a permanent fashion. The sanctity of England and its empire was once more secure, a fact that filled Hugo with pride.

He served three masters: king, country, and control. A man must always defend his king, protect his country, and maintain his control.

"Daniel, find out what you can about the rules for the men who fight in Lewis Street boxing rings, assuming they have any. The smugglers run it, but I want to know how they allow men to fight in the rings, and what the stakes usually are."

Daniel moved deeper into the crowds, and Hugo continued to watch the tables, the turn of cards, the cries of victory and, more often, defeat. Then his breath caught as he saw a golden-haired man at a table, one that for an instant made him think...

But no, it was not the Earl of Lonsdale. It was his younger brother, Graham Humphrey. They shared their father's fair hair and eyes, but upon a closer examination, Graham's looks came from his mother, not his father.

For a moment Hugo was disappointed. He was hungry for revenge tonight, and facing Lonsdale would have given him a chance to lash out. Not that he would enact his endgame here. No, when it came time to kill Lonsdale, it would be at a time and place of his own choosing.

Lonsdale had more lives than a bloody tomcat, but those lives were running out. It wouldn't be long before Hugo had Charles right where he wanted him. And then, the final stroke.

Daniel returned, his lips in a firm line.

"Well?" Hugo asked.

"The smugglers who run Lewis Street boxing rings are the worst sort. The type to double-cross a man for a simple ill look."

"That's not unexpected. What else?"

"Those in charge"—Daniel lowered his voice and leaned in so as not to be overheard—"are known for offering a way for men to pay off debts by fighting. The wagers made are often high because there are no guarantees of safety. Sometimes quite the opposite."

"Blood sport," said Hugo.

"Indeed. And the willing men aren't always so willing. They're more desperate, I'd say. If they can't offer the smugglers what they want, their only recourse is to offer themselves...in the ring."

"Is that so?"

"Yes, sir."

Hugo pointed to the man sitting beside Graham Humphrey. "You see that man?"

Daniel eyed the young aristocrat sitting next to Graham. "Phillip Wilkes, the Earl of Kent?" He and Graham were laughing and enjoying a night out at a table playing faro.

"Yes. Sampson is running the table. Set the earl up to lose. I want him to owe you a vast sum of money. When he can't pay, demand he settle the score by fighting at Lewis Street."

Daniel frowned. "I should point out, these boxers have been known to kill men in these fights."

"That's something we shall allow fate to decide. It is required to move a more important piece into position."

"I understand."

"And Daniel?"

"Yes, sir?"

"Be sure to use your real name."

Hugo didn't miss the resignation in Daniel's eyes. He was loyal to the core, yet he'd been showing some reluctance to his methods as of late.

Daniel wandered to the faro table and took a seat beside Kent, nodding at him in silent greeting as the game began. Hugo collected a glass of brandy from a passing wench's tray and tasted the liquid. Subpar, but better than he expected for this place.

He began to think of other games, other pieces, and

other moves yet to be made. Word from his men working within the League households was that they were finally ready to fight back.

No doubt Ashton Lennox was leading the charge. He was the only member of the group who ever had any ability to play the game like Hugo did, but it did not matter. The baron was far too late, and even this turn of events had been expected. Necessary, in fact. There would be no stopping the firestorm from raining down upon the League of Rogues and everyone they loved.

❧

Graham Humphrey folded his cards and watched his friend Phillip, the Earl of Kent, anxiously. The faro table had thinned out, and the real match was now between his friend and a dark-haired man who played with considerable skill. He'd introduced himself as Daniel Sheffield, a manager down by the docks.

Kent leaned forward, frowning as he examined the cards the dealer turned up on the green felt tabletop. Faro was half skill, half luck, and usually Kent was blessed with both, but not tonight. Sheffield was winning almost every hand it seemed, and racking up debts against Kent.

"Another round?" Sheffield challenged Kent. "One good hand would set you right."

Graham gripped his friend's arm, giving a shake of his head, but Kent shoved him off.

"Another." Once more the dealer laid out thirteen cards, and the bets were placed as to what card the dealer would turn up next.

Graham's stomach knotted as Kent placed a hefty sum, which Sheffield quietly doubled. A hush settled around the table as a small crowd gathered to watch.

The dealer turned the card over, and Kent's face turned the color of birch.

"I..." he stammered. "I may need a few days to collect the finances for you, Mr. Sheffield." Kent was not poor, but no man could afford so much without sufficient time.

"I'm afraid I'm leaving in a day's time," said Sheffield. "But perhaps we can come to an arrangement." Sheffield leaned in and whispered something in the earl's ear. Kent nodded hastily. Then Sheffield rose and departed.

"Phillip, what did he say?" Graham demanded in an urgent whisper.

Kent rose from the table and pulled on his coat. "Not here."

Graham followed him out the door, sliding his own coat over his shoulders. Once outside in the icy wind, Graham jerked his friend to a halt.

"Phillip, what the devil did he say?"

The Earl of Kent couldn't meet his gaze. "I've no means to pay his debt in a timely fashion, and he offered..."

"What?" Graham feared the answer his friend might

give. If he was so hesitant, it had to be something dreadful.

"He has *other* interests and finds himself in need of someone."

"What do you mean? What interests?"

"Boxing. He feels that I could repay the debt if I agree to fight in the rings on Lewis Street. He has some sort of financial arrangement with those who organize the fights."

"Lewis Street?" Graham echoed. He'd only heard rumors of the place. It was a bad place to be a boxer. The men there had no honor and showed no mercy. It was not a place where anyone should go.

"I'm bound there now. Win or lose, he says my debt will be considered paid in full."

"No, Kent, you cannot—"

His friend spun to face him. "What would you have me do? Better to face a brute in the ring than have every note called in by every financier in London. Once word was out that I had allowed such a debt to be owed, my name would be ruined." He looked away. "Thank you for trying to stop me from that last hand. I should have listened to you. I'm sorry."

Kent went to call for a hackney, Graham following on his heels.

"Well, I won't let you go there alone," Graham announced. "Someone's going to have to drag you to a doctor afterward."

The two exchanged a moment of cold laughter.

"Thank you, but I'd rather prefer to think I stand a chance of winning."

Graham didn't want to think about what might happen in the tunnels tonight. He feared that once it was over, he might be calling on a priest rather than a doctor.

LILY WANDERED DOWN THE HALL OF THE GRAND townhouse, smiling as she admired her new place of employment. Her first place of employment. Working as the lady's maid to the wife of a prominent man in society had been an unexpected turn of good fortune. Melanie Waverly was exquisitely beautiful, the sort of woman all men found desirable. Her flashing eyes and coquettish smile had earned her many admirers.

Lily paused in front of the door to her lady's bedchamber and smoothed a hand down her pale-lilac day gown. It was pretty enough, yet it hung loose on her body. She'd grown taller in the last few years, yet she still had a rather coltish body with smaller breasts and hips than most women her age. She would never draw the kind of attention her mistress had, but perhaps that was a good thing. She'd only planned to stay in service long enough to meet a decent man, another person in service, and hopefully marry. She had no expectations beyond that, and working in the Waverly household would be an excellent way to start.

She knocked lightly on the bedchamber door. It wasn't her mistress who opened it, however, but her master. Sir Hugo was a handsome but intimidating man, with dark hair and even darker eyes. There was an aura of power about him that Lily sensed immediately, and it made the hairs on her neck stand on end.

"You must be the new maid. Lily, is it?" He stepped aside, and Lily slipped past him.

"There you are. You're late." Melanie's tone was curt as she eyed herself critically in the mirror of her vanity table. "Come and fix my hair. Don't just stand there."

"Check your temper, my sweet," Hugo warned his wife, and he offered Lily a pleasant smile. Perhaps his bark was worse than his bite? Still, Lily knew better than to trust men, at least when it came to maids in service. She'd been warned that it was in a man's nature to take advantage if he was in a position of power. And a woman in service was on the lowest end of that power as one could get.

"Quickly now," Melanie snapped.

Lily carefully picked up an expensive silver hairbrush and began to comb through the thick waves of her mistress's hair. The moment she did, her mistress began to relax. When she had finished and was done with her other duties within the bedchamber, it was early evening.

Sir Hugo had left earlier to visit his mother and was expected back for dinner, though it was possible he would spend the evening at his club, Boodle's. The staff would spend the afternoon and evening catching up on their work if neither the master nor mistress returned until late.

Lily had finished changing the linens and exited her lady's bedchamber. But as she passed by the master's room, she heard sounds, a man muttering to himself.

She pushed open the door wider and saw Sir Hugo. He was pacing in his bedchamber. She started to close the door, but it creaked and she froze.

"Who's there?"

She guiltily pushed the door open and revealed herself.

"Oh, it's you. Bring me some brandy," he said without emotion.

Lily rushed to fetch a decanter and glass from his study and handed them to him. He had settled himself in the chair by the fireplace, which wasn't lit.

"Shall I fetch someone to light it for you?" she asked. His distant gaze told her his thoughts were miles away.

"Sir?" she prompted.

"No, leave it," he muttered, looking at the dead hearth. "It seems strangely appropriate."

Lily could see he was troubled, and she wanted to help. There was a terrible pain inside he was trying to hold back.

"Sir, was your mother not well when you saw her?"

"Oh, she was well." His reply was cold. "Her life has been just fine without me in it."

"She was not happy to see you?"

Sir Hugo huffed. "She was quite happy to see me. I thought perhaps things would be different between us now. Only she then proceeded to ruin everything."

For a second Lily didn't know what to make of his snapping outburst. She reached out to touch his shoulder, the way she would a friend.

"I'm so sorry, sir. I'm sure she didn't mean any harm."

Hugo's hand was white-knuckled around the glass as he

slowly set it down on the table by his chair. "Perhaps. But it does not change the facts laid before me."

Lily wasn't sure what she wanted to say, but she wanted to offer him some words of comfort. "Sir, I know it's not my place, but...is there anything I can do? To help?"

His eyes flicked to her hand, which still rested on his shoulder. "Help? You think you can help me?"

"Sometimes it helps when people talk about what pains them. Takes the weight off their shoulders."

Hugo slowly rose from his chair, and her hand dropped from his shoulder. She watched him quietly close the door to his chamber, blocking the only way out of the room.

"Who sent you?"

"Sir?"

Hugo approached her. She felt powerless to move, even as he reached up and took her by the throat, though he didn't squeeze.

"Who. Sent. You?"

"I don't understand, sir. I was leaving my lady's room when I heard you in distress. I only wished to help."

Hugo looked her over, eyes narrowed. For a moment he looked ashamed, as if he realized he'd made a mistake. She thought he would let her go. Then his eyes hardened, and he began to squeeze.

"You think because you see me upset, that you can help me? Do you presume to think you understand anything *about me? You know* nothing *about pain or suffering." His dark eyes raked over her body.*

"But you will."

"Sir? Please don't." She whispered the words, not understanding anything except that she was in danger.

Before she knew what was happening, she was dragged into the mistress's bedchamber and thrown onto the bed. Minutes later she lay on the bed, her skirts tossed up past her hips, pain coursing through her. But she dared not move, dared not do anything but draw shallow breaths and try not to think. He gripped her waist tight, the hold hard enough that her skin would blacken with bruises in a few hours.

Hugo finally climbed off her. "You know when to be quiet. That's good. I could find other uses for someone who can control themselves like that."

A tear leaked from her eye and dampened the pillow below her chin. She stared at the fibers of the pillow as the reality of what had happened set in.

"Tell my wife anything and you will lose both your wages and your employment. I will see to it that no one else hires you." He nodded at the box on his wife's bedside table, the one that held Melanie's collection of jewels.

Hugo exited the bedchamber. Lily stayed still, like a frightened rabbit hiding from a fox, knowing the danger was all too near.

When she finally got up, she dropped her dress back down and used the cloth and the water from the washstand to clean herself up. There was blood on her thighs and the sheets. Sheets she would be expected to clean.

It was that thought, the idea of her doing all the work to hide this shame while he pretended that nothing happened, that broke her. She rushed down the hall and through the kitchens, fighting off tears. She could not stay here. She could not work for that monster. Without a word to anyone, she slipped out the back door and fled into the streets, never looking back...

LILY JERKED AWAKE. HER THROAT FILLED WITH A scream that would not come. Then she remembered where she was. She was in Charles's home. Safe. At least for now. She wasn't within Hugo's easy reach, not here.

Yet in truth she was always within his reach. She was his puppet, dancing on his strings. She leaned down over her baby and brushed the backs of her fingers over Katherine's velvety cheeks. She should have been a horrific reminder of that night, a black spot in her memory, but Lily refused to see Katherine that way.

You are my child. Mine. You will never be his.

She kissed her baby's forehead before she slipped out of bed. Night had fallen, and only embers were left in the tiny fireplace. Lily used a poker to stir the flames back to life, adding a fresh log from the pile. Lily smiled. Davis must have brought them up sometime earlier that day. She stoked the flames until they burned steadily. When she returned to her bed, she picked up her daughter, carrying her over to her crib and setting her down inside.

Lily had let the afternoon escape. She still had work to do, including polishing the boots, as she had promised for Davis. With a heavy sigh, she left her chamber and walked down the hall. It was quiet. Most of the staff were now attending to their own supper down by the kitchens. But Lily wasn't hungry.

She was just coming down to the ground floor when she heard the front door knocker. The usual footman wasn't there since Charles was supposed to be out for the evening. Lily hastily smoothed her clothes to look presentable and rushed to open it in his place. A dark shape lurched inside, grabbing at her as he collapsed. At first she tried to dodge the man's hold, but for a second she thought it was Charles who was reaching for her. She tried to grab him as he tumbled to the ground.

"Charles..." the body on the floor groaned. "Need... help." The man soon sank into unconsciousness.

Lily rolled him onto his back and got a better look at him. He was badly beaten, his face bruised and swollen, but there was no mistaking the familial resemblance. It was Graham, Charles's younger brother. She'd only seen the man a few times in the last year, and Charles rarely spoke of him. Whatever had happened between the brothers had been so bad they continued to keep their distance. Now Graham was here, begging for his older brother's help.

"Mr. Humphrey?" she asked, but the man didn't stir. She checked his wounds, but there was no evidence that he had been stabbed, only beaten. She ran for the kitchens, calling for the butler. Mr. Ramsey rushed to meet her just outside the servants' dining room.

"Tom? What on earth?"

"It's Mr. Humphrey, his lordship's brother. We must fetch the doctor." Lily led Ramsey back to the entryway. The butler cursed as he knelt by the fallen man.

"I'll get him to the drawing room. There's a couch there. Have Davis fetch Dr. Shreve on Duke Street."

"Yes, Mr. Ramsey." The butler shouldered Graham into the drawing room. She'd never been more thankful that Ramsey was a strong, fit man, albeit in his fifties. He had no trouble getting Graham into a place where he could rest safely. By the time Lily had sent Davis to Duke Street and returned to the drawing room, Ramsey had removed Graham's coat and waistcoat and was examining him for further injuries.

"How did you find him, Tom?" Ramsey asked.

"He was pounding on the door. When I opened it, he collapsed on me. He asked for help before he passed out. He wanted to see his lordship."

Ramsey removed Graham's neckcloth and winced at the dark-blue finger marks that circled Graham's throat.

"Someone tried to strangle him," Lily said.

Ramsey nodded. "I believe so."

Lily's hands rose to her own neck reflexively. Vivid, painful memories of when Hugo had her by the throat. How she had tried to escape him, but that escape had been short-lived.

"I wish his lordship was here," Ramsey muttered.

"Where is he? I could fetch him," Lily offered.

"I'm not sure. He left for Vauxhall, but you know how

he is. The man changes his direction like the wind. He could be anywhere now. You would never find him."

"What should we do?" Lily asked. Graham lay still, but his breathing was deep, not shallow.

"Once the doctor assesses him, we shall put him up in one of the spare rooms. When his lordship returns, we will explain the matter to him and he will decide how to proceed."

Lily nodded. Ramsey was aware, even more so than she was, of the precarious nature of the relationship between the two brothers.

In an effort to help, Lily brought clean cloths and a basin of water and wiped the blood on Graham's split lip and the dirt on his face. It looked as though he'd fallen a few times before arriving at Charles's doorstep.

The drawing room door opened and Davis entered, followed by Dr. Shreve. The doctor was hardly a stranger to the Lonsdale household, given Charles's fondness for boxing.

"Over here," the butler said. Lily shifted over but kept close to watch the doctor as he lifted Graham's shirt. More bruises and welts covered his chest.

"Someone beat this man quite severely." The doctor's sharp eyes assessed Graham's condition. "He has a few broken ribs, here. It is important that he rest in bed as much as possible for the next few weeks." The doctor leaned close, touching Graham's throat. Graham suddenly stirred, tossing restlessly like a fitful child.

"Charles?" Graham groaned. The sound was oddly pitiful, like a boy desperate for his older brother, because he was the only person who could make things right. Lily brushed a wet cloth over Graham's brow, trying to comfort him. His eyes opened, and she glimpsed those light-gray eyes, so much like Charles's.

"Easy," the doctor said. "Rest, Mr. Humphrey. You are out of danger, but you need to sleep. You understand?"

"Yes," Graham replied.

"If it hurts to speak, then rest your voice as well," said Dr. Shreve. "It looks like someone tried to crush your windpipe."

Ramsey joined Lily near Graham's head. "His lordship isn't here, but we will bring him straight to you once he has returned."

"Phillip...is dead." He coughed and seized with pain, no doubt from his broken ribs. Lily stroked her fingertips over his forehead, trying to calm him. Then she smoothed a wet cloth over his brow.

"Who is Phillip?" asked the doctor.

"The Earl of Kent... They beat him to death... Lewis Street... I barely escaped." Graham's eyes rolled back into his head, and he slumped on the couch.

"Lord Kent? Dead?" Ramsey whispered, his eyes wide.

"Who is he?" Lily asked the butler.

"A friend of Mr. Humphrey's. Since they were just lads. A good man."

Lily shuddered. A man was dead, and Graham was

badly beaten. She feared Hugo was somehow involved, making another move in his deadly game. Had he intended for Graham to die as well? Or was it important for him to live, to be here, battered and bruised?

"Put him to bed and I'll leave some laudanum for the pain." Dr. Shreve and Mr. Ramsey picked Graham up, one arm around each of their shoulders, and carried him from the drawing room. It was a tricky thing to get him up the stairs, but they managed it.

Lily remained with Graham for an hour, keeping a vigil at his bedside. She owed it to Charles, after everything he'd done for her and Katherine.

Graham woke as she was bathing his forehead with a cloth. His eyes fixed on her, a feverish gaze, but no less intense.

"Does he know?" Graham asked drowsily.

She put a glass of water to his lips. "Know?"

"Yes..." Graham caught her wrist, his thumb touching her racing pulse. "Your eyes...too kind." He fell back asleep, leaving Lily to wonder what it was he meant.

7

"This is a terrible idea," Cedric muttered as he followed Godric, Ashton, and Lucien down a hedgerow in Vauxhall Gardens.

"I'd like to point out that *most* of Godric's ideas are terrible," Lucien replied in a low whisper. "But it hasn't stopped any of us from participating before."

"I don't see any of you with better ideas," Godric snapped, glowering at Lucien and Cedric.

Cedric smiled. It was like old times, when he and Godric had run wild in Cambridge, before they had been pulled into Charles's orbit like four moons, before Peter had been lost to them all forever. It had been a binding of five souls over the loss of one. And tonight, like they had the night they'd saved Charles all those years ago, they were once again trying to rescue Charles, this time from himself.

"How do we even know Charles is here?" Cedric asked.

"I have reason to believe he may be searching for companionship tonight," Ashton replied.

"Hold on, the last thing I want to walk in on is Charles naked and—"

"Oh hush," Lucien laughed. "One of us will go then."

Cedric followed his friends through the dark gravel walkways of the expansive gardens. They came to a path that had three distinctive archways featuring a realistic painting of the ruins of Palmyra. As a lad when he had first visited, Cedric had been convinced that the paintings had been real ruins.

"Should we check the dark walk?" Godric suggested.

"Might as well," Ashton whispered. "Best place for trysts." They tried to move unnoticed in the paths until they reached the farthest promenade. The dark walk, or lovers' walk, was narrow and offered a clandestine, very close place for lovers to meet in the evening. Cedric had brought a lady or two here himself, before he had married Anne. He imagined taking her here, pushing her into the velvety leaves of the bushes and hiking up her skirts. The fantasy brought a smile to his lips. Perhaps once Hugo was finally dealt with, he could bring Anne here and show her some of his more wicked fantasies.

"Cedric." Lucien's hiss pulled him from his thoughts. He realized that his friends had all ducked across the crossway of merging paths and were waiting for him to join them. He glanced down the path, making sure that no one was watching, then hastily ducked in beside the others as they proceeded once more in single file. The sudden clang of a clear bell froze them in their tracks.

"Bloody hell," Godric growled. "We forgot. It's nine o'clock. The show."

All around them the paths began to fill with ladies and gentlemen who moved toward the famous cascade at the center of the garden, which could only be viewed at nine o'clock for fifteen minutes. A miller's house had been constructed there with a rippling waterfall that created a heavy froth at the bottom as the wheel turned.

Colored dyes had been added to the water, and floating luminaries created a beautiful sight of dancing light and colored water. People clapped and cheered as fireworks exploded overhead.

The four of them were pushed toward the water's edge of the massive fountain. Cedric cursed. They would not be able to escape the crush until the spectacle was over. He scanned the crowd and caught a glimpse of a familiar face.

Charles.

He stood at the back of the crowd, half in shadow. Only the fireworks illuminated him. But he was alone. No woman was with him, and his face was... Cedric tried to read his expression, but it proved difficult in the growing gloom. Charles never had trouble securing companionship, yet tonight during the Vauxhall magic of the fountains and the fireworks he was alone, decidedly so.

Cedric had the strange feeling that he was intruding

upon something intimate and personal. Whatever had brought Charles here tonight was not meant for anyone else to witness. A man's loneliness was somehow sacred, belonging only to him, and it was not right for others to witness it like this.

"We should go," Cedric said to Ashton once they were able to push their way past the visitors to the gardens and reach their other companions.

"We all agreed he needs intervention," Godric reminded him. The duke's eyes were full of a pain that Cedric felt deep in his bones. When one man in the League hurt, they all hurt. It wasn't easy to explain, but it was undeniably true.

Resigned to his duty, Cedric pointed out Charles. They turned to look where he was pointing. All the faces in the crowd were turned skyward to watch the fireworks, but something was amiss. A man about twenty feet from Charles was watching Charles. Then he seemed to notice the League watching him.

"My God, it's him," Cedric said, half to himself.

"Who?" asked Godric.

"Gordon." Cedric would never forget the face of the man who'd almost murdered him and his sister Horatia. He remembered the gardener's cottage burning all around them, and how he'd been left blind for months afterward.

The man locked eyes with Cedric and gave him a nod, then turned his attention back on Charles and reached into his coat.

"Who is Gordon?" Godric asked.

"My former footman," said Lucien. "One of Hugo's assassins!"

Ashton spurred them into action. "Go! Stop him!"

The League broke apart, each man shoving at the crowds around them, trying to find the quickest path to Charles and the man stalking him.

Charles turned away and slipped into the hedgerows, vanishing from view, unaware of his peril. The assassin followed him like a black wraith into the shadows. Cedric was not a man to dwell on fanciful notions. He was a sportsman who needed to believe in things he could feel and touch, but the sight of that man haunting Charles's steps in the cloaked gloom made Cedric wonder if devils were in fact real.

Cedric shouldered a rather plump woman out of his way, who harrumphed in indignation, swinging at him with her fan, but he was already out of her way. Lucien, however, caught the woman's fan right in his face. Cedric dodged the edge of the massive fountain, leapt over a bench facing the garden path, and kept running.

Godric was now a step behind him and the dark stranger they pursued perhaps fifteen feet away. But there was no sign of Charles. If they couldn't reach the man soon, he would vanish. Without warning Gordon spun, a blade in his palm as he lunged straight for Cedric.

"Hello again!" said Gordon.

Godric grasped Cedric by his coat and hauled him

backward, preventing him from being slashed by the man's blade. Too late, Cedric realized the position they'd let themselves be caught in.

"It's a trap!"

Gordon hadn't been trying to catch up with Charles—he'd been luring them all away from him. How easily Cedric saw it now. That was why Gordon had waited until Cedric saw him to make his move.

Cedric and Godric prepared to fight the man, though they were both unarmed.

"Two of you, eh?" he said. "Hardly seems like a fair fight." Out of nowhere a second blade appeared in his other hand. "That's better. Now, who would like to die first?"

Thump! Gordon collapsed to the ground with a muffled cry as someone tackled him from the side. Ashton had somehow found a way to cut the man off from a different path, and he struggled with him now.

"Careful! He has two knives!" Godric cried out. There was a sudden yelp. Ashton leapt back, a knife in his hand.

The other was buried in Gordon's thigh. Gordon staggered to his feet, only to drop to his knees.

"Well...that wasn't...supposed to happen."

"It's over, Gordon," said Ashton.

The man smiled darkly. "You can't be everywhere, Lennox," Gordon said, his voice harsh, but growing weak.

"You might be surprised," Ashton growled. Cedric

couldn't understand why the man didn't stand up or fight back. The wound was not a fatal one.

Ashton raised the blade to his nose, inhaling carefully, then his eyes widened in shock.

"What is it?" Lucien asked.

"Belladonna." Ashton dropped the blade as though burned and checked his clothes.

"Did he cut you?" Cedric asked.

Ashton sighed in relief and shook his head.

"Poison? Why would he…"

Ashton bent over the dying man. "Spare your soul some damnation and tell us what you know. Who were you really after?"

The assassin smiled weakly. "I believe you know," Gordon replied simply. "And if you don't, well, it won't really matter much longer." Then he convulsed on the ground, and his eyes rolled back into his head.

Ashton punched the gravel beside the man's head. "Damn it all!" He sat back on his heels and cursed again under his breath.

"We'd best go now, before someone sees us," Godric said quietly. "We can't be tied to this. It would be too easy for Hugo to use it against us."

"Agreed." Lucien gripped Ashton by the arm and hauled him up to his feet. "Let's go."

They sank back into the security of a smaller path, one that would lead them out of the gardens. Cedric prayed that Charles would be safe wherever he was, at least for tonight.

I AM A BLOODY FOOL.

Charles sighed heavily as he walked up the steps to his townhouse. He had spent nearly two hours scouring Vauxhall Gardens, hoping to see the woman in the red gown again. It was a silly notion to think he could find her there simply because that was where she had been when those brutes from Lewis Street had taken her, but he had no idea where else to look. He had only her first name to go by, and no one he'd met remembered seeing anyone of her description with that name. She was an enigma he feared he would never unravel.

Was she a gentle-born lady? The conservative cut of her fine red silk gown suggested so, but her defiance and bravery were not traits often found in a gentle-born woman. Certainly, he had known brave women, the wives of his friends were excellent examples, but their bravery had been tempered by their positions in life, even when they dared to reach beyond it.

Lily had been different. When she broke free of her captors, something about her reminded him of himself, and where he drew his own strength from, and that feeling had only strengthened as they spoke. She had experienced things in her past, dark things, he was sure of it. It had created a strange longing for her, for the sense of kinship the woman gave him.

"Who are you?" he whispered into the darkness. For the first time in his life, he felt his heart race like a boy in love. But that was ridiculous. He'd experienced infatuation, lust, and a myriad of other emotions for the women he'd been with over the years, but this was the first time something...pure seemed to burn inside him, an emotion so deep and clear it rang like a bell.

Have I ever been in love? No, not in the way the poets put to paper. He certainly had been in lust, but never love.

He was still lost in these ruminations as he returned home. The lamps had been extinguished, except for a few nearest him. He felt an emptiness in his home; the servants were likely downstairs seeing to their own supper.

Ramsey exited the door to the servants' quarters. "My lord. Thank God you are home."

Charles tensed. He recognized that tone. "What happened?"

"Come upstairs and I'll explain." Ramsey motioned for Charles to follow behind. "Your brother arrived an hour or so ago, presumably on foot. He was badly beaten."

"By whom?"

"We do not know. We only know that the men involved were connected to Lewis Street. Does that mean anything to you?"

"Yes, I fear it does." Charles followed Ramsey to a guest bedchamber. Inside, he found Graham lying on the bed, Tom Linley at his side. The lad had been holding Graham's hand. Tom withdrew his hand from Graham's grasp, his face reddening as he backed away.

"We had the doctor here to check him over. A few broken ribs and a bruised throat. The greatest concern is whether he's bleeding inside. He will need to rest for a few weeks, at least."

Charles sat on the edge of the bed close to his brother.

"Graham..." He touched his brother's shoulder and Graham stirred, his eyes opening.

"Charles. Thank God..." Graham's voice was rough, but he continued to talk. "Kent is dead. They killed him."

Pain lanced his heart. The Earl of Kent was dead? Charles had known Phillip a long time, almost as long as Graham, and had counted him among his friends.

He grasped his brother's hand, holding it, wishing he could lend Graham his strength. "What happened? Tell me everything."

"We were gambling at the Cockerel. Do you know it?"

"I do. By the docks."

"A man sat down beside us and started winning. You know Phillip—he has the devil's own luck at cards. But not tonight. I tried to get him to quit, but this man would always egg him on into another hand, until he lost more than he could repay." Graham winced as he shifted in the bed.

"What happened then?"

"The man told Phillip there was a way he could pay

back his debts to avoid becoming a public spectacle. He could fight in the Lewis Street boxing rings. I went with him and..." Graham closed his eyes as he fought to keep his composure. "He never stood a chance. They put him in a ring and wouldn't let him out, even after he won the match. They kept sending in another, and another, and the betting grew higher and higher. They wore him down, and when he couldn't stand... The last one kicked him until he didn't move again. I tried to stop them, but they..." He couldn't finish, but his injuries made this part of the story clear.

"How did you get out?" One could easily become lost in the Lewis Street underground.

"Lucky, I suppose. I didn't know where I was going. But eventually I felt the breeze, stumbled my way through until I could see the torch lights flicker." Graham choked on his next words. "I left him, Charles. I couldn't get his body out...I..."

Flashes of another dark and terrible night returned to Charles. The chill of the river, cutting like a knife as he splashed to the surface, finally free of the ropes that had bound him to the heavy stone Hugo tried to drown him with.

But at what cost? Peter... He couldn't find him. He struggled, cried out Peter's name. Had he hurt Peter in his struggles? Had he...? The fear of what he might have done that night never left him. He'd been about to dive back down after Peter, even though he had no strength left in him, but Godric had grabbed him and swum to the bank. He surrendered to exhaustion and let the others get him to shore. They clawed their way onto the muddy bank and collapsed onto their backs.

Still gasping for air, he had stared at the sky above, the wild array of stars so thick they filled the sky. Their cold, distant light choked him with emotions. Peter would never again see them, and he would, because of the four men who lay beside him. He raised his head, and there, on the opposite bank, his would-be murderer was also climbing out of the water, swearing his revenge upon them all. Their war wasn't over; it had only just begun.

"Graham," Charles spoke soothingly. He better than anyone knew the pain Graham was going through emotionally and physically. "Who was the man who bet against Phillip?"

"David...or Daniel... Sheffield. Yes, that was his name."

Charles closed his eyes, trying to mask his reaction. That was the man who had betrayed Jonathan and Audrey in Calais. Hugo's second-in-command.

Once I find him, he will pay for Phillip.

Graham looked away, his face full of shame. "Charles, I know I shouldn't have come"

"You are right where you belong, brother," Charles said. "We are blood, and we are always here for each other." He gave Graham's hand another squeeze. "Rest now. I need you alive and well to help me see justice done."

Graham closed his eyes, and sleep claimed him once again.

Charles watched his brother for a moment before he nodded for Ramsey to leave, then turned to Tom.

"Thank you for staying here with him. You are a good man." He paused, his emotions still raw. "You don't know how much I *need* to have friends who are loyal and true."

"I'm your valet, sir. It's my duty."

"You are far more than that, Tom. We are friends."

"Friends, sir?"

"Yes. I believe we have been for some time now." He smiled ruefully. He had needed a friend desperately the night he met Tom.

Tom frowned, as if uncertain about what he was about to say. "Then may I ask a personal question, as a friend?"

Their gazes locked. Something about Tom's eyes reminded him of late-summer storm clouds. The kind of storm he had loved as a boy, one where he would dash into the meadows, reckless and unafraid, to watch the clouds climb upon one another, the rumbling thunder building and the feeling of a static charge in the air. He'd felt invincible then, ready to face any challenge by man or nature, and life had seemed endless. That innocent boy was gone. Dead long ago. But when he looked into Linley's eyes, he saw flashes of that boy, as though the lightning from the storm had struck him and brought him back to life.

"Ask me anything, Tom."

"What happened between you and your brother?"

Charles looked to Graham again.

"He never forgave me for the death of our father."

Tom sucked in a breath, but didn't interrupt him.

"My father fought in a duel in my stead. I was a boy, only seventeen at the time, and I challenged someone to a duel. My father knew I would get myself killed and took my place instead."

Tom reached out and put a hand on his shoulder. "He died in the duel?"

"No. He killed the other man, but that death haunted him. Broke him. He felt like he had murdered that man in cold blood. He died a year later, from grief and guilt." Charles hadn't spoken these details to anyone, not even the League. But Tom had been here with Graham and knew of the ill will his brother held. He deserved to know the truth as to why.

"Graham blames me, and rightly so. If I hadn't lost my temper, our father might still be alive."

And I wouldn't have broken my family apart. His reckless temperament had hurt so many people and ruined so many lives. His father's, Peter's, even Hugo's, the man now determined to destroy him.

"You were practically a child." Tom gave Charles's shoulder a squeeze. In that moment, Charles knew he had a bond with Tom much like he had with Godric and the others. Something that he couldn't define, but it was there, tying them together. Someday he hoped Tom would return the favor and talk about his own past.

"Some sins are unforgivable, no matter the age."

He looked at his brother's face, hating the void that had stretched between them. He had been too afraid to try to get close to Graham after their father died, too filled with guilt to believe he could make things right.

Tom must have read his thoughts. "My lord, it isn't too late. He came to *you* in his hour of need."

"I hope you are right," Charles said. He had to make things right before it was too late, before Hugo triumphed. Charles knew how it would be in the end. Too much darkness surrounded them for either he or Hugo to ever forgive the other. In the end, one of them would die.

I can't afford any more innocent lives lost, not to him.

"You don't have to stay," he told Tom. "I'll watch over him now."

Tom said nothing, but did not move from his post. His quiet determination filled Charles with a sense of hope. Surely so long as good men and women with noble minds and pure hearts stood by one another, they could keep the darkness of those like Hugo at bay.

He had to believe that, or all was lost.

8

Lily slipped out of the guest bedchamber a few hours before dawn, after Charles ordered her to go to bed. She was happy to obey; she was dead on her feet by this point.

As she reached her room, she saw Davis leaving his. He froze when he saw her. Something flashed in his eyes that put her on her guard.

"Tom, a word, please."

She followed him into her room, heart pounding. Davis closed the door. Kat was still asleep in her crib.

Davis crossed his arms over his chest. "I know."

Lily had to fight to conceal her panic. "Know what?"

"You want me to say it?" His voice softened, but she remained mute. He sighed. "You are a woman." He kept his voice quiet, aware that his words would carry through the hall if he spoke much louder.

"I'm not"

Davis jerked the cap off her head and pulled at her hair. She winced as the pins keeping the wig tight to her scalp pulled free. She felt naked and covered her head where her long blonde hair was tightly pinned down. Hugo had considered having her crop her hair short, but decided she was more useful to him if she could play more roles than just a young boy. She wondered if he would ever admit to his mistake if he found out.

Lily was faced with a terrible choice. Right now, Davis was vulnerable. His real hand was clutching her wig, leaving only his wooden hand free. She weighed her options, based on what she had learned from Hugo's teachers.

She didn't want to kill him, but she could. However, that would create further complications, far too many to allow her to remain here without suspicion. She would have to escape with Kat and report to Hugo, and she feared how that would end.

She could knock him unconscious and escape, but that would lead to the same problem. Confession could not save her, nor would bribery. Davis was too loyal for such things. She didn't want to hurt him. He was the closest thing to a friend she had among the Lonsdale staff, and he was a father.

Her one hope lay in the fact that Davis didn't know *why* she was here.

"Please... Please don't tell," she begged him. "This was

the only way I could provide for Katherine. She's everything to me."

He handed her back the wig and looked over at Katherine. "She's your daughter, not your sister, is that correct?"

Lily cast her eyes downward. "Yes. How did you know?"

Davis's eyes softened for an instant. "When you think no one is looking, you change. It's very slight. I recognized it because my wife looked that way at Oliver before she died. There's no mistaking a mother's look. You nearly hid it from me. I thought more than once I was mad, but I convinced myself I had to be right."

Lily nodded. It seemed not all the training in the world could hide her motherly instincts completely. "And the father?" Davis asked. "Is it Lonsdale? Some of us have wondered. The timing of your arrival and the baby, we thought perhaps he had fathered the child and was only just now taking care of it. Such things are not unheard of."

"No, she isn't his."

Davis pursed his lips and closed his eyes, rubbing them with the thumb and forefinger. "Why the deception?"

Lily walked over to the cradle and leaned lightly on the edge. "You know why. A woman with a child can find no easy, honest way to make a living without a husband to give her credence."

"Why not a maid?"

"I was going to be a scullery maid at Berkley's, but I

learned being a footman paid far better, especially during the holidays. And it was safer too. That was how it began. And then Lord Lonsdale asked me to be his valet. I could hardly say no."

"But a young man?" Davis shook his head slowly. "Unfair as it is, I see how you made your choice. But I pity you for it."

"I neither need nor want your pity, Davis. I ask only for your silence. Katherine is well cared for, and I enjoy my position."

The footman waved a hand in surrender. "I understand, really, Tom—wait, what is your real name?"

She considered lying, but remembered that too many lies could trip you up when you least expected it. "Lily. But please, you must swear to me that you won't breathe a word of this to anyone. If you do, then the nurse Lonsdale hired will be able to look after both our children." She pointed at her child. "Don't do it for me, but for Katherine. I need to keep her safe."

"Safe from what?" Davis's eyes narrowed. "Are you in danger?"

Lily nodded. She could be almost entirely honest with him on this point. "Her father. He won't hesitate to use her or put her in harm's way if it's to his advantage."

Davis was quiet a long moment, then nodded to himself as he came to a decision.

"You're a good lad...er, lass, and his lordship is a better

man with you watching over him. I'll help in whatever way I can."

She was overcome with relief and fell back to sit on her bed. "Thank you, Davis."

"Now, you've been up all night with Lonsdale and his brother. Rest. I'll take Katherine when she wakes."

Lily thanked him and collapsed onto her bed. She had sealed the crack, but too many knew her secret. Everything could fall apart at any moment. She might not be able to remain Tom Linley for much longer. And that would make Hugo question her continued usefulness.

She would have to tell Hugo that Lady Essex desired to see her come out as a lady. It would fit into his current designs for using her easily enough. But she dreaded the idea of letting Charles see her as a woman again. Not because of what she would have to do, but because of how he made her feel. Like she was wanted, *cared* about. It was a dangerous reminder of how easy it would be to fall in love with him.

LADY ESSEX SMILED AT LILY AS THEY MET IN THE drawing room. Lily was still in her valet disguise, and she stood in front of the lovely young duchess the way that would be expected of Tom Linley.

"How are you?" the duchess asked.

"Fine, Your Grace," Lily replied. This morning she had

received an encrypted note from her master, informing her to take Emily's help, but to proceed with caution. No doubt he had concerns of his involvement being exposed, but he recognized this as an opportunity too good to miss. If he had any true fears, however, he would have arranged to meet with her first.

"Please, no need to pretend. No one is here but the two of us." Emily had sent away her servants after tea had been served.

Lily had examined the nooks and crannies of the room with a sweeping gaze before she agreed to sit down. The duchess poured tea and handed her a cup. Emily's violet eyes were sharp with intelligence, but they softened as she gave her a warm smile.

"Have you thought over my offer?"

Lily took a sip of tea before slowly nodding. "Yes, Your Grace. I think I would like to do it."

Emily clasped her hands together. "Oh, this is splendid. I was hoping you would agree. I have already been making preparations, you see."

"Preparations?" Lily almost squeaked the word and cleared her throat. "What sort of preparations?"

"I have dreamed up your background." The duchess produced a small bit of paper and handed it to Lily. "And I have a seamstress waiting just outside."

Lily could only stare as the duchess went to the door and opened it. She poked her head into the hall, speaking to someone. A young woman entered, in her early twenties, with kind eyes and a manner that put Lily at ease.

"This is Everly. She's a wonderful modiste and most discreet," Emily promised. "I adore Madame Ella, but when I saw Everly's designs when she arrived in London a few weeks ago, I knew I wanted to hire her. Now I have a good reason to."

Lily stared at Everly and Everly stared back, sizing her up. "Well, come now. Let's see what we are working with. Surely not a boy's figure under all that."

Lily came forward, like she was drifting through a curious dream as Everly turned her around removed her coat. "Remove your waistcoat as well. Are you bound?" Everly nodded at Lily's bosom.

"I am."

"Do you happen to know your size, in inches? That way we won't need to unbind you."

Lily gave Everly her measurements and then kept still while the woman worked, examining her from head to foot.

"How many dresses?" she asked the duchess.

"At least a dozen to start, as well as all the necessities. Boots, cloak, riding habit, gloves, reticules."

"Understood, Your Grace." Everly flashed Lily a smile and exited the room. Lily snatched up her waistcoat and quickly drew it back on. She felt oddly naked without it, as though her disguise was no longer complete.

"Now." Emily nodded at the paper Lily had set aside. "Let's review your history, shall we?"

Lily examined the sheet. "My name is Lily Wycliff?"

Emily grinned. "I do actually have a distant Wycliff cousin. It is much easier to sell a lie when it's concealed within a truth, don't you think?"

Lily felt a chill. Hugo often said the same thing. "Yes, it is." She looked over the next few lines.

"I'm a widow? With a daughter?"

"Yes. That part will be more difficult. But it's necessary for your daughter's sake. Does she have any middle names? Something she could go by? We can't have anyone hearing the name Katherine and make the connection as to who you are."

"Yes, of course. Sophia, that's her middle name."

"Sophia Wycliff," Emily repeated the name.

Lily read the rest of the notes. She was the widow of a man named Aaron Wycliff. "And we are second cousins?"

"By marriage. Aaron was a second cousin of mine that I met as a girl. Now, after his death, you are coming to stay with me."

"Stay with you?" Lily handed back the note she had been given. She had learned under Hugo's employ to quickly memorize anything given to her.

"Yes. I believe you should move into my residence and bring Sophia with you." The duchess had seamlessly transitioned to calling Katherine by her middle name.

"But Lord Lonsdale will be expecting me to—"

"I've already thought of that. You shall tell him an aunt of yours has taken ill and likely will die soon. Request a few weeks off. He will give them to you."

Emily had thought of everything. "And His Grace won't mind my being here?"

"Godric? Heavens, no." The duchess touched her rounded belly. "He will likely be relieved if I tell him that you will be here to help me through the delivery. After Lord Rochester and his wife had an early birth, well, it's left my husband somewhat shaken."

Lily had been there the night Charles helped deliver Lord Rochester's child when it arrived almost a month early. He had been a hero to her, though she'd never been able to tell him that.

She thought back to the night she had lain in her small room above the gambling hell with only a tavern maid to help her bring Katherine into the world.

She'd managed to survive her escape from Hugo, despite having no money and no references, by finding work down below and a room she could afford above a gambling hell. It had been far from easy, and even the barmaid with her now had marveled at her resilience. She lay there on the bed, bleeding and exhausted, holding the babe in her arms, wondering if now she could finally rest.

Then Hugo entered the room. She hadn't seen him since the day he had stolen her innocence, yet somehow he had found her.

She hadn't known then that he was a spymaster and had her movements followed for the last nine months.

He waved the tavern wench out of the room. "I'm sorry I wasn't here sooner."

"Sorry?"

"I know how you must feel about me, but I am not without compassion. I had hoped to make this moment easier for you, if it were within my power."

She choked on her tongue, clutching the tiny baby to her chest, fear screaming inside her hard enough to make her bones rattle. "I..." Why was he being...amicable? It didn't fit with the way he'd stolen her innocence nine months ago.

"So, tell me, do I have a son?" Hugo held out his hands, his face reflecting an unexpected look of hope that stunned her. Lily stared at him, her body frozen, hands locked around the wool blanket that swaddled her newborn child.

"Not a son..." she whispered.

Hugo's interest dampened, and his lips wilted into a frown. "A girl? That is unfortunate."

His meaning was clear. He had a son, but he'd hoped for a spare, and a girl was not useful to him. All the better. It meant he wouldn't want her.

"I have nothing you want, Sir Hugo. Please leave. She's mine." Lily would not let this man have anything to do with her child.

He placed one hand on the headboard of the small bed and leaned over her.

"That's not up to you. She's mine if I wish her to be. No court would deny me. Do you understand?"

Lily closed her eyes. She hadn't even named the child yet, and already she was to be taken away from her?

"Please...I must keep her." She swallowed her humiliation and begged Hugo for mercy.

"Perhaps. You see, you were wrong a moment before. You do have something I want." His tone was less cold and more curious now.

"I'll give you anything," she replied instantly. She would do anything for her child.

"I have been watching you, you see. You are resourceful, in your own limited fashion. You understand what it takes to survive, the sacrifices and compromises required for survival." He looked around at her meager surroundings. "You might consider your conditions poor, but if I were to thrust ten other women into the same conditions, I'd wager none would have made it this far. I can use someone like you." Hugo stood, appraising her in a far different way than the night he'd stolen her virtue. "Yes. You could be most useful."

He turned and left for the door. "You may keep the child...for now. I will come for you both in a few months." He stopped and turned back to her. "Do not delude yourself into believing you can flee. Do as I say, and I will see to it you and the child are compensated."

Lily clutched her child the rest of the night, too terrified to sleep.

. . .

"LILY?" EMILY CLEARED HER THROAT, JERKING LILY away from her thoughts of the past.

"Yes, Your Grace?"

"Call me Emily. If we are to be cousins, then you must play the part."

"Of course, Emily." Lily still couldn't believe that the duchess was helping her. A bitter taste filled her mouth, and her palms moistened with sweat. Lord, how was she going to survive this?

Emily touched her arm in concern. "Are you all right? You've grown very pale."

"It's simply the stress of the situation, Your Grace. I mean, Emily."

"Oh, then you must sit." Emily tried to tug her into a chair, but Lily shook her head.

"I'm sorry. I must return to Lonsdale and make my plans to leave."

"Then do try to come tomorrow. Do you have a dress to wear? I can't have you appear here as Tom every day."

"I do." Lily had some dresses at her old room above the gambling hell.

"Then come tomorrow, assuming Charles agrees to give you time away." Emily gave her arm a gentle squeeze. "We will help you, Lily. I promise. There are many wonderful young gentlemen who will be most excited to meet you."

"Thank you." Lily collected her cap and secured it on her head. "You've been most kind."

Emily followed her to the door. "Of course. We rebellious ladies must stick together, after all."

As Lily exited the Essex household, she wished desperately that she was more like Emily and the others. But she could never be one of them. She was unworthy of their warmth and generosity. Someday they would know who she really was, and they would curse her name.

9

"How are you feeling?" Charles carried a tray of food into the guest bedchamber for Graham. His younger brother sat up in bed, his face still a messy mix of blue and purple bruises. One eye was almost swollen shut.

Graham winced as he reached for the toast on the tray Charles placed on his lap. "I feel like the devil himself trod all over me with his cloven hooves."

"Eat, even if it hurts. Food will help you heal." Charles pulled the chair up to the side of the bed and watched as Graham ate. It'd been so long since he and Graham had talked, let alone been in the same room like this.

Graham paused in his breakfast to look at him. "You don't have to stay and watch me eat."

"I know. I suppose I am just glad you came to me." He

didn't have the courage to confess how much it meant to him that his brother had sought him out.

"I didn't *plan* on coming here," Graham said a bit gruffly. "But I knew I couldn't go home to Mother and Ella." Graham put his hand to his chest in obvious pain. Charles understood Graham's concerns. Charles had lived in this home for the last ten years. It was a bachelor residence, but a large one. He hadn't wanted his mother and sister under the same roof because he often brought ladies home for a night. It was deuced uncomfortable to come down for breakfast after a tumble in bed, only to find your mother scowling at you over a cup of tea. If Graham had shown up at their mother's house in his condition, it would have been disastrous.

"No, I suppose you couldn't. Mother would have had a fit. Then she'd want to storm the Lewis Street tunnels herself. And Ella..."

"Would've been terribly upset," Graham finished.

"Yes." Charles's little sister was not good at handling difficult news. She was a tiny fae-like woman with a soft heart much too big for her. She had been often ill as a child, and while it hadn't done any overt damage, it had made her more delicate. If she were to see Graham injured, it would destroy her.

"Charles," Graham said, his eyes downcast. "What are we going to do about Phillip?"

"I'm going to handle it. I will find him if he's still there."

Graham's eyes went wide with terror. "But you can't go down there. You'll get killed."

Charles stood and walked over to the window, bracing one hand on the frame. "I've been down there before. I know my way."

"What?"

Charles couldn't look his brother in the eye. "I...have been known to box in the rings down there from time to time."

He turned at the sudden sound of dishes clattering as Graham shoved the tray aside to try to get out of bed. He made it to his feet, but he had to lean against the bedpost for support. His face was ashen.

"Why... *Why* would you fight down there? You have Fives Court. Why would you seek out a place like that?"

Why? Because I feel alive only when there are risks involved, when there is a chance to truly get hurt. Because I deserve to hurt. I deserve it.

"Charles..." Graham spoke his name softly. It reminded Charles so much of when they were boys, before he had ruined everything between them.

"Don't worry yourself. I always win. They haven't found a man yet who could beat me." His falsely cheerful boast made his brother frown.

"I'm going to put aside the part where it is clear you want to get yourself killed. You truly believe you could explore the tunnels and find Phillip?"

"Yes." Charles pointed at the bed. "Eat and rest. I'll

take care of everything." It was midday, so the tunnels would be empty and quiet, aside for the occasional thief or fighter waiting for night to fall.

"Don't go alone. *Please*. I cannot lose you as well." Graham grabbed his sleeve, jerking him to a stop.

"I'll take someone with me," he promised. Graham released him, and Charles left the bedchamber. He was in the hall putting on his greatcoat when Tom arrived through the service entrance.

"My lord, I need to speak with you." The young lad's voice was breathless, as though he'd been running.

"No time, Tom, I'm off for the day. Won't be back for a few hours, if not longer." There was no way he would take the boy with him. He could fight, it was true, but this required someone experienced with danger. Ashton, perhaps, or Cedric. Not the whole League, of course. That would attract too much attention.

"I'm sorry, sir. I'm afraid my aunt has fallen ill. Aunt Miriam needs me."

Charles froze. "You've never mentioned an aunt before." Then again, he'd only learned of Tom's uncle yesterday.

Tom's gaze fell. "She was my mother's sister. They quarreled a lot when I was a boy. Now that she is dying, she has summoned me to make amends. I'm sorry to leave you on such short notice, my lord."

Part of Charles wanted to make Tom stay, but that would be selfish. "You will come back, of course?"

A strange mixture of emotions crossed Tom's face, too fast for Charles to decipher. "Oh, yes, sir. Davis has agreed to see to your needs until I return."

Charles nodded. "Go on then, but write me when you reach your aunt. I want to know you arrived safely. And I expect you to return as soon as possible."

The tension in Tom's face eased. "Thank you, my lord. I will."

Charles wanted to say something more, but there was no time. He turned his back on Tom and closed the door behind himself as he left.

He walked down the street and up the steps to Ashton's door, never more relieved that most of the League lived so close to each other when they were in London. He tapped the knocker. When the butler answered, Charles was shown inside immediately, another one of the benefits of the League's close-knit relationship. So long as the gentleman in question was home, they would be shown inside with none of the usual pretense of having to pay formal calls. Charles waited in the drawing room. But when the door opened, he instead saw Rosalind, Ashton's fiery Scottish wife.

"Charles?" Rosalind came over to him. "What's the matter? The butler said you seemed ill."

"Ill with concern, perhaps," he murmured, catching sight of his pale face in the wall mirror, Rosalind now beside him. When he'd first met her, he hadn't wanted to trust her love for Ashton, going so far as to try to bribe her to leave, but he'd been wrong about her. She loved Ashton as fiercely as he loved her.

That didn't stop him from feeling frustrated, though. As much as he was glad for his friends settling down with wives who were worthy of them, those same wives created complications. Before marriage, his friends would have willingly dashed off with him to a place like the Lewis Street tunnels, but now? Now his friends had other considerations before they put their lives in danger, such as the safety of their families. Resentment crawled beneath his skin. He hated that part of himself, knowing it was wrong to feel that way.

"Ash will be down soon. I just want to be sure that you are all right." Rosalind touched his arm. He covered her hand with his, patting it once before he let go and so did she.

"I'm quite fine."

But he wasn't fine. Right now his greatest fear was that he would ask Ashton for his help, and Rosalind would forbid it. Rosalind nodded and left him alone. Perhaps she had sensed something in his tone. A few minutes later, Ashton joined him.

"Charles?" There was a note of concern in his voice. "I heard you aren't feeling well?"

"It's not what you think." He paused, making sure Rosalind wasn't lurking near the door. "I need your help. I have to go into the Lewis Street tunnels to retrieve a body. It's a matter of honor and respect for a friend."

Ashton's face went blank. "A *body*?"

"Lord Kent. He was most likely killed there last night. My brother was with him and almost met the same fate. I promised I would retrieve him, come what may. I know the tunnels well, but it would be unwise to go alone. Especially once you learn who was behind it."

Ashton waved for them to leave. "You had best tell me everything that happened on the way."

They soon caught a hackney to Lewis Street. By the time they were at the entrance to the tunnels, he had told Ashton everything he knew. When they knocked on the door, Charles expected the gatekeeper to slide open the hatch and peer at them. But he wasn't there. Charles tried the door handle, and the door opened with a heavy groan. The gate was unguarded. That left him with an unsettled pit in his stomach.

"Sheffield had to have had a reason to maneuver Lord Kent into such a position." Ashton kept close to Charles as they moved deeper into the dark bowels below Lewis Street. Lamps hung every twenty feet along the craggy walls, illuminating just enough of their path for them to keep walking.

"Obviously it was on Hugo's orders."

"Obviously," Ashton agreed. "But why? A message? Then why not Graham instead?"

"I'm not sure," Charles whispered. The tunnels had ears, and he did not want to risk being overheard.

"Perhaps it is because Lord Kent is a man without a family. There is no one to seek answers for his death."

Charles scowled. "Or perhaps Hugo wants to remind us that *no one* is far enough removed for his designs. He planned for Graham to be there, to witness everything, and to come to me for help. No one with any connection to us, no matter how remote, can be considered safe anymore."

Ashton started walking again, and Charles led him deeper into the dark. "I believe Hugo is starting his endgame now."

The narrow tunnel opened into a cavernous space with several boxing rings. At the far end of the room there was a group of iron cells meant to keep people locked up. In the times of the Tudors, this space had been a dungeon used for keeping political prisoners too influential to be kept in more visible prisons. When the monarchs wanted someone to disappear quietly, they ended up in the tunnels.

Charles shivered at the empty quiet of the room. It was usually so thick with sweating bodies that a man could barely get through.

Ashton pointed toward a lumpy object toward the back by the cells. There was a body inside wearing what had once been fine clothes. "There."

Heart pounding, Charles hurried over and knelt by the corpse, rolling him over onto his back. The face was almost unrecognizable, but it was Lord Kent.

"His leg has been broken," Ashton observed. "What animals would do this and call it sport?" Ashton's calm demeanor was crumbling at the sight of Phillip's tortured body.

"Graham said they beat him until he stopped moving." Fury swept through him. Hugo may have believed no one would avenge Phillip, but he was wrong, so very wrong.

The man suddenly moved. His body seized, and a gasp of air escaped his lips.

"Bloody Christ!" Charles fell back onto his backside in alarm.

"He's not dead!" Ashton pulled Charles to his feet. Together, they lifted Phillip up by his arms, taking one over each of their shoulders.

"Phillip? Can you hear me?" Charles asked.

"G-Graham...?" The croaked whisper was full of pain.

"Graham sent me," said Charles. "Good God, Ash. We've got to get him out."

They lifted him up, trying to keep any pressure off his legs while they carried him back up the sloping tunnel. There was still no sign of the gatekeeper. It was as though the tunnels has been abandoned. Charles was grateful for the ease of their escape, but he couldn't help but feel that they were being played somehow. Or watched. Once they reached the portal to the street, Charles stayed with Phillip while Ash summoned a coach, and then they carefully lifted him inside.

"Take him to your home," Ash said. "I'll get the doctor."

Charles nodded. Time was of the essence if they were going to save him.

10

Lily carried Katherine out of the servants' quarters, saying her goodbyes to the staff. It took every bit of her self-control not to cry. These men and women were good, loyal people who had helped her settle into a life here, a life that had become a happy dream, at least when she was wasn't reminded that she was the cuckoo in their nest.

She looked back upon the house before she summoned a coach. The beautiful townhouse looked much like the other houses on the street, but the red door with a lion's head knocker would always be home for her, and leaving it made her heart ache.

"Mama?" Katherine whispered drowsily and burrowed closer to her.

She stroked a hand up and down Katherine's head before she climbed into the coach. "Sleep, love."

When they reached the gambling hell, it was late afternoon. Lily carried her daughter up the back stairs and slipped out a brass key to unlock the door. This time she was careful to check the shadows in the room, half expecting to find Hugo lurking here again.

She set Katherine down on the bed and changed out of her clothes. Removing the bindings around her breasts, she drew in a deep breath. Then she pulled on her stockings, stays, petticoats, and a dark-blue day gown that buttoned up the front. She removed the cap and wig and took some time to brush out her long gold locks, then washed off the colored powder that concealed her more feminine features. It was a relief to look like herself again and not have to spend an hour each morning changing her face to hide.

She finished cleaning her face and then worked her hair into a simple coiffure. She studied herself in the cracked mirror. It wasn't perfect, but it would have to do.

She collected her Tom Linley disguise and tucked it under the bed, out of the view of casual eyes in case someone got into the room while she was gone. She glanced at herself once more in the mirror, and it began to sink in that the end was coming. Hugo intended for her to seduce Charles, and then his final plan would be set in motion. There would be no more Tom and no more life in Charles's home.

No more Charles.

And then what? she wondered. Would she at last be free

of Hugo? He had promised her as much. He'd said he would allow her and Katherine to live in the country and to do what she wanted. She would be free, free to carry the guilt of her actions with her forever.

But she also knew how Hugo thought. He had invested time and money into her education, and he hated wasting resources. Part of her knew that she would hear a familiar sound a year or two later, that of a cane being stuck against her door, and a new task would require her attention.

She would never be truly free.

With a heavy sigh, she picked up her daughter and left the room Katherine had been born in, locking it behind her. She hired another coach to take her to the Essex townhouse. There she was let in by a footman, and Emily rushed down the stairs to greet her.

"Lily! You came." Emily embraced her as though they were cousins and not plotting a deception to fool the *ton* about her identity. Emily gave Katherine a little kiss on the forehead just as her husband came down the stairs.

Lily had been around Godric many times, but she'd always been somewhat invisible as a servant. Now she was facing him in a dress, holding her daughter and feeling exposed. Would he recognize her?

"Mrs. Wycliff?" Godric beamed at her. His green eyes and natural charm hit her hard. No wonder Emily adored this man. When he smiled, it was like the sun came out after days of rain. Of course, it was nothing compared to when Charles smiled. If Godric was sunshine, Charles was the sun himself. All heat, light, and raw power that consumed her completely. Lord, she'd only just left him, and she already missed him.

"Your Grace." She dropped into a curtsy, which proved difficult since she still held Katherine in her arms. The child stirred and rubbed her eyes and blinked owlishly at Godric.

"And who is this then?" Godric rubbed Katherine's chin, beaming at the child. Lily could already tell he would make an indulgent, loving, and protective father.

"Sophia, Your Grace." She kissed the crown of Katherine's blonde head. "Sophia, this is Lord Essex."

"Shush. You may call me Uncle Godric." He winked at the girl, and she smiled at him, clapping her hands together.

"I have a nurse for her upstairs in the nursery if you would like to get her settled," Emily offered.

"Thank you, Emily." She curtsied again to Godric and followed Emily upstairs.

A matronly woman named Mrs. Yorke took charge of Katherine and set her down in a room full of toys. A large wooden crib was prepared, with a warm fire lit in the hearth. It looked so inviting and wonderful that Lily's eyes burned with tears.

"Emily, it's..."

"Please say it's all right. Godric and I have been

preparing this for the last two months, and I'm so glad Sophia will be able to use it before our own child arrives."

Katherine reached for a toy horse and waved it at the nurse, who chuckled and sat down next to her, picking up a doll to join in play with Katherine.

"It's more than I ever could have dreamed. More than we deserve." Lily clutched her hands to her chest, her throat tight as she watched her daughter play.

"Nonsense. You deserve this. Everyone does." Emily hugged her shoulders. "Now, come down and have some tea. I want to tell you about the ball tonight."

"A ball? So soon?" Lily waved to Katherine as she left the nursery, but the child was completely engrossed playing with Mrs. Yorke.

"Yes. I apologize for the short notice. Lord Sanderson and his wife are hosting one tonight, and I thought it would be a perfect opportunity for you to meet some decent gentlemen. I've already spoken to Lady Sanderson, and she's thrilled to have you attend."

"But I don't have a suitable dress..." She had left the red gown in the room above the gambling hell, afraid Charles would recognize it if she wore it. But she realized now she should have brought it so he *would* recognize her. Why hadn't she? Was she trying to sabotage herself?

"Everly had your first dress and a cloak delivered an hour ago. It's a ready-made one she was able to tailor to your measurements. I spent the morning shopping for you. There are stockings, slippers, and anything else you might need before Everly can bring you more gowns."

Emily and Lily came into the drawing room. Godric was reading a newspaper by the fire, and Emily's foxhound was resting on the cushions of a chair opposite him. The dog lifted her head as Emily approached, wagging her tail furiously, thumping against the cushions. Emily brushed her fingertips over the dog's head, whispering sweetly to it.

"Did little Sophia like the nursery?" Godric inquired.

"Yes, Your Grace. She was very excited. Thank you for letting us trespass upon your hospitality."

"Nonsense. You're family. I was sorry to hear that your husband passed. Emily said Aaron was a good man."

"He was." Lily followed Emily as she sat down on one of the settees and poured two cups of tea. The foxhound leapt up and came to sit by Emily's leg, eyeing the tray of small biscuits hopefully.

"Not now, Penelope," said Emily. The poor dog sighed and rested her head on Emily's knee, eyes rolling between Emily and the tray. "Did you remember to invite the League to the ball tonight?" she asked her husband. "Lady Sanderson expects them all to attend."

Godric frowned as he folded up his paper. "I did, darling, but do *we* have to go? What if you—?"

"I'll be fine. You may carry me up any icy steps, and I promise not to dance." Emily touched her swollen belly. "This little one isn't due for another month. She will be staying put, won't you?" She spoke this to her belly with a warm smile.

Godric looked to his wife with amused contemplation. "Emily swears our child is a girl, but I'm not so sure."

It was clear that Godric did not suspect anything unusual about her. Lily was able to relax in Godric and Emily's company and laughed as they teased each other about their coming child.

"Did you know Sophia was a girl before she was born?" Emily asked.

Lily shook her head. "No. I had no idea what to expect. I only knew that I loved the child, no matter what." Having Katherine inside her had been like sharing her heart, her breath. Loving her child was like loving herself. There'd been no question about that.

"I will certainly love a girl if we have it," Godric said as he opened his paper again. "But Lord, such a child will give me gray hair if she's anything like her mother."

"And if it's a boy who's anything like his father, I will go gray first," Emily countered. "Now, Lily, about tonight—" A knock on the drawing room door interrupted whatever Emily had been about to say. Simpkins's face appeared around the edge of the door.

"Forgive the intrusion, Your Grace, but an urgent letter has arrived from Lord Lennox."

Godric was on his feet in an instant, taking the letter. "Thank you, Simpkins." He tore the wax seal open and read the letter. His face paled. "My God."

Emily watched her husband intensely, as though she could almost read his thoughts. "Trouble, my dear?"

"Ash needs to see me at once. He and Charles retrieved Lord Kent from the tunnels on Lewis Street. He's been beaten nearly to death."

"Lord Kent?" Emily's eyes widened. "What on earth was he doing down there?"

Godric folded the letter up. "It's an underground boxing ring for those who like to fight and wager without restrictions. Charles has been there a few times. It's vicious and dangerous. It's unclear why Kent went in, however."

Lily's heart thundered madly against her ribs. Charles had gone back down there to find Kent? Her instinct was to run straight back to Charles to help. But she remembered where she was, and *who* she was now. Tom was gone forever. She was Lily Wycliff. She was trapped here. A stranger in skirts.

"This has Hugo's shadow over it, I'm sure of it," said Emily.

"I fear you are right," said Godric. "But you are not to concern yourself with this. Not in your condition."

"Are you going now?" Emily asked.

He nodded and came over to her, stealing a lingering kiss that left Lily feeling envious. If only she could have that with someone like Charles...

"The League will be meeting shortly to discuss this, but I should be home for the ball." He turned and strode from the room. Emily didn't speak for a moment. She kept quiet, her head cocked as though listening for anyone who might be close enough to hear them. When she seemed satisfied, she finally spoke.

"This does not bode well." She rubbed her temples. "I trust you know from Charles about Hugo Waverly and the danger he presents?"

Lily's throat constricted. "Yes."

"This must be his doing. Everything seems to come back to him." Emily scowled. "But the mystery is *why*. I wish they would tell me what happened that night."

Lily leaned forward. "What do you mean? How much do you know?" She'd known for a long time there was a secret, one that Charles kept buried deep. She knew Hugo was at the root of it, but neither Charles nor Hugo had ever explained what made them hate each other so.

"It was long ago, when Godric and the others were at Cambridge. Hugo kidnapped Charles from his room, bound his arms and legs, and dragged him to the river."

Lily's blood turned to ice when she pictured Hugo trying to drown Charles so viciously. "That much I know. I've heard him cry out in his sleep to that effect. But what I don't understand is why."

Emily shrugged. "I wish I knew. I'm not even sure my husband knows the full reason. Charles is a man of many secrets. He is all laughing and teasing on the surface, but when no one is looking he's a man made entirely of steel."

That was true. Lily had glimpsed that man of resolve

and courage like no one she'd ever seen before. But there were secrets there, ones that left shadows in his gray eyes. She wondered at times if his secrets were as damning as hers. Perhaps they were. She remembered how he'd cry out in the night, shuddering with nightmares and whispering the name Peter over and over until tears coated his cheeks and he slipped back into sleep. Those nights haunted her.

"Does the name Peter mean anything to you?" she asked Emily.

"Peter? Yes...I believe he was a friend of Godric's at Cambridge, but he died. Godric doesn't like to talk about it. Why do you ask?"

"It's something Charles says when he has nightmares—he whispers the name. But he never talks about Peter when he's awake."

Emily's gaze turned distant, as though she was lost in thought for a few minutes. Then she shook her head and looked at Lily.

"The two must be connected, but that's a mystery for another time. For now, we have other pressing matters. Let's go up and look at that dress for tonight. I have a feeling it will be splendid."

Emily was back to business she could handle, the ball and the task of finding Lily a husband. Despite Lily's anxiety, she managed to turn her focus to the ball as well. After all, she would see him there tonight.

Her heart gave a wild flutter. And then what? Would

she have a chance to kiss Charles again? The first time had been so wild and quick that she wasn't sure she hadn't dreamed it.

For now, she would try not to think of Hugo or his plans. She would think only of Charles and the way he made her feel whole again.

11

"How is he?" Charles asked the doctor.

Dr. Shreve shut the door to the bedchamber where Phillip had been settled and removed his spectacles, folding them carefully and tucking them away in a slender leather case before he met Charles's gaze.

"He has several broken ribs, and his left leg is fractured in two places, but I'm most concerned about the injuries inflicted to his skull. I reset the leg and bound it, but the rest?" He shook his head. "If he survives the next week, he may well yet recover, but it is in God's hands now."

Charles released a breath he hadn't realized he'd been holding. "Thank you, Doctor. I'm certain you've done everything you can." He shook Shreve's hand, and then Ramsey escorted him to the door.

"Phillip is a tough man," Ashton said, placing a hand on Charles's shoulder. "He may surprise us all."

"I hope you're right." Charles leaned against the wall and closed his eyes. God, would this nightmare ever end? Was there no crevice Hugo's tentacles could not reach? People were being hurt because of him, all because Charles been a foolish child playing adult games, thinking a duel would solve his problems. Instead, it had been the cause of all the misery that had followed him ever since. Because of that mistake, he would never know safety for himself or for the people he loved.

"I cannot do this any longer," he said quietly.

Ashton said nothing, but he joined Charles in leaning against the wall.

"If Hugo wants me, maybe I should surrender. We can't let things go on like this. What if he comes after Rosalind next? Or Lucien's newborn? He is escalating his attacks."

"Perhaps he is desperate," Ashton said, though he didn't sound convinced.

"Or he simply wishes to further tighten the screws until I beg for mercy."

Ashton said nothing in reply at first, staring off into the distance. Then he looked to Charles. "I think it's time."

"To give up?"

"No. We've always known you had a past when we saved you. None of us regret that day. But we never pushed you to tell us more than you were prepared to. But now I think, prepared or otherwise, you must tell the League everything that happened between you and Hugo. Only then can we know for certain how to proceed."

Charles often had nightmares of the night he'd almost drowned, when Peter died, but there was perhaps an even greater fear than that. To confess his sins, to explain why Hugo wanted him to suffer endless torment? Though he knew they would stand by him, part of him feared that they might in some small fashion side with Hugo and hold Charles to blame. Just as he held himself to blame.

And yet, Charles was tired of keeping his secrets. Of being a coward. Perhaps the only way to destroy the demons still haunting him was to face them.

Charles nodded slowly. "Summon them all here."

Ashton smiled. "They're already on their way. I sent the letters half an hour ago."

"One step ahead of me again?"

Ashton shook his head. "Simply being prepared. We have much to discuss, regardless."

Charles sighed. "I suppose we do." He would tell the League everything, but he would not stop there. He would free them of their vows. He would not ask them to stand by him any longer. The danger was too great, and they all had too much to lose. They had been his shield long enough. It was time for him to be theirs.

Charles and Ash went to the billiard room. He poured himself a glass of port and offered one to his friend.

Ashton politely refused and sat in a chair by the fire. A quarter of an hour passed before the others began to arrive. Godric came in first and joined Charles by the decanters. Cedric and Jonathan came in together, followed soon by Lucien.

"How is Phillip?" Lucien asked, breaking the silence.

"Alive...for now," Ashton said. "He's in a bad way. The doctor says if he lives out the week, there is hope he will survive."

"What the devil happened?" Cedric asked, looking between Charles and Ashton.

"He was lured into Lewis Street by Hugo's second-in-command," Ashton explained. "Sheffield convinced Phillip to pay off the debt he owed to him in the ring. It wasn't about money, of course."

"Then what was it about?" Jonathan asked. "Why Lord Kent?"

"Because Charles's brother, Graham, was with him. He's sending a message, without laying a finger on Charles's family directly," Ashton explained.

Charles finally spoke. "He wants me." He finished his port and stared at his closest friends. He felt he had let them down, let them get too close to him, and because of that they were all marked men.

Unless he gave himself over to Hugo.

"Well we know that," said Godric. "But why do I get the impression that you summoned us here for a different reason? I assume this has something to do with your plans, Ash?"

Ashton had long been working secretly, learning everything he could about Hugo and how best to take the fight to him. Recently, he had tasked them all with an assignment, but as of yet none of them honestly knew what Ashton was planning.

"Charles, it's time," Ashton said. Once he told them about his past, they would have every right to be done with him. And if they didn't, he would have to leave them. At least then they might be safe.

"Time for what?" Cedric asked.

"For me to tell you the truth about myself and Hugo Waverly. The reason he tried to drown me in the river Cam."

Charles poured himself another glass as every eye in the room fixed on him. He took a long, burning gulp, avoiding their gaze. He didn't want to face them, but he had to. For the sake of his soul if nothing else. Would they understand? Would they cast him out of their lives forever because of his foolishness? Fear took root in him like a blackened oak tree suffering from some disease that turned it rotten at its core. But he had to do this, had to face his friends and break the seal holding back the horrors of the past.

"It was the summer of 1807. I was seventeen, and my father had come home early from the bank. I knew right away something was wrong..."

London, April 1807

Charles glanced up from the essay he was writing for his entrance exams to Cambridge and saw his father rushing down the corridor into his study. He was home early.

"Father?" Charles abandoned his books and rushed to see his father. Guy Humphrey stood behind his desk, shoving pound notes into a small bag. When he saw Charles, he frowned.

"Father, what's wrong?"

"Not now, dear boy." He opened a drawer in in his desk and removed a pistol. He hastily primed it for a shot and tucked it inside his coat. He'd never seen his father touch the pistol in his desk before.

"Father, you're frightening me. Please, tell me what is happening."

Guy sighed heavily. "Someone I know is in trouble." His tone made Charles tense. It was one of resignation and regret.

"Trouble? Let me come, Father. I can help."

"No." His father brushed past him. "You must stay here. You must take care of your mother, as well as Graham and Ella."

"But—"

Guy turned to Charles as he reached the front door.

"For God's sake, boy, do as I say just this once! Stay

here. I will return as soon as I can." His father rushed down to grab the reins of a horse held by a waiting groom.

Charles should have listened to his father, but he knew he needed help. He couldn't let him go alone. He waved for a passing coach and pointed at his father in the distance.

"Follow that man." Then he tossed a few coins to the driver and climbed inside. The coach rumbled on the cobblestone streets for half an hour before they finally stopped. Twilight had fallen, and Charles slipped out of the vehicle and handed the man another couple of shillings.

"He went into that house, two doors down," the driver whispered.

"Thank you." Charles walked calmly down the street, trying not to appear conspicuous. When he reached the townhouse the driver had pointed out, he heard shouting from inside. His father's voice came clearly through one of the windows facing the street. Charles rushed up to the door and tried the handle. It turned, and he burst inside. The scene that met him was chaotic.

His father was at the foot of the stairs. A woman close to his mother's age leaned against him, her face stained with tears. She held one hand against a reddening cheek. At the top of the stairs a tall, dark-haired man his father's age glared down at them.

"Baltus, you bloody bastard!" Guy yelled.

Charles was baffled as to what he was witnessing.

There was fury in his father's eyes, a murderous rage that was reflected in the gaze of the man at the top of the stairs.

"You want the bitch? She's yours. I'll not have that whore under my roof anymore!"

Charles didn't know who this woman was or what she was to his father, but whoever that man was, he had hit her. If there was one thing Charles knew as a law in his heart, one did not ever hit a woman.

"How *dare* you!" Charles shouted, stepping up beside his father at the foot of the stairs.

"Charles!" Guy hissed. "Go home. Now!"

The woman stared at Charles in terror.

"Ah, so you brought the boy," Baltus sneered as he stomped down the stairs. "How fitting."

Charles held his ground, not flinching under the man's cruel inspection.

"You shouldn't even be here, boy. Did your father ever tell you that?" Baltus snapped. "He never planned on marrying your mother. He was the second son, the spare. He wanted Jane here, you see, but couldn't have her. Not when he wasn't going to be an earl. But me? I *was* good enough to have her." He pounded a fist against his chest as he continued. "And that burned him up inside. He still wants her. Even now."

"You lie," Charles growled.

"Your father married your mother and gave birth to you, the son he never wanted. And yet *my* wife..." His dark eyes pinned Jane in place. "She still pines for him like a dog. *My* son will never see you again, do you hear me, Jane? You can join Lonsdale's bloody harem for all I care. You are dead to me."

Before Charles realized what he was doing, he swung a balled fist at Baltus. When his fist connected, Baltus stumbled back a little, but recovered quickly.

"Why you little bastard. You call that a punch?"

"I call that a challenge," Charles spat in Baltus's face. "I demand satisfaction."

Jane's husband laughed darkly. "Very well. I accept. It will be a pleasure to kill you. I'll even have your father watch."

"No!" Guy released Jane and stepped between Charles and Baltus. "If it's blood you want, you can try to take mine. It is *my* honor that needs satisfaction, not his."

"Father—?" Charles started, but Guy glared at him.

"As you wish. I will kill you," Baltus warned. "And then I'll let the boy challenge me again, and I will kill him too."

"You will do no such thing," Guy said, his tone as hard as steel. "Jane, go with Charles. I trust there is a coach waiting outside?"

Charles nodded. "Yes, Father."

"Good. Take Jane outside, now."

Charles escorted the woman outside, but he was still afraid for his father.

"Th—thank you," Jane whispered as they settled into the coach outside.

"Of course. I just wish I could do more, Madam..." He didn't know what name to call her.

"Waverly, Jane Waverly. I'm a friend of your mother's. Violet and I grew up together."

"My mother?" Relief swept through him. No wonder his father wanted to protect her. She was a friend of his mother's. He didn't want to think about that nonsense Baltus had said about his father being in love with this woman. He had been trying to upset Charles, and unfortunately it had worked.

"Violet warned me to leave my husband years ago, but we both knew that wasn't possible. A husband has his rights and a woman has none." The words came in bitterness and sorrow. He'd never thought much about a woman's place in society, or her lack of power, perhaps because his parents had always treated each other as equals.

"My father will protect you," Charles promised her.

She gave him a soft and melancholy smile. "I know he will, but I cannot ask him to. I lost that privilege long ago." She touched Charles's hand in a way that reminded him of his own mother.

A moment later his father climbed into the coach, and it jolted forward.

"Jane, are you all right?" Guy opened his arms, and Jane went into his embrace.

Charles's jaw slowly fell. It was true. Jane and his father *had* been more than friends. His father had wanted to marry this woman? He gazed at them and the way they clung to each other. A sudden ache filled his heart, burning like fire.

"Does...does Mother know?" Charles asked when he finally found the strength to speak.

Guy stared at Jane, cupping her face in his hands, not speaking.

"Tell him, Guy. He deserves the truth. He's no longer a child." Jane gripped his wrists and closed her eyes.

Guy turned to Charles. "I was the second son in my family. My older brother, Stephen, died in a riding accident when I was twenty-five. You were only two years old then."

Charles nodded. He remembered Uncle Stephen, or at least he thought he did. The man had the same gray eyes as Guy and Charles did. He swore he could remember Uncle Stephen smiling at him through the haze of dim childhood memories.

"Jane and I had been sweethearts since we were children. I loved her with all my heart, but she was the daughter of a duke and I was the spare. Jane's parents wouldn't consent to let me marry her, and she was betrothed instead to Baltus Waverly. He had curried much favor with the Crown, and Jane's father preferred him over me."

Guy's face was edged with grief. "So Jane married Baltus, and I married your mother."

"Do—do you even love my mother?" Charles didn't

want to know the answer, but he had to find a way to understand all this.

"Yes. Of course I do. I never once regretted marrying her and building a life with her, but..." Guy looked to Jane. "I will always love Jane as well."

Jane's eyes said what her lips would not, that she would always love Guy as well.

"Are you going to duel with him?" Charles asked his father.

"Please don't," said Jane. "I don't want you to get hurt because of me."

"No, Jane. This is something I should've done long ago. He's hurt you long enough." Guy brushed a hand over the bruise on her cheek, and she leaned into his caress.

"Father, no. *I* challenged him. I will face him."

"*You will not.*" The harsh edge of his father's voice softened. "You are too young, Charles. And I owe him much for the pain he has caused Jane. To both of us."

Charles fell back against the coach cushions, lost in thoughts and worries.

When they reached home, Guy escorted Jane inside, and Charles tried to listen at the door as Guy explained things to his mother. All he heard were murmurs. His mother escorted Jane to the spare bedroom, and Charles was told to go to his own room.

He was given dinner in his chamber that night, in punishment for disobeying his father. He stared glumly at the cold bowl of soup. The bedchamber door opened, and Graham slipped in. He scowled at his little brother. Graham, only twelve, was quick-witted and usually amusing to have around. But Charles wasn't in a good mood tonight.

"Graham, back to bed with you."

His little brother ignored him. He climbed onto Charles's bed and sat next to him. "Father's upset."

"He is." Charles had never felt so dreadful in his life. The look his father had given him before he'd been sent off to bed haunted him. Guy was disappointed. All of his life, Charles had only ever wanted to be like his father, to make him proud. And tonight he'd failed. Not only that, but his father's life was now in danger because of his impulsive temper.

"Why is he upset?" Graham eyed Charles's tray, looking eagerly at the biscuits there.

Charles took a biscuit and gave it to Graham. "Because I did something foolish."

"What did you do?" his little brother asked between bites.

"I challenged a bad man to a duel."

His brother's eyes widened. "You're going to fight a duel?"

"No. I wanted to, but Father won't let me. He is taking my place."

"You're not a very good shot," Graham observed. "You'd probably get killed."

"I am an excellent shot," Charles snapped, unhappy at his brother's lack of confidence.

"You are not. That's why he's mad, I bet. You'd probably get killed."

"Stop saying that!"

"Do you think Father will win?" The concern in Graham's voice made Charles uncomfortable. He'd been trying to avoid that same question all night.

"He will. He has to."

Charles let Graham stay. He fell asleep around midnight. An hour before dawn, Charles crept out of his room and hid by the stairs to wait for his father. When Guy came down, dressed in black trousers and a white shirt, he didn't seem to be surprised to find Charles there.

"Come on, then," he said, and they headed to the door.

"I can come?"

"Yes. Because you caused this, Charles, you should see the consequences." His father's voice was cold and heavy. Charles looked down at his boots glumly as he followed his father to the horses.

They rode to a field at the edge of town, where Baltus was waiting for them. He wasn't alone. A young man, perhaps three years older than Charles, was there with him.

"My son, Hugo, wanted to see me kill you, Lonsdale," Baltus boasted.

Charles stared at the young man. His dark eyes were almost black as he looked upon his father with pride, smiling. The pair were like a dark mirrored reflection of how Charles felt about his own father, but where they were filled with confidence, Charles felt only fear and doubt.

Guy opened a box containing two pistols. "Choose your weapon." Baltus took one and loaded it.

"Twenty paces?" Baltus growled.

"Agreed." The two men turned back-to-back and paced away from each other. Charles moved out of the way. Baltus's son did the same. Charles's heart thudded against his ribs as he counted the paces with his father. He curled his hands into fists and prayed for it to be over.

Please let Father survive.

When his father stopped and turned, he looked to Charles, a calm confidence in his eyes.

"Be strong, Charles."

Baltus and Guy lowered their weapons at each other. The air thundered with the sound of two gunshots. Charles blinked in a daze as he stared at his father as the smoke cleared.

"No!" But the cry didn't come from Guy's lips, but Baltus's son. "Father!" Hugo rushed to Baltus as he sagged and crumpled to the ground.

Guy lowered his weapon and watched as Baltus took in a few ragged breaths, crimson blossoming on his lips as his lungs filled with blood. Charles couldn't tear his eyes away from the scene. He'd never seen a man die before, had never seen blood like this before. His vision swam, but he stayed rooted to the ground. Hugo dragged his father into his arms, tears streaking down his face. It made Charles feel like he was watching something he should not.

Hugo held him as he died, and the young man murmured soft, comforting words over and over long after the light had left his father's eyes. Guy approached them and knelt down. He whispered something to Hugo, and when the young man violently shook his head, Guy pressed a bag of coins into his hand.

After a moment of hesitation, the young man took the coins and gripped the pouch so tightly Charles thought he'd squeeze the coins into solid metal. The young man looked directly at them. Pure hatred loomed there, so clear and black that it filled his face. But the rage was not directed at Guy. It was at Charles.

Because I started this. I challenged his father. Had I said nothing, none of this would have happened. I killed him...

When Guy reached Charles, he placed a hand on his shoulder. "Come home now."

Charles didn't look back. He couldn't bear to see that young man cradling the body of his father, and he couldn't look at his own father. Some part of the light inside Guy died the moment he killed Baltus.

Nothing would ever be the same again. And it was all his fault.

12

"Good God," someone muttered. Lucien, perhaps.

Charles held his breath, unable to focus, waiting for his friends to judge him, knowing he would deserve it if any of them walked out of this room. An inner torment twisted sharply inside him, because part of him wanted them to. At least then he'd know he was right all along, that he didn't deserve them.

"I have regretted that decision every day of my life," he said at last. "And I will understand if any of you wish to leave."

"Leave?" Jonathan spoke up. "Why would we leave?"

Charles finally managed to look at the faces of his friends. There was no derision there, no disgust, no outrage. Only understanding.

"You challenged a man who beat his wife," Godric said slowly. "That is not something to be ashamed of."

"There are other ways to handle men like him," Charles countered.

"Sometimes I wonder," Cedric said. "But you didn't kill him, your father did."

"No, I killed him. If I had kept my temper, none of this would have happened." Charles expected Cedric at least to understand the horror of his sin. But Cedric merely stroked his chin, his face pensive.

Ashton spoke next. "So, that night at Cambridge. He saw you and those feelings of hatred resurfaced?"

Charles nodded. "He followed me to my room, and when I fell asleep, he bound my hands and wrists and dragged me to the river. But Peter caught up with us."

Peter Maltby, the boy who was a friend to both him and Hugo. A loyal man with a heart of gold. The men in this room knew what had happened next. They'd all been there, drawn by his screams. And Peter's.

Lucien steepled his fingers. "Charles, no one here is leaving you. Ever. We are blood brothers."

"He's right," Godric said. "We began down this road with you and will follow you to the end, no matter how dark a place it might lead."

"Things are different now," Charles said. "You all have families..." He had to make them understand the danger they all faced. It wasn't just their lives—the lives of anyone who touched them were at risk.

"You forget the women we've married are far from helpless."

"Certainly not mine," Jonathan chuckled.

"Nor mine," Godric laughed.

Ashton placed a hand on Charles's shoulder. "Charles, rest easy. We will not desert you in your hour of need."

A lump formed in Charles's throat. How could he ever deserve these men as friends?

Ashton stood before the room, like a general addressing his troops. "And now we come to the other reason I've called you here. I've given you all assignments. What have you been able to discover?"

Lucien spoke up first. "I've been working with Avery. Ever since Hugo tried to have him killed in France, he's had to keep his distance at the Foreign Office. Officially, the two have called the incident in France a misunderstanding. Unofficially, they both know the score. Hugo has had him reassigned to Scotland, but Avery is not without his supporters. He has compiled a list of men he believes are under Hugo's direct control, and I'm having them followed to see if any come near our homes or our families."

"I've been checking into his financial position," Ashton said. "Most of his wealth is tied up in investments with the Crown and is unfortunately secure." That meant he couldn't be financially ruined like most other men.

"Godric and I have been making inquiries with gentlemen who have crossed paths with Hugo in the past and suffered for it. We might have some legal cause of action if we could convince the other men to stand with us," Cedric offered hopefully, and Godric nodded.

"That would be ideal, but I fear it won't be enough," Ashton sighed. "Hugo's position protects him in ways we cannot assail legally. As I feared, the solution available to us won't be honorable."

"It's not as if Hugo has shown a damned ounce of honor toward us," growled Cedric. "Why should we be honorable toward him? Hit below the belt, I say."

"We're supposed to be better than that," said Charles, much to his own surprise. The others looked to him, and he suddenly felt on the spot as to what to say. "I mean, if it were just us, I would say we should not stoop to his level, no matter the cost. But...it has never been just us, has it? At every turn Hugo has shown that anyone associated with us is also at risk."

"Then you agree we must do whatever is necessary?" asked Ashton.

With a touch of reluctance, Charles nodded, as did the others.

"Good." Ashton turned to the room. "I know you're all wondering what it is I have planned. The truth is, I am still weighing options. I cannot say more, for reasons that will become clear in the near future. For now, I must ask you all to trust me."

Godric huffed. "Of course we trust you. It's damned unsettling not to know what we're trusting you with."

"Other than our lives," Lucien added.

"But we do trust you," said Cedric. "Take the time you need."

Ashton nodded. "Thank you. Now, with that settled, and with Phillip resting and Graham keeping watch over him, I believe we are all due to attend the ball at the Sandersons' tonight."

Jonathan and Cedric both groaned, and Lucien muttered something about damned debutantes.

"A ball? Ash, you must be joking," Cedric said. "We're talking about taking one of the most powerful men in England down, and you're talking about dancing?"

Ashton smiled darkly. "You know me better than that, Cedric. I never go to balls simply to dance. They are hives of information. I have reason to believe that a man in Hugo's employ will be there, a man I am certain is having doubts about his employment. I want to see if I can convince him to turn to our side, or at least provide us with something useful. The ball provides a perfect cover to meet with him."

"And while you're off playing the hero, the rest of us will be dancing." Lucien crossed his arms over his chest, scowling.

"Now, now, I need you all to act as distractions, and I think dancing would do us all a bit of good." Ashton cut in over the dramatic sounds of the men bemoaning their fates as dance partners. "Besides, I'm told Godric is going to be escorting Mrs. Wycliff, and I'd rather like to meet her."

Lucien sat up an open interest. "As in Aaron Wycliff? I knew the fellow. Didn't know that he'd married. Wonder who the lady is." Though he was happily married, he prided himself on knowing every lady in London by name or at the least by reputation.

"Emily's cousin, by marriage," Godric explained to the others. "Aaron Wycliff was Emily's second cousin, but she was apparently quite fond of him. He died a little over a year ago and left his wife a widow and mother to a little girl. Emily invited her to stay with us now that she is out of mourning." Godric glared at Charles. "Which means she's *not* for you. She is a sweet creature who needs a decent husband to care for her and her daughter."

Charles huffed. "If she's hunting for a second husband, I'll be sure to keep my distance. A wife is the last thing I need."

"Ash, how do you know about Mrs. Wycliff?" Godric demanded. "She only arrived a few hours ago, and I haven't told anyone."

"Hugo has his spies, and I have mine. I thought it best to keep ears to the ground as it were, on all fronts."

"You have spies in our households?" Cedric asked.

Ashton smiled. "I told you to trust me. Think of them more as willing accomplices who wish to remain anonymous. It's important to stay ahead of Hugo and make sure he can't hurt anyone we care about. After the incident with Gordon last Christmas, I realized it was only fitting to make sure I did as well."

There were a few grumbles, but Ash turned the focus back to the ball. "Dancing it is, then. Unless there any objections?"

Lucien huffed. "I always object to dancing, unless it's with my wife, and she's still recovering from Evan's birth." Jonathan and Cedric both chuckled at his gloomy reaction.

"A quadrille or two won't kill you," Ashton reminded Lucien.

Charles walked his friends to the door. After they left, he headed upstairs to check on Phillip and his brother. Phillip was asleep in bed. Graham was in a chair, also asleep, or so he thought. When he moved to close the door, Graham spoke up.

"Charles?"

"Yes?" He slipped inside the darkened bedchamber.

"Thank you for saving him. He's my closest friend, and I..." Graham swallowed audibly. Charles wished he could have spared his brother this pain swirling inside his head. He'd felt it too often himself in the past.

"I wish we'd found him sooner." Charles was afraid the injuries would be too much for Phillip, but there was still hope he would pull through. Phillip had always been a tough bastard. He'd lost his parents to scarlet fever at a young age, and he'd always been alone. It had made him a damned strong fellow.

Graham stifled a yawn. "Are you going out? I thought I heard a footman say something in the hall just now."

"I had planned on it, yes, but I'm happy to stay if you need me."

"No, you should go. I'll watch over Phillip." He lifted a book up from his lap. "I have plenty of reading to fill my hours."

Charles let out a breath. Graham was still keeping his distance, it seemed, but he was relieved his brother was speaking to him again. "Very well. If you need me, I'll be at Lord Sanderson's."

Graham nodded and returned to his book.

Charles slipped out of the room and went upstairs to dress. He would humor Ashton and attend this ball, but afterward, he needed to find a quiet place to sit and think.

Two hours later, Charles was at the Sanderson residence. He straightened his coat and faced the Palladian house before him. It was a freestanding home, not built wall-to-wall against its neighbors like most houses were these days. Lights illuminated the windows facing the street, and strains of music escaped the doors. A footman met him at the top of the stairs and collected his hat and coat.

Charles lingered just inside the doorway a moment, listening to the songs and sounds of gaiety. There was an odd melancholy that he experienced at times like this. It was as though he were the long-forgotten ruler of a shadow realm, doomed to never feel the sunlight upon his skin or the breeze ruffle his hair. It was a foolish thing to think, perhaps, but he felt it so strongly in that moment that his breath was trapped in his lungs, making him light-headed.

He drew in a deep breath, painted a smile on his face, and entered the ballroom. Light bathed the room, and dancers swirled past him in fluttering colors like the wings of parrots from a tropical paradise. He'd once seen a dozen parrots in a gentleman's hothouse garden, and the experience here was not dissimilar. There was something life-affirming about it all.

Charles felt a little better now. Perhaps a dance or two with a pretty girl would raise his spirits. His gaze swept the room as he searched for familiar faces. He saw Miss Breckton, a lovely young lady who was most excellent company, so long as one did not talk politics. Her father was a vocal lord in the House of Lords. There were the attractive but shy wallflower twins, Amelia and Augusta Pepperidge. He'd always loved the idea of being in the company of twins, but right now he had only one woman on his mind, a woman he was quite convinced he'd never see again.

Charles caught a glimpse of his friends now. Ashton was on the edge of the ring of spectators, Rosalind at his side, smiling widely. Ash was no doubt waiting for the opportune moment to meet with Hugo's man. Deeper in the room, Cedric and Anne were already twirling in a dance, along with Jonathan and Audrey, though it seemed those two were fighting over who should lead whom. Godric stood near the refreshments with Emily, who had one hand resting on her belly.

It was unusual to see a woman with child in public so close to when the babe was due, but Emily had always been unconventional, and the Sandersons adored her. Here she could breach any etiquette rule she damned well liked. Lucien was with them, as was Horatia, who leaned against his side. That meant their new son was under the care of a nursemaid for the evening. She seemed quite content to talk to friends at the moment rather than dance. Charles smiled, pleased that Horatia was looking so well. He'd helped bring her son, Evan, in to the world. The babe had almost not made it because he'd come a month too soon. Thankfully, he was strong like his parents and was adjusting quite well, and he was now a healthy little tyke.

Everyone he cared about was in this room tonight, all laughter and smiles upon their faces. This was a moment that he could have dwelt in forever. If he could have trapped it all within a glass and kept it preserved for centuries he would have. The darkness and worries of the future were nowhere to be found here tonight. There was only dancing in the company of friends.

If Hugo was gone, perhaps it *would* always be like this. Days in the sun and nights beneath the chandeliers, dancing wild and free. No more looking over their shoulders with concern. Despair suddenly rose up within him.

Ashton might have felt confident he could outwit Hugo, but Charles was not so certain. And if tonight did not go as planned, then what? If Ashton's plans fell apart, Charles knew what he would have to do. He would do whatever he had to in order to protect them all. If it meant facing Hugo alone like a lamb to the slaughter, then so be it. He would give his life for them all. He could not ask them to do the same.

"Charles! Glad to see you old boy!" He turned to see which man had called his name, only to have his heart stutter to a stop.

There by the tall veranda doors was a woman in a blue gown the color of midnight, with silver netting over her skirts like a blanket of stars. Her long blonde hair was pulled back in soft waves and bound with ribbons in a Grecian fashion. He struggled to breathe.

It was her. His angel from Lewis Street, the one who'd kissed him as though it had been her dying wish and then had vanished like a ghost. Of all the places he thought to find her, he had never once imagined it would be here.

13

Charles's heart began to race as he started walking toward the woman in the midnight-blue dress, like a man lost in a most exquisite dream.

She'd told him her name was Lily, but had that been the truth? He tried to think of all the ladies who might be acquainted with Lord Sanderson, and yet he knew of no woman like her. A haunting vision, a woman built by God just for him. The crowd thinned as he moved through it, ignoring every call of his name as he tried to catch sight of the woman again. When he reached the veranda, she was gone.

Vanished again, as though she had slipped into another realm through a beam of moonlight. Charles opened the veranda door, shivering as he walked out onto the terrace overlooking the gardens. The tall hedges that formed a labyrinth were covered in frost, and the moon rose high above him as he stepped down onto the garden path. Had she come out here? He kept his steps light as he traversed the winding path.

Snap! He froze at the sound of a twig breaking and turned to look behind him. There she stood, staring at him, blue eyes wide and dark as a northern sea.

"You..." he whispered, knowing he sounded foolish. "It's really you."

Her hands fisted into her skirts, and she started to retreat. The silver netting shimmered like clouds shot through with condensed moonlight.

"No! Please, don't go. I didn't mean to scare you." It sounded like he was begging, but he didn't care. If she disappeared again, who knew if he'd find her a third time?

He raised his hands in the air to show he didn't mean to hurt her. "Please. I'm just happy to see you are well."

She looked around and slowly let go of her skirts, her eyes softening.

"My name is Charles. Charles Humphrey. Do you remember me, from the other night at Lewis Street? It's Lily, isn't it?"

She nodded. "Yes. How could I forget my savior?" Her breathy voice was just as he'd remembered.

"I was so worried after you vanished. I only wished to see you safely home."

"I know." She paused. "But I was ashamed that..."

"You kissed me?" Charles finished, smiling a little. It had been one of the best kisses of his life, the kind that changed a man down to his very bones, the kind that etched itself onto one's soul.

"Yes." Lily smiled a little. The expression stirred something deep within him, a shadow of a memory, but he couldn't quite bring it into the light. All he knew was that winning a smile from her was a reward unlike anything else.

"Never be ashamed of a kiss, not one such as that." He flashed a grin that'd had many a woman rushing into his arms with weak knees and starry eyes. Lily, however, tilted her head and eyed him with curiosity.

"May I escort you back inside?" He had seen her shiver. She wasn't wearing a cloak and had to be freezing.

"I suppose you may."

"Excellent—"

"Lily!" A voice carried through the gardens, one Charles recognized. Emily was calling for her? How on earth did she know her while he did not?

"Over here!" Lily called out. A moment later Emily joined them within the labyrinth.

"Charles!" Emily beamed at him. "I see you've met my cousin. I'm so glad."

"Cousin?" He almost choked on the word. No, hellfire and damnation, *this* could not be the widowed cousin looking for a husband, could it?

"Yes. My cousin by marriage, Mrs. Wycliff."

He blinked, suddenly dazed. His mysterious angel was a quaint little widow from the country?

"It's a pleasure to...*officially* meet you, Mrs. Wycliff." Charles made a courtly bow.

"It's a pleasure to meet you as well, Lord Lonsdale," Lily replied. Charles studied her curiously. Unless she was an avid reader of gossip columns, she would not necessarily know he was the Earl of Lonsdale. Lily smiled. "Emily has told me much about you and your friends."

"Why don't we go back inside?" Emily said. "I'm afraid I'll catch a chill out here."

Charles nodded and turned to Lily. "Of course. Mrs. Wycliff, do you have any dances open on your card?"

Lily opened her mouth, but no words came out. Emily answered for her. "I'm afraid she's quite full. Not a single dance is free. Even if you *had* arrived on time." Emily gave him a disapproving look that would have made his mother proud.

"Right. Well... Perhaps I shall have a bit of luck later this evening." He caught Lily's hand and turned the tiny card up in the moonlight, peering at the list of names, recognizing most of them. He bit his lip to hide a smile as he escorted them back inside. Emily steered Lily away from him, seeking to protect her cousin from his bad influence, no doubt.

As she should, I suppose. She needs a proper husband. And that isn't me.

Then something Godric had said came back to him. Lily had only just arrived in London today. Yet he had seen her two days ago. There was more to this woman than perhaps even Emily knew. Perhaps Godric meant she had only called upon them today. She may have stayed elsewhere before that.

The mystery behind her lingered, just as the kiss they had shared on Lewis Street. He might not be husband material, but his curiosity about her was too strong to be denied. Tonight he would uncover Lily Wycliff's secrets.

But first he had to knock a few men off her dance card.

❧

"That went rather well, wouldn't you agree?" Emily whispered to Lily as they walked away from Charles.

Lily's heart was still pounding. Standing before him now, as close to her true self as she'd ever been, she'd felt incredibly vulnerable.

"At least he did not recognize me," said Lily. "Thank you for rescuing me."

"Yes, I was worried that if he spent too much time with you, he might see through the ruse. You spoke differently around him, I noticed."

"It's a tone I've heard ladies in the *ton* use around men," Lily said.

"It is something of a fashion," Emily noted. "It may serve you well tonight."

She smoothed her hands down her gown and peered around at the guests in the ballroom.

"Must I really dance with all these strangers?" she whispered back to Emily. She was supposed to find a way to dance with Charles, yet when she'd seen him spot her in the ballroom she'd fled to the gardens, hoping he wouldn't follow.

"Well, I thought it would be good for you to meet some eligible bachelors. The Sandersons only invite the very best gentlemen."

"Does that include Lord Lonsdale?" Lily inquired with half a smile. "We both know *his* reputation."

Emily laughed. "Yes, well, he is still a gentleman, and quite sought after. But we both know he is not likely to settle down. I mean, you worked as his valet. You've no doubt seen sides of him that would make me blush crimson. Besides, I'm sure you'd never be interested in a man you'd spent so long serving."

Lily wanted to disagree. Being Charles's valet had never felt like servitude. It had been more about companionship. Charles was lonely, despite his roguish ways and the ladies he bedded. And when the opportunity arose, she was going to have to use that against him.

"Lord Kerrigan is your first partner for the waltz," Emily announced with a hint of excitement. "He's a bit wicked, but I think he's quite wonderful." As if on cue, a tall blond man strode toward them, a thunderous expression clouding his sky-blue eyes. His entire front, however, was dripping with ratafia. His clothes were ruined.

Emily smiled. "Ah, Lord Kerrigan, I was just about to... Good Lord, what happened?"

"Your Grace." Kerrigan bowed before Emily, then turned to Lily, doing his best to hide his frustration. "Mrs. Wycliff, I must apologize. There was an incident at the refreshment table. I cannot ask you to dance with me, not when there is a chance I may damage such a lovely gown. I'm afraid I must return home at once and remove these clothes before my valet curses me for all eternity." Kerrigan bent over Lily's hand and pressed a kiss to her knuckles.

"We will have that waltz another time," Lily assured him.

"I hope so. Don't fall in love with anyone else until then." He winked at her and took his leave of his hosts.

Lily sighed, somewhat disappointed. It would have been a delight to dance with a tall charming man like Lord Kerrigan. But it did open a slot on her card, and with it, an opportunity.

"Drat!" Emily slapped her silk fan closed. "I was so hoping you would have a chance to dance with him. I wonder what happened?"

I have my suspicions. Lily glanced at the refreshment table and saw Charles there watching her. He held a nearly empty goblet of ratafia to his lips, and with it, the most wicked smile she'd ever seen. He raised his glass to her in a silent toast. It was *exactly* what she expected Charles to do if his goal was to find a way onto her dance card. Without even meaning to, she smiled and giggled.

"So, no Lord Kerrigan then." Emily tapped her fan into one palm like a military general would a riding crop.

Lily kept one eye on Charles. "Perhaps I can find another to take his place?"

Emily shook her head. "I'm afraid that wouldn't be appropriate. When a gentleman and lady do not end up dancing, one cannot replace one's intended partner for another. Silly, I know. Besides, they've already begun the dance."

"The next is a quadrille," Lily observed, studying the card attached to her wrist by a string. The name *Mr. MacGuire* was written beneath her dance number.

"Oh, excellent. Mr. MacGuire is a handsome and wealthy banker from Drummonds and a close friend of Ashton's. There he is—oh, for heaven's sake..." Again Emily's hopeful tone soured. A handsome red-haired man crossed the ballroom toward them, limping heavily.

"My deepest apologies, Your Grace." Mr. MacGuire's rich brogue was as captivating as his green eyes, but all Lily could think of was Charles, and she wondered what he had done to the poor Scotsman.

"Oh, dear. What happened, Mr. MacGuire? Are you hurt?" Emily held out a hand to him, but he waved her off.

"I'm fine, just a wee accident. I tripped and hit one of the steps from the terrace. I'm afraid I won't be much fun to dance with tonight." He looked to Lily apologetically. "Next time, Mrs. Wycliff?"

"Yes, of course. Please feel better, Mr. MacGuire." Lily let him press a kiss to her hand as well. She looked toward the French doors leading to the terrace and saw Charles leaning against the wall, his arms crossed and a smug smile on his lips.

Of course.

Surely he didn't plan on maiming everyone at the ball tonight? What was his goal here? As Emily had said, it wasn't appropriate to accept a new offer, even if a partner had to bow out. Did he wish to shame her by forcing her to sit out all the dances, or was he simply sending her a message of his interest in her? At this point she feared she would have no partners and no dances. And that fear was fully realized a few minutes later when the rest of her dance partners filed up to her and Emily one by one, each with an excuse for leaving the dance. Charles, damn him, was still by the refreshment table, smirking.

"I think I shall sit down. It seems I won't be dancing for a while." Lily walked toward a group of chairs by the wall, where a number of frightened wallflowers timidly watched the proceedings. Lily eased into a chair in their midst. These poor girls lacked any confidence, it seemed, which was why they had remained without dance partners.

"You're Mrs. Wycliff, aren't you?" one of the ladies asked.

Lily nodded glumly. On the one hand, Charles's interference was a good thing. It showed he was interested in her, which would make her task all the easier to complete.

And that was the problem. She didn't want to.

This was almost as bad as the night Charles had insisted she accompany him as Tom to a gambling hell. He'd found himself a woman for the night, and when Lily had found him, Charles had shoved a coin purse into her chest and told her to bed a woman as well.

He'd meant it as a kindness, she supposed. Charles had often remarked on how Tom still had a ways to go before reaching manhood. But all she could see was Charles with another woman, trying to buy her off for some privacy.

I suppose I loved him even then.

It hadn't started that way. At first she was simply supposed to watch the movements of Charles and his friends at the gentlemen's club they frequented. Then he'd taken pity on her and made her his valet, just as Hugo had hoped. Most of the spies within the League's households had obtained their positions because Hugo knew how each of them thought, what qualities they sought, and the weaknesses they had.

Guilt and generosity were Charles's weaknesses.

She'd tried to keep her distance from Charles at first, to keep their relationship professional, but she soon realized that he did not need a valet—he needed a friend. And she had been that for him, even though it pained her. It pained her because she feared she might develop feelings for him. And she had.

How could she not? He was perfect. Perfectly handsome, perfectly amusing, perfectly adventurous. He was everything a woman could want—he was everything *she* wanted.

"Is Lord Lonsdale yours?" the girl to her left asked.

Lily stared at her, confused. "I beg your pardon?"

The girl blushed. "Well, we've been watching him stare at you all night, and it seems he's managed to keep some of the most handsome men here from dancing with you. Do you have an understanding with him?"

"No, I don't think so." Before she could say more, the girls around her gasped as Charles appeared from nowhere, as if he'd been summoned.

"Ladies." He smiled, and each of the shy girls looked ready to faint, but thankfully they were all seated in chairs.

"My lord," the garden of wallflowers murmured back to him.

"Mrs. Wycliff, it would seem you have a few dances open. May I?" He held out a hand, and Lily almost leapt to her feet, but resisted the urge. She could not seem too eager. That had been one of Miss Mirabeau's first lessons. The French courtesan had once worked for Hugo, training women in the art of seduction. *"If you wish to stoke a flame into a raging fire, you cannot give it all the fuel it wants at once. You must make it work a little, yes?"*

"Well?" Charles curled his fingers in invitation, his gray eyes sparkling. Suddenly Lily had a stroke of genius, though it required a touch of lying.

"I'm afraid only my very last dance is free, but it seems none of these ladies have partners. If you wish to dance with me for the final waltz, then you will do me a kindness and dance with my new friends."

The wallflowers chittered like a flock of cream-colored songbirds. Charles's eyes narrowed, as if trying to understand her game, and then he gave a slow nod.

"I would be honored. Ladies, who is to be first?" He took charge of the timid ladies and chose the most frightened one first, leading her out to the group of dancers lining up. Charles only looked at Lily once before the music started, and then he became an enchanting dancer, engrossed in the company of his young partner.

The girl next to Lily sighed and bumped her shoulder against Lily's. "He really is smitten with you. I don't think any rake would dance with so many just for one waltz."

"He's not a rake, he's a rogue." Lily laughed to herself, but she couldn't deny the warmth she felt in her chest as she watched him take on dance after dance, making each young lady stand out and shine. The other gentlemen in the room couldn't help but notice them now. By the final dance, each of the wallflowers had been asked by several young men to step out on the floor with them as well.

Charles joined her by the now empty rows of chairs. "So, was that your wicked scheme all along?"

Lily feigned shock. "Whatever do you mean?"

"I think I may have single-handedly made no less than

several matches for those wallflowers tonight, thanks to you." Charles grinned like a proud peacock.

Lily smiled at the crowd. "They were all so wretched here, but now look at them. Smiles on every face." She peeped up at him from beneath her lashes. "You did that."

"I did." He crossed his arms and watched the dancers with some small satisfaction. "Now, have I earned my waltz?"

"Indeed you have." She held out a hand, and he escorted her to the floor.

Her breath caught as he pulled her close. It felt wonderful to be in his arms. She'd never been held by him before. They had wrestled, sparred, even splashed in a lake before, but he'd never held her, never danced with her. Her mother had often told her before she'd passed that if a man could dance like an angel, Lily ought to marry him. *"The man who dances well loves even better."*

Lily stared up into Charles's face as he slid an arm around her waist and the waltz began.

"I can feel how tense you are," he said.

"How could I not be around someone like you?" she answered coyly. Charles enjoyed being toyed with in verbal banter. It made him try harder. But he didn't reply with a witty retort like she'd expected.

"Whatever worries you carry, let them go," Charles whispered. "Dance with me and let everything else fade."

If only it were so easy...

How she longed to really let go of the past and her fear

of the future. She wished only to shine a light upon the darkness inside her. For just one dance, she didn't want to let anything destroy their moment.

They danced in perfect rhythm. She was taller than most ladies, and her legs kept up easily with Charles's longer strides. His fingers on her waist crept down to her lower back. His eyes never left hers, except when they lowered to her lips. And just like that she was lost in dreams of him kissing her again. For a moment, she really did let go.

He held her close in his arms. Her skirts swirled around her ankles in whispers of satin, and the light from the chandeliers seem to make the world glow in an unimaginable way, like the gates to their own private heaven had opened up and she and Charles were dancing through the clouds.

When the orchestra faded into silence, the crowd in the ballroom broke into applause. Why did it have to end? But Charles kept hold of her, his eyes halfway closed as he released a slow, shaky breath that mirrored her own.

"I don't wish to let you go," he confessed.

"I'm afraid you must," Lily said. "The music has ended."

His gray eyes clung to hers. "I'm afraid if I do, you'll vanish again."

All these years she'd heard other ladies whisper of love and how it consumed one's soul. Now she truly understood it.

"I won't go anywhere," she promised him. "I'm staying with Emily, remember?"

"If I arrive at Godric's tomorrow, you will be there? You will agree to see me?" His face lowered as though he intended to kiss her. They were in the middle of the ballroom and they couldn't, but he seemed oblivious to this fact and stopped just inches from her lips. She glanced to the side and already saw guests staring at them, talking amongst themselves.

She forced herself to pull away before the scandal they were causing grew any further. "I will be there and I will see you."

"Then I will see you tomorrow." He raised her hand to his lips and feathered a kiss over it. The heat of the moment made her a little dizzy. How could he make something so innocent seem so wicked?

Because you're in love with him, and he with you.

Lily rejoined Emily as the crowds in the ballroom dispersed. Soon everyone would be headed home to warm beds, hot fires, biscuits, and tea. For the first time it would be her chance to enjoy coming home to such things, rather than being the one to prepare it for others.

"Well, how was it?" Emily asked with a teasing smile.

"My first ball?" Lily asked.

"No, dancing with Charles." Emily's smile was far too sneaky, but Lily didn't care. Let Emily matchmake away if she liked.

"Wonderful," she admitted.

"I saw what you did," Emily said. "At first I thought you were rejecting Charles by forcing those other girls on him. Then I knew you were not only helping those girls find some attention, but testing Charles as well. Am I right?"

Lily smiled. "After a fashion."

"It seems to have worked. He is certainly infatuated with you. Perhaps I was wrong about him. Maybe Charles is ready for marriage. I did promise I would sail to the ends of the earth to find the woman destiny set for him." Emily gave her a hug and whispered in her ear, "Perhaps destiny was right in front of him all along."

Lily tried to swallow down the knifing pain in her heart. She feared more than anything that it had been, but not the destiny any of them had been hoping for.

14

"uite a night, eh?" Cedric clapped Charles on the shoulder as they left the Sanderson home. "Far less painful than I feared."

"Quite a night indeed," Charles agreed. He hadn't thought his spirits could be buoyed after the attacks on Phillip and Graham. But coming here tonight and finding Lily... Even her name made his blood hum and his head dizzy, as though he'd drunk too much whisky. She had given him a glimpse of hope again.

"It seems to have pulled you out of your black mood for a while, at least. I saw you danced with a number of fine ladies. I don't suppose any of them caught your fancy?"

"One flower," he admitted. "Lily Wycliff."

"Emily's cousin from the country?" Cedric chuckled.

"Well, Godric forbade you from wooing her, so I guess it was only natural that you would. That must have been the blonde beauty you were with during the last waltz."

Charles smiled to himself. "That she was." He'd seen stunning women before, that was nothing new. But there was something more to Lily that drew him toward her, something that called to him. Like he sensed in her a kindred spirit, perhaps even someone wounded as he was. If she was, then perhaps there was a chance of them healing each other.

He resolved to call upon her first thing tomorrow, but a problem occurred to him. What the devil did a man do when he called upon a woman properly? Sit in a parlor and drink tea under the watchful eyes of a chaperone? Then he realized Emily was going to be Lily's chaperone. He would never live down the humiliation of that.

"You know she has a child?" Cedric asked, his tone colored with caution.

Charles nodded. "I heard. But I am exceptional with children. Just ask Tom. I've been known to take care of his baby sister from time to time."

"Speaking of Tom, where is he? It's not like you to be without your valet."

Charles's heart sank as he remembered Tom's less than happy circumstances. "Tom's favorite aunt is dying. I gave the lad leave to stay with her. He took young Kat with him."

"Oh, that's a shame."

"It is. And I feel damned guilty for wanting him here."

Cedric shrugged. "A good valet is worth his weight in gold."

This was true enough, but the boy had also become a part of his life, more like a young protégé. His confidant. His friend. And outside of the League, he didn't have many he counted as such.

"Ah, there you are." Anne joined them outside, stifling a yawn as she leaned against her husband.

"Oh dear, best get you home, lady wife." Cedric chuckled and shot Charles a wink.

"Yes, you should. Good night, Charles." Anne smiled at him, and the couple headed to their waiting coach.

Charles sighed, watching his breath form a brief cloud before he tightened his gloves. Alone again. He waved a groom over, and the man led his horse up to the bottom step of the house.

He rode home on the darkened streets, humming the tune of that last waltz. He didn't want to forget a moment of his time with Lily Wycliff.

Damnation, he was falling hard for the woman, and he didn't even know her. She was a stranger to him, albeit a beautiful one, yet he could almost swear that he *did* know her. But that was impossible. True, he had wooed many women over the years, but how would he forget someone like her? And she would have had to have forgotten him, which was simply unthinkable. It seemed she would remain his mysterious blonde angel for another night.

But come tomorrow, he would learn everything he could about her.

Once safely home, he saw that his horse was taken care of and then stole some biscuits from the kitchen before retiring to bed. His nightclothes had been laid out by Davis, and he stripped out of his evening attire, tossing them over the back of the chair. The fire was lit in the hearth, but the chair beside it was empty. The chair he often found Tom asleep in on the nights he didn't accompany Charles out.

Charles pulled on his nightshirt and climbed into bed. Despite his exhaustion, he rolled restlessly from side to side, stretching his legs and arms to get comfortable, yet sleep still eluded him. His eyes kept slipping open as his mind played over the events at the ball.

He sat up and watched the firelight create shadows on the canopy draperies over his bed. An awful thought crept in on his happiness. If Hugo learned of his interest in Lily, it could put her in danger, just like everyone else.

She was safe enough under Godric's roof for now, but there was no telling what would happen in the days to come. He only knew that Hugo would try to make another move soon. When he did, Charles would have to be ready to stop him...or die trying.

Hugo Waverly was in his study reading over the latest dispatches from Paris when the door opened. Daniel Sheffield slipped inside without a knock or word of greeting. Daniel was an extension of Hugo, and a weapon to be wielded whenever necessary.

He pushed the stack of dispatches away and leaned back in his chair. "Anything to report?"

"Kilkenny, the man you feared was sympathetic toward the League, was hit by a coach this evening on his way to the Sanderson ball. He did not survive."

"Pity that. Coaches are a dangerous thing at night," Hugo mused with a cold smile. Kilkenny wouldn't be missed. "What else?"

"Lord Kent still lives. Lonsdale and Lennox went into the tunnels and found him, and word from our source is that he clings to life. I could have our man correct that."

Hugo considered it. Letting Kent die under Charles's roof would be horrific, but he didn't want his agent to risk exposure.

"Unnecessary. The message was sent and received, as planned. That is all that matters. What else?"

Daniel smiled now. "Lonsdale was seen dancing with a woman named Mrs. Wycliff."

He paused for a beat, knowing Hugo did not know that name. "Mrs. *Lily* Wycliff. She is said to be a distant country cousin to the Duchess of Essex."

Hugo tapped his fingers on the desk. "So, the plan worked. I was hoping it would." Her suggestion to pose as a cousin to Lady Essex was quite brilliant. And allowing the duchess to do half the work for him was nothing short of delicious. The so-called League of Rogues would soon welcome Lily with open arms. And then…

"I believe that news deserves a drink." Hugo stood and retrieved a set of glasses and a decanter of scotch. He poured two glasses and handed one to Daniel.

"To Mrs. Lily Wycliff." Hugo chuckled. "May she weave a seductive web around Lonsdale's vile heart."

Once she did, Hugo would be the spider at the center of that web, ready to strike.

15

Charles stared at his outfit in the mirror of his bedchamber, his nerves running rampant. He'd woken early, *far* too early, and had lain in bed for hours planning in detail how he wanted to spend the day with Lily. He'd accounted for Emily's usual games. No doubt the woman would try to play matchmaker and have her own agenda, but Charles was determined to see things through his own way.

He looked over his bottle-green waistcoat embroidered with gold stags, his buff breeches and dark-blue coat. Would Lily approve? He'd never thought his appearance questionable before, but now he was doubting every choice he made.

"My lord?" Davis stood there at his right side, frowning. "Did I choose something incorrectly?"

Charles frowned now as well. "No. I'm simply unsure

of myself. Do you think I look impressive? If you were a lady, I mean."

Davis gave a half smile. "I think you quite handsome, my lord. If I were a lady, that is."

"I'm so bloody nervous after all these years."

"Nervous, sir? I've never seen you nervous meeting a lady before."

"This is different. None of my usual games, secret rendezvous, or sneaking in through windows. I wish to do things right."

"I see, my lord. Well, that *would* be a change for you."

Charles turned to face Davis slowly, and the man's smile vanished.

"I'm sorry, my lord, I didn't mean..."

"No, you're right, of course. Lord, I don't even know what a proper time to call on a lady is. Do you?"

"I believe late morning to the early afternoon is considered acceptable." Davis used a small brush to remove some dust from the coat, not that Charles saw any.

"Late morning. Early afternoon." Charles slipped his pocket watch out and glanced at it. It was only half past nine. Bloody hell, how was he going to spend the next two hours?

His butler appeared in the doorway. "My lord?"

"Yes?"

"There's a Mrs. Ellis here to see you," said Ramsey.

"She said she's answering the notice you posted seeking a governess and nurse for Katherine and little Oliver."

"Right!" He'd forgotten about his quest for a nurse after everything else that had happened.

"I put her in the drawing room, and I'll have a maid bring in some tea."

"Thank you, Ramsey." Charles tugged his waistcoat down to smooth out any wrinkles and tucked his watch back in his pocket. Then he headed to the drawing room.

He found a middle-aged woman waiting patiently in a chair. She moved to stand when he entered, but he waved for her to remain seated.

"Mrs. Ellis?" he asked.

"Yes, it's a pleasure to meet you, my lord." The woman's blue eyes were gentle and her smile open. He liked that. Nurses who didn't smile weren't always the best for children. He took a seat across from her and studied her more closely. Plain clothes, good hair, but styled in a plain chignon, and a pleasing face and voice. All good, but he still had questions, ones that mattered more than her appearance.

"Now, how long have you been a nurse and governess?"

"Ten years," she said. "I was employed by Viscount Richmond and his wife for their children, but they are now grown enough to attend Eton."

"I see. And have you worked with younger children? Say two or three years old?"

She nodded. "I worked with one of the boys since he

was three and the other since he was five. I'm quite comfortable with the little ones."

"Good, good. Now"

"Pardon me, my lord, but I should like to meet the little ones."

"Ah… Well, one child is not here. You see, the child is the little sister of my valet. Their mother died, leaving the young man to care for child, and I look after my people. I'm fond of Katherine and wanted her to have the best care."

Mrs. Ellis's brows rose in surprise. "You want me to care for a servant's child?"

Charles frowned a little.

"Ah, I see…" Mrs. Ellis's gaze turned shrewd. "She's the child of a liaison?"

The question was bold and inappropriate, but he couldn't blame the woman for the assumption.

"Forgive me," she quickly added. "But it is important to know these things ahead of time, for the child's sake."

It certainly wasn't an implausible scenario. He had known men in that very situation. But he did not sleep with servants. It was not an issue of class but of power and choosing not to wield it over those who had none. And Tom's mother had been a lady's maid to a countess.

"She isn't mine, but you will find, Mrs. Ellis, that I have an open heart when it comes to children. One of my best footmen lost his wife last year and is raising a son on his own. He'll be your other young charge."

"It's about time we had lords taking care of children. I think it's a fine thing indeed, my lord."

He sensed she was teasing him, though he couldn't fathom why.

"So, you will take the position?"

Mrs. Ellis didn't immediately answer. She took a moment to study him, and finally nodded.

"Excellent. Even though the lad and his sister aren't here, I'd like you to start right away with Davis's son so you will be settled in when Tom and his sister return."

"Thank you, my lord." She held up a carpet bag. "I had hoped this position would be suitable, and I came prepared."

"Good. Have the housekeeper show you to your room, and you will have a chance to meet the staff and little Oliver."

He waited for her to proceed him. Once he was sure she would be seen to, he checked his pocket watch again. That hadn't taken nearly enough time.

"Sir?" Davis spoke up as he exited the servants' stairs. "I just met with Mrs. Ellis. She and Oliver took to each other right away. I don't know how I can ever thank you." Charles's face heated a little. It was always a bit embarrassing when they thanked him for his generosity. In his mind, his actions should be considered normal, not something exceptional.

"You're welcome, Davis. I believe she'll suit the children very well. But if you'd like to repay the favor, I could use some advice as to how to spend my time before paying a call on my intended lady."

"Perhaps you could buy the young lady flowers?" the footman suggested hopefully. "That will take at least half an hour, and it would bring a smile to her face."

"Davis, you are a smart man." He winked at the footman, grabbed his greatcoat, and left to summon his coach. The best flowers were on Bond Street.

At the flower shop he met a young lady with doe-brown eyes and honey-blonde hair who was artfully arranging stems in a vase by one of the bloom-filled windows. He noted the quality of the cloth of her gown, even though it was a season or two old. It was possible the young lady had fallen on hard times and had sought out employment here. Well, he'd be sure to reward her for any help she could give him today.

"Excuse me, miss?" He cleared his throat, and the young lady gasped, almost toppling the vase of flowers. Charles steadied the vase and set it securely back on the table. The woman faced him, a blush coloring her cheeks.

Charles grinned. "I'm terribly sorry." At least he still had some ability to dazzle the ladies left with him. With Lily he felt untried and ineffective, but it seemed she was the only woman not completely dazzled by him.

"What may I help you with?" The girl waved at the flowers that covered every surface of the store.

"I need a bouquet," he began uncertainly. It had been longer than he could remember since he'd had to work at winning a woman over. All too often, they fell head over feet for him with no effort on his part, but it was different with Lily. He wanted to be a shining knight for her, a man who would give her the world or perish in the attempt.

"For a lady you admire? Or shall this be for a proposal?" The woman waited patiently for Charles to decide.

"This would be...a courting...bouquet?" He prayed there was such a thing.

The woman tried to fight off a little smile. "Ah... First time to call upon your lady?"

He nodded, feeling a little jolt of nervousness.

The woman watched him, her hands hovering near a pot of gardenias. "Tell me about her."

"She's beautiful. She's golden-haired, as though the sun kissed her, and her eyes are as blue as cornflowers. She's tall and graceful..." He noticed the woman staring at him, and he realized praising Lily's physical beauty was not what she had in mind. "She's witty, intelligent, and most definitely wily. She ties me in knots. But she's had hardships. Her late husband died after an illness and left her alone with their young daughter. She dances like a dream, but she's also kind and thoughtful and mysterious..." He couldn't resist smiling now. "When she laughs, the candlelight seems brighter, and when I hear her voice, the rest of the world falls away."

"She's made you into a poet, I see." She was already moving about the shop, plucking colorful flowers one by one and tucking them into a vase. "That tells me all I need to know." Then she returned and pointed out each selection.

"Gladiolas for strength and faithfulness. Calla lilies for innocence and purity, amaryllis for splendid beauty, and daffodils for unrequited love."

"Unrequited?" Charles asked.

"Think of it as a plea for it to *be* requited," she answered with a wink.

Charles noticed she missed one flower, a flower he recognized. "And the gardenias? What do they mean?"

The young florist smiled and touched his gloved hand. "Secret love...and the sender of gardenias is lonely." The woman's gaze drifted to the flowers, and he realized she must be lonely as well. Loneliness was so tragic in such a shop such as this.

"Is it that obvious that I'm lonely?" Charles asked.

"It's in your eyes and how you speak about your love."

Charles chuckled wryly. "Perhaps not much longer. How much for the bouquet?"

"Five shillings." The florist carefully tied the bouquet with a blue satin ribbon and removed it from the vase, then handed it to him.

Charles handed her ten pounds.

"From one gardenia sender to another." He gave her a grateful smile before he left the shop and returned to his coach.

He felt like a silly fool sitting in his coach with a massive bouquet in his hands, but he couldn't think of any other way to show Lily he wanted to be a proper gentleman toward her. Thanks to Emily, his reputation no doubt preceded him.

As the coach stopped in front of Godric's townhouse, a swarm of butterflies flapped madly inside his stomach. He checked his pocket watch yet again and sighed with relief. Almost eleven. Finally. Surely if he went up and knocked, Godric would let him in, even if he was a tad early.

His hand shook as he lifted the knocker and rapped on the door. When Godric's butler, Simkins, answered, Charles grinned.

"Simkins, you old devil! Still alive, are we?" He slapped the man on the shoulder.

Simkins smiled indulgently. "No thanks to you. You are expected. I should warn you that all beverages have been put out of your reach. Should you be thirsty, I will bring you whatever you require—in a *very* small glass."

"Then you'll simply need to bring many of them."

The butler's gaze dropped to the massive bouquet. "Flowers? Well, now, you must be serious about this one," Simpkins teased.

"I certainly am," Charles admitted.

"God have mercy upon her. The ladies are in the morning room. Let me announce your arrival." Simpkins left him standing in the foyer.

"Charles?" Godric's booming laugh made him cringe.

"Good Lord, are those *flowers*?" He came down the stairs, green eyes bright with humor.

"Not one more bloody word," Charles warned. "I've had enough of that from your butler. Why hasn't he retired yet?"

"He fears the day my rugs are left undefended from one of your visits. It's what keeps him going."

"Lord Lonsdale, the ladies will see you now," Simkins announced as he returned to the hall.

Charles squared his shoulders and headed for the morning room. Godric stood at attention and gave a mock salute as he passed, then trailed behind him. Charles shot him a questioning look.

"Oh, I wouldn't miss *this* for anything," said Godric.

Charles cursed under his breath and opened the door, prepared to face Emily as their chaperone and Lily, the woman fast stealing his heart.

16

The morning room's peach-colored walls glowed with the bright winter sunlight flooding the room through the tall windows. Emily was seated on a chair by a crackling fire, a book in her hands. She beamed at him as he entered, then nodded toward Lily, who was on a couch by the window, also reading. No doubt Emily had wanted them to be seen in this exact way when he entered.

Charles cleared his throat, and Lily glanced up, the gaze of her blue eyes caressing him. He wanted to drag her into his arms and kiss her senseless behind the curtains. But no, indulging in brief meaningless passions was what the other Charles would do. He had to be more than that for her.

Lily's eyes widened when she saw what he held. Feeling like a bloody fool, he thrust the bouquet out awkwardly.

"Here." It was the only word he could get out at first. His heart was hammering so loudly he could barely think.

Lily blinked. "Pardon?"

Charles heard Godric snort behind him. Emily put a hand to her face, trying to hide her smile.

Oh God, he would never hear the end of this, would he?

"These are for you," he said correctly.

Lily set the book aside and took the bouquet. She buried her face in the brightly colored flowers. Charles's breath caught as the sunlight illuminated her. She was simply the most exquisite woman he'd ever met. The beauty inside her shone in the merry twinkle of her eyes as she slowly raised her gaze to his as she basked in the sheer feminine delight of her brushing her face against the petals. He couldn't look away, didn't want to. He was lost in Lily, this beautiful stranger who yet seemed so familiar. Could a man love a woman at first sight? He felt as though it was possible, when she looked at him the way she was doing now, as though he'd answered some silent, secret prayer she'd held deep within her heart.

I feel the same way. She is the answer to my loneliness.

"These are lovely." Lily glanced at Emily, her cheeks reddening as she displayed the flowers to her cousin with embarrassed pride.

"They are indeed." Emily smiled at them and then stood to leave. She gave Charles a slow, meaningful look, but he wasn't quite sure what she was telling him. Be on his best behavior? Couldn't she tell he was trying?

"Excuse me. I shall return in a moment with a vase." Emily joined Godric in the hallway and closed the door.

She'd left him alone with Lily. That was unexpected. Either she trusted him to be a gentleman, which was unlikely, or she was expecting him to be himself and seduce Lily, which he might very well do if he had the chance.

He sat down on the opposite end of the couch, his heart still racing, his palms sweating. He'd never felt nervous around a woman like he did now. Yet he was also full of a tranquility that he'd never believed possible. Something about all this, as frightening and alien as it was to him, felt right.

Lily sighed dreamily. "Gardenias. My favorite." She rubbed her cheek against the petals and looked up at him. Her dark-gold lashes shimmered, and the soft pink of her lips were slightly parted, and all he could think of was covering those lips with his.

"Gardenias are your favorite?" He struggled past the lust of his thoughts and focused on their conversation. He wanted to know her as much as he wanted to kiss her.

"Yes, and the calla lilies too, probably because of my name." She laughed. "My mother used to put small gardenias in her hair before balls. They looked so stunning, and the aroma... She had vases of them and freesia everywhere.

My mother adored flowers. I do as well, but I haven't thought about them in years."

That sorrow he'd noticed before was in her eyes again. He slowly reached for her free hand and wrapped his fingers around hers. He marveled at how calming it was to hold her hand, with no expectations of more to come. He turned her hand over, examining the fine lines. There were several small calluses along the tops of her palm, just below the base of her fingers. He explored the calluses, wondering what events in life had led her to working with her hands.

"I'm sorry." Lily tried to pull her hand away in embarrassment, but he didn't let her. He raised it slowly to his lips, brushing his mouth gently, reverently over her knuckles. Her breath caught and his blood hummed in response.

"There is no need to apologize," Charles said. "There is no shame in hands that have seen work. Quite the opposite. I want to know everything about you. Would you tell me?"

"I can tell you some things," she said. "But not everything."

Charles smirked. "A woman of secrets, eh?"

"A woman of caution."

Charles hesitated, wondering if he could ask the question that was uppermost in his mind, knowing she likely wouldn't answer. "Very well. What were you doing alone in Vauxhall and how did find yourself kidnapped and taken to Lewis Street?"

"I had decided to arrive in London sooner than my cousin was expecting me. I did not wish to impose upon Emily's kindness more than I had to, so I took to exploring the city on my own. She had written to me about the gardens before, and I had hoped to see them myself. She had not warned me of the dangers, however."

Charles nodded. "I suppose no place in London is truly safe, which is why no woman should walk the streets alone, especially in the evening."

Her gaze grew distant for a moment. "It is a mistake I will not make again." Then she looked down at her book. "Next question, my lord."

Well, he'd tried. Perhaps a more circuitous route was required to win her trust. "What book are you reading?" He nodded at the tome she'd set aside.

"Adam Smith's *Wealth of Nations*."

"Truly?" He blinked at her. Most men he knew couldn't finish that book, and he'd never given much thought to whether a woman would read it. Not that he didn't think a woman could manage it, just that it was so bloody *boring*...

"Yes, it's a bit belabored on some of the more specific economic points, but the general discussion is rather fascinating, don't you agree?"

Charles laughed. "I wouldn't know. I tried to read it for one of my classes at Cambridge, and every time I opened the book, I would wake up hours later, my face planted on the pages. It was so bad I started using it for a pillow."

"You didn't!" Lily giggled.

"I didn't," he admitted. "But doesn't it make a good story?"

"It does," she agreed. "Why don't you tell me a true story?"

"About me?" He wanted to hear more about her, but if she wanted to hear him talk, he would do whatever she asked. "Well, let's see..."

"Would you tell me about the swans in Vauxhall?"

He shot an angry glare toward the door. "Emily! Lord, that woman. Now she's enlisting relatives to try to learn that story?" He relaxed a little and rolled his eyes. This time he was the one avoiding an answer. "No swans. Next question."

She bit her bottom lip. "Then tell me about your parents," she suggested. "Your family."

"My family..." He trailed his fingertips along her palm, tracing the fine lines in her skin. "Where to begin? My mother, Violet, is a lovely woman, and I mean that. Inside and out. She and my father had been friends long before they married. She always told me marriages based upon friendship last longer than those born of lust."

Lily nodded, her eyes searching his face. "And your father?"

"Guy Humphrey was a wonderful father, a loving and warmhearted man. It has only ever been my desire to be as good a man as he was."

"And are you?" Lily asked.

Charles wanted to smile, but found he couldn't. "I

seem to be woefully short of succeeding in that goal. But I continue to try."

Lily reached up to cup his cheek. "I think that says more than you realize." She spoke with such conviction that he almost believed her.

"Lily... May I call you Lily?" She nodded and pressed her lips together, as though this step forward had excited her. "I feel as though I know you, even though we've only just met. Does that sound strange to you?"

"Not at all," she assured him.

He smiled bashfully, feeling like a boy again. "I cannot get you out of my head, and yet I feel like I have no one I can talk to about how I feel now."

"No one? What about your friends?"

Charles chuckled. "I fear that is not possible. I have been somewhat...mocking toward them whenever they spoke about love and romance. If I were to ask them their advice now, they would no doubt have their revenge upon me."

"Oh my," Lily said, feigning shock.

"It's all in good jest, I assure you," Charles added. "Still, it must be said I have burned many a bridge this past year."

"That is a shame," said Lily. "Men often keep their feelings to themselves, and that simply cannot be healthy. You truly have no one to talk to?"

Charles thought about it. "Well, perhaps my valet."

"Your valet?"

"Yes, I trust my valet as much as I would any of my friends."

"He must be quite the valet. Would you tell *him* about the swans at Vauxhall?" Lily teased, gently nudging him in the ribs with a finger.

"Lord, why does every lady I meet want to know about the bloody swans?" He let out a groan and settled back on the couch, shifting her closer to him in the process, but only just. She didn't pull away, and he crowed inwardly at his small victory. Her fingers were still dancing along his skin. He was lost in her, in the swell of her breasts as she breathed and the pulse beating in her throat and faint floral aroma that clung to her skin since she'd buried her face in the bouquet. He wanted to kiss her so badly that his entire body ached with the primal need to taste her. He knew that if he took her into his arms, captured her mouth with his, that he would feel her heartbeat against his lips and he would be truly lost forever.

"Because the tale of the swans is legendary," she answered. "Just as *you* are legendary, my lord."

Her amused smirk made him want to laugh out loud. It was such a familiar thing, as though he'd known this woman for years. Which was impossible, of course.

"You must call me Charles. 'Tis only fair."

Her blue eyes darkened with solemnity as she gazed at his lips. "Charles." The way she spoke his name sent a strange thrill through him, and his blood hummed in excitement.

"Lily, may I kiss you?" He half expected her to blush, then slap him for his presumption. At best he thought she might say it was too soon, or not appropriate upon their first formal meeting. Instead, she nodded eagerly.

"Yes, you may." Lily's lashes fluttered down, and her lips parted. Charles felt as though he were standing at the gates of heaven as he leaned in. Their lips brushed in a gentle burning prelude. He dug his nails into his palms, the sharp edge of pain keeping his control in check as he nudged her nose with his. Her lips parted, a draft of breath on his lower lip preceding a small moan that sailed from her throat and straight into his bones. A shudder tore through him, even as the pain in his palms receded to be replaced by lust. Fire raced between their bodies, even though he wasn't holding her in his arms the way he desperately wanted to. Lights flashed behind his closed eyes as he grew drunk on the sweet taste of her mouth—

The morning room door burst open.

"I found a vase!" Emily announced. Her violet eyes glinted as she added, "As I proclaimed loudly, *several times*, from the corridor just now."

Charles and Lily jerked away from each other. He shot Emily a frustrated scowl as the sweet lust in his veins changed into heated embarrassment.

Emily came over and took the bouquet from Lily. The flowers had fallen to her lap and were in clear danger of toppling to the floor. Emily slid the flower stems into the water-filled glass.

"There." She set the vase down on the table. "Don't they look absolutely lovely? What a perfect bouquet, Charles. Well done." Then she tilted her head to the side, as she pretended to hear Godric calling for her. "Oh, I'd best go see what my husband needs!" She stepped into the hall. "Darling? What did you need?"

"Need? What are you calling me for? I didn't say anything." Godric's voice, clearly startled, made Charles laugh.

Emily hushed him, and he next heard a masculine grunt, no doubt Godric being jabbed in the ribs by the dainty duchess. Then the door to the room closed.

Charles waited until she was gone before he turned back to Lily. Her face was flushed, her lips swollen, and a wanton hunger still gleamed in her eyes. He still struggled to play the gentleman he knew he had to be. Dragging her beneath him on the couch was what the old Charles would have done, and this woman deserved better.

"She's a terrible chaperone, but I suppose she understands that you aren't an innocent young maiden lacking knowledge of the ways of the world."

Lily's face shadowed with worry. "Does that bother you?"

"Does what bother me?" he asked, still lost in daydreams of possessing her lips with his.

"That I've been...married before?"

Her fear of his answer was plain on her face. He winced. He was making such a mess of this.

"No, not at all. I'm more worried that I won't measure up to your husband. He must have been your first love." He didn't want to think of her loving another. He wasn't the jealous sort, but knowing he wouldn't be first in a woman's heart, that there had been another before him was unnerving. What if he never measured up to her first husband?

Lily looked away. He cursed himself for reminding her of her pain. Why couldn't he have kept his mouth shut?

"He wasn't my first love. I cared about him deeply, of course, but in truth I was never in love with him."

"But you chose to marry him?" Charles asked, curious. He tried not to rejoice in the thought that he might still be the first man to win this fascinating, beautiful, and intelligent woman's heart.

Her lips curved in a wry smile. "Not everyone marries for love alone, you know. In fact, it's quite rare."

"I know. But I suppose I've always *hoped* that marriage for love would become the more expected practice." He meant it. Marriage without love sounded like torture for everyone involved. A life of commitment should be built on a positive force like love, not just a legal contract.

Lily laughed, and he swore he heard bells ringing. "You are a romantic."

"I suppose I am." He glanced at the doorway again, half expecting Emily to burst in with another distraction. He needed to hold Lily in his arms, and while he fully expected that she wouldn't let him, it was damned well worth a try.

"Stay there." He got up and dragged an armchair in front of the door, careful to butt it up against the handle. Once he was satisfied the furniture would prevent them from being interrupted, he returned to the couch. Her gaze was eager too. He saw a little thrill in her eyes as she looked at him.

"My, my, aren't we the wicked one?" Lily chuckled, and the sound went straight to his groin. Charles couldn't wait another second.

He cupped her face in his palms and captured her lips. He tried to be gentle, *was* gentle at first, but her sweet taste went straight to his head like brandy. He feathered his lips against hers, coaxing her mouth open and slipping his tongue inside, only to find hers already searching for his. His hands framed her face and slid down her body, eliciting shivers and moans as he dragged his palms across her breasts and down to her waist and then the slopes of her hips as he pulled her closer to him. Then he lifted her in one fluid motion so that she sat across his lap, which brought her closer for his kiss.

He kissed his way across the bare expanse of her delectable collarbone and down to the mounds of her breasts. His hands dug into her hips, uncaring if he wrinkled her gown. She rocked against him, straddling his body, her legs moving to either side of him. He made no effort to push things too far. Not for propriety's sake.

Propriety could hang. He simply wanted to have her, the object of his desire, the first woman he'd ever courted, to kiss him as madly and passionately as she wished with no worry as to whether to expect anything more.

Lily ran her tongue over his lower lip when his mouth returned to hers, and he growled softly, nipping at her bottom lip. She wrapped her arms tighter around his neck, pressing closer, a whimper escaping as she parted her lips wider, letting his tongue thrust as deep as he dared. He wanted her to *feel* him, to feel how it would be someday soon when he took her to bed and claimed her.

Finally their mouths parted, and he tried to catch his breath. His heart raced wildly, and he wasn't sure he would ever calm down. He was trembling. She laughed breathlessly as she placed slow, teasing kisses on his chin, his throat, his ear. The woman was a goddess, one he wished to worship for the rest of his life.

"Was that all right?" he asked as he tried to pull his thoughts together. The woman had unraveled him completely.

She pressed her forehead to his, breathing just as hard. "You know it was more than all right. It was wonderful."

The knot in his chest loosened, and a warmth spread through his body as her fingertips smoothed over his face, tracing his jaw and lips before sliding down to his neck and shoulders. He moved his hands along her lower back, exploring the gentle curve of it before he cupped her bottom, his breathing still heavy. He felt in that moment that this woman owned him, just as he owned her, and that sweet, gentle possessiveness made him bold enough to speak again.

"May I take you out tonight?"

She moved her head to rest on his shoulder, her lips teasing his ear. "What would we do?"

His hands tightened on her. "Anything you like."

"An opera?"

"Yes, an opera," he agreed. "And perhaps, until then, we could spend the entire day in this room." He waggled his eyebrows suggestively.

Her laughter made his head spin with delightful dizziness. "I think Emily and Godric might object."

"If they cannot get inside, we will not hear their objections."

Lily chuckled and nuzzled his cheek as she relaxed into him.

The tension that had seemed coiled so tight in this beautiful woman began to ease. All Charles wanted was to hold her, to let her know she was no longer alone, that he was there for as long as she wanted him.

"I don't wish to forget anything about this moment," he said, and pressed another kiss to her lips.

"My lord, that is your lust speaking." The tone of her voice hurt him, though it was a fair thing to say given his history. How could he explain what he felt to her? That this was different from anything he'd ever experienced?

"Lily, I'll be the first to admit that I know nothing of

love, but what I feel now is not simple lust." He cupped her face in his hands, making sure he had her full attention. "I have a history with women, as I assume you must know given your time spent with Emily."

"I do. But the past is the past." She laid her head on his shoulder and let out a soft sigh.

"If it doesn't matter, then why do you not trust me when I say I have feelings for you?"

She didn't immediately reply. Her slender fingers danced along the buttons of his waistcoat, tracing the ivory-colored pieces.

"It's not that I do not trust you. I do not trust the happiness I feel in your arms. It cannot last." She suddenly straightened and pulled off his lap. He tried to reach for her, but she waved for him to stay back.

"I've been here alone too long. I must go before the servants begin to gossip and ruin Emily and Godric's good names." She moved toward the door, then paused. "But...I would still like to go to the opera with you tonight."

"Even though you don't trust the happiness you feel with me?" He couldn't help but challenge her with her own words.

Her eyes burned into his. "I don't trust it, but that doesn't mean I don't *want* it." She pulled the chair away from the door and vanished into the corridor.

The room felt empty, as though she'd never been there. Vanished again. The bouquet of flowers she'd left behind was the only proof of her existence, and the gardenias seemed to mock him in his renewed state of loneliness.

Charles sat alone on the couch. He scrubbed a hand over his jaw and sighed, as though the weight of the world had been laid upon his shoulders. There was no point in staying here if he couldn't be with Lily until tonight.

Simpkins was waiting for him in the hall, holding his hat and coat. Charles accepted them silently and was halfway out the door when the butler spoke.

"Love that requires patience, understanding, and forgiveness is a love that will last long after lust is gone."

Charles stared at the butler for a long moment, and then he answered Simpkins with a nod. "Thank you."

Simpkins stared at Charles down his nose. "The beverages are still off-limits to you, my lord, but good luck."

Charles smiled and patted him on the shoulder. "And to you. I fear I scuffed up the floorboards moving some furniture around."

He could feel Simpkins's hard stare as he left. If looks could kill, Hugo's revenge would have been cut short by one furious butler.

17

Ashton Lennox sat in a chair at Berkley's club, an abandoned glass of brandy hanging precariously from his hand. His thoughts were miles away. He'd done his best to seek out the man he knew as Kilkenny, who Ashton was convinced was one of Hugo's spies, but the man hadn't shown.

Ashton had stalked the man like a master hunter would a prize buck for the last month, biding his time and convincing him to at least talk. But it had all led to nothing. Then word arrived of a carriage accident just a block away from the ball that night, and he had quickly deduced what had happened. He'd been played again, chasing phantoms in the dark, just as Hugo no doubt wished him to.

"There is something I'm not seeing. Some piece of a puzzle, a move upon the chessboard that I missed."

He had agents of his own following Hugo and his agents. Spies spying on spies. He had learned much about Hugo and the way he schemed, but there were things that did not add up. He finally understood Hugo's hatred for Charles, but there was more to it than that, he sensed it. Something that had nothing to do with Hugo or Charles directly...

He closed his eyes, remembering his own part in the events of that night.

He and Lucien had been returning from a night at a local pub, the Pickerel, when they had seen two people struggling at the edge of the river alongside Magdalene College. He and Lucien sprinted across the lawn, shouting once they realized that one man was trying to drown the other.

Then he'd seen Peter Maltby fly out of nowhere and dive into the river. Ashton and Lucien shouted more as the three splashed in the water, but they couldn't understand what they were seeing. Then a young man's gargling scream cut through the night, and Hugo crawled out of the river, gasping and smiling coldly. There was no sign of Peter or the third man. Ashton's blood had roared in his ears as he feared what had happened to Peter. His friend wasn't surfacing. Why wasn't he coming back up?

"What did you do?" Ashton had demanded of Hugo, but the question had gone unanswered. By then it had been too late.

Godric and Cedric, two young lords he'd known in

passing over the last few months, were wading into the river from the opposite side.

"Two men are in the water!" Lucien called out. "Peter and a second fellow."

"It's young Lonsdale," Godric said as he dove into the water.

Ashton and Lucien quickly dove into the watery depths as well. Hugo would have to wait.

Ashton swam deep, finding Lonsdale in the murky depths with ropes and a heavy weight secured to his feet. Peter had a knife and was cutting the ropes. When he finished Charles scrambled for the surface but it was too far off. Peter struggled for breath. Ashton saw Peter's body seize as he inhaled water and went still, his body carried away in the dark water, too far out of reach.

Ashton had been a swimmer all his life and was capable of holding his breath. He helped Charles to the surface, but by the time they broke the surface Ashton was exhausted and unable to hold on. Godric and Cedric finally reached them and took Charles to the opposite shore. He threw up a mouthful of water and lay gasping next to them.

Ashton looked back across the river. In the moonlight Hugo stared at them, furious and hateful, cursing them all. Peter was gone. He'd died trying to save young Lonsdale. A heavy cloak of despair settled over Ashton and the others as they all caught their breath.

All of them, even Hugo, had been changed that night.

And yet, that could not be the whole story. Charles's father had killed Hugo's in a duel. Hugo had never sought Charles out after that. It was a chance encounter that led to his attempt at murder. But why wait so long to come after them after that? Years had passed since that day. Had he simply been biding his time?

No. There was something more to all this. Something that had occurred before Hugo's renewed attempts at revenge. There had to be.

Ashton set his brandy on the table untouched as he rose from his chair. There was one person who might have answers, but would she even agree to see him?

He exited Berkley's and hired a coach to take him to a quiet, respectable little street in Mayfair. He'd known for years who lived in this house, but until now he'd refrained from visiting. There were lines he still did not wish to cross, but the closer Hugo got to them all, the more desperate he became.

He glanced around as he walked up the steps of the townhouse. The fine hairs on his neck rose. The street was busy with people and coaches and a few brave souls still riding horses despite the winter chill. If he was being watched, it would be impossible to tell. Ashton rapped his knuckles on the door and waited. After a minute the butler allowed him in, and he removed his hat.

"Ashton Lennox to see Mrs. Waverly."

The butler nodded and entered a room off the entryway. He returned a few minutes later.

"This way, my lord."

Ashton was shown into a drawing room. A dark-haired woman in her fifties sat at a desk, writing a letter. She looked up as Ashton entered, and he was struck by Jane Waverly's beauty.

She deposited her quill pen and stood. "Lord Lennox, how may I help you?"

"I'm afraid I need to speak with you on a delicate matter." He never thought he would be in a drawing room with the mother of their tormenter.

Jane's brows drew together. "I'm not sure I understand..."

"It's about Hugo."

At this she stiffened. "I have not spoken to my son in many years."

That, Ashton hadn't expected. "Oh?"

"Yes." She walked toward one of the drawing room windows and gazed out into the frozen world of her garden. "After his father died, I went into mourning and he returned to school. I wrote to him weekly, but he never responded and never returned home. I eventually left my old home and moved here."

"I see." Ashton cleared his throat. "I assume you know of Lord Lonsdale. Charles, I mean."

Jane nodded. "I do. I assume you know that I knew his father, Guy."

"Yes. That is part of the matter I wish to speak with you about."

"Oh?"

"Were you aware that Hugo tried to murder Charles when they were at university?"

The color drained from her face. "Murder?"

"Thankfully, he was unsuccessful. We had not heard from Hugo for ages, assumed he moved overseas. But this past year he began making moves against Charles and anyone associated with him. I would spare you the details, but the matter has become gravely serious."

Even without the details, this news visibly shook Jane to her core. "Oh, my poor dear Hugo. What have you done?"

"Charles told me about the duel between the fathers, but these renewed attacks, after so long, tell me he has new reasons to seek Charles out and punish him. I can't help but wonder if there was more to the story."

Jane nodded at the chairs in the room. "Perhaps you'd better sit."

Ashton took a seat upon the gold-and-cream brocade chair. Jane ran her hands over her skirts, nervous as to how to begin.

"I know why my son's hatred has grown so strongly against Charles." She paused, and Ashton had to prompt her with a nod before she would continue. "I grew up in the country, not far from the Lonsdale estate. I knew Guy Humphrey well, and over time an affection grew between us. But my parents did not approve of the match. It did not help that he was only the second son of the earl. They married me off instead to Baltus Waverly, who had just been knighted and was a favorite of the Crown. That was considered more valuable than anything Guy could offer. Guy married Charles's mother, Violet. She was and still is a dear friend of mine."

"I am following, madam."

"However, I..." Jane cleared her throat. "I came to my marriage in the family way."

The room seemed suddenly devoid of air. Neither of them spoke as Ashton came to grips with this news.

"You mean to say that Hugo and Charles are..."

"Brothers," Jane said quietly. "Half brothers."

"Charles doesn't know?" Ashton's question was more of a statement.

"No. After the duel, Guy told me Charles should never be told the truth, that the bitterness and resentment between Charles and my son would only drive the wedge between them deeper."

Ashton felt as though he'd been struck in the chest. It was damnably hard to breathe. He added this to what he knew of Hugo, and how this knowledge would affect him. So much made sense now. Except, how did Hugo find out?

"When did Hugo find out?"

Jane paused and swallowed hard as she met Ashton's gaze.

"Would you tell me what happened? How he discovered this?"

Jane nodded. "It was a little over three years ago..."

London, September 1819

Jane stood anxiously in the parlor, watching the clock on the mantel. A footman had brought tea in, and she kept wanting to pour herself a cup to calm her nerves. It had been so long since she'd seen her son. At last, her letters to him had finally received an answer. He was coming here to speak with her, to reconcile after his father's death all those years ago.

The door to the parlor opened, and her butler escorted her son inside. Her heart leapt at the sight. He'd grown tall and handsome, like his father. But unlike Guy, he had her dark eyes and dark hair, which had pleased her husband Baltus since he'd been dark as well. Still, it hadn't erased the pain in her marriage, knowing that she'd come into her union with Baltus while carrying the child of first love.

"Hugo," Jane breathed, her lips trembling as she held out her hands. He approached her a little stiffly, but he took her hands in his as they sat down on the settee beside each other.

"Tea?" she offered hopefully.

"No, thank you. I..." Hugo cleared his throat.

"Oh..." She sniffed, fighting back the sting of tears. But Hugo squeezed her hands gently.

"I'm glad to be here, Mother. It's been too long, and

I've little excuse for staying away." He sighed, meeting her gaze and allowing himself a smile. "Melanie and I are hoping to provide you with a grandson soon."

"A grandson?" Jane smiled widely. "What wonderful news."

"Mother...I'm sorry. I didn't mean to treat you so poorly after Father died. I held you accountable, and that was not right. Now that I'm looking toward fatherhood myself, I find I regret my behavior. I've been angry for so long, after losing Father, and...I've done things I regret and I want to make amends."

Jane shook her head, simply relieved to see and touch her son again after such an absence. But guilt dug deep within her. She had to tell him the truth she'd kept from him for so long.

"Please, tell me that you'll start by forgiving Guy Humphrey's son." He had to. If he didn't, Jane wouldn't be able to bear it.

Hugo stiffened. "Forgive Lonsdale? Mother, you know that I—"

"You have to," she said firmly, and her son's eyes narrowed slightly.

"Why?"

She paused, fortifying herself for what must be said. "Because he shares your blood."

For a long moment, Hugo stared at her. His dark eyes, so like hers, seemed to puzzle over her words.

"Shares my blood?" There was an edge of warning in his tone, one she should have listened to. But it was too late; she had to confess the rest of the secret.

"Long before I ever met your father, I loved Guy Humphrey. He was the man I wished to marry but was forbidden to. When I married your father, I was already with child. You. You were my last gift from Guy before we parted ways as lovers and had to marry other people. But Baltus loved you like you were his own, especially when he found out he could not father a child of his own. He loved you"

Hugo jerked his hands free of hers as though she'd burned him.

"No." He uttered the word in part desperation, part disbelief.

"Yes. You and Charles Humphrey are half brothers. Don't you see? You must bury the past and forgive him. He's your blood."

Hugo leapt from the settee. "No!" He shouted the word this time, as if it would somehow banish the last few minutes from his mind like a nightmare.

"Hugo, please..." Jane stood, but it was too late. Her son shot her one last dark, cold, and furious gaze before he left, slamming the door behind him so hard it rattled against the frame.

Jane slumped back onto the settee, gazing down at her hands in her lap as the tea in the pot grew cold.

JANE WAVERLY CLEARED HER THROAT AS ASHTON politely looked away while she wiped her eyes.

"Hugo never came back after that. Not even when Peter was born. I've never even held my grandson. My son never forgave me. It did not matter that Hugo was conceived in a moment of happiness, of love, with the man who will always have my heart. Hugo may have Guy's blood in him, but he was raised by my husband to have hate fill his heart. I never should have told him the truth. It's a decision that will haunt me forever." Jane's voice broke a little, and Ashton removed a handkerchief from his pocket and handed it to her. She accepted with a watery smile.

"How I envy Violet, to have a noble son with such good friends. You will have mercy on him, won't you? Do what you must to protect Charles, but please, please do not harm my son." Her heartbreaking plea shattered Ashton's heart. He was not certain he could make that promise.

"It is my fault. Mine," she whispered. "His grief has turned to madness, and I could have prevented it."

Ashton's throat swelled tight as he felt compassion for this broken, lonely woman. "We have all sworn to do what is right, Mrs. Waverly. That I can promise you." He couldn't dare tell this dear woman that it might mean killing Hugo, but the man had to be stopped.

"Thank you," Jane said, but he could see in her eyes that she knew the truth. Someone would not survive this battle.

"I'm afraid I must go. Thank you for all you have shared with me." Ashton stood, and Jane followed suit, catching his sleeve before he could leave. Her eyes were dark with emotion.

"Violet knows about Hugo. If anyone must tell Charles the truth, it should come from her."

With a nod, Ashton left Jane Waverly's drawing room. He was not prepared for the icy chill that met him as he left her home; his mind was far away, in an even colder place.

Brothers. Like Cain and Abel. This was the final piece of the puzzle. It explained why Hugo hadn't tried to hurt them after Cambridge. He'd been healing, in his own way. Trying to put the past behind him. But learning he and Charles were brothers had set him back on the path to darkness. He must have felt like a pawn in a great cosmic joke, and Hugo was not the sort of man who would ever allow himself to be a pawn in anything. He saw himself as the master of his own destiny. It all made sense now. With this, Ashton was beginning to understand what Hugo's endgame was. And that meant he could finally prepare his counter.

But what of Charles? Should they tell him?

No. Ashton did not want Charles to know the truth,

not unless he had to. It would be far too great a sorrow for Charles to bear, one that might put him in even greater danger.

18

"Tell me the truth now." Violet Humphrey stared at Charles with a sharp gaze honed by years of raising rogues for children.

"Truth? I have no idea what you're talking about." Charles hedged as best he could, but he knew he wouldn't win any argument his mother began.

"There's a woman." Violet sat perched on a settee with Charles's little sister, Ella, beside her. Ella had a book open in her lap but had not turned a page since this parental inquisition began. Her blonde hair, so much like his, framed her face as she peered blankly at her pages. She was pretty, of course, with eyes more blue than gray, like their mother's, but her features were a more feminine version of their father's. She was small and delicate, but fiercely intelligent and kindhearted.

"There are plenty of women. You...Ella...the cook..."

Teasing his mother was a favorite hobby of his. Some men collected butterflies and insects; Charles searched for new ways to provoke his mother.

"Plenty of women? Oh!" She snapped her fan shut the way a man would cock a pistol and pointed it at him menacingly.

"I believe London is full of women, or haven't you noticed?" he asked innocently.

"Ella, fetch my smelling salts. Your brother is trying to kill me."

Ella laid her book down and retrieved a tiny bottle from her reticule. Violet swatted it away like an irritating fly.

"Not *now*. Wait until I actually faint."

Charles couldn't resist grinning, which only made his mother's eyes narrow.

"The girl at the Sanderson ball. Who is she?"

"A girl now? Not a woman? I thought we were speaking of women? What interest would I possibly have in girls?"

Violet growled and chucked the fan at his head, which he easily caught.

"You know exactly what I mean, Charles Michael Edward Humphrey. Now talk."

"*Oh*," he said dramatically. "The girl from the Sanderson ball. You must mean Lily Wycliff."

"Yes. That Wycliff girl. Who is she?" His mother's brown eyes assessed him as though she was contemplating wedding plans. For the first time in his life, he wished his mother would do exactly that.

"Well, she's a widow," he began.

"A widow?"

"Her husband, Aaron Wycliff, was a favorite cousin of the Duchess of Essex."

"A country gentleman, then?" She paused in reflection, no doubt scanning her memory for any sign that she knew who he was speaking of.

"I believe so."

"And the widow? Where do her people hail from?"

Charles opened his mouth, but he realized he had no answer. "I honestly have no idea."

"You are falling in love with a woman, and you don't even know who she is?"

Charles frowned. "I didn't say I was falling in love with her. We've only just met." In truth he was, if he hadn't already, but he didn't wish for his mother to know. Not until he was certain Lily would agree to become the Countess of Lonsdale.

"You're in love, my dear boy," his mother sighed. "I've heard from more than one friend at the ball about how you looked at her and how she looked at you."

"*Radiant*, I believe someone said," Ella supplied. He had long known that she enjoyed making him squirm as much as he did their mother. "Radiant. Charming. Buoyant. Though one person did say 'a couple of lovesick fools.'"

Charles's face flushed, and he tugged at his neckcloth. How had it become so unbearably hot in this room so quickly?

"Yes, I heard that too," his mother agreed.

"I heard she has a child," Ella added.

"A child?" His mother's expression hardened slightly. "That may be a problem."

Charles hadn't forgotten she had a child. He hadn't wanted his mother to know in case she wasn't thrilled with the idea. Of course, thanks to Ella, it was too late now to avoid the subject.

"I don't see it as such. I would welcome her child as my own. If she will have me."

"Well, if you will welcome the child, then so shall I. So it seems you have decided then? After all these years, you've now found a woman worthy of your affections?"

He answered without hesitation. "Yes."

"When shall we meet her?"

He hadn't even thought that far ahead. "Er... I am taking her to the opera tonight."

His mother clapped her hands together. "Splendid! Ella and I shall accompany you and Mrs. Wycliff in your box. You shall meet us there."

"Very good," Charles said, and then he cleared his throat. "Mother, has Graham written to you?"

"Graham? Not since last week, why?" His mother's seeming happiness over Charles's upcoming nuptials thinned.

"I must ask that you not overreact, Mother, but Graham was injured. I've been taking care of him." He rushed to calm her before she panicked.

"Injured?" The word escaped from her lips.

"He's healing and safe."

Violet surged to her feet. "Safe? What do you mean? Is he in danger?"

"Mother, you really must sit. I will explain everything if you let me."

"Smelling salts, now!" Violet held her hand out to Ella, who handed her the vial of smelling salts. Violet promptly shattered it against the wall and crossed her arms over her chest, glowering.

"You will talk, *now*, dear boy."

Charles glanced at Ella and swallowed hard. Lord, sometimes he forgot his mother could be a fearsome creature.

"Graham and Lord Kent were gambling. Kent had an unusually poor streak." Charles paused, unsure how much he could tell them.

"What happened?" Ella asked.

"Kent was given the chance to fight in a boxing ring to pay off his debt, but in the process hc was gravely injured. Graham tried to help him, but they beat him as well. But Graham is going to be fine."

"Thank God," his mother said, her eyes bright with tears.

"And Lord Kent?" Ella demanded.

"He will be all right...I hope. The doctor said if he could survive a few weeks, he should pull through."

The news seemed to devastate Ella. "May I go see him?" she asked. "I mean, Graham, of course. But also Lord Kent."

Charles raised an eyebrow. He hadn't been aware that Ella was close to Phillip. "I suppose, if Mother doesn't object."

Ella gave their mother a desperate look.

"As long as you aren't underfoot while Charles is pursuing Mrs. Wycliff. Lord knows your brother will need every advantage to win this mystery woman."

"I won't," Ella replied at the same time Charles said, "She won't."

"Then you may go." Violet looked to Charles. "Graham is truly well?"

"Yes, a bit bruised, but he will be fine." It was an exaggeration, but he did not wish for her to worry more than she had to.

The significance of the moment only now seemed to dawn on his mother. "But he came to you? Of all places? Does that mean...?" Her eyes were bright with hope.

Charles gently cupped his mother's shoulders. "I think so, yes. He is still cautious, but that is only natural under the circumstances. I, for my part, will do all I can to make amends while he is under my roof."

"That's wonderful. You know how much it has broken my heart to see you two not speaking to each other."

"I know. But it will still take time."

Violet wiped her eyes. "Well, then let's focus on this evening. The opera and meeting your Mrs. Wycliff."

Charles's stomach fluttered with a sudden touch of nerves. Tonight his mother would be meeting Lily for the first time. It was quite a frightening prospect. But surely his mother would like her. She was wonderful. How could she not?

"We shall see you tonight then, dear boy." His mother kissed his cheek, then shooed him away.

Charles left his mother's home with a grin on his face, but as he stepped into his coach he had the sense he was being watched. He glanced around the street but saw no obvious signs of anyone looking at him.

In fact, he saw no one at all.

LILY HELD HER BREATH AS SHE LOOKED AT HER reflection in the mirror. She was in her guest bedchamber at the Essex house and was unable to deny she felt like a princess from one of the fairy tales she read to Katherine. The dark-rose gown she had put on was, in a word, stunning. It didn't try to hide her height, nor did it overly embellish her more gentle curves. Rather, it brought out the beauty of her willowy figure.

The dress was designed with gold bands of embroidered patterns along the sleeves and the hem. The neckline was deep and square cut, and Lily blushed as she reached up to touch her collarbone.

How long had it been since she'd played the lady? Too long. There were nights she'd escaped Charles's employment as Tom and had been able to venture to Vauxhall, even Gunter's for flavored ices, or to Bond Street for shopping. And then there had been those times Hugo had had need of her skills in a more feminine guise. But tonight she was to be out in society and would have a genuine chance to enjoy herself.

"You look lovely," Emily said from the doorway. She held Katherine high up on her side, balanced on her hip. Lily's daughter held a tiny doll and was smiling and talking to herself, chirpy little words that were too quick for Lily to understand.

"You truly wish to watch her tonight? You could leave her with the nurse." Lily couldn't believe the duchess had offered to watch the baby and miss the opera.

"Of course, but I'd rather stay home. I'm too far along to be out on icy streets tonight. Besides, Godric is in need of some paternal practice."

Lily almost laughed. One could practice all they liked, but there was no real preparation for parenthood.

"Don't forget to take your cloak." Emily nodded to one of the parcels, still wrapped on the bed. Lily removed the brown paper and unfolded a deep yellow-gold cottage cloak with a thick large hood. She wrapped it around her body and fastened it under her chin. She left the hood down for now and faced Emily, reticule in hand.

"Remember to smile!" Emily cheered. "This is supposed to be fun. You are excited to see Charles, aren't you?"

"Yes, I'm just nervous." This morning when he had paid a call on her, she had been able to do what was expected of her, but knowing he saw their future as something real, a future she secretly desired more than anything, crushed her. She wanted to believe she could have a happy life with him, but that was impossible. Not while Hugo held her daughter's life in his hands.

"You have no reason to be nervous. Charles is a good man, and I think he's quite serious about you. Godric said he has never brought a woman flowers before."

Lily couldn't help but smile. She believed that. Working as Tom, she'd grown very aware of his habits with ladies. He preferred to take more discreet and scandalous routes to a woman's affections, which had made his gesture this morning feel all the more sincere, which made her all the more conflicted. Her smile faltered.

"Mama!" Katherine held out her doll.

"For me?" Lily hugged the doll to her chest and kissed it before giving it back to Katherine. "Why don't you keep her safe while I'm gone? You'll be all right with Aunt Emily, won't you?"

Katherine nodded and burrowed her face shyly into

Emily's neck. Lily longed to hold her, but if she did she would never find the courage to leave.

"We'll be fine." Emily gave Katherine a squeeze. "Tell your mama to have a good night."

"Good night, Mama," Katherine said. Lily laughed and gazed with love at her daughter. Whenever she doubted herself, all she ever had to do was think of her, and the path became clear.

Simkins met her at the bottom of the stairs, giving her a warm smile.

"Lord Lonsdale's coach has just arrived. Would you like to wait for him to come in?"

"Oh! No, I'll go down to him." Lily thanked Simpkins and pulled the hood of her cloak up as she left. The bitter wind smelled of snow, and she saw heavy clouds, soft and gray against the dark night sky. At the coach, Charles opened the door but froze when he saw her.

"Lily, I was just about to—" He stopped, then struggled for words. "You look..."

"Yes?"

Charles looked around, as if fighting part of himself that wanted to kiss her senseless in order to be a better person for her. "You will be the envy of the opera."

Lily favored him with a smile. "Would you mind terribly if I sat beside you?"

"M-mind?" he stuttered. "Of-of course not."

"Are you cold, my lord?" She moved over and sat beside him. After a moment he carefully stretched his left arm around her shoulders. "Strange, you seem very warm to me."

"D-do I?" he asked.

She ducked her head, to make herself look embarrassed. "I'm not being too forward with you, am I? I had thought we were past all that after we..."

"Kissed?" he volunteered.

"Yes. Would you kiss me now?"

"Here?" he asked, his voice roughening a little with excitement.

"Yes, here," she cut in, moving closer to his lips.

His resolve broken, he pulled her onto his lap. Heat met heat as their lips joined. His hands explored her back, then her skirts. A wintery chill rushed up her leg as his fingers teased one of her ankles. She giggled in delight at his gentle touches. She'd never thought she could be with a man, not after what Hugo had done, but with Charles everything was different.

She felt no danger with him, no pain, no fear, only a powerful joy, tinged with a sadness she tried to suppress. She did not deserve this happiness, not even for a little while, but she could not stop herself from feeling it.

As he kissed her, she dragged her fingers down his waistcoat, wishing they were somewhere else, somewhere where she could remove it. So many nights she'd watched him bathe, seeing his glorious golden body, and she'd dreamed about moments like this, of being free to surrender her fears and feel only pleasure with this man.

He was like a bewitching elixir, one that could bring her heart back from the dead and make her whole again. He kissed her leisurely, like he had all the time in the world, which only made her more desperate.

She nibbled the lobe of his ear. "Won't you kiss me harder?"

Charles shuddered against her. "Harder?" His hands tightened a little in her hair, and she felt his erection press against her.

"Kiss me like you expect to be slapped for it."

He pulled away, concern marring the perfection of his face. "Is that what you truly want?" She nodded fiercely and curled her arms around his neck.

"Kiss me like we have no tomorrow. *Please*."

"You never cease to surprise me." He lowered his head again, and this time she saw and tasted the full hunger of the rogue she'd fallen in love with.

His mouth commanded hers, his tongue flicked inside her ear, and his hands moved everywhere. He was an unstoppable force of lust and pleasure. Lily moaned as he bit her neck, knowing it would leave a mark, but she didn't care. He knew just how to suck, to lick, to whisper his lips along her skin in unexpected places and make her womb clench and throb.

The passion he ignited within her turned into a burning firestorm. She'd never felt anything like it. She was finally getting what she wanted, and it was everything she'd hoped it would be. His rough hands were tempered by the seductive pull of his kiss, like a whirlpool eddying in a swiftly curving river. She was spinning helplessly, deliriously excited to be going along for the ride.

Then she thought of how ashamed Hugo had made her feel. How he had taken her against her will. How he had continued to use her after that. But that shame didn't have a place here in Charles's arms. There was only a sense of joy and wonder at how right it felt to be with him.

His hand crept higher up her thigh, sliding between her legs and delving into her underpinnings. She hissed in shock as he found her center and slid one finger inside her.

"Do you wish for me to stop?" he asked.

She shook her head and tried to shift closer to him, pushing his finger deeper. Her womb clenched as he explored her with that finger while they kissed. Their tongues fought a silent battle of lust, broken only by their panting breaths as he continued to stoke the fire within her. Soon it was too much, and a burst of devastating pleasure exploded through her. He silenced her cry with a slow, deep kiss, and she sagged against him.

He withdrew his hand and helped her settle her skirts back down. She was still shaking as he held her close on his lap, placing tender kisses all over her face.

"I want to burn this moment into my mind forever," he whispered.

Her heart bled, and she buried her face in his neck, holding him. They were silent for a long moment.

"Charles, could we...forget the opera?" She wanted to have him turn the coach around to take her to his home, his bed. She did not know how much time they had together, but for one night at least she wanted to believe that a life with him was possible.

He sighed heavily. "I would love nothing more, but I'm afraid my mother is quite keen on meeting you."

She jerked back. "*Mother*?"

Just then the coach stopped in front of Covent Garden. She couldn't meet his mother, not tonight. Not ever. She clutched her chest, and it took her a moment to calm.

"Yes." Charles cleared his throat and tugged on his cravat. "There's nothing to fear, my dear. My mother heard about our waltz at the Sandersons' ball and will be at the opera tonight to meet us in the box."

"Oh!" Lily had to think of an excuse, and she frantically tried to fix her hair and dress. "I can't meet her, not when I'm all—"

"Delightfully mussed?"

"Yes. Your mother, *everyone* will know what we've been up to."

"Does it matter?" Charles asked.

"Of course it does!"

"I never expected a cousin of Emily's to be so concerned with public opinion." He twined his fingers in her hair, tugging on the strands. "Would it be better if I proposed?"

Lily frowned. "Be serious, Charles."

"I'm utterly serious, darling. You're my mysterious angel. When I talk to you, when I kiss you, when I think about you, there is..." He paused, considering his words. "There's a stillness inside me, and a tranquility I've never felt before."

Lily stared at him, her lips parted. "But we have only met a few times."

"It is true. You are a mystery to me. And I adore a good mystery."

"You do not know the *real* me," she said. At his puzzled frown, she quickly added, "Please, not so soon. We all put our best foot forward when we wish to impress, do we not?"

"True. But I want to spend the rest of my life figuring you out." He sighed then. "I don't have a ring yet. I wanted to take my time choosing it."

He was serious. Lily looked away. "No. We cannot."

He didn't seem at all perturbed by her refusal. "Emily promised to find me a bride, and lo and behold, she has." He kissed the tip of her nose and gently set her on her feet so she could exit the coach. "I can be patient."

Marry him? Lily walked into the Covent Garden theater as though trapped in a hazy dream. She couldn't say yes, not with Hugo's specter looming everywhere. But if she had her freedom, she would have wept at his feet for the chance to say yes.

"My box is this way." He led her up the stairs toward an

expensive box. Lily felt the collective curious gaze of the crowds watching them.

She leaned against his arm. "Everyone is looking at us."

"Everyone is looking at *you*, darling."

Lily smiled, remembering Charles's reputation. "I rather think they're looking at me *because* of you."

Charles gazed at her with clear adoration. "Nonsense. You shine like a star fallen from the night sky. But it is as you said to me—they don't know the real you. There's so much more to you, isn't there?"

Lily bit her lip. "I'm nobody, Charles. No one so special as you imagine me to be. I fear I am only a dream you are having, and when you awaken you won't see me anymore, just an ordinary woman wondering why you are so disappointed."

"You are infinitely more than a dream, Lily. And you could never disappoint me." He stopped them just outside his box. Behind him was a fresco of Romeo climbing a balcony's ivy-colored trellis to reach Juliet. It was a play she both adored and despised in equal measure. She loved the young lovers' passion, but she hated that it ended so violently with their deaths.

And yet she could relate to it as well—for both were trapped by fate and circumstance, the hope that they felt a mere illusion. Their fates were sealed before the curtain even rose.

Charles saw what she was looking at, then bent to one knee before her. "One fairer than my love? The all-seeing sun ne'er he saw her match since first the world begun."

He gave a crooked and yet utterly charming smile, one so boyishly sweet that her heart never stood a chance. He was such a beautiful man.

Charles stood and cupped her face, leaning in close. "*Please* marry me," he said, his lips close to hers before he kissed her softly.

"I..." She needed to resist, but his sweet kisses were wearing her down. All she wanted was to burrow into him, close her eyes, forget the past, forget her pain, her sorrow, and find only the joy his love would bring.

I loved you at first sight, without shame without regret. But it comes at such a high cost for us both...

"My heart will be for no other," he vowed.

Lily shook her head. "Stop it. Every man can carry a book full of fancy words, especially a man like you."

She expected this to upset him, but he only chuckled. "Fancy words, yes, but inviting my mother? That, my darling, comes from a true desire to commit to you. There is no way I would ever subject you to my mother's scrutiny unless I was serious about you. And scrutinize you she will."

Lily swallowed hard, a shiver of dread rolling through her. She'd only glimpsed Lady Lonsdale once or twice before, and even then only at a distance.

"If you won't say yes tonight, please know that I will keep asking every day until we are both old and gray. By then I'll be too old to get down on one knee, but I will still ask until my last breath." His gentle, earnest words surprised her. He meant it. Lord, she wanted so much to say yes. But she couldn't forget Hugo, couldn't forget her daughter's safety. Her daughter had to come first.

"Now, let me introduce you to my mother and sister." He opened the box door and ushered her inside.

The Countess of Lonsdale and Lady Ella Humphrey rose from their seats as Lily and Charles entered.

"Mother, may I present to you Mrs. Wycliff. Lily, this is my mother, the Countess of Lonsdale."

The countess was a stunning woman in her fifties. Lily did her best to smile despite her nerves.

"You may call me Violet, Mrs. Wycliff. It's a pleasure to meet you."

"And please call me Lily." Lily's tone betrayed none of her inner turmoil.

Violet smiled warmly. "Lily. A lovely name for a lovely woman." Violet turned to her daughter. "This is Ella."

Lily nodded. "Ella." Charles's sister beamed at her.

"Now, to business. My son told me that you are a widow?" Violet mused, her gaze sweeping critically over Lily. "Is your mourning period over?"

"Mother!" Charles hissed in warning.

Lily placed a hand on his arm. "It's all right." Her first husband was, after all, nothing more than a fabrication. "Yes. He died almost a year and a half ago."

"And you are a mother as well?" Violet asked.

"Yes. I have a daughter, Sophia. She's three years old," Lily answered.

"That's lovely." There was no hint of sarcasm in Violet's tone. "Charles does very well with children, don't you, Charles?"

"Possibly because he is still one himself," Ella said half to herself with a chuckle.

Charles's face went as red as a ripe strawberry. "Mother," he groaned, staring at his boots, looking bashful. Lily nearly laughed. How she adored him, even when he was completely flustered.

"But it is true," Ella added. "He's quite wonderful with children."

"I know." Lily laughed, remembering all the times Charles and Kat had played together, and how Kat seemed to glow whenever he interacted with her.

"You know? Charles, have you met her daughter?"

"No, he hasn't." Lily realized her mistake. "I meant, Emily has told me how good he is with children."

"Oh, I see." Before anything more could be said, the orchestra below began to play, signaling that the opera was soon to begin. Charles ushered her to a chair by the edge of the box and sat beside her.

A hush fell over the crowd. Lily accepted one of the small cards Charles handed her and examined the title in the candlelight: *The Devil to Pay*.

The title made her shiver. Charles reached over and

curled his fingers through hers. She could feel the heat of his palm through her silk gloves.

As the opening overture began, she squeezed his hand back and favored him with a smile. Everything would be all right. It was only an opera. She had to try to enjoy it or else Charles would sense something was wrong.

19

Hugo sat in his private box, his wife, Melanie, beside him. But as the opera began his gaze was not on the stage. Rather, it was on the balcony across from them. Charles, his mother, and his sister were all in the Lonsdale box, but when Hugo recognized the fourth among them he smiled. His little spy was in place, playing her part as the lovely widow. Word was already spreading among the *ton* that Charles soon would propose. No one had ever seen him so besotted before. Perfect.

He rose from his seat.

"Hugo? Where you going?" Melanie demanded in a harsh whisper.

"Apologies. I have business to attend to. I shall return shortly." He slipped out of his seat and into the corridor, waving down a serving boy.

"Yes, sir?" the boy asked.

"Do you have pen and paper?" Sometimes the boys came prepared with such items to help the opera patrons pass notes to one another.

"Yes, sir." The boy provided him with pen, paper, and a small polished board to write upon. Hugo scrawled a note to Lily, folded it, and handed it to the boy.

"You are to deliver this to Mrs. Wycliff. She is in Lord Lonsdale's box. No one else must read it. See to it and I will pay you double this." He handed the boy ten shillings. The boy rushed off to deliver the note. Hugo returned to his box and took a seat. Melanie glanced at him once he sat down.

"Sorry, my love." He leaned over to kiss her cheek, but that was simply a formality. His marriage had grown cold even before the birth of their son. After his failed attempt at reconciliation with his mother.

After he had learned the truth.

At first he had missed such comforts from her, but as work and the desire for revenge consumed him, he realized there were plenty of women in London who could see to those needs. He was a servant of the empire, and as such he came to see such things as his due.

He had been careless with Lily, however. He'd mistaken her overtures of kindness and sympathy as an emotional ploy, and he'd assumed she had been planted in his home by one of his rivals. By the time he realized the truth, that she had been sincere, rage had consumed him, and he had lost control.

Though he would not admit to feeling shame or regret at the act, he did recognize it for what it was—a mistake. She had seen into his heart when he had spent his life perfecting the means to disguising it. That was no easy task. And she had kept her wits about her when he had been most savage to her, which was equally impressive.

So instead of dealing with her right away, he'd had her followed to see how she would cope without money or connections. To his surprise, she did well for herself, even though she was with child. She had begun with begging, of course, but she did not stop there. She connected with people, talked to them, and eventually found employment as a barmaid at the gambling hell that became her home.

It would have been preferable if she had given birth to a son, one he could raise to succeed him at the Home Office, while Peter took the family name and title, but that was not to be. Still, the woman herself had shown her worth, and he did not waste things of value.

On her own, the girl served little purpose except to potentially expose him to scandal. But she did allow him to force her mother into obedience. If he hadn't, she might have tried to use the whelp against him someday. He had simply gotten there first.

Hugo's lips curved as he watched Charles and Lily in their box. They were entering the endgame now. Soon he would strike at Charles's heart, and there would be no stopping him.

DURING THE FIRST INTERMISSION, A SMALL BOY approached Lily, slipping a note into her hand carefully, unseen by Charles or his family. Only a few words were hastily written in a hand she recognized with dread.

When he proposes, say yes.

Lily tore up the paper and disposed of the pieces behind a potted plant near the entrance to the box.

"Everything all right?" Charles asked as she returned to her seat. She glanced across the theater, and her heart stuttered to a halt. Hugo was here. He was watching her, but where? She scanned the private boxes and soon spied Mrs. Waverly across the theater. But no Hugo.

"I...I'm afraid I'm not feeling well. Might you escort me home?" It was still the intermission, and it wouldn't be too disruptive if they slipped away now.

"Of course." Charles studied her with concern. "Mother, Lily is feeling poorly. I am escorting her home."

Violet and Ella both stood. "Are you all right, my dear? Anything we can do?"

Lily shook her head. "No, no, thank you. I'll be fine once I'm able to rest."

Violet clasped her hands and gave them a squeeze.

"Well, please let us know if we can help. It was lovely to meet you."

"And you, Lady Lonsdale. Thank you."

Lily took Charles's arm, and they exited the box. They passed through the mingling crowds and had reached the top of the stairs when Lily stopped. Hugo was there at the bottom of the stairs. He raised a glass of champagne toward her. Charles had his back to Hugo and did not see him.

"Charles..."

"Yes?" he asked.

There was no turning back. "Yes," she echoed declaratively.

He raised a brow, still confused. "Yes?"

"*Yes*," she replied more emphatically. "Yes to your question in the coach."

Suddenly the anxiety and concern in his eyes vanished. "Yes?"

Before she could finish nodding, he grabbed her by the waist and twirled her in the air, laughing. The bold action attracted stares and gasps, but Lily didn't care. For one brief moment she allowed herself to believe she had said yes for herself, not for Hugo. She buried her face in his neck as he slowly set her down and held her.

"I'm so happy I can scarcely breathe." He chuckled in her ear. "Let's get you back to Emily's so you may rest. We have much to prepare. Will a wedding in a few days be suitable? I can procure a special license."

"So soon?" she gasped.

"Yes. I'm quite set about this business, and I see no reason to wait unless you do. Do you want to wait?"

"Well..." She would have to tell him the truth, at least enough of it that he would know he was marrying Lily Linley and not Lily Wycliff. But that was a concern for tomorrow. Charles caressed her cheek, smiling so brightly it made her chest ache.

"A few days," she finally agreed.

He took her arm in his as they started down the stairs. She could feel his happiness emanating off him. How she wanted to be with him in that same place of joy, but she couldn't; she could only pretend to share it.

Charles froze when he spotted Hugo at the base of the stairs. Their eyes met, but neither made the first move toward or away from the other. What was he still doing there? Lily had hoped he would vanish back into the shadows where he belonged.

Slowly, Charles began to move again, but he kept Lily as far from Hugo as possible. When they reached him, Hugo smiled broadly.

"Well now, this is quite a lovely picture, Lord Lonsdale." Hugo offered a grin as cold as the winter wind. "And who might you be, madam?"

Charles stepped between them. "Do not speak to her."

Hugo ignored the comment. "I heard about Lord Kent. Terrible news. Wasn't he a friend of your brother's?"

Lily felt Charles's arm tense. "You know he is. Just as I

know you were behind it. And if I were free to do so, I would see to it that you paid for that."

"Are you threatening me? My, my, Lonsdale, one might think you want to *duel* me."

"Would that put an end to this?" Charles growled.

Hugo's broad smile made Lily's stomach turn. "No. I'm afraid not."

"Because you know I'm a crack shot. And you aren't."

"Believe what you will." Hugo's eyes slid to Lily's, lingering a little too long, before he looked back to Charles.

Lily couldn't believe she was finally seeing these two men face each other down. There was so much venom and rage between them, hidden behind polite smiles and formal postures, that she was surprised they hadn't come to blows.

"Whatever happened to your valet? Tom, was it? I heard he left London. I wonder...did he ever reach his destination? Would be a damned shame if that boy and his sister went missing."

Lily swallowed hard. She hadn't sent the letter to Charles like she'd promised, telling him that she'd reached her aunt's home safely.

Fury, the likes of which Lily had never seen, blackened Charles's eyes. He took a step toward Hugo, and for a moment Hugo seemed uncertain if he should retreat.

"If that boy or anyone else goes missing, I *will* come for you. I'm not afraid to risk a trial for murder, not if it removes a black spot like you from this world." Charles didn't even raise his voice. He didn't need to.

Hugo's lips curled in a snarl, but Lily intervened, tugging on Charles's arm.

"*Please*, take me home." Lily could feel the press of their mutual hatred from all sides, suffocating her. If she couldn't get Charles to leave, he might do something rash.

"Charles, please!" She jerked harder on his arm, until his focus was back to her.

Charles reluctantly gave in. They left the theater and the danger behind them, but as Lily glanced back, she still saw Hugo's face.

When Hugo had recruited her, he had promised her a chance to someday retire in the country with Kat. Her service bought her silence. In his twisted mind, he saw himself as being generous toward her. Perhaps it was his sick way to forgive himself the violence he'd wrought upon her.

But now, seeing Hugo's face as they left, she was no longer convinced he would keep that promise. His hatred of Lonsdale was all-consuming, and in the end she knew he did not care who burned alongside him. And Hugo always took care of loose ends. So when Hugo was finished with Charles, wasn't that what she and Kat would be to him?

I must tell Charles everything. If he knows and doesn't despise me, then I may yet at least save my child.

They entered a coach, but Charles still hadn't said a word. "Charles?"

He didn't look at her; his mind was miles away. "I'm sorry, Lily. You must think my outburst earlier to be highly inappropriate. This night has turned out most wretched. I must see you home at once, and I fear then I must go."

"Charles, wait. Please, listen to me first."

He continued, still lost in his own black mood. "That man, Sir Hugo, he's not a good man. You do not know what he has done to me, to my friends... He's..."

"Evil. I know."

Charles stared at her. "What do you mean? Has Emily spoken of him?"

Lily reached across the coach and covered one of his hands that rested on his knee.

"Charles, please. I must make a confession."

"Darling, there's nothing to—"

"Yes, there is. You will likely cast me out of this coach once I tell you, but before you do, know this. Everything that we shared, all of it, has been real to me. Please do not forget that."

Charles leaned forward, studying her in the dim light. "Lily, love, you're starting to frighten me."

"Charles." Her tongue felt thick. The words weighed heavily upon her. "I'm not who you think I am."

He didn't speak, but his eyes narrowed. She pressed on.

"I'm not a widow. I'm not Mrs. Wycliff."

"You're not Emily's cousin?"

"Emily was helping me find a husband. My real name is Lily. Lily...Linley." She waited, holding her breath.

"Linley?" He whispered the name. "You're not related to Tom Linley in any way..."

"Charles," she almost groaned. "I *am* Tom."

He stared at her blankly. "What?"

"Tom isn't real."

"But..." He trailed off, and his gray eyes widened in complete bafflement.

"I am Tom, but I've never *been* Tom. Lily is who I truly am." She dropped her affected feminine voice to better demonstrate how she'd played the part of a young man. It was perhaps the first time Charles had ever heard her true voice, neither that of Tom the valet nor the mysterious Mrs. Wycliff.

He scanned her again, this time in open concern. "Tom?"

"Tom was simply a disguise." She drew in a deep breath, steeling herself for what had to come next. What he was already figuring out, no matter how much he tried not to.

"This whole time you've been..." Charles raked a hand through his hair.

"Charles, please, you must listen to me."

"Lily, please don't tell me you've been... Not him."

"Yes. I'm working for Hugo." She wanted to cry as the words escaped her.

His face turned ghostly white. "No... No..."

"I'm sorry. I'm so sorry." She reached out, but he stared at her hand like she held a poisonous viper, so she dropped her hand.

"This is a dream...a nightmare," he stammered. "Why...*why* can't I wake up?" He bent forward again and covered his face with his hands.

Lily bit her lip, pain cutting deep inside her. "Charles, listen to me. I never wanted this. I never wanted to hurt you. From the beginning, I cared about you."

Charles jerked away from her, a flicker of anger in his eyes. "How *dare* you say such a thing? You confess to working for a man who wishes me dead and yet speak of caring for me? While you stood by and did *nothing* as he attacked my friends and their families time and again?"

"You do not understand. He will take my daughter from me if I don't do as he says."

The anger in Charles's eyes softened a little. "Katherine? Why would Hugo care about a babe? He has assassins ready to be called in. Spies in every nation. What use to him is a woman and her child?"

Lily closed her eyes. "Because the child is his. Hugo is Katherine's father."

Charles let out a bitter, cold laugh. "Of course he is. And now he's using his former lover to bait me so he can take away the last of my joy. Is that it?" His tone was so cold that Lily expected the inside of the coach to frost over.

"We were *never* lovers!" She spat the words out with such violence that he recoiled. It took her a second to calm before she could continue. "I was a maid in his house, and he...he *took* me." She couldn't bring herself to elaborate. The harsh winter of his gray eyes melted a fraction. Turning her face away, she wiped at the angry tears that trailed down her cheeks.

Charles's voice softened. "He forced himself upon you?"

She nodded. "I ran from him. I begged on the streets to survive until I could find work. Many months later he found me...and my baby. He can take her away anytime he wishes, Charles. He can claim Katherine and take her away, because she's his."

Charles frowned. "And so he forced you into his sick and twisted game? Why?"

Lily swallowed. "He saw value in me. My height and build and how I faced a crisis told him I could be useful in his service. And so he trained me to fight, to hide my appearance, to find all that is secret. And because of Katherine, I could not refuse. For nearly three years, I have not been able to refuse. And I have done terrible things, both to those who deserved it and those who deserved better. But when I met you, I..." She swallowed again. "You are a wonderful man. A loving kind man with a noble heart, and I died inside each day seeing the torments Hugo put you through."

"And yet you said nothing," Charles said. "Why speak now? What changed your mind?"

Lily looked to the carriage floor. "After you confronted Hugo, I knew I would never be free of him, no matter what happened. I realized I was helping him destroy a good man, selling my soul to the devil himself, without even being given my daughter's safety in exchange. I know you no longer feel anything for me, but please, help me protect my daughter. I beg you. She is the only thing I have left in this world. I cannot lose her."

Though she had killed whatever feelings he'd once had for her, she prayed that his noble spirit would still be in control, that he'd help her save her child in exchange for what she could tell him about Hugo's plans.

Charles was quiet a long moment. Then he opened the coach window and called for the driver to change course.

Fear spiked inside her. "Where we going?"

"To someone Ashton trusts. We will need absolute secrecy if we are to have a war council."

20

Charles couldn't look at Lily after he helped her out of the coach, so he turned his focus on their destination. They faced a lovely townhouse with dead ivy crawling up the walls. He rapped the knocker, and a tall, muscular middle-aged butler met them at the door.

"Lord Lonsdale to see Lord Darlington."

"Is there a message to take to Lord Darlington?" the butler asked.

"Tell him, *Cam*."

They were allowed inside and waited in the entryway while the butler went upstairs. Charles kept himself at attention, still trying not to look at Lily. A few minutes later, the butler returned.

"I'm to show you to the library. His lordship will be down as soon as he is dressed. He also told me to deliver these." He held a handful of letters, addressed to all of the League members.

"Yes, that's correct."

"I'll have my quickest lads deliver them at once."

Charles and Lily were shown into the library. Charles found himself torn between wanting to speak to her and wanting to be as far away as possible.

"Charles," Lily whispered and glanced his way. She looked somehow *more* beautiful. "Please, say something. Anything."

God help me, I think I still love her, the woman who would bring about my destruction.

"Was any of it real?" he asked, his voice hoarse.

She wiped a tear and sniffed. "Every minute."

"I asked you to *marry* me." He still didn't believe her, even though he wanted to. She'd admitted to her deception, so what did any of it truly mean now?

"And I wanted to. I still do, but I know that's impossible." She turned away, looking out the window at the frosted garden outside, lit by moonlight. "Still, I cannot regret telling you the truth. As painful as this is, despite everything I have lost in telling you, it has also lifted a great weight off me."

He thought of the long carriage ride to this house, how she'd spent the ride curled up the corner, taking up so little space, as though she thought she didn't deserve it. The misery in her eyes had cut him to the core. He was hurt, it was true. He had been compromised and betrayed.

But he also had to try to see the world through her eyes. It was not as if she had ended up here by choice.

Hugo had taken her, hurt her, forced a child on her, and then threatened to take that child away. She had never had a choice in any of this, not from the moment Hugo had had his way with her. It was unfair to hold her accountable for his actions. She had made a choice to confess all to him. Wouldn't that include how she truly felt?

His hands curled into fists as he fought off conflicting emotions.

Charles moved toward her. Before he could think twice, he grabbed her shoulders and spun her around to face him. He didn't know what to say, so he didn't speak. He jerked her to him, slamming his mouth down over hers.

Part of him wanted to punish her for her betrayal, show her how furious he was, but an animal hunger took over and all he now wanted was *her*. Lily in his arms, in his bed, beneath him, with him, part of him. Life was a cruel mistress who showed him no mercy.

"Charles." Lily gasped his name.

"Tell me to stop and I will." He moved their bodies back so they were pressed flush against the nearest bookshelf. He fisted a hand in her hair and moved his lips down the smooth column of her throat, wanting to explore her more than ever.

"Please, *don't* stop. Not ever," Lily whimpered as he

nipped her collarbone. Charles tore the ties to her cloak apart, and it fell to the floor at her feet. The swell of her perfect breasts made him hungry. She'd bound these beauties flat for an entire year? It was a crime against nature, one that he would make her pay for by spending hours exploring them with his mouth and hands.

"I should hate you," he said as his lips returned to hers in another violent kiss. Their mouths broke apart, and she gazed at him with those blue eyes of hers that were infinitely bewitching.

"You have every right to hate me," she replied. Tears coated her lashes now as she blinked rapidly.

"I hate how weak you make me feel," he said, and each word tasted bitter on his lips. "I hate everything Hugo has made you do. But I don't hate *you*."

Lily curled her fingers into the lapels of his coat and leaned into him. "There were so many nights I wanted to crawl into your bed and lie against you. You made me feel safe. I am trusting you now, tonight, to protect not only me but my child. Please, Charles, I know my betrayal is unforgivable, but Katherine is innocent in all this."

The anger that had mingled with his lust faded, leaving only a softer, deeper desire that frightened him. He wrapped his arms around Lily.

"I will protect you both."

They were quiet a moment, simply holding each other in quiet desperation. The library door opened, and a blond-haired man entered. He wore slightly shabby clothes, but Charles knew they'd been fine once. Darlington had fallen on hard times of late.

"Lord Darlington." Charles greeted the viscount with a nod. "Thank you for allowing us to impose upon you."

Darlington flashed them a rakish grin as he looked at Lily. "Of course. No trouble. I imagine your friends will be arriving shortly. Tea is on the way, such as it is." Darlington chuckled. Charles didn't miss the rumpled clothes and mussed hair. He'd obviously come from sleeping, and Charles and Lily had interrupted him.

"Lord Darlington, I'd like to introduce you to Lily, Lily Linley." He nodded at his woman.

Darlington came over and kissed her hand. "*Enchantée*."

Lilly blushed and smiled. Charles tried to stop himself from feeling jealous. Darlington was a rogue with a wicked reputation almost on par with his own.

"Linley, you say? The rumors said you were head over heels for a widow named Wycliff," Darlington observed.

"Yes, quite head over heels, considering she's the same woman," Charles murmured and glanced toward Lily. She paled, and he wondered what she was thinking.

Darlington's gaze drifted between them a moment. "Well, make yourselves comfortable. My butler will show the others in when they arrive."

"Thank you." Charles waited until Darlington was gone before he took Lily into his arms again. "You must tell me everything. The others too. Can you do that?"

Lily nodded. "I'm afraid it will only make you angry...to know everything."

"Just answer me this." Charles steeled himself for the answer he suspected she would give them. "Did Hugo send you to me as Lily? Did he want me to fall for you? Was this all planned in advance, even our encounter in the tunnels?"

She paused, and her hesitation drove a dagger into his heart.

"You did not rescue me at Lewis Street. I was there on a separate mission for Hugo. He sometimes calls upon me on my days off as Tom. But when Hugo learned that you had encountered me as Lily and that you were intrigued by me..."

Charles frowned. "He knew he could use you against me."

"His original idea was for me to pose as *his* cousin, hoping you'd try to use me to learn information about him. But when Emily came to me with her own plan, Hugo decided to embrace it instead. He knew you would trust Emily far more than anyone else."

Charles sighed, an unbearable weight settling on his chest. "He's not wrong. I would trust Emily with anything,"

"But I never meant for you to meet me in the Lewis Street tunnels that night," she quickly added. "Not as myself."

The misery he had tried to keep at bay broke through.

"Hugo has always known how to hurt me, to make me bleed." He moved on shaky legs to a chair and collapsed into it. Lily was suddenly at his feet, resting her cheek against his knee as she clung to his legs.

"Again, I know you can't believe me or even trust me." Her voice was so broken that it nearly killed him. "But I *do* love you. I never hid that fact. I never acted beyond what I felt. If anything, I held myself back as much as I could."

I can forgive you, but how can I trust you?

He reached out to touch her hair, to ground himself by touching those golden strands. But before he could, Lily was up and walking back to the window.

He would see to Lily and Kat's safety, that much he knew. They were as much victims in this tragedy as anyone, and he would not let Hugo harm a hair on her or Katherine's head. But beyond that? He knew he would spend the rest of his life missing her once she and her daughter were able to leave London safely. He would never feel like this with any other woman again, not ever.

He stared at the toes of his boots and she watched the garden, both of them ignoring the silence that had grown into a thickening fog between them.

Ashton was the first to arrive. He strode into the library and nodded to Charles.

"Glad to see my rendezvous plan was executed properly—" He froze when he saw Lily. "However," he began again, "normally one does not invite one's lover to a war council, no matter how attractive she is."

"Believe me, Ash, she is more a part of this than you realize."

Ashton folded his arms over his chest. "I assume you'll explain?"

"I will, once the others are here," Charles promised.

"Very well."

Soon Godric and Lucien arrived, and right on their heels were Jonathan and Cedric. None of the League were smiling, but that was understandable. This was a summoning, a war council that Ashton had arranged long ago. They were all to meet at Lord Darlington's should they receive a message from Darlington with the word *Cam* in it—the river they'd rescued Charles from all those years ago. Anyone watching their letters or their communications would likely not see the significance of a letter from Darlington because he was outside of their immediate circle.

"What's Mrs. Wycliff doing here?" Godric asked when he saw Lily. "Emily is expecting you home any minute to see Sophia to bed."

Charles saw Lily stiffen.

"Is she all right?" Lily asked Godric.

"Sophia is fine," Godric assured her. "But I still don't understand why you are here?"

"I promise you, Lily's presence here is necessary," said Charles told his friends.

"Everyone, take a seat," Ashton said. "Charles, I believe, has some information to share with us."

Charles stood. His palms were slick with sweat, but he had to tell his friends the truth.

He cleared his throat. "I know you're wondering why Lily is here."

He waited for her to join him, and she did, her face downcast. He understood her concern. He was about to explain how she'd betrayed him, betrayed them all, and how she was now begging for their help.

"Lily's real name is Lily Linley." He paused. "For the last year, she has been living under my roof as my valet, Tom Linley."

This caused murmurs of concern to break out among the League. At another time or another place, there would have been a lot of good-natured ribbing at Charles's expense over the matter. But given why they were here, they knew the significance of this revelation went far beyond an amusing social farce.

"I was not aware of her deception until tonight," Charles said. "She was sent by Hugo to work at Berkley's Club to be a spy, and on his orders she eventually infiltrated my house as a servant."

The silence that descended on the room was deafening. Only the grandfather clock out in the hall could be heard ticking slowly.

"Hugo hired you?" Ashton's tone was that of ice.

Charles reached out and took one of Lily's hands in his, squeezing it gently.

"She wasn't hired," Charles said. "I want every man in this room to understand this. Lily was a maid in Hugo's house when he..."

"Hugo Waverly raped me." Lily raised her eyes and looked at everyone in the room. Her voice was strong and fearless at a time when she had every right to be afraid. "I escaped from him and gave birth to his child in private, but he found me again. He pressed me into his service, threatening to take my child if I did not do as he commanded."

Charles squeezed her hand again. He was proud of her courage.

"Hugo trained me to be useful to him. To become a tool, a weapon in service of the Crown. Only he soon decided to use me for his own personal aims, to use me against you all."

"It's perhaps unchristian of me, but I would like to throw Hugo in the Thames," Lucien growled. "To rape a woman?"

Godric slammed a balled fist onto the reading table he sat at. "And then threaten her child?"

"And then force her to work for him?" Cedric howled. "Villain!"

"So why did you stop being Tom?" Ashton asked, the calmest of them all. "I assume Hugo changed his orders?"

"Yes. He wished for me to secure Charles's affections, with the intention of having me betray him just before—"

"Before the endgame," Ashton finished for her.

"This man is the devil himself," Jonathan muttered.

"Yes, but the devil is clever and not to be underestimated. Such a betrayal, revealed at a time of Hugo's choosing, would have broken Charles, made him incapable of defending himself." Ashton still stared at Lily with a coldness that Charles didn't like.

He was the only one who had any right to be furious with Lily. He was the fool who had fallen for her, the one who'd proposed to her after only a few brief encounters. Now when he looked at her, he saw a familiarity, the eyes he'd gazed into often enough over the last year, the eyes of a dear friend. And now he loved her, loved her madly. But how was he to know Lily's true feelings? He could never fully trust her until the day Hugo stopped breathing.

"So, now we know something of Hugo's plan and that his final stroke must be coming soon. How do we respond?" Cedric asked. He toyed with his cane.

Ashton still stared at Lily. "That depends on Miss Linley."

Lily nodded, understanding. "What do you need of me?" Charles kept hold of her hand, hoping he could keep her calm, but the nervousness she had shown before had faded.

"How far did Hugo want you to go with your seduction?"

Her hand tightened in Charles's grasp as she looked at him, pain in her blue eyes. "He wanted me to accept Charles's proposal."

A wave of despair washed over him, even though he had sensed with building dread that she would make this confession.

She squeezed his hand again. "The truth is, I wanted to say yes, even before Hugo ordered me to do so. But I had hoped to refuse as long as I could, to protect you," she whispered. "Please, believe me."

Charles's eyes burned as he looked to Ashton. "Then perhaps we should give Hugo what he wants. A bloody wedding. The only way to end this is to make him believe all is going according to plan."

"Quite right," Ashton agreed. "But that means everyone in this room will be in grave danger. It is very likely that your wives, children, sisters, brothers, and mothers will all be at risk. No one will be judged if they choose to take their families and leave London."

Charles stepped toward his friends. "You saved my life once, and that debt grows deeper each day. But this burden is mine alone to bear. You've helped me carry it long enough. I would beg all of you to leave."

There was a long, heavy silence, again punctuated only by the ticking of the clock in the hall.

"We all went into the river that night," Lucien said. "*All of us.* I'm staying here until the matter is settled once and for all."

"As am I," Cedric added with a nod.

Godric smirked. "I never liked that bastard, and I've been meaning to settle the score if I was offered the chance."

"I may not have been part of your League until recently, but I am here now, and I'm not leaving either," Jonathan said.

Ashton smiled grimly. "Then I believe it's now a matter of seeing to the safety of our families. We should consider sending them away."

"But you must be careful," Lily interrupted. "Hugo has servants in each of your houses."

"More men like Gordon?" Lucien demanded.

Lily nodded. "Yes. I do not know who they are, only that he has at least one in each townhouse in London."

"What about the country homes?" Cedric asked.

She paused, uncertain. "I don't believe so. But it is impossible to be sure."

"And their job is to report back to him?" Ashton asked.

"Yes, anything they overhear, what they learn of your movements."

"Might they attack us, like Gordon did?"

"They will do whatever Hugo asks of them, either out of loyalty or fear."

"Wonderful," said Godric. "Assassins in our midst."

"If you send all your families away, Hugo will become suspicious," said Lily. "You must stagger their trips. Come up with mundane reasons, play disappointed when they choose to leave. If Hugo senses you are trying to protect them, it will draw his attention."

"Unless we distract him with the wedding," Charles added. He knew Hugo would be thrilled to see his spy marry his hated enemy. All else would cease to matter once Hugo achieved that goal, because he'd have Charles exactly where he wanted him.

"Charles, you don't need to" Lily began, but Ashton spoke over her.

"No, Charles is right. We'll keep his mind plenty occupied if he thinks his plan is working. Lily, you will need to keep sending him reports, play his game, reluctantly, of course. Change nothing about your behavior, but I will advise you what to say about our plans."

Charles balked. "I don't want Lily involved aside from the wedding. She's been a pawn in this long enough. She needs to be safe." He owed her that much, at least. She was a victim of Hugo as much as he was. Perhaps in a way that made them even. Her life destroyed, his life betrayed.

They were perfectly matched by tragedy.

"No, Charles. Lord Lennox is right. I must play my part. Kat is the only thing that matters now. She must be kept safe." She grasped both of his hands, and for a moment as he gazed into those cornflower-blue eyes, he saw Lily and Tom both there, begging him to trust them. It was an eerie thing to see a friend in a stranger's eyes. Everything around them faded as he lost himself momentarily in her face, wishing more than anything that he'd met her in a world where Hugo didn't exist.

"It is too dangerous. I'm not about to let you risk your life for me—"

She suddenly lunged at the hearth, retrieving a poker and swinging it so that it stopped a mere inch from his face. She wasn't breathing hard, and something about her expert control over that fire poker made his blood sing with desire. Who knew he loved such a dangerous woman?

"Don't forget, you fought me more than once when I was Tom. I was trained to fight long before I ever met you. I am not weak."

"I know, but this shouldn't be your fight, Lily. You deserve to be safe...after everything you've been through."

Her eyes lowered until all he could see were her dark-gold lashes. "I don't know about that. I've done things working for Hugo. Things I am not proud of."

"I do not hold those things against you," said Charles. "Anything you did was to protect your daughter from his clutches. How could I not understand that?" If he'd been alone with her and none of his friends were watching them like they were some sort of play, he would have pulled her into his arms, breathed in her sweet scent, and reassured her that he understood her actions with a kiss.

"I suppose a wedding will suit, since you two can't keep your eyes or hands off each other," Lucien said with a wry chuckle.

"Agreed," Ashton said. "You and Lily indeed sell your attraction quite well."

"Then you will need someone willing to aid you in your ruse," Lily said. "A priest who can officiate, but agree not to finalize the marriage. I do not know how the church will look upon such fraud."

"I may know someone," said Ashton. "His parish is in the country, but I'm sure he will come here if I asked."

"You will not need to," said Charles suddenly, surprising even himself. "I intend to go through with this marriage without any deceptions."

The other men in the room seemed a little puzzled by Charles's bold statement.

"You cannot really wish to marry me," Lily said.

"I do." Not that he could say why. He knew there were reasons, but right now he was too afraid to examine them.

"But a wedding would be binding. It would truly make us..."

"Man and wife. Yes, I'm well aware of how weddings work."

"It's why he's run the other way from them all his life." Cedric snickered.

"You're not helping," said Godric. Charles heard Cedric curse as the duke kicked him in the shin.

"So we plan the wedding," Ashton said. "We will keep Darlington's house as a rendezvous point in case we must reconvene. The new code word will be..."

"Gardenias," Charles said, thinking of what the shopkeeper had said the flower meant. The call of loneliness. And here he was, willing to marry a spy sent to betray him in an effort to cure that loneliness.

"Very well. *Gardenias.* But remember, you *must* continue to act normally. Assume *everything* you say outside of this house will reach Hugo's ears. Not even Berkley's is safe. Make no changes in staff. It would only alert him to our actions, and there would be no way to be sure you'd found the spy in your household."

They soon came to an understanding of what had to be done. Charles shook the hand of each man as they left. Godric paused as they reached him.

"Lily, will you be returning home to my residence?"

Lily glanced at Charles. "Yes, I believe I must."

"She will," Charles agreed. "And I shall come with her."

"But—" she began.

"Given the public announcement of our engagement, it will not seem out of place. There's no chance that I will leave you and Kat alone."

Godric nodded. "I will have a separate room prepared for you. I will see you both at the house then."

Now only Ashton was left, who watched Charles carefully. He then turned to Lily. "I need a minute with Charles. Would you mind?"

"No, of course not." She nodded and left the library. Charles instantly felt her absence. He feared that she would vanish all over again.

"Charles, I need to know where you truly stand on

this." Ashton placed a firm but gentle palm on his shoulder, grounding him in a way he hadn't realized he needed. Tonight's revelations had left him feeling oddly adrift.

"Where I stand?" he echoed.

"Yes. This marriage will be real. She will be your wife. I understand why you wish to protect her from Hugo, but are you certain you want to tie yourself to a woman who may not love you?" Ashton's voice softened. "I know your heart, Charles. You put on a carefree demeanor, but you've always questioned whether you deserve love. I'm telling you, you *do* deserve love and happiness, like the rest of us. I can't stand by and let you marry someone simply because of guilt, or because it makes the fight with Hugo a little easier."

Ashton's eyes seemed to glow in the reflection of the firelight in the hearth of Darlington's library. Charles's throat constricted as he spoke.

"Don't worry about me. I am more concerned that you will all face this danger with me. I never meant for any of this to happen. It's my fault."

"The fault's not with you, but Hugo. Every sin lies upon his head. Now, about Lily..."

"I know it makes me sound like a fool, or perhaps a madman, but I think I love her. And I suppose she knows me better than any woman ever has. As Tom she was a friend, a confidant. I never hid myself from her. Now that I've been around her as she truly is, as Lily, I find that strangely liberating." He smiled ruefully. "Do you know how many women I've been with over the years, the famed courtesans, wicked widows, passionate spinsters? None of them knew any more about me than the smile I wished to present. Lily has seen me in my darkest moods, stayed with me through my nightmares, and never once abandoned me. I am still certain she cares for me. That must count for something, mustn't it?"

How could he put into words the way Lily glowed as she entered a room, how his breath caught and he could barely remember his own name? It wasn't merely that he wished it might be more. It *was* more. Had *always* been more.

"You are certain then?" Ashton asked.

"I am."

"Well then, we shall make preparations for a wedding, and you will play the part of the smitten fiancé."

For the first time in what felt like hours, he managed a smile. "That will not be hard," Charles said. He would spend time with Lily and Kat. He would make sure that they were safe. His future wife and future child. Knowing how Katherine had been conceived only made him care more about the child. She needed love, security, and a father who would give her both.

And that man is me.

21

Lily fidgeted during the entire coach ride back to Godric's townhouse. She had learned to steel her nerves in the most dangerous of situations, and yet those same nerves fluttered wildly whenever Charles glanced her way.

Did he truly mean to marry her? After what she had done? It was madness. He wouldn't...would he?

When the coach stopped, he helped her down, his hands gripping her waist the same way he had when they'd gone to the opera. Like everything was normal. How she wished that were true. She fought off a shiver, longing to burrow into his warmth.

Godric was waiting for them in the drawing room, as was Emily. When she saw Emily's face, she knew Godric had found some safe way of explaining the deception to her. Lily expected any number of furious reactions.

Instead, Emily came up to her and embraced her tightly and whispered in her ear.

"You are far braver than I even knew. Godric and I shall protect you and Kat with our lives."

Lily began to protest, but Emily placed a finger to her lips, warning her to be silent.

"It's quite late. Perhaps we should retire? I shall have some food sent to your rooms. Charles, I've had a bedroom prepared, and a footman is waiting to assist you if needed."

Charles nodded his thanks as he bid everyone good night and went upstairs.

Lily stayed in the drawing room for a time, even after Emily and Godric retired to bed, looking out the window and wondering what would come next. Any sense of security she'd had these past three years had been a lie. She had always been walking a knife's edge of obeying Hugo's instructions and avoiding detection. By all rights she was in the most perilous state she had ever been in, and yet she also felt strangely at peace about it. Come what may, the course she was now on promised an end.

She came to the nursery. Katherine was asleep in the large crib, tucked between several thick soft blankets, a new doll cuddled under one arm. Love blossomed in Lily's chest as she bent over and stroked the curls back from her daughter's face. She heard footsteps behind her and recognized the shoes that made them. She'd polished them often enough.

"I understand now," Charles said.

She stood up, still looking down at Kat's sleeping face. "What do you understand?"

He joined her at the edge of the crib. "You know, I thought for a time that perhaps she was my daughter. That perhaps I had slept with your—I mean, Tom's—mother?"

Lily smiled, resisting the urge to make a joke about the odds of such an occurrence.

"She looked so familiar, but now I see it's Hugo I recognized in her features."

Lily stiffened. "Does that trouble you?" she asked, moving a little between him and Katherine.

He sighed and leaned down to brush the backs of his fingers over Kat's cheeks. The baby stirred but didn't wake.

"She may share his features, but inside I see only her mother's heart." Charles's gaze shifted to Lily. His eyes moved over her sensually. Her pulse quickened. She should have tamped down her reaction to him. This was not the time for such things, but the heady, heavy warmth of that desire flowed through her nonetheless, drugging her thoughts and senses.

He reached up and cupped the back of her neck, his warm fingers curling around her skin. "If I am the only one holding love within my heart, you must tell me, Lily. It will not change the vow I made to you and your child."

She swallowed, feeling dizzy as the world seem to spin on its axis.

"You are not the only one," said Lily. "I'm quite certain I loved you the moment I first saw you, as foolish and dangerous as it was to do so." She placed a hand on his chest, feeling the silk of his waistcoat beneath her fingertips. He lifted her other hand to his lips, kissing the calluses at the top of her palm beneath the base of each finger. How could he make her feel so cherished with such a simple act?

"You've worked so hard, haven't you?" he murmured, pity and compassion in his voice.

She pulled her hand away. "I did what I had to. I don't want your pity."

"What do you want then?" he asked, his gray eyes sparking with silver.

What did she want? She wanted to sleep without keeping a knife tucked away under her pillow. She wanted Katherine to grow up and know a happiness she feared she'd never have herself. She wanted this, all of this, to be over. But as Charles's hands moved to her shoulders, she wanted one thing more than all of that combined.

"You." She thrust herself forward and kissed him, and he kissed her back in equal measure. Despite the glitter of danger in his eyes, she knew he would never hurt her, not like Hugo had. It was only pleasure, pure and potent, as timeless and unending as the moon pulling the tides. The masculine energy that emanated from him was a comfort, an enticement, not a threat. Heat uncurled in her abdomen as she leaned deeper into the kiss. He suddenly bent, scooping her up in his arms as he carried her.

"Which room is yours?"

"The one on the left of the nursery."

He carried her into her bedchamber and set her down with infinite gentleness before he closed the door. A fire burned in the hearth and a tray of cheese and fruit sat on a plate, but Lily wasn't hungry. Charles came back and stood in front of her, cupping her face in his hands. Their gazes locked, stormy gray meeting turbulent blue.

"Know this. I will stop if you tell me to," said Charles. "I don't want... I don't want you to fear anything that happens in this bed between us."

She gripped his wrists and gave them a light squeeze. "It's all right. I trust you. I always have."

"We'll go slow," he vowed as he knelt at her feet.

She couldn't help but laugh. "You, slow? Why do I find that hard to believe?" She had seen and heard enough of his romantic lifestyle to know he preferred his lovemaking fast and furious.

He looked up at her as he slid one of her dark-red slippers off her foot. He gave a cocksure grin that made her stomach flutter more wildly.

"I can make love with *infinite* slowness when I wish to," he assured her. "Savoring each inch of skin I bare." He removed her other slipper in his hands and began to massage her feet—the arches, the ankles, even the balls of her stocking-covered feet—and it felt like heaven. She moaned in pleasure as she collapsed back on the bed and propped herself up on her elbows. He unfastened the ribbons above her knees and slowly rolled down her stockings, pausing to look at the plain silk.

"When we're married, I will have all your stockings embroidered with lilies."

She tried not to think of the future they might share. It would hurt too much if it became real and was then torn away from her.

"Would you wear lilies on your waistcoat?" She was half teasing, half trying to distract herself as he bared her skin and let her stockings drop to the floor.

"I would tattoo them upon my body like a sailor, if you wish." He was so serious as he said this that her throat tightened as a flood of conflicting emotions battled for control inside her.

Charles ran his palms up her calves, playing silent melodies upon her flesh as he explored her, then pushed her skirts up her thighs as he stood. He caught her face in his hands and bent to kiss her. Fire raced from his body to hers, and she sighed at the exquisite perfection of his kiss—hard, then soft, then playful, then exploring. It was as though he was trying to make up for a lifetime of missed opportunities. His passions made her the sole focus of his attention, and she knew she would never have enough of it in this life.

She tried to lock her legs around his hips, but he

stepped back and pulled her onto her feet, trying to turn her so her back was to him. Then she understood his intention, how he wished to take her, and she faced away from him. Her heart began to race, and fear collided with desire. She'd been hurt this way before, but if he wanted, she would try it. She would try anything.

She started to lift her skirts up. "You want to...?"

"What? No, love, please." He pushed her skirts back down and wrapped his arms around her waist, holding onto her, his body radiating heat like her own private sun. He trailed kisses on her neck until her pulse calmed and her breathing stabilized again. He slowly let go of her, and his hands began to unlace the back of her gown.

A flash of embarrassment filled her. She'd been foolish in assuming he wanted to take her that way. He'd merely wanted to undo her gown. When he finished unlacing the gown, it dropped into a pool of cloth at her feet.

"Still with me?" he whispered before kissing her cheek.

"Y-yes." She placed her palms on the bed to steady herself as he unlaced her stays and let those drop as well. She wore only a chemise now, and she somehow felt more vulnerable than ever before in her life. She rotated in his arms to face him, unable to stop trembling.

"You're afraid."

How could she not be? What they'd shared in the coach on the way to the opera had been wonderful, but it had only been his finger, not...the rest of him. She didn't want this night to be one of pain, not with him.

"I am," she admitted, "but not of you. It's just that I've only ever..." Her face heated. "It hurt before. The pain was with me for days."

Charles wrapped his arms around her, holding her flush against him in a fierce embrace.

"I wish..." His whispered voice was rough with emotion. "I wish he'd never hurt you, never touched you. All I can do is promise it won't be like that with me."

Lily could feel in his touch and hear in his voice that this wasn't about possession. He spoke out of a desire to ease her concerns, to protect her, to care for her. A true lover would never hurt a woman, and Charles, she suspected, was perhaps the best lover any woman could ever have.

"I *want* you, and that want is stronger than any fear." She nuzzled his throat before placing a soft kiss above his cravat, then began to untie the neckcloth. She had done this many times for him before, and each time it had made her body flush. He let her slide the neckcloth off, holding still, a smile on his lips.

"I forgot. You undressed me often."

"I did." She knew she was blushing, but she couldn't help it. "And all those times you bathed and—"

This time it was he who blushed. "Lord, I made you massage my shoulders only a few nights ago."

"I didn't mind. But it always made me so nervous. I was certain you would see the desire in my eyes, feel it in my touch," she admitted. Charles let her unbutton his waistcoat, and her fingers trembled a little on the pearly silver buttons.

He reached up to twine his fingers in her hair. "How did you hide all these gold locks from me? I saw you with short cropped hair often enough."

She bit her lip to hide a smile. "Do you really wish to discuss how I pretended to be a boy in front of you? Now?"

Charles chuckled. "I fear my curiosity has gotten the better of me."

"Wigs and a hundred hairpins," Lily confessed. "It made my head ache. I had considered cutting my hair, but Hugo wished for me to keep my hair long for other occasions."

Charles threaded his fingers through her hair, gently removing pins while she finished unbuttoning his waistcoat. "I'm glad. Your hair is radiant." He shed his waistcoat, then lifted his white lawn shirt over and off his head.

"I have to kiss you again," he warned, a teasing glint in his eyes.

She smiled up at him. "I won't object."

Charles kissed away all doubt and fear, leaving only tenderness, heat, and light in his wake. He broke the kiss to nibble at her bottom lip, the light sting of his bite flooding her with warmth between her thighs. She clung to his bare shoulders, feeling his taut muscles shift beneath her hands as he drew her closer.

He swept his hands down her back, then her backside,

cupping her bottom through her chemise, then lifted her up and sat her on the bed again. When he broke the kiss this time, it was to remove his boots and stockings. His hands paused at his trousers, and he looked at her.

"Go on," she teased, and smiled as he pulled them off. She'd seen him naked more than once as Tom and knew how well-endowed he was. How often she'd had to hold her feelings back before, and now she didn't. Already she burned with longing.

"Lie back," he whispered. She slid back on the bed and crawled beneath the sheets. He joined her, and she began to slip her chemise off. He helped to remove it and then pulled her into his arms. Their bare forms pressed against each other for the first time, skin to skin, with nothing, not even secrets, standing between them.

The fine hairs on his chest tickled her breasts, and she shifted closer against him. Their legs twined together, and he stroked one hand from her shoulder slowly down to her calf before he hooked her leg around his hips. He lay in the cradle of her thighs as he covered her body with his.

"I want to explore every inch of you." His mouth moved down to her throat. He paused to kiss her collarbone, then moved toward her breasts. Heat flowed through her as he sucked one nipple between his lips. She couldn't stop the moan that escaped her lips as he tugged gently at it. Her head flew back as he cupped and kneaded her other breast. Light flashed behind her closed eyelids as pleasure began a slow, delicious build inside her. His mouth and hands roved over her more aggressively, but only just enough that she started writhing and panting. She'd always longed for larger breasts, as if those would somehow make up for her height, but Charles seemed enraptured by those she possessed, and for once she didn't feel ashamed of her figure.

"You're exquisite," he said as he nuzzled her sensitive mounds. "Like you were made just for me." His thumb rested against one hardened peak before he flicked his tongue against it.

Lily whimpered. "Please, stop teasing me." She fisted her hands into his hair and tugged. With one last playful lick, he slid down her body to her thighs. She tried to close her legs, embarrassed that he would see the marks on her skin where having a child had stretched her.

"Please, I know I'm not..." She trailed off, shame strangling the words.

"Every mark on your body defines you, Lily," he whispered. "It speaks of your courage, your strength, your love. Motherhood has only made you more lovely. I've always longed for someone real, someone who would accept me the same way."

Charles's sweet words were killing her. "But you have no scars." He had only one scar along his chin, but it was old and barely visible. She'd seen the masculine muscled perfection of his body so many times, she would've remembered if he'd had any others.

"They're on the inside," he said, his gray eyes showing

a hint of sorrow. He nuzzled down to the inside of her thigh, and she tensed as his mouth moved closer to her.

"What are you...?"

"Be at ease, love," he said soothingly just as his mouth settled on her center. The soft heat of his mouth and tongue exploring her consumed her in a flood of liquid fire. His tongue teased her folds, questing and conquering. It felt like heaven, yet she couldn't lie still. She wriggled and gasped with each delicate shift of his tongue. No man had ever been between her thighs like this, and she gloried shamelessly in the ecstasy of this moment. He kept her prisoner to the sweet torture of his mouth, and the bold swipes of his tongue sent her spiraling. Her need for him was more urgent than ever.

"Charles...I need you...inside me, please."

His reply was to fasten his mouth on the small pearl peeping between her folds while pushing two fingers gently into her channel.

She cried out at the sensations that overwhelmed her. So much was happening too fast. It was too much. Too good.

He moved up her body, and she spread her thighs, feeling his weight atop her as his shaft nudged her entrance. Emboldened by her own reckless desires, she raised her hips as he guided his shaft into her. He teased her folds, coating himself in her wetness, and she blushed wildly, her womb throbbing in anticipation. Then he pressed in, slow, his length hard as he entered the heated core of her body. She felt a slight whisper of pain as his shaft, thick and long, pushed deeper into her. Her legs trembled as she tried to relax, but it felt like he was spearing her.

"You feel like heaven."

The sight of his face, full of affection and desire, spiked her own arousal, and she relaxed, letting him sink all the way inside her. "So do you." She'd been so afraid of how it would hurt, how it would be like before, but it was nothing like that. She felt connected to Charles in the most intimate way possible.

"Tell me if I hurt you." He leaned down, bracing his arms on either side of her head.

For once she loved that she was taller than most ladies. Her lips were even with his, and she could kiss him while he gently rode her. As their eyes met, she was drawn in, consumed by the vitality and sensual dominance of his gaze as he lowered his mouth to hers.

This time when he kissed her, it felt different. Deeper, more unifying, as though he wanted to mold himself to her into one being. Love, hope, and desire all hummed in her like a chord plucked on a harp, the harmonious notes vibrating long after being struck. She had never felt so in tune with another soul, as though she could match her breath and the beat of her heart to his.

She kissed him back, trying to tell him with her lips what she was too afraid to say in words.

I love you. Love you so much I cannot envision life without you.

They shared a sigh of pleasure as she caressed the strong tendons in the back of his neck and gasped in sweet agony as he entered her again and again. The friction of their connection penetrated every nerve, and she finally understood what she had missed when she'd lost her innocence. *This* was what lovemaking truly was supposed to be like. The exquisite rush of physical joy that poured through her was magic. And it only kept building, higher and higher, like the tower of Babel, reaching toward heaven itself until...

She careened over the edge into impossible pleasure as she climaxed. Her soul shattered and reformed. He quickened his thrusts, whispering her name like a prayer. And then he came apart above her. She drank in the sight of his eyes, the way he held nothing back from her. It was so beautiful—*he* was so beautiful—that it overwhelmed her. A sob escaped her lips.

"Lily. I'm so sorry. What did I do?" He brushed the pads of his thumbs over her cheeks, which were wet with tears. "Please don't cry," he whispered. "I can bear anything but your tears."

She sniffed, unable to stop, and buried her face in his neck, clinging to him. He didn't understand. She felt free for the first time in years. She calmed, and her breathing hitched only slightly as she let go of her tight grip on his shoulders.

He kissed her temple. "I'm so sorry."

"No!" She cupped his face, offering a watery smile. "I didn't mean to upset you. I'm happy. I feel... I feel *free*." Perhaps not free of Hugo's clutches, but free of the pain and fear that he had left her with. Charles had shown her a way out of the darkness and into the light.

"I didn't hurt you?"

"No," she promised. "You showed me what it should've been like that first time."

His jaw clenched, and she saw a flash of anger in his eyes. "His crime will not go unpunished." His growling threat, despite its violence, was oddly endearing. Yet it also worried her.

"You can't let your anger rule over you," she warned.

Lily brushed a lock of hair out of his eyes. He turned his face into her hand so he could kiss her palm.

"I'm sorry. You're right. Anger has no place here. I promise you only pleasure from now on." He nuzzled her nose before stealing a kiss. He shifted as though to move, and she wrapped her legs tighter around his waist.

"Please don't move. I like the feel of you on top of me."

"I'm not too heavy?" he asked.

"No, you're perfect. I want to stay just"—she yawned—"like this." Despite her best intentions to stay awake, she sank into a blissful sleep, her body still wrapped around her tender rogue.

CHARLES WAS A DEAD MAN.

One night in bed with Lily had sent him to heaven's gates because there could be no place on earth as perfect as this. He watched her drift off to sleep, counting the tears that still clung to her lashes. Tears of joy. He had done that. For all the pleasure he'd given women over the years, there had never been anything like this.

But he hadn't freed her as she claimed—she was the one who'd freed him. Freed him from the heavy burden of a broken and lonely heart. Now he felt like he had been given wings to fly. He had never thought it was possible to feel like this.

He looked down at Lily, his beautiful, brave angel. She would never know what a gift she was to him. Every breath, every look, every smile was his undoing. She broke him apart and reforged him into something infinitely more than he had been before. Anything was possible. Anything, so long as he had her in his arms.

He rolled their bodies to one side and tucked her close to his chest, taking in her soft, feminine scent. It was a scent he now realized he should have recognized because it was hers, had always been hers, even when she'd scampered about his home disguised as Tom.

"Do you love me the way I love you?" he whispered, stroking her hair back from her sleeping face. He knew she couldn't possibly hear him in the land of dreams, yet her lips curved up in a smile that sent his pulse racing and a wild joy fluttering through him.

"I hope so, because you are my heart now. I live and breathe only for you." He kissed her lips and closed his eyes. He felt as though he'd been a dreamer, half-awake his entire life, and now he was truly alive because he'd finally found his other half. He finally understood the power love wielded in a man's heart.

His father was right. Love was stronger than hate. Love was everything.

22

Charles slipped out of bed in the early morning. After donning his clothes, he crept to the nursery. Katherine was awake and being tended to by Emily's nurse.

The nurse curtseyed. "Good morning, my lord."

Kat ran toward him, and he caught her up in his arms. "Unca Charles!"

"I'll be your papa soon. Would you like that?"

She studied him, then laid one tiny hand on his jaw and nodded. "Papa Charles?"

"That's right." He pressed a kiss to her forehead and held her close, his heart fit to burst as she curled her arms around his neck, hugging him back.

"I have to go downstairs now, but you stay here and play with your nurse, all right?"

The nurse's eyes lit up as she smiled. "What a lucky

child you are, Katherine, to have such a wonderful papa soon." She led Katherine back to her pile of toys by the fire as Charles took his leave.

He paused in the doorway, watching his daughter-to-be. It didn't matter that she was Hugo's by birth; she would belong to Charles in every way that mattered.

As he came down the main stairs, he expected to find the house mostly empty, with everyone still asleep after their late and stressful evening. This was not the case.

"Didn't expect to see you up and about this early," Godric said as he exited his study. "Breakfast?"

"Very well, but then I must go. There's much to be done today." Charles followed Godric into the dining room. A sideboard laden with chafing dishes awaited them, fresh from the kitchen. As they ate in silence, Godric watched him.

"No nightmares last night?" he finally asked. The question had been phrased casually, but they both knew the significance. Nightmares of that night in the Cam far too often haunted his dreams. Last night he'd drifted to sleep and hadn't stirred once.

"No, it was peaceful."

"Good. I was worried."

"She gives me peace, Godric. I don't quite understand it, but I damn sure won't question it."

Godric's green eyes glinted with amusement. "You were always so convinced that love was going to destroy the League, that it would make us weaker. I trust you see now that isn't true?"

Charles sipped his tea and nodded, a rueful smile on his lips. "And I'm sure I won't hear the end of that, either. But what if I'd never found someone who would be to me what Emily is to you? If I alone never found it, was never worthy of it. I do not think I could have endured that."

"But you have her now, and all will be well."

"That is my hope." They shared a knowing look as Charles got up from the table. "I must return home and make preparations for the wedding." He looked up at the ceiling, a sense of dread edging at the corners of his mind. "You'll keep my ladies safe?"

"With my life," Godric vowed.

"Thank you." His throat always felt tight when his friends showed such loyalty and friendship to him. He could trust Lily and Kat's safety to no one better.

A footman brought him his hat and coat as he left the house. It was hard not to study the footman and wonder if this man might be in Hugo's employ. How could he know which servants to trust? What about in his own household? Could there be another working for Hugo that Lily did not know about? Davis had served in the military. What if...? He repressed a shudder as he rushed down to his coach.

Once home, he found Graham eating breakfast. His bruises had turned an ugly shade of black, and his arms moved stiffly as he buttered some toast.

"How are you feeling?" Charles asked. "How's Phillip?"

"Still alive, thank the Lord, but he is so...broken. Not just in body, but in spirit. He hasn't even woken yet except for once or twice to have a bit of water and broth. I'm worried, Charles. Phillip and I have been friends since we were boys. What if he doesn't..." Graham dropped his toast on his plate and pushed it away, his appetite clearly gone.

Charles came over and placed a hand on Graham's shoulder. "He will rally. He's a strong man, as are you."

"Strong? I daresay I am not. If I had been, he would not be lying bedridden upstairs."

"Don't blame yourself," Charles said. "I know the sort of men he fought. They are strong, but they have no honor. You were damned the moment Phillip lost that hand of cards. I suspect Sheffield told them to break him. And you."

"Perhaps, but it doesn't ease my guilt." Graham covered his face with his hands.

Charles looked away, not wanting to intrude on his brother's grief. When the moment had passed, he gripped Graham's shoulder tight and then leaned down to softly whisper in his ear. "I need you to be strong now, brother. The man responsible is coming for me soon. I need you to find an excuse to take Ella and Mother north to Scotland, as far as you can in a week. Ashton's brothers-in-law are there. They will take you in. Hopefully the roads will be passable for traveling. But you must act calm, play as though it's a trip to see the sights. Do you understand?"

"But—" Graham began, but Charles held a finger to his lips.

"Shhh. The walls have ears." He pretended to reach for a plate of food beside Graham.

"Scotland?" Graham whispered back.

"Yes. There will be a wedding soon. After that, you must go quickly."

Graham reached for his cup of tea. "A wedding? Whose?"

Charles waited for him to take a deep sip. "Mine, of course."

Tea shot all over the table. "*Yours?*"

"Yes. Congratulate me, brother." Charles spoke in a normal voice now.

"Good God, the world must be ending. Is it the woman Mother wanted to meet at the opera last night?"

"Yes, Mrs. Lily Wycliff. She's a widow, formerly married to a cousin of the Duchess of Essex. How did you know of the opera?"

"Ella came by last night. She said Mrs. Wycliff looked stunning and was very sweet-natured."

Charles grinned. "She is certainly the most beautiful woman the world has ever seen. She puts Helen of Troy to shame." She had even launched the proverbial thousand ships to war, just as Helen did.

Graham stood and held out a hand to his brother. "I

never thought I would see the day, but I am truly happy for you."

"Would you..." Charles swallowed hard. "Would you stand with me, at the wedding?"

Graham was taken aback, his lips parted as he hesitated. "You want me there beside you?"

"You're my brother," Charles said. "There's no more deserving place for you than at my side."

Graham's smile dropped as he looked away. "I'm sorry, I cannot."

Charles's heart fell. "Why not?"

"I have not been a proper brother to you. Too much time has passed for me to take this place so easily. I wish for things to improve between us, but I must insist on one of your friends being there instead. They have been there for you when I have not."

Charles clasped his brother on the shoulder. "There is room enough for all of you, I wager. Don't see it as a reflection of the past for us, but a promise for the future. Please, say you will stand by me."

Graham hugged Charles. "I happily accept the honor." Charles smiled, feeling that wellspring of hope inside him again. Meeting Lily had changed everything in his life for the better. Well, almost everything. "Remember, after the wedding you must take Mother and Ella north."

Graham nodded as he let go of Charles. "Understood."

"Now, I must meet Ashton to acquire a special license

from the Doctors' Commons. I'll see you later this evening."

Charles returned to his chamber and had Davis lay out a fresh set of clothes. After he bathed and dressed, he walked to Ashton's house. Ash's residence was on was Half Moon Street, only one block over from Charles's home.

Ashton was coming down the stairs as Charles was let in. "Charles!" He smiled as if he were genuinely surprised to see him there, ever the actor when it was required. There was a reason no one in the League played cards or chess with the man.

"I thought you might like to accompany me to the Doctors' Commons for a special license."

"I'd be honored. I heard the news only this morning. Rosalind is thrilled, of course." He took a hat and coat from his footman and followed Charles outside to wait for Ashton's coach. They both stood outside, the cold morning air cutting through them, but at least they were reasonably sure they were alone.

"Graham will stand up with me for the wedding, as will you all, I hope. He's going to take my mother and Ella to your wife's relations in the north. Can you have Rosalind notify your brothers?"

"Yes. I think it's a splendid idea."

"What about Kent?" Charles asked. "It won't be easy for him to move from my home."

"We may have to risk leaving him under your roof. I'm not sure there's any other option." Ashton tightened his gloves as his coach stopped at the base of the steps. Charles followed him inside and waited until the vehicle was in motion again so the clatter of hooves would keep the driver from eavesdropping.

"What is our next move?"

"There's only one left to make. Lily must go back to Hugo."

Terror squeezed Charles's heart. "What? She can't. That's too dangerous. What if her deception has been noticed?"

"She must or else her deception *will* be noticed. He will expect her to report on the wedding plans so that he may make his own. With luck, he may reveal to her what his next move will be, and that is information we desperately need."

Charles wanted to argue the point, but Ashton was right. "I don't like it."

"I know this will be hard for you, Charles. You're finally feeling what the rest of us feel, that wild, desperate desire to protect the woman you love. It makes us irrational and unpredictable at times, but if you cannot learn to control it, you will only make things more dangerous for her. You must trust her. She has been well trained. She would have to be to escape my detection for almost a year."

"I suppose that is true." The last thing he wanted was to put Lily in any more danger because he couldn't control himself.

"Now, *you* should focus on the wedding. There's still much to be done. Leave the game of chess to me and your future wife." Ashton's grim smile only made Charles more nervous. Ashton was welcome to play games all he liked, but not at the expense of Lily's safety.

She comes first. Always.

23

Lily's hands trembled slightly as she entered a bookshop just off Bond Street. The dark-rose gown and yellow-gold cloak she wore made her feel out of place amid the shanty shelves and dusty tomes. Motes of dust danced and swirled in the beams of light cutting through the windows and illuminating the gilded spines of the books stacked thickly behind her.

An old man sat behind the counter, sleeping, the soft repetitive sound of his snores a comfort in the thick silence of the musty little shop. In the last year she'd grown accustomed to meeting Hugo in clandestine, often dangerous places. To meet now in such a quaint little shop, just a street away from the where most of the *ton* were shopping for Christmas, was strange. But this was where his message had instructed her to meet.

She leaned against the nearest shelf and looked out onto the street. Lily closed her eyes but a moment, replaying how Charles had looked just before she left Emily's house to come here. He had pulled her into an alcove and wrapped her in his arms. He hadn't wanted her to go, but Ashton was right—she had to. The moment she had confessed herself to Charles, this had become her battle as much as his. She had pressed herself into him, letting the beat of her heart match his.

The memory of their making love had left a beautiful magic that seemed to run beneath her skin whenever Charles was near. It was as though she could summon the feel of their union in her mind and body over and over. She'd always remember the bliss of looking into his eyes and seeing the world born anew. It was *his* memory she would carry into this meeting like a shield against Hugo.

With a stolen kiss, she had vowed to come back safe to him. He had promised to spend the afternoon with Kat and his mother, making their wedding plans.

Lily tensed as the shop door opened, and her heart stuttered to a stop. Hugo had arrived. He removed his hat and glanced calmly around the room. He meandered toward her, pausing every few seconds to look at the ramshackle shelves as though perusing the titles. Lily glanced at the old man behind the counter, who was still snoring rhythmically.

When he finally reached her, Lily went rigid. Every muscle coiled tight. She forced the black memories of what he'd done to her deep into the recesses of her mind and instead wrapped herself in memories of Charles. The way he'd lingered with her in the alcove, his hands clinging to her before he finally let her go.

"I hear wedding bells will finally ring?" Hugo said casually.

"Yes. The wedding is to be in a few days."

"So soon? I'd have preferred more time to prepare. Is this your doing?"

She shook her head. "Given the time of year, he wishes to honeymoon here in London with his friends before their families leave for the holidays."

Hugo gave a cold smile. "I will manage." Lily wished she'd brought one of Emily's muffs instead of only wearing gloves.

"What must I do next?" she asked, careful to keep her tone calm. He could not suspect any change in her demeanor, or she would doom herself and destroy any advantage the League had.

His eyes narrowed. "Eager for orders?"

"Eager for this to end." She allowed her weariness to show. It was no act. "I want to be free of you and this life. I want to take my child away from London and never look back."

He studied her a long moment, assessing her for any hint of deception. But every word had been the truth, just not the way he thought.

"That was the agreement. Fear not, plans are being

made. I'll give him his precious honeymoon. Then perhaps I'll take away something he loves, to remind him he will never be safe."

"Still with the games?" Lily said, though she knew she was in danger of angering Hugo by saying it. "I thought you were ready to move against him? To end this once and for all?"

"I *am* ready," said Hugo. "I have already decided on an appropriate venue. Someplace Charles will think he has a...fighting chance. But I have no desire to end things too quickly."

Lily sighed inwardly. He was still not done with his torturous games? "What do you wish for me to do next?" she pressed carefully, not wanting him to know she was trying to glean further hints of his plans.

Hugo grabbed her upper arm, his hand squeezing hard. He dragged her close to him, and the familiar scent of his soap made bile rise in her throat. She hadn't been able to clean the scent off her skin fast enough after that night with him.

"You are to give Lonsdale a *very* satisfying honeymoon. I want him to have a taste of marital bliss. That will make his downfall all the sweeter." He released her arm, and his gaze shot to the window at the front of the shop, then back to her.

"Soon this will all be over," he said, a distracted look now in his eyes. "And you will have earned your freedom."

Then he left her, exiting the shop before Lily could say

anything else. She sagged against the bookshelves, clutching her arm, which still throbbed. It was going to bruise and Charles would be furious, but at least she was safe.

She waited several minutes, giving Hugo time to leave the immediate area. Her gaze turned to the gilded spines gleaming in the sunlight streaming through the window. She wished now more than ever that she could slip between the pages of a book and vanish into a story. But there was no escaping this. She could only see it through to the end.

Taking a deep breath to clear her head, she pulled the hood of her cloak up and exited the shop, calling a hackney back to Emily's house. Inside, she heard voices coming from the drawing room.

Katherine was screaming.

The sound sent a flash of terror through Lily. She burst into the drawing room and froze. Charles was holding Kat up in the air, spinning her in circles. She was screaming in delight, not from fear.

"Again, Unca Charles! Again!" Kat waved her chubby arms as he carefully lowered her back onto his chest. The look of relief on his face when he saw Lily in the doorway stirred her heart.

"You're back!" he exclaimed and rushed over.

"Mama!" Kat waved, and Charles transferred the squirming child into her arms.

"Sweetheart." She buried her face in Kat's hair, taking

in her child's sweet scent, letting it bury the memory of Hugo's.

Charles curled an arm around her shoulders, drawing her and Kat into a loose but comforting embrace. "How did it go?"

She checked the room and the hall. There was no place close enough for someone to overhear them. She laid her head on his shoulder and sighed. "He wants the wedding to go ahead. Whatever he's planning will be after the honeymoon." She closed her eyes, weary. "He wouldn't tell me what he wants to do next. He's being close-lipped, more so than usual. It makes me afraid, Charles. So very afraid."

"I know." He kissed her forehead. "Emily has volunteered to take over for you if you need to rest. She adores Kat."

She shifted Kat from her right hip to her left. "I would like that, but I don't want her out of my sight."

"Why don't we go to your chamber? I'll watch over her while you sleep."

"You don't mind?" She hated that she wanted to rely on him like this. Looking after Kat was her responsibility.

"She will be my daughter in a few days. It's my duty and honor to look after her," Charles said. They exited the drawing room, and Lily paused at the foot of the stairs.

"You really do not mind that she's...?" She couldn't bring herself to say the words.

Charles shook his head. "She isn't his. She is and always will be yours. That's all that will ever matter to me." His vow, so softly worded, was delivered with such intensity that it stole her breath.

"You are..." She choked on the words. "You are the most wonderful man. I do not deserve you."

"Nonsense. *I* do not deserve you."

He took Kat from her, and the three of them went upstairs to her bedroom. Lily gratefully lay on the bed, at first intending to simply watch Charles and her daughter play, but when her head settled on the pillow, her eyes shut and she drifted to a state of dreams.

THEY WERE DANCING. THE BALLROOM, ONCE SO FULL OF people, had darkened around the edges as people faded and wall sconces and candles were extinguished.

"What do you treasure most?" Charles asked, a smile hovering about his lips.

"I think you know..." she said.

Suddenly, the world around her changed, and she was standing in a dark hall facing a gilded mirror. The glass was foggy, but it cleared when she placed her palms on it, revealing Charles holding Kat. They were both watching her, smiling. Then for a moment Charles's face changed into Hugo's before it changed back again.

The world around her changed again. Charles was running

away from her, down the Lewis Street tunnels, his harsh and panicked breath echoing down the stone corridor. He vanished right before her eyes, and Hugo's voice followed her into deeper sleep, murmuring words that would never stop haunting her.

"Soon this will all be over."

24

It was an absolutely perfect day to be married. The skies were clear, and the ground was covered with freshly fallen snow. It was a day that Charles never thought he would see. He stood at the front of the church, wearing his best blue waistcoat and finest trousers. Beside him, Graham stood quiet and alert. The bruises on his face had turned a sickly yellow as they started to heal. The rest of his friends had initially taken their places beside him. This was a momentous occasion for them all, and it didn't feel right for them not to stand with Charles. But before the ceremony had started, due to the general crowding and already anxious clergyman, they'd taken their places in the front pews with their wives. Beside them were his mother and sister.

Charles scanned the crowd seated in St. George's, astonished at the number of guests who could arrive on such short notice. His mother caught his eye and smiled encouragingly. He answered her with a wink, and then his gaze drifted to the front of the church.

I never thought this day would come. I never dreamed that I would know love or share it with another person.

Yet here he was, waiting for Lily to come down the aisle. He wasn't nervous, not like many of his friends had been on their wedding days. He had no doubts, no fears, no worries, not when it came to Lily. She was his North Star, a gleaming beacon that he could set his course to for the rest of his life. Tying his life to hers...well, in a sense it had happened long before today. Despite the deceptions she'd been forced to play out, there had been a deeper bond between them, which had ultimately set her free. This ceremony was only a formality. In his mind, he and Lily had been husband and wife since the moment she'd agreed to marry him. Though the ceremony and documents would use her assumed name as Emily's cousin, a second set of documents had been added with Lily's true name, which would be set aside and hidden until their business with Hugo was concluded.

Graham leaned in close to whisper, "You seem so certain about this."

Charles offered a smile. "Why would I have any doubts? She is my life, my breath, my every hope and dream. A smart man knows better than to question his destiny."

"Father said that about Mother once."

"He did?" Charles had wanted to believe his parents' marriage had been a love match. They'd insisted it was, but he'd always had his doubts after his father had rescued Jane Waverly. He had seen so much love between his father and Jane that day, so much pain over the life they never had a chance to have together. Knowing his father had settled by marrying his mother had always hurt him deeply.

Graham's lips curled up in a smile. "He once told me that he knew Mother was his destiny because of the way she danced with him. He told me he hadn't known at first that love could grow softly over time, until the day he danced with her and he realized they were perfectly in tune. I was worried I might never find that, but it seems you have. That gives me hope."

"Love does grow softly and sweetly." He thought of all the times Lily, as Tom, had provided him not just with her physical presence but an emotional tether. She'd cared for him all that time, bearing the burden of her secrets alone. That hadn't been part of Hugo's plan, he knew that. Her support had saved him from despair and madness. Had Hugo known of their bond, he no doubt would have used it to poison their affection for each other further.

It is my turn now to bear her burdens and to care for her.

The doors opened at the far end of the church. Everyone turned as Lily stepped into the church, one hand curled around Godric's arm.

The world froze as he gazed upon his future. Even the

motes of dust dancing in the sunbeams from the windows seemed to stand still.

I've been so blind. My heart's desire was with me all along.

The wedding gown Lily wore was of the softest pale-blue silk, like ice over a frozen pond, reflecting the winter skies above it. Belgian lace trimmed her bodice and the edges of her skirts, which billowed out as she walked toward him. His eyes lifted to her face, nervous about what he would see when she looked at him. Lily's face shone with an eagerness that echoed his own. One would think that Godric was the only thing keeping her from running into his arms. Relief and giddiness rippled through him, and he had to remind himself to stay where he was and not run to her.

Godric passed Lily's hand carefully into Charles's. The sunlight illuminated her gold hair like a halo. She was indeed his angel, but no fragile creature with delicate wings. His Lily was an archangel, a warrior who fought the darkness.

She gazed at his chest and his waistcoat, which had gleaming white lilies sewn into the blue silk. "You wore lilies?"

"Of course. I had it tailored just for you."

The clergyman coughed for their attention. They shared a sheepish glance before facing him.

"Well, let's get on with this, before I get struck by lightning," Charles said, loud enough for the room to hear.

"I touched the holy water on the way in, and I fear that it may have burned me."

Lily giggled and covered her mouth with a gloved hand.

With an aggrieved sigh, the clergyman began the ceremony that would forever change Charles's life.

Emily St. Laurent felt tears trail down her cheeks. For as long as she'd known Charles, she'd seen his pain and the way he'd masked it with humor and roguish wickedness. But now there was finally hope. No, more than hope—there was joy. She saw it in his eyes when Lily all but raced to him at the altar.

I said I would find someone who would love you as you deserved, Charles. But the truth is that she found you.

Lily and Charles shared a laugh after he jested about being struck by lightning, much to the clergyman's dismay. Emily chuckled as Godric curled an arm around her shoulders and gave her a gentle squeeze.

"You did this, darling," he whispered in her ear. "You were the beginning for all of us." He pressed his lips to her cheek and nodded at their row of friends.

Emily leaned forward, looking at those who had become her family, her world.

Wicked Lucien and his sweet Horatia, and their little son, Evan.

Adventurous Cedric with his wife, Anne.

Calculating Ashton and his fiery Scottish wife, Rosalind.

And, of course, Jonathan, Godric's half brother, alongside Lady Society herself, Audrey.

Because of Lady Society, she had known long before she'd even met Godric that he and his friends were bound together by a deep bond of friendship. The speculation of that bond had been a recurring theme in her early articles.

But it was a spontaneous decision by Godric to kidnap her over her uncle's debt that had led to the League's salvation.

"To think, if I'd never abducted you that night..." Godric said as his arm curled around hers. "I don't know where any of us would be without you. Especially Charles."

Emily wiped at her tears. "You think yourselves wicked, but in truth you have all been the most noble and wonderful men. Even if during our first encounter you were all acting incredibly foolish." She smiled up at him. "But it did lead to the most wonderful things."

"*You* led to the most wonderful things," Godric corrected her. "You and your lady friends. I fear we all would have been lost without you."

Godric placed a hand on her swollen belly, feeling the tiny life within her flutter in excitement. The baby loved the sound of Godric's voice, she was sure of it, and she'd felt it stirring more and more in recent days.

"Everything will be different now," Godric said.

Emily smiled. "Of course it will. Charles is in love. Nothing could possibly be the same."

Emily prayed that he would be safe. That they would all be safe. But with Hugo lurking in the shadows, these glorious moments seemed all too fleeting. Soon the League would face their greatest danger yet.

LILY WAS CAUGHT IN A DREAM, LIKE A GLISTENING dewdrop suspended on the length of a shimmering strand of spiderweb at dawn. She felt the magic of this day infusing her with strength and hope. All around her the wedding guests talked and laughed, the sounds of their gaiety filling her heart with an intense warmth.

And yet part of her felt like a fraud. She was not truly free to be herself. She was not Lily Wycliff, after all, but Lily Linley. She was not free to act as though she knew all their guests by name, even though she did. As Tom, she'd met most of them, but she was supposed to be a stranger in Charles's world. She couldn't forget to play the part.

And then, of course, there was the specter of Hugo lurking in the back of her mind.

"You seem a bit dazed, my dear." Violet, Charles's mother, joined her in one of the few semi-secluded spots in the large dining room of Charles's townhouse.

"I think you're right," Lily confessed. She smoothed

down her pale-blue skirts, even though they were already perfectly flat. It had become a nervous habit of hers, ever since she'd grown used to her Tom disguise. She felt rather exposed wearing a dress.

"Wedding breakfasts can be overwhelming," Violet agreed and put her arm around Lily's shoulder, giving her a squeeze. "You're doing well. Just remember to breathe and smile. You'll have your privacy soon enough."

"Thank you," Lily whispered, but when Violet moved to leave, Lily caught her hand. "May I ask... Do you approve of me, Lady Lonsdale?"

Violet's brows knit in confusion. "Approve of you?"

"Do you believe I am good enough for your son?" She still felt she was not and never would be good enough. Charles had told his mother much of the truth of who she was, leaving out only Hugo's role in things and explaining her deception as Tom as a desperate attempt to provide for her daughter.

Violet cupped Lily's face in a motherly way, peering deep into her eyes. "Do you love him?"

"More than anything in my life, except Katherine. I would die for him," Lily promised.

Violet chuckled gently. "I'm sure that won't be necessary. Neither of you need be so silly or do anything so Shakespearean. But I see your love for him. As though he's your world and you are caught up in his gravity." Violet looked at Charles, who was a ways off talking to a few guests. "He's exactly the same with you. I daresay you are both worthy of each other, and that is good. Marriage should be a union of equals, in heart, body, mind, and soul." Violet kissed her cheek. "And I am proud to call you daughter. Now, where is my grandchild?" She looked around the room. Kat was in Emily's arms, playing with a lock of Emily's auburn hair.

Lily watched with joy as Violet retrieved the child from Emily and held her close, whispering in Kat's ear. The baby squealed in delight, catching the attention of several guests, though no one seemed particularly upset that a child was at an adult gathering. Charles had insisted Katherine be present. He'd already shown Kat off to his friends, which had filled Lily with the greatest joy.

After a long moment of watching the guests around her, she needed a minute to catch her breath. She slipped outside the room unnoticed, walked down to the library, and sat down on one of the couches. Drawing a deep breath, she tried to convince herself this fairy-tale moment was in fact happening. It wasn't a dream. She was married to Charles.

She heard footsteps behind her and saw Charles standing in the doorway, holding two plates of wedding cake. Orange rose petals covered the top of the cake, and the floral scent it created was intoxicating. He kicked the door to the library closed and flipped the latch while juggling the plates.

"Finally, my own bloody wedding cake." He grinned and held out one plate to her. She took it, unable to hide a smile as she remembered how he had brought her a slice at Jonathan and Audrey's wedding breakfast a few months ago. It was something he'd done at every wedding she'd attended with him in the last year.

"What amuses you, wife?" Charles asked. The way he caressed the word *wife* made her heart tremble and quake with pent-up longing.

"You," she replied. "It seems you are always bringing me cake." She dipped her fork into the cake and sampled a bite. Heavenly. A few bites later, her plate was gently taken from her and set out of reach.

Charles pulled her close and kissed her. His arms cradled her body, and she lost all sense of time around her as she surrendered to him. She could feel his heart against her and an excitement that tingled from her head down to her toes as he kindled a fire within her. He moved his lips to her ear, whispering soft sweet things to her. She nearly wept at the bittersweet perfection she felt being in his arms, knowing the perils that tomorrow might bring.

I would give anything for today to never end.

Then his mouth was on hers again, sending new spirals of passion through her as he banished her fears. He explored her with a hungry eagerness that her own body echoed with equal urgency. She parted her lips, eager for a deeper kiss. Their tongues played together, each still tasting the sugary sweetness of their wedding cake lingering upon the other's lips.

Lily threw her arms around his neck and pulled him

flush against her. He lay back on the couch, pulling her to lie on top of him. Her tired soul seemed to sink into him. She relaxed and kissed his chin, his cheeks, his throat. She wanted him to feel how grateful she was to be his, how blessed she felt to call him hers in this moment. His masculine scent, carrying that hint of sandalwood and leather, belonged to her now. The way his gray eyes twinkled and the twitch of an almost smile—they were hers now to enjoy. Charles belonged to her in every way, and knowing that filled her with joy. She planted a kiss in the hollow of his neck before returning to his lips. He chuckled softly, and she could taste his smile.

"This is rather nice—to be the one eagerly seduced for a change, I mean." He gently dug his fingers into her hair, holding her still as he gazed upon her startled face.

She felt her face heat up. Perhaps it was bad for a wife to be intent on seducing her husband. "You don't mind that I...?"

"Mind? Lord, no. This is a fantasy to end all fantasies, my love. You may do this every day if you like. In fact, I *insist* you do." He brushed the pad of his thumb along her bottom lip. "The others would be insanely jealous to know what an *aggressive* wife I have." His eyes glinted with merriment, and she couldn't resist smiling back.

"You're terribly wicked," she reminded him.

"I certainly am." He moved his hands up her skirts, lifting them, and then he cupped her bottom. Her pulse quickened as desire began to overrule rational thought.

"Could we...here?" she whispered, scandalized and yet hopeful.

"It is our house. We can *anywhere*." The glint in Charles's gray eyes promised her wicked, wonderful things. And she knew he would deliver.

25

There was a brief tearing sound, and Lily's undergarments were conveniently out of the way. She eased back from him, allowing him to unfasten his trousers. She lifted herself up against him and moaned softly as he entered her. The now familiar sensation of fullness was all that she asked for.

Charles panted against her neck as they began to move as one. She set the pace, riding him slowly, relishing the feel of their bodies rubbing together and the way he clutched her tight to his chest as though she were precious to him. They were a single being, composed of hunger, need, and love. Without words they spoke of what they meant to each other. She wet her lips with her tongue and dug her fingers into his shoulders, the ache between her thighs sharp with her need.

Lily would always be a slave to this desire for him,

would do anything to have more of it. Heat pooled within her as he began to thrust deeper, harder, with almost savage lust. Yet she was the one in control. She was with Charles, the man she trusted more than anyone, even herself, and with him nothing frightened her anymore. His shaft seared her, plunging deep, so much that she thought she might perish from the overwhelming sensations of that almost violent friction where they were joined. She pressed down harder, faster, moving her hips as they both sucked in ragged breaths.

His possession of her was relentless, and she fell headlong into the dark passion of her own animalistic needs. Waves of pleasure exploded inside her. She felt scorched inside, and yet she didn't wish to feel any other way.

At last she collapsed on top of him, and he thrust deep once more before he hissed out a breath and fell back against the couch. Charles stroked her hair and watched her with sleepy, leonine eyes. She envied him and how at ease he was with his own sensuality. Perhaps someday she would feel as comfortable as he did.

"Now that is how one should spend their time at a wedding breakfast." His soft, rich laugh flooded her with butterflies and she sighed, only to suddenly stiffen.

"Oh Lord, the guests!"

"Easy, love. I locked the library door when I came in here. No one will disturb us."

"But aren't we expected to be there?"

"I've been to enough of these to know that by now

everyone is content with interacting with one another in their own little groups. We will hardly be missed. Besides, anyone who knows me even a little would be shocked to discover I stayed so long. Mother will see that the guests are shown home."

She climbed off him and took a moment to sigh over her ruined undergarments as he put his own clothes to rights. Then he opened his arms for her to return to him, and they both stretched out on the couch. She lay against his side, an easy peace settling upon them. She wasn't afraid, wasn't cold, wasn't unloved. Charles had given her the world when he'd married her today, and he would never know how much she loved him for that. There simply weren't enough words in the world to tell him.

"Lily, now that we are married, perhaps you should tell me about yourself," Charles said with a half grin, but he was also serious. "There should be no more secrets between us."

She agreed. There was no more need to keep anything from him now. "What do you wish to know?"

"Where were you born? Who are your parents? What was your childhood like? Tell me everything." He stroked her hair, the sensation both soothing and hypnotic.

"I was born in a town called Rose Heath in Cornwall. My father's name was Alan. He was a gentleman and my mother a lady."

"Truly now?" Charles was taken aback. "How did you end up in service?"

"My father died when I was twelve. Mother and I had no means to support ourselves, and what money we had after Papa died was transferred to a distant cousin who wanted nothing to do with us. My mother was able to secure work as a lady's maid in London for a friend who was a countess. She was wonderful to my mother and me. She even let me go to school with her children, as they were about my age. But the countess fell ill and died, and my mother, who was ill herself, passed on only a month later. I was eighteen by then and had, I thought at the time, the good fortune to acquire a reference to work for Sir Hugo Waverly's wife."

She paused, steeling herself. "I believe I was the only one he ever...hurt. None of the other maids seemed skittish or anxious around him." She gritted her teeth. "But the day it...happened, he was hiding a black mood, though I was the only one who saw it."

"What do mean, you were the only one?"

"He had come back from a visit with his mother. He was cold, but in a formal way few would have noticed. But beneath that he hid a deeper pain he didn't want to talk about. He was so sad and angry... I just wanted to help him, but when I showed him sympathy, he..." She shook her head, holding back her tears. She couldn't relive that moment. Not now.

"I wish I could do something, *anything* to take that moment back for you," Charles whispered.

"No, don't say that. I have Katherine. She is my gift,

my miracle. I will not let the past define me, Charles. Not anymore. And had none of that happened, I never would have met you."

"I suppose you are right." He curled his fingers under her chin, lifting her head so he could kiss her. "We should stay here all day. What do you think?"

"I think I would prefer your bed."

"*Our* bed," he corrected. "I shall make few proclamations in our marriage, but this shall be one. I insist we share a bed. None of that sleeping apart nonsense. That's one of the privileges of being married—I can debauch you whenever I like." His eyes twinkled with amorous mischief layered with a deeper lust that made her flush all over.

"You certainly may." Lily giggled, feeling girlish and delightfully silly for the first time in years. She'd never dreamed she would feel joy like this, yet here she was.

"I thought Kat might stay another night or two at Godric's, if you are amenable to that?" His eyes twinkled hopefully. "We could have a few days together, just us, if you like. Emily thinks the time with Kat will be good practice for Godric. He's always been terribly awkward around children."

Lily thought it over. It really would be nice to have Charles all to herself for a few days, and if Emily and Godric didn't mind...

"Is it safe? To leave her with them? Hugo might..."

Charles's eyes darkened. "She's probably safer with Godric than she would be with us."

Lily realized this was true. Godric was a duke, after all, with more staff on hand than Charles at any given time.

"I wish there was somewhere completely safe we could send her," said Lily. "But there isn't, is there?"

"Not yet," said Charles. "But soon."

Lily rested her chin on her chest, closing her eyes. "I don't want today to be over."

He brushed the backs of his fingers along her cheek. "Nor do I." There was another long moment of silence. Finally, Charles looked toward the locked door. "Why don't we see if we can slip upstairs without being noticed by the guests?"

"Yes, let's."

Lily and Charles climbed off the couch and headed for the door, trying not to giggle lest they be caught.

LUCIEN BOUNCED HIS SON IN HIS ARMS, CHUCKLING AS Evan cooed and gurgled, a grin on his chubby cheeks. Evan's brown eyes were his mother's, and that made him even more irresistible. Lucien sought out his wife in the crowd and soon found her speaking to the other ladies, who were gathered in a tight circle.

"That spells trouble," Cedric grumbled from beside Lucien.

Lucien agreed. "Can you believe they all knew that Lily

was Tom and kept it a secret from us?" Lucien whispered this after checking to see that no servants were close by.

"Yes, well, they did not know *everything* about her," Cedric said. "Otherwise, they would have warned us of her ties to Hugo."

"True. Still, I wonder how they figured it out? If anyone was going to see through Tom's disguise, I would have thought it would have been Ashton."

Cedric smiled, pointing out Audrey in the group. "Yes, well, we might have Ashton, but they have Lady Society herself. She knows more than Ash does when it comes to women. And no doubt her active imagination led her down that path for reasons Ashton would never have considered."

Lucien nodded. "Indeed."

"We really shouldn't be surprised, should we? With Emily in charge, the ladies are bound to know everything before we do."

"And sometimes more." Lucien shifted Evan in his hold as the baby started to drift off to sleep.

Cedric snickered. "At least we have something to celebrate. It's not every day a man marries his valet."

"Indeed it is not." Lucien started to say something more, but the sight he caught through the open door across the room stopped him short. Charles was carrying Lily in his arms and slinking up the stairs, glancing around in the hopes of not being caught.

Lucien broke into a grin. "Escaping his own breakfast? Why am I not surprised?"

Cedric laughed. "Wish I'd done that with Anne. But no, we were a well-behaved couple."

"As was I," Lucien agreed. "But this is Charles. We should know better by now."

Ashton and Godric joined them, Godric carrying little Kat in his arms.

"Good practice, this," Godric said as he balanced the child on his hip.

"It certainly is, but I daresay nothing truly prepares you for it." Lucien laughed and peered down at Evan's face. There was nothing more beautiful in this world than his newborn son, aside from his wife, of course.

"Do you think having children will change everything?" Cedric asked, a slightly worried look in his eyes.

"Of course it will." Ashton smiled as he joined them. "But change is not something to be feared. Marriage changed all of us for the better, after all."

Lucien nodded, thoughtful. "I want London to be safe for them. Our children need to have lives of adventure, not fear. And so long as Hugo shadows us, they won't be safe." He held Evan closer.

"The endgame is coming soon," Ashton warned. "We must be ready. All of us."

"What do you know?" asked Godric.

"Too much and not enough," Ashton said cryptically. "But know this: when Hugo makes his move, it won't be against Charles alone." The men exchanged glances, and more than one man clenched his jaw as Ashton continued.

"Though his quarrel began with Charles, Hugo sees us all as one collective group now. We represent something vile to him. Something that must be wiped out." Ashton lowered his voice even more. "But we have one advantage that he does not realize. He will treat us like pawns, and we will continue to let him. But remember, we are knights, and knights can jump over all the other pieces."

HUGO LEANED BACK IN HIS CHAIR, EYES FOCUSED ON THE black-and-white marble chess set in front of him. Beside him was a piece of paper, the words "It is done" scrawled in Daniel Sheffield's elegant hand.

Charles was married.

Despite the fact that this had been his plan, Hugo felt rage vibrate through him. The man he hated more than anything was enjoying bliss in the arms of his new wife. A bliss he did not deserve.

The door to his study opened, and Melanie stood there, looking radiant as always, but there was a nervousness in her eyes.

"Yes, my dove?" He spoke the endearment sweetly, playing the part of a doting husband.

"Hugo, I'm leaving."

"For how long?" he asked, assuming she meant to spend a week in the country.

She kept a hand on the door latch, and he could hear the metal handle tremble. "Forever."

She'd made the threat before, whenever she didn't get enough attention. "No, you're not."

"You don't have to believe me," she said.

At this, he tilted his head, studying her more carefully. The pretty wife he'd purchased with his reputation and his fortune had aged well and was possibly more beautiful than the day he married her. What had changed about her? In the last few months, Melanie had seemed happier than he'd ever remembered, and she hadn't been with him. She'd been off to dinner parties and balls alone.

No...not alone. Of course. Melanie had taken a lover.

"Who is he?" Hugo asked, not daring to move from his chair. If he did, he might strangle his wife.

"All that matters is that I'm happy. I have found what you could never give me."

"Oh? And what, pray tell, is that?" He'd given his wife everything—jewels, power, expensive clothes, trips to the continent, priceless art...

"Hugo, you closed your heart off long ago, even before we married." Melanie spoke with a quiet honesty that stunned him. In this final hour of their marriage, she was challenging him. "I wanted you to love me. I wanted it to be you, but you never... *You never let me in.*" She looked down at the floor now. And much to his own surprise, so did Hugo.

There had been a time he had hoped to hold on to her affections, only to be consumed by his work. Serving the empire. Protecting the Crown. He knew that he had closed himself off, because he had to. It was easier than dealing with the pain.

But when he'd learned she was carrying Peter, he had hoped to mend all that between them. He'd become more attentive and had even reached out to his mother for the first time in years, hoping to bring them all closer together. To be what a family should be.

But Melanie and his mother had brought that hope crashing down into ruin.

"I'm leaving for my mother's estate in the country, and I'm taking my son."

Hugo's fists shook. "If you insist on being a fool, then go, but you will *not* take my son. Peter will have a far better life in London. The best education, the best tutors, the best introduction to society. He could rise to become a lord. Why would you take all that away from him?"

"Because if he stays, I fear he will become just like you."

For a long moment, Hugo didn't move, didn't breathe. He'd expected fury, he'd expected rage. He had not expected sorrow to steal his breath.

What would he provide Peter? Money, power, position,

yes—but what else? What lessons would he teach? Revenge? Guile? Treachery?

What could he give his son that would make him a better man?

He stared at his wife and uttered one word, because it was all he was capable of.

"Go."

Melanie fled and Hugo closed his eyes, trying desperately to bury the pain. Was this how his father had felt all those years ago when he'd learned his wife, Hugo's mother, had never loved him? That Hugo hadn't even been his son by birth? Yet his father had fought for him, taken him under his wing and raised him as his own.

And yet when he'd lost his father, he'd come close to ending his own life. He'd always looked to him for guidance, and without him he had nothing. He'd gone to school, done his duty, and yet day by day he had considered ending it all. It would be so much easier.

Peter Maltby found him on one of his darkest days, befriended him, showed him that life was something you created for yourself. It was all a matter of will. It was the reason he'd named his son after him. It was the least he could do, considering how things had ended between them.

Perhaps it was for the best if young Peter went with his mother. Perhaps he would be a corrupting influence on him. Perhaps later, when this was all over, he could heal. Perhaps then he could be the right sort of father for him.

But that did not mean he had nothing to contribute. His life had value. It had to. To suggest otherwise was insulting. He had served his country. He had bled for it. He had sacrificed *everything* for it. Did he deserve nothing in return?

But what if he could raise another in Peter's place? He had promised Lily a pension to raise Katherine with in exchange for her service, but he could do so much more than that.

His son would carry his name, but his daughter could be his legacy. Perhaps it was time he took her back. To give Katherine a better life than anything she could expect to have as the child of a servant.

"Is that what you truly want? To hurt a child by taking her away from her mother?" Peter Maltby's voice haunted him, just as it always did when he was close to breaking down. Even as a ghost, Peter could still talk to him.

"But what life can Lily give her? She was raised above a gambling hell, for God's sake."

"That is the life you forced her into."

"We all live with our mistakes," Hugo muttered. "I'm trying to make amends for mine. I can provide her far more than she can. The mother will be compensated. I will make things right."

"If you want to make things right, let her go. Let them all go."

Hugo's lip curled. "I can't."

"*Why?*"

"You know damn well why."

Lord, he wished Peter were truly here, not just a voice inside his head. Peter had always softened the hate inside him. He'd saved Hugo's life at a time when he'd been ready to give in to despair. But Peter was dead; he lived only in the past now.

Hugo closed his eyes, and the memories of his days at Cambridge surfaced.

"Well, that was an odd coincidence," said Peter.

"You couldn't have known it was him," said Hugo.

"Why do you hate him so?" Peter asked.

Hugo pulled his glare away from Charles, where he sat a few tables away at the pub. After their chilly reintroduction, Peter had taken him aside to talk in private to calm him down.

"I don't want to talk about him," Hugo muttered and glared at Peter. "Why are you so nice to him?"

Peter grinned, his good mood infectious. "I believe every man is essentially good. You've read John Locke, haven't you?" Peter tapped the cover of a thick book he was carrying.

Hugo snorted. "Hobbes is more realistic, less romantic. Mankind is destined for violence and driven by animal urges. At best, we can control those urges."

Peter's laugh was warm and his eyes bright. "You know, Hugo, if you smiled more, you'd be sitting at a table with more friends."

Hugo glared at Peter, but Peter never took his scowls personally. He always saw the good in people, just as he had said. It was impossible not to like Peter. When Hugo had arrived at Cambridge, he saw no future for himself. He had considered putting his head in a noose or jumping from the bell tower. But Peter had been there, had talked to him, had been a friend when Hugo believed he was utterly alone. Peter had saved him.

"Tell me, what did Lonsdale do to you? You haven't told me the whole story." Peter slid closer to him. All around them the cacophony of robust voices from the young men enjoying the pub and laughing bounced off the stone walls.

"Hugo, we're friends," Peter reminded him.

Hugo wanted to lash out, to tell Peter they weren't friends, but it wasn't true.

"He killed my father."

Peter's eyes dropped to the table awkwardly. "I thought you said his father killed him."

"Charles challenged my father. But he was a coward. His father fought in his stead and killed mine. But it never would have happened if he hadn't challenged him."

Peter looked toward the table where Lonsdale was sitting. He was alone now, but he tried to smile hopefully at the patrons around him. For a moment Hugo realized he could have pitied Lonsdale for having no friends, just like him, and for looking too eagerly for company. But Hugo hardened his heart.

"Either man could have called off the duel," Peter reminded him. "And would your father shooting a boy have made him a better man in your eyes?"

Hugo frowned but didn't answer.

"Forgiveness is one of the most powerful forces there is," Peter

said, his gaze locked on Hugo's face. "Second only to love. You don't have to love him; you need only to forgive him."

Hugo snarled and threw his plate of food so hard it hit the wall and shattered.

"I CAN'T!"

Hugo had said the words aloud without realizing it. He looked around to see if anyone had overheard him, but he was alone.

Alone.

He let the memories of the past fade as he stared at the chessboard once more. His fingers flicked the white king over onto its side. The king rolled lazily in a half circle before coming to a stop. Then Hugo curled his fingers around the white queen piece.

With his other hand he retrieved a set of five letters that had been written days ago and rang the bell for a footman. He'd intended to give Charles a few days to enjoy married life before Hugo ripped it all away, but now he couldn't wait. He wanted this to end. He wanted a new beginning.

When the servant he'd summoned appeared, he gave the letters to him.

"Deliver these at once."

Until now, Hugo had been playing with Charles and his friends. They no doubt thought that they'd foiled his plans at every turn, but what they did not see was the fact he had been putting his pieces into position the whole time. Every gambit that had failed had been accompanied by other moves unseen.

Five letters to five agents lying in wait. By midnight, he would have every rogue in the League under his control. They would be on their guard now, of course, but it didn't matter. There would be no one to save Charles this time.

He opened his hand to stare at the white marble chess piece, brilliantly pale against the skin of his palm.

"Checkmate, Charles."

26

The night was still and cold, no breeze to stir the mane of Cedric Sheridan's horse as he reached his home. Tucked safely in his coat was a carefully wrapped package containing a set of ruby earrings for Anne. An early Christmas present he couldn't help but get when he'd seen them earlier that day in a little shop on Bond Street. He grinned rakishly as he thought of how she would thank him, hopefully with ecstatic kisses, and he could then sweep her into his arms and carry her off to bed.

He dismounted just as the darkness deepened and clouds swept over the stars above. No lights could be seen from the windows, which meant Anne had gone to bed early. Given her condition, it was for the best. She needed more sleep. Cedric looked around, expecting his groom, Joel, to see to his horse, but the lad was nowhere in sight.

With a sigh, Cedric led the horse around the side of the house himself to the small stable he kept for his and Anne's horses. He saw to the gelding's needs, ensuring that it had oats and water in two buckets before he removed the saddle and blanketed him.

The stable door creaked open. A figure stood at the entrance, but he couldn't see the man's face because he was silhouetted against the purple sky outside. The hairs on the back of Cedric's neck rose in warning. He kept his back to the stall, making sure he couldn't be attacked from behind.

"Joel?"

"I'm sorry, my lord. I was seeing to my needs when you arrived." Joel's cheerful voice allayed Cedric's unease, and he relaxed.

"Oh, yes. No worries, lad. It's late as it is." He stepped away from the stall, cursing Ashton and his cryptic biblical-like warnings.

Joel chuckled as he took over seeing to the horse. "Cold night tonight."

"Indeed. All quiet at the house?"

"Aye. Her ladyship retired nigh on two hours ago."

Cedric smiled a little, picturing himself sneaking into bed, curling his body around Anne's, and kissing her sweetly until she woke up. He wouldn't keep her awake for long, but he did want to steal a few kisses from her before falling asleep himself.

He shivered suddenly, as though someone had stepped over his grave.

I am overreacting. Ash has made me suspicious of everything, the damned fool. Yet he couldn't shake the sense that something wasn't right.

As he left the stable, he could hear Joel humming as he worked. Then the humming ceased and a heavy silence cloaked the stable. Cedric spun. He saw Joel's limp body lying on the straw-covered ground.

A dark figure lunged at him and struck him hard in the face. Cedric grunted as he fell back against the stone floor. Darkness sucked him down into an abyss.

LUCIEN SANG SOFTLY TO EVAN AS HE PLACED HIM IN HIS bassinet. The baby gazed up at him with a dreamy smile.

"You spoil him, you know." Horatia chuckled as she leaned against his side.

"You disapprove?"

"Hardly. I think we should spoil him more."

She wore a dark-red dressing gown, belted loosely at her waist, and her hair hung down in soft waves around her shoulders. Lord, he had the most beautiful wife. Lucien curled an arm around her, pulling her into his side so he could kiss her.

"I love you."

"And I you." Her brow wrinkled in concern. Horatia

placed a hand on his chest. "What is wrong? You seem anxious."

"I am. I'm afraid for you and Evan. I can't shake the feeling that whatever will happen is going to happen soon."

Horatia hugged him close. "I know. It's frightening. But we will be safe. Ashton will—" The door to the bedchamber opened, and a footman stepped in. He held a pistol, aimed at Lucien's chest.

"Matthew?" Horatia whispered the man's name.

"I need only you, my lord. Leave quietly with me, and no harm will come to the lady or the child."

Lucien moved in front of Horatia and the bassinet.

"Don't think of calling for help, my lord. There's more than one man outside, and they will come if necessary. If you leave, I'll make sure they come with us and leave your wife and child alone."

"Lucien, *no*," Horatia breathed, already knowing his intentions.

"Where are we going?" Lucien asked.

Matthew's expressionless face chilled Lucien's blood. "We are going to see *him*. That's all you need to know. Now come." He flicked the barrel of his gun toward the door. Lucien turned, catching Horatia's trembling body, and kissed her.

"More than my own life," he whispered as he pulled away from her. "More than anything." He couldn't bring himself to say anything more, for fear he would break.

"Lucien…" Horatia put herself in front of the baby's bassinet, reaching out to him, and his heart shattered when he couldn't reach back. They shared one last lingering look before he faced Hugo's man.

It was late enough that the servants would be at their dinners belowstairs. No one would be harmed. That was the only good thought he could have tonight.

Matthew pointed at the front door. "Open it and go out to the waiting coach."

Lucien did as he was commanded. He was almost to the coach when something hit him hard from behind. He fell against the side of the coach and half turned as two men leapt at him, their fists striking him over and over until he crumpled to his knees. Then he was grabbed by the arms and lifted into the coach.

Lucien blacked out moments later.

GODRIC SAT IN HIS STUDY, QUIETLY THINKING OVER THE day's events. Ashton's warning had left him sick with worry. Charles's wedding had been a pleasant enough reprieve, but it hadn't removed the danger to Emily and their unborn child. He was terrified that there was nothing he could do, and he couldn't send them away. Even if Emily could travel the harsh winter roads in her condition, he knew better than to try. She would only find her way back and perhaps land in even more trouble trying to help him. Then there was little Katherine they were watching over for Lily and Charles. He couldn't let anything happen to the child.

A soft sound, like footsteps on carpet, drew his focus. He looked up through the open door of his study and saw a figure in the hall slink past. Godric glanced at the clock on the mantel. It was almost midnight. His servants would normally be in bed.

Ordinarily this would be of little concern, but his mind connected what he was seeing with the possibility of what he had been fearing. He got up from his desk, moving silently as he followed the man up the stairs. The gleam of a pistol in his hands froze Godric's blood as he realized that the man was heading toward the nursery. He rushed up the stairs and launched himself at the man. They hit the steps, bodies crunching against the carpet and wood. Their limbs tangled as they fought. Godric punched the man in the jaw and soon recognized him as one of his gardeners.

"You—" he grunted. The man kicked him in the stomach, and Godric tumbled down the stairs, groaning as he hit the bottom. He blinked, trying to clear his vision of the black spots that shrank and grew in turns. Body aching, he scrambled to his hands and knees, his gaze darting frantically up the stairs.

"Emily! Simpkins!" he bellowed. "Protect Katherine!" He prayed his wife could hear him. Why was no one coming to his aid? Where were Simpkins and the others?

Could they not hear the commotion? Godric was halfway up the stairs when he saw the man throw himself at the door to the nursery, but it did not budge.

"Open this door!" the man shouted. Silence answered him. Good—Emily had heard his warning. The man hissed and raised the pistol at him.

"I was here for you and the child, but you will have to be enough for now. Get on your knees so I can tie your hands."

Godric had no wish to comply, but he knew Emily and Katherine needed to be safe, and they would be safest if he left. He fell heavily to his knees and slowly raised his hands. He heard the man shuffle behind him seconds before the man hit him with the pistol. Godric grunted as pain exploded through him. He crumpled to the floor, his vision blurring.

"Emily—" He raised one hand toward the closed nursery door, fingers straining for the three lives safe behind that impenetrable oak. The man stood over him, peering down with a scowl.

"You are one tough bastard, I'll grant you that," he muttered. Then he raised his boot and brought it swiftly down on Godric's face, and everything went dark.

EMILY HELD KAT IN HER ARMS, TREMBLING AS SHE heard Godric shout out a warning. She slid the door latch in place, sealing off the nursery. She flinched at the sudden pounding and muffled shouts of whoever was outside. It was not her husband.

"Mama...want Mama," Kat whispered, her tiny hands digging into Emily's arms.

"I know. Mama is safe, but we aren't. Hush. You must stay quiet. Do you understand?" Kat's cheeks were coated with tears, but she nodded.

Emily carried Kat across the room to the tall dresser in one corner. She opened the highest drawer, one well out of Kat's curious reach, and dug through the baby blankets until her fingers brushed against cold metal.

The sound of her husband's pained shout from the other side of the nursery door made her freeze. Her heart nearly stuttered to a stop. She pulled out a pistol from the folds of the blankets.

Godric...

She dared not breathe. They had made a vow to each other. No matter what happened, she was to protect Katherine and their unborn child at any cost, even if it meant leaving him to danger. It was a vow she'd never wanted to obey, but she had to. She pointed the pistol toward the door and waited.

There were no more sounds outside, but she couldn't bring herself to open the door. What if the intruder was waiting for her to show herself?

"Want Mama," Kat whispered against Emily's neck.

"I know, I know," Emily crooned, curling her arm

around Kat's body as she eased them down onto the floor to wait. The only sounds she heard now was the haunting tick of the mantel clock and the sound of her heart fracturing as she feared for Godric's life.

JONATHAN ST. LAURENT HELD AUDREY IN HIS ARMS, placing teasing kisses on her lips as she finally fell into sleep. He tenderly placed her beneath the covers and blew out the candles. She caught hold of his hand as he started to rise from the bed.

"I'll be back, sweetheart," he said, and her hand dropped to the sheets.

He left the bed and donned his clothes in the dark, then exited the bedchamber and headed down the stairs, hoping to find himself a glass of brandy. He was having the worst time getting to sleep ever since Ashton had told them all they were in imminent danger. He didn't fear for his own life, but he did fear for his brother and his friends, and most importantly for Audrey. She'd been targeted once by Hugo already, simply to hurt the League, and he wouldn't let that happen again.

Something felt wrong. It was like a change in the air of a coming storm. He slipped outside unnoticed, hoping that the brisk air would clear his head. Having once been a servant, he knew how to be both quick-footed and quiet as a mouse. Even his own servants rarely were able to find him when he didn't wish to be seen or heard. He ducked out into the street and saw down the moonlit road toward Godric's house, a coach out front. Two men were carrying a body. They lifted it into the coach, which then headed down the street toward his home.

"No..."

The end was here, and sooner than any of them had expected. He used the tall rhododendrons to shield himself by the steps up to his house, but the coach rolled past and kept going. Jonathan glanced down the street to Godric's home and then at the coach, torn between wanting to see if everyone in the house was all right and fearing that Godric was in that coach and needed him.

He could hear Ashton's voice in his head. *"If Hugo wished to assassinate us, we would all be dead. Even his attacks so far have been feints. He won't try to trick us all to be at the same place, either. But he will want us together, and he will want it to be violent. You must let them take you. It is safer for everyone if we surrender. Remember, this game isn't over yet."*

"Then I must be one move Hugo didn't take into consideration," Jonathan said to himself. "He didn't come for me."

Jonathan began to run, keeping the slow-moving coach in sight. As long as it didn't speed up, he might be able to follow it. He only prayed that the League would survive the night. Evil could not be allowed to prevail.

THE CHESS PIECES ON THE ORNATE MARBLE BOARD gleamed in the firelight. Ashton stared at the board, his mind clear of all thoughts as he focused on the moves. The white king was exposed, with no knights in a position to save him.

It was a metaphor. This match symbolized his struggle with Hugo, but he wouldn't presume to equate the game to their true situation. Still, it gave him a point of focus. He could picture Hugo playing a similar game, because that was the way he viewed the world. Objects to be moved, stratagems to be played, pieces to be sacrificed.

Ashton thought back to a private conversation he'd had with Lily, before the wedding breakfast had begun.

"YOU KNOW WHAT HE WANTS."

Lily nodded. "Charles's death. After he feels he's suffered enough."

"And he wishes to do it himself."

She nodded again. "Eventually."

"How do you think he will do it? What is his idea of suffering?"

Lily hesitated. "By killing all of you in front of him, with him powerless to stop it."

Ashton nodded. "Correct. This is a war of the mind. It always has been." He paused a moment. Lily was attentive, listening. She wasn't giving in to feelings of despair, simply watching him for an opportunity to contribute. He could understand why Hugo had found her useful.

"The moves, the stratagems, even the players must be seen through that lens. Every move Hugo makes in his endgame will be calculated to take something away from Charles. To hurt him, and yet leave him powerless to retaliate, for fear of losing more. There will always be just enough hope left to believe that things will end differently, until he has nothing and realizes all the times before that he should have acted but did not. He will blame himself for each and every tragedy that has befallen him. Only then will Hugo kill him."

Lily's resolve wavered, and she looked to the ground. He could hardly blame her. Being inside Hugo's mind had sickened him, but it had been necessary. Hugo's past had been the key all along. Once Ashton had understood Hugo's motivations, the rest had fallen into place, and a weakness had shown itself.

Ashton lifted her chin with his fingers. "But...if he loses you first..."

Lily swallowed but didn't speak.

"Do you understand what I'm telling you?"

Lily turned her gaze to where Charles stood, talking to guests. Her eyes narrowed in grim understanding.

"I do."

Ashton had been impressed by Lily's courage. Few men would make such a sacrifice easily, but she hadn't hesitated.

The door to his study opened, and a tall dark-haired man stood in the doorway, a pistol with two barrels side by side gleaming in the firelight. Ashton slowly stood, slipping the chess piece into his waistcoat pocket. Upstairs, Rosalind slept safe and sound. He'd locked her door from the outside and slipped the key under her door as a precaution, but the truth was he hadn't expected anything to happen for at least a couple more days.

"You're early," Ashton said calmly to the man in the doorway. He recognized the fellow as one of his grooms—or rather, one of Hugo's spies who'd spent two years here as a groom. So, Hugo had been moving people into position long before they had even learned of his return.

"Not going to fight?" the man asked.

"I'd rather not, Baxter, if it's all the same to you. Besides, you need me alive."

"Aye, I do." The man flicked the pistol. "I was supposed to rough you up a bit, but I think we can dispense with that. For old times' sake. Let's be off. He wants you there by midnight."

"Very well." Ashton exited the evening room.

The weight of the white queen in his pocket seemed to grow with every step he took. "Baxter, if you don't mind me asking, what is your impression of your mission?"

"How do you mean?"

"You've known me for two years, worked as my groom, sometimes as my footman. What possible reason do you think Hugo has to act against us? Have you ever seen me as a threat to the country?"

"Not my place to say, sir. But with all the secret meetings you lot have had and adventures off in other parts, I reckon you must be up to something no good."

Ashton almost chuckled. That, at least, confirmed his belief that Hugo had convinced his men that the League were dangerous in some way. "Fair enough."

Tonight he would face the darkness of Hugo Waverly's heart, and the League would be tested like they had never been before. His mind flashed back to the river, the darkness, the sucking depths, and the fear that what had happened that night would repeat itself.

I did my best to predict all the moves. The game is now out of my hands. Please let me be right. The white queen could be the key to everything.

27

Charles brushed his fingertips over Lily's cheeks, picturing himself as an old man, still holding her in his arms and marveling that he had been granted a long and happy life with her. She watched him, her eyes the purest blue he'd ever seen.

He pulled her body beneath his, covering her with slow, soft kisses. She tilted her head back, exposing her throat, and he ran his fingertips down the delicate column until he reached her collarbone. She sighed dreamily and stroked her hands up and down his arms as he nibbled on her throat. Each time he gave her little love bites, she giggled and then moaned. He slid one hand down to her breasts, exploring the peaks. The pale-pink nipples were perfect tips, and he shifted down her body so he could take them into his mouth, sucking on them until they were hard and Lily's breath came out faster.

Charles wanted to linger over every inch of her skin, learning her secret spots that made her moan and call out his name. The ticklish spots on her lower waist, the flare of her hips, and the soft skin behind her knees—all of it was a gift to him, a precious thing he feared he had so little time to enjoy.

"Do you want me to make love to you, wife?" he whispered.

She lifted her head from her pillow and nodded slowly. "Yes...husband." She whispered the word tentatively, like a child afraid to speak about Christmas lest Christmas never come. But she need not ever worry. He would stay her husband as long as he drew breath. He sat back on his heels and pulled her up onto his body. She was less afraid now, growing bolder in bed now that she knew there would only ever be pleasure between them.

She watched him slowly enter her and then moaned so sweetly, it made his body rigid with a desperate need to draw out this final climax. He wanted to bask in the glow that seemed to emanate off her as she gave in to her pleasure and abandoned her fear. Lily gripped the pillow on either side of her head, her back arching, her breasts on perfect display as he claimed her, and she in turn claimed him in a way no other woman ever had.

I am yours, will always be yours.

His body trembled as she came apart beneath him, and then he followed her over the edge of bliss. His vision turned white for an instant as he surrendered to their shared passion. He hoped, deep within his soul, that they had created a life between them in this moment, that something of him would remain with her if he didn't survive whatever Hugo had planned.

"I love you." The words trembled on her lips as though she might weep, as though she feared she'd never have another chance to say them.

He bent his head and covered her lips with his, wanting to ease the ache he saw in her face. Danger was coming, he could feel it, yet he felt strangely calm. Not unlike a man condemned to die who had been given his fill of a glorious sunrise—the brilliant colors, the vibrant skies, all of it. He would soak up the glory of those final glimpses. That was how he felt with Lily. He would worship her now and take that memory into battle with him like a shield.

She drifted to sleep, and he held her a long while before he slipped from bed and dressed. Despite what Ashton had told him, he sensed within his bones that whatever was coming was coming tonight, and he wanted to be ready.

He'd just finished buttoning up his waistcoat when the door handle to his bedchamber began to turn. As the door opened, he raised his fists, expecting...well, he had no idea what would come through the door.

When it did open, a man he recognized stood before him.

"So, it's you," he said to Daniel Sheffield.

Daniel's grim smile looked bleak in the candlelight. "He didn't trust anyone else to bring you to him." He held no weapons. Charles tensed, wondering if he could stop this man in a fight if it came to it. No one could match him when it came to boxing, but at the same time, he was no assassin. Lily had bested him in fencing because she knew when to break the rules.

"You won't fight me." Daniel said this without arrogance but rather with a calm assurance.

Charles didn't lower his fists. "I won't?"

"You might make a show of it, but we both know you're going to come. Because the others have. Because you know I'm not truly alone. And because he has the child."

Every muscle in Charles's body went rigid, and he glanced toward the bed behind him. Thankfully, Lily hadn't awakened. He couldn't let anything happen to that child.

"Very well." Charles lowered his fists, and he and Daniel exited the chamber with Lily still lost in the land of dreams.

Daniel had a coach waiting outside, and Charles followed him into it. Neither man spoke as the coach lurched forward. Daniel watched the streets through the windows, and Charles stared at his hands clasped in front of him. His fingers trembled slightly, but he hid it easily enough by clenching them tightly together.

"You say the others came willingly?" asked Charles.

Daniel gave a half smile. "I never said that. But it was far too easy to capture you all. Of course, that was expected."

"Expected?"

"Sir Hugo has a more cunning mind than you realize, Lonsdale. He anticipated Ashton's plan to let you all be taken easily long ago, I'm afraid."

Charles leaned forward. "What does he hold over you, Sheffield? Or did he buy your loyalty?" He asked this not with anger but curiosity.

"He has no hold over me, nor did he buy me. He saved me at a time I thought I couldn't be saved. That sort of debt is far stronger."

"I understand." Charles thought of the debts he owed to every man in the League, and to Peter as well. Some debts could never be repaid.

"Do you?" Daniel asked, but his question was not sarcastic, rather ponderous.

Charles found it easier to speak of the past now. Facing death now made such secrets seem irrelevant.

"I made a foolish mistake as a boy, and it took Hugo's father from him. And I lost my own father in the bargain —it just took longer to happen. But it wasn't enough for Hugo that we both lost our fathers. Did he ever tell you that he tried to drown me at Cambridge?"

Daniel was quiet a moment and then spoke. "He did, but I'm curious to hear your side of it, if I may."

"It was a quirk of fate that brought our circles back

together. I had a friend, Peter, one of my few friends at school. And, it turned out, he was a friend of Hugo's as well. He had us meet one day, thinking we would hit it off, not realizing we shared a common past. Something about that meeting set him off. That night, Hugo dragged me from my room and bound my hands and wrists." Charles rubbed his wrists, feeling the ropes as if it were fifteen years ago. "He dragged me into the shallows of the river Cam and tied me to a heavy stone. I never stood a chance." As he spoke, he was borne back into the past, feeling the water swallowing him up and feeling his throat burn with his cries for help.

"Peter Maltby came to my rescue. He was one of the finest men I've ever known. He died saving me. My other friends arrived, pulling me from the water, but Peter was lost. I had taken another life from Hugo." He paused, drawing in a slow, painful breath. "I owe my friends everything for saving me."

Daniel was quiet a long moment as his gaze met Charles's.

"He's going to kill you tonight."

"I know."

Daniel paused, as if it physically hurt him to divulge part of his master's plans. "You don't. Not really."

"What about my wife?" Charles asked.

"Unharmed. She and the child will be allowed to live. You discovered her deception then?"

"Yes," he lied. He was not about to admit that she'd

confessed Hugo's plans to him, or that she was now on his side. But was it possible he already knew? What if Daniel's words were just a ploy to coerce him into cooperation?

The coach stopped and they climbed out, but his shoulders slumped at the sight of the entrance to the Lewis Street tunnels. Daniel glanced at him, a hesitant look in his eyes. Charles grabbed his arm, hoping he could appeal to this man's honor in some way.

"Please, do not let him harm the child or Lily. They are innocent. I need to know, whatever happens, that they will escape his wrath."

Daniel's dark-brown eyes studied him. "I have spent my life serving my country and repaying the man who saved my life. But this past year I've watched him succumb to his own madness. You have my word I will do what I can for them." His lips turned down in a cold frown, but the frustration seemed to be turned inward.

"Thank you." Charles released Daniel's arm, and they descended into the tunnels, which were surprisingly empty, much like when they'd rescued the Earl of Kent. No doubt Hugo's men had cleared them out. Perhaps even now they were stationed in the shadows, ensuring no one interrupted this private meeting.

When they reached one of the open areas that held the rings for fighting, Charles skidded to a stop. Hugo stood in the center ring.

"Welcome, Charles," Hugo said with a laugh. "I've arranged for a little party here tonight, and you're the guest of honor." He waved for Charles to look beyond him.

Behind him in the three usually empty tall metal cells were his friends. Ashton stood in the middle cell, pressed up against the bars, proud and unafraid. Cedric sat on the ground behind him, holding a hand to the back of his head and groaning. In the second cell Lucien was slumped, barely conscious, against the wall, his face bruised. Beside him, Godric was also seated, angry, sweat and blood dripping down his brow. Ashton curled his fingers around the bars, his blue eyes intense with sorrow as he and Charles looked at each other.

"I'm sorry," Charles whispered loudly enough that they could hear.

Hugo only chuckled. "Come now, I never said this was a surprise party. You were expecting this as much as I was looking forward to it. You knew they would be here, because they carry the guilt of their sins as much as you do."

Charles stood at the edge of the boxing ring. Despair cloaked him like a shroud. What if Hugo had anticipated Ashton's every move? Could all his planning have been for nothing?

"Where is she? The child?" Charles asked, not seeing Katherine among them.

"She's safe." Godric's voice was hoarse. "Emily has her."

"Silence!" Hugo bellowed. "Or I'll have you shot before your time."

Thank the heavens, Kat was safe. So not all of Hugo's plans had gone as they should. He took a small amount of pleasure in that. It proved Hugo was fallible, and that gave Charles faith in Ashton's plan once more.

"The time has come, Charles. After what you did to my father, to Peter...it's time for you to pay. A pound of flesh from each of you. The wages of sin, with interest." Hugo turned to the League in the cages, a gleam of triumph in his dark eyes. Ashton stepped forward, shielding Cedric and the others as much as he could.

"This won't work, Hugo. You're trying to tear us apart, just as you always have. Haven't you learned yet that we only get stronger?"

"Do you really?" Hugo asked. "Or have I worn you down so gradually that you don't even see where you will break?"

Charles's soul splintered, like ice over a swift-moving river. He would not survive, not if he lost them. He stepped into the ring, arms held open wide, exposing himself.

"Take me, kill me."

Hugo looked to Ashton and smiled. "Crack."

Charles looked to each of his friends. He would do anything for them to have another day with their wives, their families. He would give his life without hesitation to give them but another few seconds of happiness. He owed them that. He owed them everything.

"You want me, Hugo. It's only ever been about the two of us. Kill me and let this be ended."

"Loud and impulsive. Foolhardy as always. You're failing to see the lesson, Charles." Hugo paced before him, like a lion waiting to be set free from his cage. There was a horrifying confidence in his eyes. "And, as you will see, suffering is the greatest teacher."

Hugo turned his back on Charles and studied the trapped rogues with a cold, speculative appraisal. The men in the cages tensed, sensing their danger.

Ashton never took his eyes off Hugo. Lucien struggled to his feet, as did Godric and Cedric. None of them wished to die on their knees. Daniel watched from the edge of the ring, his arms crossed, his face impassive.

What can I do to save them? Charles had never felt more helpless in his life, except that night in the river. The past was repeating itself, but this time they couldn't swim to the opposite shore.

"Lennox, Rochester, Essex, Sheridan... Which of you will stand by him now? He's brought death and ruin to you all. Surely you would not stand at his side," Hugo said with a sneer. Then his expression changed. "I am feeling magnanimous. His life is forfeit, but yours do not have to be. I offer you your lives—*if* you renounce him and walk away."

"Do it!" Charles begged them, eyes burning with tears. "Leave...*please*."

Ashton shot Charles a glance with an expression Charles couldn't read. Then Ashton cocked his head, as if considering Hugo's offer.

"You've never understood true friendship, have you, Hugo?"

"Oh, shut up, Lennox. You've been beaten. You're *all* dying tonight unless you agree to leave. Now, if you are wondering why you should believe me, consider this: Having to explain the disappearances of so many of the gentry is a huge inconvenience for me. Abandon Charles to his fate, and I will have no more to do with you, because I know you will never move against me. If you did, your complicity would become public. Therefore, I have nothing to fear from you. Of course, I rather hope you stay because I'll thoroughly enjoy watching the light vanish from your eyes."

Ashton chuckled softly, as though amused at Hugo's offer. "All these years you've hated us, but not because you lost Peter or your father. You filled yourself with hate because you knew you would never have what Charles had that night. Love, love from strangers. Our bond is based on love, and sacrifice when called upon."

"You *dare* speak of love? Peter was my friend. I loved him, and you fools took him from me! He was my only friend, the—"

"*He was my friend as well!*" Ashton shouted, in a

surprising burst of rage. "And he died trying to save your most hated enemy. You hated Charles even more for that, but what you should have seen from the start was what Peter's death really meant. He wasn't trying to save Charles that night—he was trying to save *you*." Ashton paused, drawing in a breath. "Because he knew, as your only friend, that your soul would never survive murdering your own brother."

The wind rushed out of Charles's lungs. He was suddenly dizzy as he swayed on his feet. What had Ashton meant by that? Brother? No. They weren't...they couldn't be...

He stared at Hugo, tracing the lines of Hugo's face, seeking a familiarity and, to his own horror, finding it. Hugo was a dark-haired version of Charles's father. He hadn't wanted to see the truth, had denied those thoughts from ever surfacing. Yet hadn't he looked upon Kat and sworn he'd seen something of himself in her little face?

I'm her uncle.

Hugo gave Ashton a slow, deliberate clap. "Half brother. Accuracy is important, wouldn't you agree?" He began pacing again, but he still seemed completely in control. "His mongrel father seduced my mother and she bore me, yet my true father raised me, *loved* me. He died protecting my honor." Hugo looked at Ashton again. "Honestly, just whose confidence did you expect to shake with that revelation? It seems to be news only to Charles.

And we are *not* brothers, no matter what blood might tie us together."

Charles couldn't have agreed more. Brothers were not made by blood, but love. The men trapped in the cells here were his true brothers.

Hugo stopped pacing and looked slowly, deliberately at Charles. "Since your friends seem reluctant to denounce you, I should by all rights kill them all. Those were the rules, after all."

Charles said nothing. What could he say that wouldn't make things worse?

"But perhaps blood should count for something," Hugo continued, as if considering a new possibility. "Choose one. Choose one of your friends to leave, and I'll choose one to kill. A fair trade, wouldn't you say?"

Charles's teeth felt like they were grinding into powder. "I'd tell you to go to hell, Hugo, but it seems you already rule there."

Hugo smirked. "Choose no one, and I will kill two."

"*What do you want from me?!*" Charles screamed. "My life? I will throw myself upon your sword. My title? You are the elder brother. I will surrender it."

"Even if that were within your power, I want nothing of yours. Make your choice, *brother*, and I will make mine."

Charles looked to his captive friends and back to Hugo. "I..."

"It won't matter," said Ashton. "It's a trick. Choose

one of us to leave, Charles, and that's the one he'll choose to kill. Whatever he says, it will be a trick."

Hugo sagged and sighed. "Oh, for God's sake, must you *always* be such a bloody know-it-all? Choose, Charles, or Ashton dies first."

Charles closed his eyes and took a deep breath. He looked to Hugo.

"I choose...to apologize."

Ashton smiled. Hugo blinked. "What?"

"I know this will not change anything, that you are set upon this path. I know nothing will satisfy you but my death, but...I am sorry. I am sorry I challenged your father. I'm sorry I am the reason for his death and Peter's. If I could undo it all, I would. I would have found another way to protect your mother from the man you called your father. I am sorry for the pain you have suffered."

Hugo's composure began to fail him. He strode over to Charles and struck him with the back of his hand. Charles did not resist, taking the blow, but standing his ground. For the first time since they'd arrived, Hugo began to shake with anger.

"Your apology means *nothing*!" Hugo roared. "You think you can save yourself with *words*? Your words killed those closest to me. And now they have sealed the fate of those closest to you. Daniel, a pistol." Hugo waved a hand imperiously, and Daniel held out a loaded gun. Hugo briefly examined it and then raised the barrel toward the men in the cells.

"No!" Charles's voice echoed through the cavern. He leapt across the ring, putting himself between Hugo's line of sight and his friends. "End this, Hugo. But leave them out of it."

"Charles, don't," Godric cried out from behind him.

"You're only prolonging your pain, Charles," said Hugo, as if explaining the situation to a child. "Don't you see that?"

Charles had a flash of inspiration. "This all began because I made a challenge. Let it end the same way. I challenge you, Hugo."

Hugo snorted. "To a duel?"

"To a fight. You think yourself better than me? Then prove it. Let us settle this, just you and me. Or are you too much of a coward, *brother*?" He emphasized the word, wanting to draw Hugo's wrath upon himself and away from his friends.

Hugo's lips pulled back in an animalistic snarl. "As you wish."

He handed the pistol back to Daniel and gave his lieutenant the smallest nod. Daniel tucked the pistol in his coat and walked past Charles, only to suddenly turn and lunge.

Pain lanced through Charles's lower back. He grunted, his legs trembling as Daniel gripped him by the shoulders, holding him with one arm, while his other dug painfully into his lower back. Charles could feel the blade of a knife inside him. Daniel had *stabbed* him.

For a moment, Charles shuddered as he stared into Daniel's eyes, feeling the cold steel blur together with white-hot agony. It felt wrong, foreign. He was a dead man. In an oddly detached moment, he wondered how long would it be before he bled out.

He was dimly aware of the shouting of his friends and the rattling of the metal cages as they tried to get to him. Yet all he could focus on was that he had been killed by the man who'd promised to protect Lily and Katherine from Hugo. How stupid he'd been to think he could trust him.

He wanted to close his eyes, to surrender now and let it be over. He couldn't win a fight, not with a fatal wound—that was beyond even him.

Daniel leaned in close to whisper in his ear, his soft voice surprisingly clear. "It's not fatal, Lonsdale. You can survive this. So fight. End this, for all of us." Then he stepped back, a bloodied dagger gripped loosely in his hands.

"Charles!" Ashton shouted, terror coloring his voice.

Charles staggered, covering the wound in his back. When he removed his hand, it came away slick with blood. He raised his eyes to Hugo, who merely smiled.

"You...you won't even face me in a fair fight." Charles tried to ignore the way his muscles cramped around the wound and how it made his legs feel wobbly.

"I never agreed to fight *fair*." Hugo rolled up his sleeves and waved a hand at Charles, mockingly inviting him to attack. "Come on now. Fight for your friends' lives. They're all counting on you."

Charles tried to bury the pain from his wound, and raised his fists. His breath was shortening. He knew he couldn't have much time as he felt the hot blood trickling down his back.

This is no different from any other match. Fight him with everything you have left.

He only prayed it would be enough.

28

Lily was lost in a dream of kisses and whispered words of love as she and Charles watched the sunrise through the bay windows. Her husband leaned over her, his gray eyes alight with passion.

Then the sun sank back below the horizon and darkness cloaked them. Charles cried out as dark, shadowy hands pulled him from the bed and dragged him under the floor, which had become the surface of an icy river.

"Charles!" Lily screamed.

She bolted upright in the bed. The empty bed. Charles was gone.

Lily threw back the covers and glanced around the room. The fire had died in the hearth, and everything was quiet. Charles would never have left her, not tonight. Not while they all waited for Hugo to make his move. He had to have been taken. They all had.

But so soon? She had been sure he would wait at least a few days. Why now? No, the *why* didn't matter. What mattered was *where*. She believed she knew where Hugo would take them. A place where he could arrange for privacy and have dramatic effect. A place where Charles would think he had a "fighting" chance.

The Lewis Street tunnels.

Lily's hands shook as she rushed upstairs to her old room and dug around for Tom's valet clothes. She needed the ease of her breeches and waistcoat to run. Then she pocketed the one thing she was certain she would need tonight and rushed from the room.

I always knew my time with him would be short, but I never believed I would have him for only a day. It isn't enough.

Then she remembered her meeting with Ashton.

"It's never enough when you are guided by love," Ashton said. "But if you have the strength, you can save him. You can save all of them."

A ghost of a smile crossed her lips. "Including yourself."

Ashton sighed heavily. "I do not enjoy playing Hugo's games on his terms. I would take your place if I could, but I'm not the one who owns Charles's heart."

Lily nodded. "I understand."

. . .

SHE STILL UNDERSTOOD. SHE KNEW WHAT SHE HAD to do.

Please don't let me be too late.

JONATHAN HID IN THE SHADOWS OF THE TUNNEL entrance that fed into a large cavern with boxing rings. He'd had to evade some of Hugo's men who were keeping away the riffraff, but that did not prove too difficult. Now he was watching Charles fighting for his life. And losing. Twice he had gone to the ground, and twice he had gotten back up.

With every punch Charles grew weaker. Blood trailed down his lower back, leaving a sickly crimson pattern on the floor as he fought Hugo. It was surprising to see Hugo fight. He was good, perhaps as good as Charles, but the injury to Charles's back had made him weak. His sluggish steps and off-kilter feints weren't working. Again he dropped to his knees. Hugo crowed and took a step back, taunting him to get back up.

Jonathan looked toward the cages. The League were watching, all of them silent. Jonathan checked each man over and froze at the sight of Godric, who had blood trickling down one side of his face from his temple.

Someone grabbed him from behind, taking his arm and pulling him back. He raised a fist to strike but halted when he saw Tom...or Lily dressed as Tom.

"What are you—?"

"There's no time. I'm going to distract Hugo. Do nothing to interfere. No matter what happens, you must stay here. When you see an opportunity, set the others free, but do not try to leave the tunnels until it's safe. Hugo's men are still patrolling the surface. Do you understand?"

"How will I know when it's safe?"

"When Hugo is gone." It was all she said before she slipped back into the shadows.

❧

CHARLES COULD BARELY BREATHE, HIS WOUND ACHED, and sweat rolled down his forehead into his eyes, making them burn. Hugo's fist connected with Charles's jaw with a *crack!* and he fell onto his back. Again.

"That's four!" Hugo said, triumphant. "Lucien's life is now forfeit as well. Four falls, four lives. All you had to do was stay on your feet, Charles, and you couldn't even do that. Now, let's end this."

Charles wasn't sure he could get up this time. His arms were like lead, and his muscles were seizing. Blood rolled down his back, leaving the rest of him feeling cold, so damned cold. He couldn't seem to catch his breath. Part of him wanted to just stay there on the ground, sucking in air until he could move again.

He looked toward his friends, all of them pressed

against the bars. Ashton, Lucien, Godric, Cedric. They were all doomed. Because he'd failed them. Everything seemed to be slowing down. White dots colored his vision.

"Charles!" Lily's face was suddenly over his, her cool fingers on his hot forehead. "You must get up," she said, just loud enough for him to hear. "You must fight."

Hugo grabbed Lily by the arm, dragging her up to her feet. "At last, my spy returns. Unexpected, but fortuitous. Did she tell you, Charles? She works for me."

"Hugo, you don't have to do this," Lily said, pleading. "Has he not suffered enough?"

Hugo looked to Charles with a knowing smile. "What do you think, Charles? Have you?"

Charles had managed to roll over, and he was on his hands and knees now, blood pouring from his lip and pooling on the floor. "Don't..." he gasped.

Hugo turned back to Lily. "My dear, I am glad you came, regardless of your true motives. I'm not angry with you for developing feelings for Charles. He is pitiable, I know. But you have done your job well, and I keep to my agreements. You will have your pension and your quiet life in the country."

"I don't want your money, you monster," Lily spat.

Hugo ignored her. "And I will raise our daughter here in London. Give her a life you would never be able to. She will have privilege and status befitting a Waverly."

Lily's face drained in horror. "No... You can't."

Daniel approached, reaching out to take Lily away from the ring, but she stomped on his foot and struck his nose with the flat of her hand. With Daniel momentarily blinded, Lily reached into his waistband and took one of his pistols away, cocking it and aiming it at Hugo.

Hugo grabbed her arm and wrestled with her for control of the pistol. But she could not match Hugo's strength as he bent the pistol around, turning it toward Lily's chest.

Crack!

Charles's heart stopped as Lily crumpled to the ground.

"No..."

Hugo tossed the spent pistol to the ground and advanced on Charles, murder in Hugo's eyes. It was like Charles was back in the river, the dark water closing around his head, the heavy stones pulling him down. No one would come back this time. There were no more miracles left.

My world, my whole world is gone.

Black despair clawed at his chest, squeezing tight. He thought of Katherine, *his* child, motherless, to be taken in by Hugo and raised as his own. She needed him now more than ever.

Rage electrified his body, and he surged to his feet. A roar escaped his lips as he launched himself toward Hugo. Hugo stopped dead in his tracks. The rage Hugo had stored over the decades shrank and cowered in the face of

Charles's fury. Death itself had arrived, and in the face of it, Hugo Waverly did the only thing he could do.

He ran.

Charles bellowed in rage and chased after him. His boots were slick with his own blood, but he did not stumble across the rough stone floors. He sprinted after Hugo in the darkness, the intermittent torches offering glimpses of Hugo's retreating form.

The ground began to rise beneath Charles's feet as they moved upward. They were leaving the tunnels. Suddenly he and Hugo were outside, the freezing air cutting his breath off as he got his bearings. They were close to the Thames.

Hugo skidded down the icy bank, panting as he got ahead of Charles. The Thames looked solid, and Hugo dashed across the ice, Charles just behind him. Twilight bled over the wintry landscape ahead of him, creating eerie shadows from the figure just beyond his reach.

"Stop!" Charles shouted. Pain and rage filled him to the point where nothing else existed within him any longer. He was a beast driven only with one purpose: to kill the man he pursued.

The deafening sound of ice breaking was all around him, echoing across the Thames. Hugo stopped, his boots sliding on the ice. Charles did the same, listening for another warning sound, but he could see no obvious cracks.

"Not another step, brother," Hugo warned, his voice firm and cold.

The rage within him came roaring back. "Brother? You dare call me that? You took *everything* from me. She was my world." Charles's fingers curled into fists. He dared not close his eyes. If he did, he would see her, his beautiful love, dying in front of him.

"It's no less than you deserve. You took *my* world from me," Hugo practically growled, and Charles saw the pain beneath Hugo's icy glare. "You and your father destroyed my life."

"He was your father too. He was trying to save you." *Save you from your hate. Like Peter.*

"He left me to save myself," Hugo said. "You are a disgrace."

Charles kept his fury at bay. "I've never had a problem with the man I am, but you? You are a murderer. If we're listing sins, yours will come first." Charles took another step toward Hugo. This had to end. They could not go on like this.

"*Murderer?* How *dare* you—"

Crack! The ice broke, and Hugo cried out and plunged into the icy depths below.

"No!"

That should have been it. He should have moved back to where the ice was more solid, back toward the shore. But in that moment he pictured Hugo suffering the fate he'd feared for himself for so long, and what might have happened if Peter and Godric and Cedric and Lucien and Ashton had done nothing.

Charles rushed toward the hand sticking up from the break in the ice, but it gave way and he collapsed into the river as well.

Darkness, ice, and cold enveloped him. He could see another figure struggling in the murky depths. Charles reached for Hugo, his fingers brushing the tip of his shoulder, but the current was too strong.

We're going to die.

Every nightmare he'd had since university was coming true. His lungs burned, and soon he would be inhaling water. It was the end, for both of them.

Hugo was close enough for Charles to see the puzzled look on his face. The question in his eyes.

Why?

Why try to save him now? Charles had no answer; he just knew he had to try.

And then Hugo's mouth opened as if he'd had one final revelation. Air escaped as he choked, his pale face contorting as he drew in water. Charles feared he would not be far behind him.

It was always going to come to this. Death in the dark. And this time he had killed his own brother, his enemy, his blood. But the rage that had driven Hugo was one that could have consumed Charles had the duel gone differently. Everything would have been averted if he had not challenged Hugo's father to a duel.

Perhaps he had been the villain of this story all along...

Charles moved his arms, frantically clawing toward the ice above him, trying to find the opening he'd fallen through. His eyes closed, and he stopped fighting. Lily's face filled his mind.

I love you.

He'd be joining her soon. There was that to be thankful for. He felt his body flying toward a growing light, moving at a blinding speed, white and black flashing across his closed eyelids as he soared.

I'll find you, Lily, I promise.

Icy cold pain exploded through him, and something hit his chest hard.

"Breathe! Breathe, you bastard!"

Charles coughed violently, panting and retching as he rolled onto his side. He was lying on the edge of the frozen river, twenty feet from where he'd fallen in. Godric. It had to be Godric. Or Lucien, perhaps. He was the stronger swimmer.

The man beside him was scowling, and when Charles's hazy mind connected him with a name, he tried to attack the man.

"Stop, you fool. You're too bloody weak," Daniel snapped in irritation, holding Charles down until he stopped thrashing. "You're welcome, Lonsdale."

"Why?" Charles groaned as he forced his aching, freezing body to a sitting position.

"I owed Hugo everything. My oath of loyalty was one

I could not break. But that loyalty died with him. Consider this my offer of a truce. I will see to it that no final orders are carried out posthumously on Hugo's behalf. It is over."

Daniel climbed to his feet and walked up the slope of the riverbank. He did not look back and soon vanished down a mews out of sight. Charles followed only until he saw his way back to the entrance of the Lewis Street tunnels.

Every stiff joint and bone cracked as he moved back through the stone passageways. The flow of blood from the wound to his back had slowed from the cold. He was numb, his thoughts trapped beneath a heavy cloud, but he knew he couldn't give up. His friends still needed him, and Katherine still needed a father.

And Lily... He needed to hold her one last time.

With Hugo's sentries gone, the tunnels were beginning to fill with its usual denizens. A few straggling pickpockets had already returned. Charles stumbled toward the group of men leaving the cells. Jonathan was there, unlocking the cell doors as fast as he could. No one spoke as Charles fell to his knees beside Lily's body.

She wore her valet's trousers and a waistcoat with his family's livery, Tom coming to his aid one last time. She lay on her side, eyes closed, her face pale and solemn, as though she were asleep. With a shaking hand, he reached out and cupped her face. Her skin was still warm. It tortured him with memories of mere hours ago, when she'd been alive in his arms, kissing him in his bed. His beloved wife. She'd lasted only a day.

A hand settled on his shoulder. Someone crouched beside him.

"She was the final move," Ashton said, as if to himself.

"Move? This wasn't a bloody *game*, Ashton," Charles growled.

"It was," said Ashton. "A most bloody one." His fingers tightened on Charles's shoulder. "Lily's presence here was no accident. She knew what she was doing. She gave her life for yours. For all of us."

"I don't understand."

"Hugo knew that as long as you still had something left to lose, you would not commit yourself to destroy him the way you had to. Your fear for our lives would always hold you back, allowing him to chip away at us all until there was nothing left. But to lose her?"

A chill filled the air. Charles slowly turned to Ashton, his fists tightening. "You...*told* her to sacrifice herself?"

"I told her how events would play out, and she saw the mistake he'd made, just as I had. She understood Hugo almost as well as I did. You must believe me—if I could have taken her place, I would have."

Charles wanted to strike Ashton down, but behind the calm words he could see the pain his friend was feeling. He had made himself think like Hugo, *be* Hugo for a time, and that had cost him a piece of his soul.

The League now came in a silent ring around him, and

for a moment he felt connected to them all. They were one body, one soul, as they mourned with him. Never had any man been blessed with such friends, and yet they had paid an unspeakable price. Lily's life given for him, for *all* of them. He reached out to brush a fingertip down Lily's cheek, his eyes clouding with tears.

"Hang on," said Jonathan, his brow furrowed. "Where's the blood?"

"Blood?" Lucien muttered from beside him.

Lily gasped and spasmed. "*Ahh!*"

Everyone around her cursed and fell back, including Charles. For the first time in his life, he nearly fainted.

"Oh..." she groaned and tore at her waistcoat. She ripped the buttons aside, moaning as she exposed a thick layer of leather and a small metal breastplate.

"What in God's name...?" Cedric began.

A bullet was wedged into the metal, and Lily gingerly touched it, but it was firmly pressed into the plate.

"Well done, Lily." Lucien chuckled. "Well done. Never face a dangerous situation without protection, I always say."

Lily's eyes locked on to Charles. She smiled and then winced, covering her chest. "You're alive," she whispered.

"So are you," he murmured in disbelief. "But how?"

Lily nodded toward Ashton and Cedric. "I remembered Lord Sheridan's duel last year. I heard about the armor and thought there was a chance this might work. Mind you, I had hoped to shoot him dead, but once we were struggling, I made sure he shot me where I wanted him to."

"It shouldn't have worked," Ashton said. "You should be dead." When everyone glared at him, he shook his head. "I'm sorry, but it is true." He knelt down and examined the dent and the bullet still wedged inside it. "Had it been a glancing blow, then yes. But at such close range and straight on? It should not have worked."

Charles had a revelation. "It was Daniel's pistol," he said, remembering the way Hugo's lieutenant had stabbed him. He wouldn't be surprised to learn that the pistol had not had a full charge of gunpowder. But it didn't matter. None of that mattered right now.

"You'll still be bruised," Lucien warned. "Possibly have a broken rib or two."

"It certainly feels like it." Lily reached for Charles, and he pulled her into his arms. He buried his face in her hair. His body quaked as he started to cry. He couldn't hold it back any longer—there was no stopping this flood. She curled her arms around him, holding him like a child, and he didn't care.

"It's okay, my love," she said.

"I know," said Charles. "I know."

Hugo was dead.

Lily was alive.

It was finally over.

29

Charles never wanted to see another bloody doctor ever again. He lay back in his bed, his torso heavily bandaged. It was just as Daniel had told him—the knife wound wasn't fatal. It had stopped at his hip bone. Painful, but shallow. He'd known exactly where to strike to make a convincing, bleeding wound without killing Charles. The man had spared him and then saved him.

"You're frowning again," Lily whispered.

She lay in bed beside him, her own body bandaged to support her broken ribs. What a pair they were. Broken and bruised and bedridden on their honeymoon. But alive and together. He turned his face toward her, still overcome with love and relief. She leaned into him and pressed her forehead against his, closing her eyes.

"By all rights we should be dead, and yet we are not."

He reached up to hold her face in one hand. "I'm so grateful."

She curled her fingers around his wrist. "As am I."

"But it doesn't make our good fortune any less remarkable—or puzzling."

"Puzzling?"

"We lived essentially because Hugo hated me so much. You would think that more hate would hasten things, yet instead it caused him to draw things out, make it into a game he believed only he could win."

"He never wanted to just kill you," said Lily. "I think, on some level, he had to prove that he was better than you. That his values were superior."

This only confused Charles more. "What do you mean?"

"In the last few years, I learned more about Hugo than I ever wished to. As monstrous as his actions could be, Hugo held duty, loyalty, and service above all else. You and your friends value friendship, honor, and freedom. I think he hated what you stood for as much as he hated you yourself. Yet you won."

Charles thought back to the river, reaching out to Hugo despite all that he had done, and that last moment of revelation upon his brother's face. Realizing, too late, that he'd been wrong all along.

They were quiet a long moment, holding hands, fingers interlaced, before Lily spoke.

"Still happy to be married to me?" Her words were

playful, but there was a hint of fear in her eyes, a fear that he would push her away.

"More than ever, wife," he promised. "More than you will ever know. I waited a lifetime to find you. Did you know that? I've been waiting, your name carved upon my heart."

She flashed a smile free of sorrow, free of hesitation. This was the woman Lily was always meant to be. Unbroken. Unafraid. Courageous.

"I've been talking to Emily about you, you know."

"Should I be worried?" Charles asked, raising an eyebrow.

She trailed her fingertips along his jaw. "She says you're the last one."

"The last what?"

"Wicked rogue." She bit her bottom lip. "And you're all mine, my lord."

"Is that so?" He tilted her chin up and lowered his head to hers.

Their kiss carried the slow heat of a late-spring sun. All the pain he'd borne since his father's death faded in the wake of that all-powerful kiss. In that gentle passion, Charles was reborn. "How did I ever have the good fortune to find you?" he asked Lily.

She gripped his neck, gazing at him as though lost in dreams of her own. "We found each other because it was meant to be. Call it fate."

"Fate," he said solemnly, his heart filled with hope for the future. "And I'll never let you go."

She kissed him again, and he felt the world suddenly open up with a lifetime of possibilities and wonders yet to come.

This was love. This was what the poets wrote about. He may have been the last rogue to fall in love, but he was also the luckiest.

The past could remain in the past. He could mourn those he had lost. He could learn from his mistakes. And he could be thankful for his friends and family, who always stood by him. But he would no longer let the past define him. Everything was going to be different from now on. For once, he could look eagerly toward the future.

He held his wife in his arms and kissed her as though the world was ending, even though he knew it was just beginning.

EPILOGUE

Five months later

"She has the loveliest green eyes, Emily. Just like Godric's," Charles teased as he stared down at Emily and Godric's daughter, Sierra. They were by a small lake in Hyde Park, taking in the glorious spring sunshine.

"She's going to be so spoiled." Emily's complaint was followed by an indulgent chuckle.

"Of course she is," Lily replied. She held a hand over her slightly rounded stomach protectively. She sat on a bench not far from where Charles and Emily stood by the small lake in the middle of the park, and held Kat on her lap. The child wiggled her legs in excitement, more eager to run about then sit still.

When Charles looked her way, his heart turned over in

his chest. He would soon be a father twice over, and he couldn't think of anything more wonderful.

I love you, he mouthed. She mouthed the words back and set Katherine down on the ground, nudging her toward Charles. He knelt and opened his arms.

"Kat, come to Papa." Kat ran over to him. He lifted her into his arms and hoisted her into the air. She squealed and laughed as he held her close.

"Do you want to see the baby?" he asked her.

Katherine nodded, suddenly serious. She leaned over Emily's shoulder to peer down at the baby.

"So pretty," she said to Emily, then tucked her head shyly against Charles's neck. Lily rose from the bench and joined Charles and Emily and the rest of the League by the lake.

Ashton and Rosalind lounged on a blanket, both of them in an animated discussion about banking. *Lord, if that is their idea of pillow talk...* Cedric and Anne stood at the water's edge, talking to a gentleman about horse breeding. Their newborn twins, Sean and Hartley, named after their valiant footman who'd once saved Cedric and Anne's lives, were safely at home in the nursery being looked after so the new mother could have a moment outside in the fresh spring air.

Lucien, Horatia, and little Evan were feeding ducks. Evan, safe in his mother's arms, watched in fascination while the white ducks huddled around their legs, quacking incessantly. Jonathan and Audrey stood beneath the shade of a tree, their faces close as they whispered to each other. Audrey grinned mischievously, and Jonathan had one hand on her hip, his fingers toying with her skirts.

There's trouble afoot there. Charles smiled and looked to Godric, who rolled his eyes and took Sierra from his wife, cooing as he kissed the babe's forehead.

Everything was as it should be. Finally.

He looked around the park and saw Daniel Sheffield and Melanie, Hugo's widow, escorting Hugo's son, Peter, to the lake's edge. Daniel had married Melanie scandalously fast after Hugo's death, but the rumors about their union died quickly as new gossip spread to take its place.

Daniel knelt by the boy's side and pointed at the swans in the center of the lake, smiling as the little boy talked to him.

Charles wondered for a moment whether Peter would follow in Hugo's footsteps. But if there was one lesson he had learned, it was this: blood does not make us who we are. It was up to Daniel and Melanie to see that Peter was raised a better man than his father.

Daniel glanced at him, nodded once, and Charles answered with a tilt of his own head. Their war was over. There were no enemies left, only friends and, perhaps, cautious allies.

Let every rogue have their day, Charles thought, looking over everyone in the park, *and let them be blessed with a life full of friends and love, as I have been.*

He almost laughed, realizing he sounded like he was praying, and added, *Amen*.

"What's so amusing?" Lily asked.

"I was thinking about how my prayers have been answered, and how I was fortunate enough not to be struck by lightning, seeing as how I've been so wicked. I always feared I might be destined for the fires below." He was teasing, of course, but deep down part of him had feared he'd caused too much pain to ever deserve such joy.

Lily gazed at him, her blue eyes filled with an ancient understanding. "A man like you, Charles? There's only one thing you're destined for."

"And what is that?"

She leaned up on her tiptoes and brushed her lips over his and whispered, "Love."

EXCERPT FROM THE *QUIZZING GLASS GAZETTE*, December 18, 1822, the Lady Society column:

Never fret, my dears, Lady Society has returned. Lord Lonsdale has finally gotten leg-shackled, it is true, but there are many other rogues in the world with hearts that need taming. Too many for me to deal with on my own. Remember, ladies, it is up to you to do your part. Perhaps your rogue is still out there somewhere, waiting to be discovered.

. . .

WORRIED THIS IS THE LAST LEAGUE OF ROGUES novel? Don't worry! It isn't! The League continues on, starting with the story *Never Kiss a Scot* starring Brock (Rosalind's Scottish brother) and Joanna (Ashton's sister). Turn the page to see the cover as well as some special Character Art of Charles and Lily. And be sure to keep turning the pages after the art because I'm sharing the first three chapters of *Never Kiss a Scot* with you!

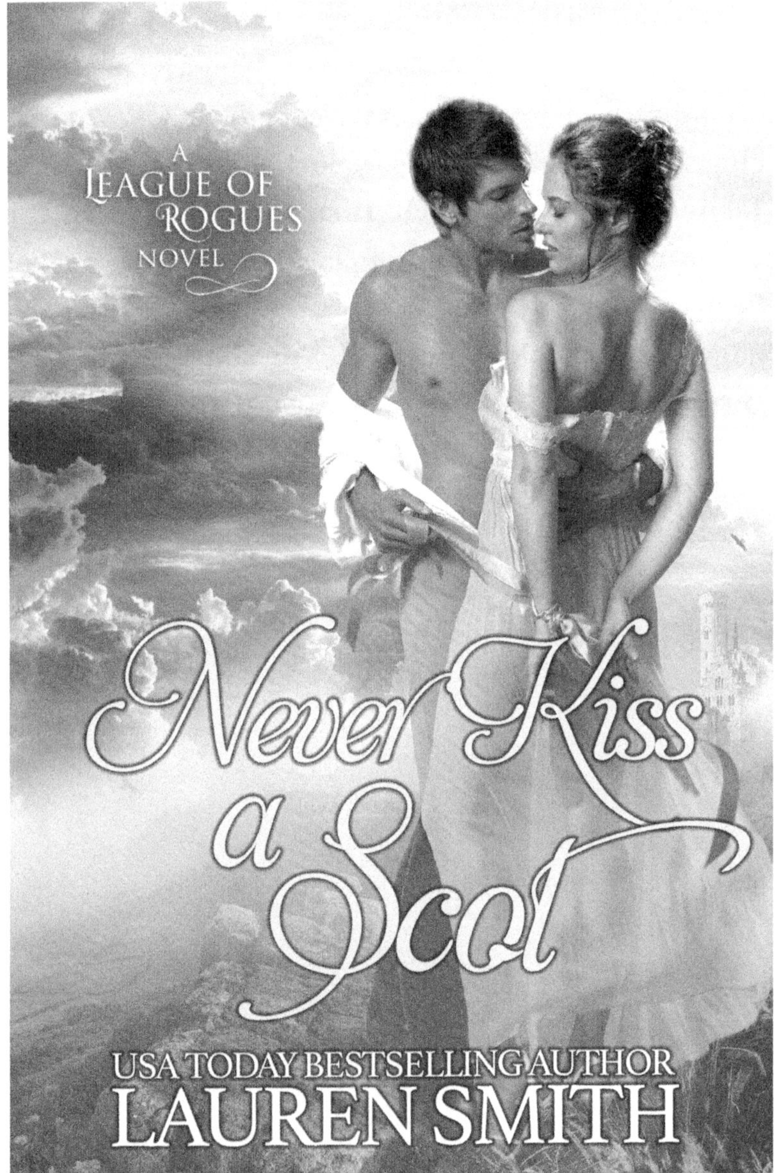

A
LEAGUE OF
ROGUES
NOVEL
Never Kiss a Scot
USA TODAY BESTSELLING AUTHOR
LAUREN SMITH

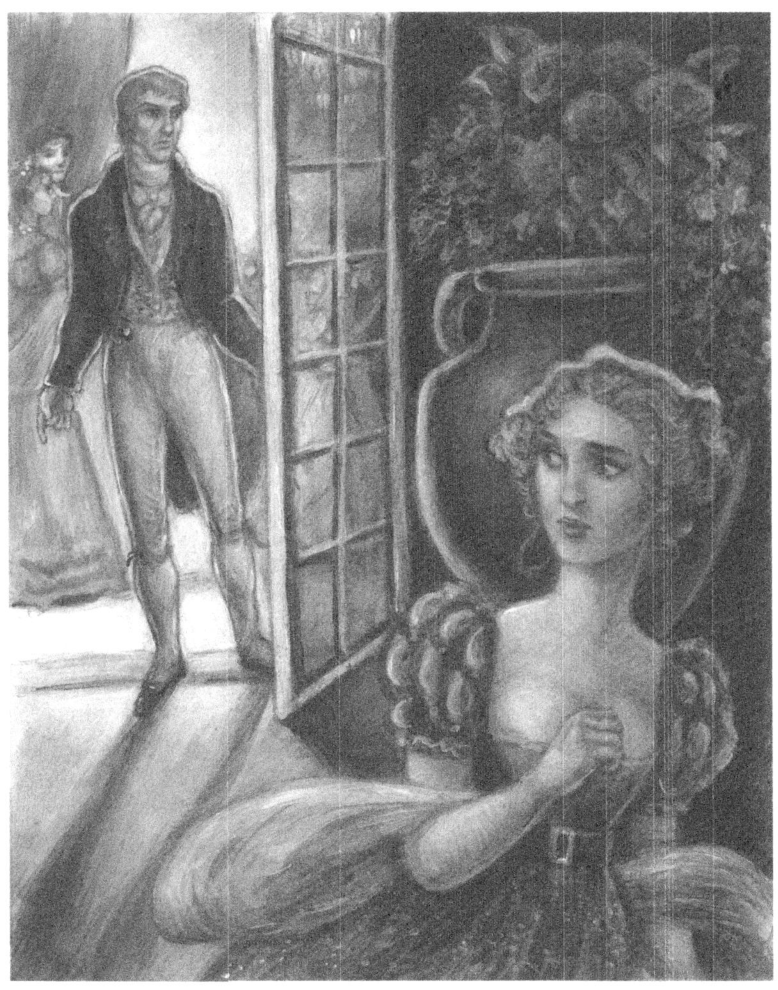

The best way to know when a new book is released is to do one or all of the following:

Join my Newsletter: http://laurensmithbooks.com/free-books-and-newsletter/

Follow Me on BookBub: https://www.bookbub.com/authors/lauren-smith

Join my Facebook VIP Reader Group called Lauren Smith's League: https://www.facebook.com/groups/400377546765661/

Are you read for a taste of Brock and Joanna's love story for the next book in the League of Rogues series?!

NEVER KISS A SCOT

CHAPTER 1

Excerpt from the *Quizzing Glass Gazette*, June 30, 1821, the Lady Society column:

Lady Society has been hearing the most delicious tales. Dare I say rumor has it that Lord Kincade—a Scottish earl—and his two brothers have recently come to Bath and are setting the fans aflutter and the matrons atwitter? I'm tempted to suggest matches for these Scottish rogues, but then again, if I know anything about Scots, they will take what they want, when they want it. Ladies of Bath, if you desire one of them for a husband, I wish you the best of luck!

Hampshire, June, 1821

. . .

The wild Highland lord grasped the woman in his arms, pressing his lips to hers. Wind tore at her skirts as they stood upon the highest point of the heather-covered hill, embracing each other. There was nothing so wondrous as this, nothing so fulfilling as a perfect kiss…

"A perfect kiss?" Joanna Lennox glared at the last page of her Gothic novel, *Lady Jade's Wild Lord*. "There is no such thing as a perfect kiss." A perfect kiss was a myth. She was sure there wasn't, because if there were, she would have been kissed by now and known that, wouldn't she? Yet here she was at twenty years old, unkissed, uncourted, and utterly *alone*.

She stared into the depths of the fireplace in her library, her heart empty. After three arduous seasons in London, she was a failure as far as the standards of the marriage mart were concerned. The rumor mill had begun to spin tales of why she was still single. London society loved to mock a woman who could not catch a man, especially a woman with a large dowry. Desperate men would overlook any number of problems with a woman so long as her dowry was bountiful.

So what is it that I lack that sends even fortune hunters running to the hills?

It wasn't that she hoped to be married for the sake of marriage itself, or to stop those silly peahens from gossiping. She was an independent, intelligent, opinionated woman. Yet something was missing within her, some grand secret that only someone in love was privy to. At least, if the books she had read were any indication. She wanted to love and be loved by a man, but she knew just how rare love matches were.

She tried to focus on the book in her lap as she pulled her tartan shawl tight around her shoulders. The library in her old country home was a little chilly, even with the fire lit. She usually could lose herself in a book, but not tonight. Her older brother, Ashton, had fallen ill with the grippe, and his fiancée, Rosalind, was tending to him. But the house was quiet, an awful quiet that lent itself to restless nights and melancholy thoughts.

Joanna had witnessed Ashton banish the depths of his coldness and shed the burdens of the past so that he might embrace a warm future with his bride-to-be. It was clear that her brother loved Rosalind dearly, even if he was too damn stubborn to admit it.

Will someone ever love me like that? She blew out a frustrated breath. It wasn't as though she hadn't *tried* to find the perfect gentleman. She'd been charming, polite, and endearing. Men loved to engage her in conversation, yet no man came to call on her, and none sent flowers. There was not one flicker of hope that she was to be courted.

The worries plagued her more and more, leaving her sleepless at night and irritable during the day. But she wasn't the sort of woman to sit and mope, which was why she found her current mood most irritating. Joanna knew she ought to be doing more to distract herself from these doldrums.

Perhaps the Society of Rebellious Ladies would appreciate another member.

Joanna giggled at the thought and turned to the last page in her book. That would at least keep her distracted from her unsuccessful husband hunt. The society was a secretive and increasingly sought-after group for young ladies of the *ton*, and yet joining it was also considered scandalous—which was part of its appeal to those who were members. Rumors suggested that the Society was always in the midst of schemes, some of which even graced the pages of the *Quizzing Glass Gazette*, and they seemed quite happy to be off on adventures of their own without men shadowing them. Their husbands hadn't the faintest idea that the balls, teas, and dinners were often a ruse for the Society's activities.

Since Joanna had no man who was eager to shadow her, she would be a perfect candidate to join the Society. They had been known to accept single ladies, married women, and even declared spinsters among their ranks. Each member of the Society had to possess the characteristics of strength of will and purpose, and they understood that loyalty to the other members was paramount.

A sudden creak of the wood floor startled her. No one should be about at this hour, yet there were any number of reasonable situations in which someone might be. She was still up, after all. Slowly, she peered around the edge of her chair.

A tall, broad-shouldered man in black trousers and a long black shirt stood in the doorway, staring at her. His eyes were a mercurial grayish-blue, and intensely focused on her. For a moment, Joanna was arrested by the sight of his chiseled jaw and aquiline nose, his dark hair a tad too long to be considered respectable.

A splash of clarity hit her. A strange man had just walked into the library close to midnight—and she was there alone. She kept calm. If she needed help, she could cry out. A servant would hear her, surely.

"Who are you?" she asked. He wasn't one of her brother's friends. Ashton belonged to an infamous band of English peers known in some circles as the League of Rogues. She knew nearly all of his friends, as well as the members of the League, and this man was neither. So who was he?

"It doesn't matter who I am. Who are *you*?" His voice was low, silky, yet the brogue was thick enough that she knew he had to be Scottish. Was he perhaps tied to Ashton's fiancée? She was Scottish.

"I'm Joanna Lennox." She closed her book and set it aside with her blue tartan shawl on the chair as she stood.

"I know that clan," the man said, noticing the tartan. "MacLeod. Are you Scottish?"

"What? Oh no, my family has relatives who are, but not

me." She thought of how very *not* Scottish she was, and the idea amused her. She had to admit she'd often dreamt of living in the Highlands, not caring a whit what London society or its damned rules thought about her. She put those thoughts aside to focus on the stranger in black. She came closer, wanting to see him better. Logically, she knew she ought to be shouting for help, but she didn't feel as though she was in any danger. "You didn't answer me. Who are you?"

The man glanced about, clearly struggling to think of an answer.

"I..." He hesitated, and then his eyes narrowed. "Is Lady Melbourne here?"

"Why yes, she's—wait a moment." Joanna knew then why she was so fascinated by him. There was something acutely familiar about his eyes, that same serious shade of grayishblue. And the way he frowned was so like Rosalind, who was quite a serious woman.

"Are you one of her brothers? Did you come down for the wedding?" That had to be it. In all the excitement of her brother's unexpected engagement and then his sudden illness, they must have forgotten to tell her that Rosalind's three brothers had been invited from Scotland for the wedding.

"Aye. I received a letter from my sister and came down to attend the wedding. I only just arrived and didn't wish to disturb the household." He widened his stance, the move strangely aggressive. Joanna had the sudden concern that he might try to grab her, but that was silly.

He was Rosalind's brother, not some villain, even if he was dressed like a highwayman. Perhaps he'd only just arrived and wasn't prepared to meet her, which would explain his interesting choice of clothing. He would be exhausted from travel and need time to rest, and here she was judging him as though he was a man sent to cause trouble.

"Oh dear, you must be tired after such a long ride. Have the servants taken your things to your chambers?"

"Thank you, my lady, I've already been seen to. I was just looking for a room to warm up in a bit before going to bed." His gaze searched hers, and she had a suspicion he was expecting her to challenge him, but she had no reason to. He was Rosalind's brother and quite welcome here.

"Well then, come sit by this fire. I just finished my novel and was planning to retire soon. I'd be happy to lend it to you—if you enjoy novels, that is." She returned to her chair and picked up her book, then came back and placed it in his hands. "It's one of my favorites."

He stared at the title. "*Lady Jade's Wild Lord*? Thank you."

It was an L. R. Gloucester novel, a torrid Gothic novel, and he was staring at it with a reverent expression that tugged at her heart. Like a man who hadn't held a book in his hands in years.

"I'm afraid I'm still at a loss as to your name. Which one of Rosalind's brothers are you?"

His storm cloud colored eyes darted around the room

before they came back to her. "How do you know about us?"

"Oh, she told me all about the three of you. Let me guess..." She tapped her chin, grinning. "Are you Aiden, Brodie, or Brock? I shall guess...Aiden."

He snorted. "Like hell. Do I look like some young pup?"

He certainly didn't. He looked more like a Scottish Highlander out of her girlish fantasies.

"Brock then," she said. "You look like a Brock. It's a very old name, Brock. I like learning about names and their meanings. Did you know Brock means badger?" She stared at his lips, surprised at how full they looked. Then she wanted to kick herself. She should not be dreaming about this man's lips. He was a guest, and she needed to act like a proper lady, not some wanton creature obsessed with someone's mouth.

"Badger?" He tilted his head. "I didn't know that." Those full lips curved into a smile, and she couldn't help but grin back. Her heart raced wildly as she met his eyes. His devil-may-care grin hit her so hard that she had trouble standing. Brock set the book down and suddenly caught her by the waist, pulling her flush against his body.

"It's a custom from my village to offer a kiss to those whose families are about to be joined."

A kiss? Excitement shot through her like quicksilver. Perhaps she would finally get to know whether her Gothic novels were telling the truth about kisses.

"Really? I've read about parts of Scotland, but I've never—"

His arm around her waist tightened, and she pressed against his body, feeling the hard muscles of his tall frame against her soft curves.

"Shush, lass, and let me keep with tradition," he whispered, then bent his head and slanted his mouth over hers.

His taste exploded upon her tongue, seducing her with dark excitement. A hint of brandy was still on his lips, and she relished it. One of his hands dropped from her waist to cup her bottom. She squeaked in surprise against him and then moaned as he fisted his other hand in her hair, pulling her head back so he could deepen the kiss. Her knees buckled treacherously, and she tried to think, but it was hard to be rational when her stomach was filled with such a wonderful swooping feeling. She was kissing Rosalind's brother...

Joanna pulled herself away enough to separate their lips. She was amazed at the riotous sensations she was experiencing from just a single kiss. Maybe kisses really could be perfect. How could she feel something invisible yet so tangible when she didn't even know this man? It didn't make sense, and she liked things to make sense.

Get control, Joanna—you don't swoon at kisses. Kisses can't be nearly as good as they are described on paper.

Yet Brock's kiss had been exactly that—devastatingly perfect. Of course, she had no way of knowing if all kisses were like that or just his, given that this was her first.

"This is traditional where you come from?" If all the ladies in Scotland were kissed like this upon meeting a man...*Lord*...

His lips twitched. "Old as the bones in the hills."

She kept her palms pressed on his chest, knowing she ought to push away, to behave like the English lady she had been raised to be. But part of her, a much stronger part, wanted to toss the rules of good behavior aside and do anything for just one more kiss. She looked up, gazing into his grayish-blue eyes.

"And I suppose it would be rude of me to break with tradition."

His now arrogant smile would've made her slap him if she wasn't so desperate to lose herself in his kiss again.

"Incredibly rude. You'd be insulting my entire clan."

Her pulse fluttered, and she sucked in her lower lip briefly as she anticipated another kiss. "Well, Mother did raise me to respect other cultures." She slid her palms up his chest and curled her fingers into his black shirt as their mouths met and that addictive fire burned through her all over again. She clung to Brock, exploring his mouth with hers, their tongues touching gently before the kiss became more insistent.

His hands moved back to her waist, tugging at the blue sash above her hips as his other hand pulled pins loose from her hair until he was able to slide her hair ribbon free. Then he was pulling her wrists together, winding the sash around them. Her body melted at the sudden domination and the thrill of him binding her, but she tried to react rationally.

"What are you doing?" she asked in a breathless mixture of anger, fear, and arousal. "This can't be traditional." She tugged on her now bound wrists, staring at him, hoping he would explain himself.

"I'm sorry about this, lass, but I can't have you calling for Lennox."

Lennox? He had to mean her brother, but why was he restraining her?

"Call for—" She was silenced as he slid her hair ribbon between her parted lips and tied it around her head, gagging her. With gentle hands, he guided her to the chair by the fire and pushed her into it. She fell back with a muffled cry, not one of pain but indignation. How *dare* he truss her up and—

"Move from here in the next few minutes and I fear you will regret it," Brock warned.

She tried to curse him, but the gag muffled the noise. He gazed down at her a moment longer, a sharp flash of regret in those gray eyes that made her still. He didn't want to leave her tied up. This wasn't part of some game of seduction, so why had he? More importantly, what was the thing he was about to do that he clearly did not want her to see? A cold wave of dread swept through her, but she dared not move, not until she saw him vanish through the library door and into the corridor outside.

Joanna waited only a moment before she leapt up from

the chair and rushed to the door. She pulled at the handle and stumbled into the hallway, tripping over a wrinkle in the carpet and twisting her ankle. She yelped as she took a step on the injured ankle.

At the sound of footsteps, she glanced up, expecting to see Brock, but instead it was Charles Humphrey, or as London knew him, the Earl of Lonsdale. Charles was a member of the League of Rogues and one of her brother's closest friends.

He jerked to a halt when he saw her hands were bound and her mouth gagged. "Joanna? What the devil?" He tugged the ribbon free from her lips and unbound her wrists. "What happened?"

"There's a man here...one of Rosalind's brothers..." She tried to explain, but she honestly had no idea what was really going on.

"You mean a Scotsman is in this house?" Charles snapped.

"Yes, he said he was invited to the wedding, but then he tied me up and—"

"He's not invited. The bloody bastard shouldn't even be here. We must tell Ashton at once."

"What? Why?"

"Because Rosalind's brothers are damned dangerous. They've come to take Rosalind back to her father in Scotland. He's a rotten excuse for a human being." Charles looked her over. "The man didn't touch you, did he? I mean, aside from binding you?"

Joanna swallowed hard and shook her head. She wasn't about to admit that she'd been passionately kissing a dangerous Scotsman.

"Thank God. Your brother would never let one of those brutes hurt you," Charles muttered as he helped her down the hallway. She clutched the silk sash that had been around her wrists as they strode down the hall, calling for her brother.

"What sort of a man is her father?"

"The sort who beats his own defenseless daughter."

"Did her brothers hurt Rosalind? Or was it just her father?"

"Just her father, as far as I understand. But I've tussled with them once before. One of the bastards broke a chair over my back."

"My God! What was that all about?"

Charles hesitated in answering, but not for long. "As you might expect with me. A woman. Take my word on this—you don't ever want to be alone with any of them. They'd seduce you before you had a chance to think."

Joanna swallowed the sudden lump in her throat. Brock was dangerous? She shouldn't have been surprised. Any man who could kiss like that had to be. It was just her luck that she found a man who made her feel alive, and he was someone she should never marry.

CHAPTER 2

Bath, one month later

"She'll never marry, not that one, unless she sets her sights low, and maybe not even then." A society mama *tsked* a little too loudly as Joanna passed by her in the assembly room.

"Quite right," another woman whispered back. "No one ever asks her to dance. Must be something wrong with her." The words cut deep because Joanna knew the woman was talking about her, and she knew the woman was right.

There was only one man in England who seemed to be interested in her at all—a rather boring but decently attractive man named Edmund Lindsey. He was only a gentleman, no title but plenty of fortune. Still, Joanna was hesitant to consider him. She felt no passion for him, no great fire in her belly or flutter in her chest. She didn't want to marry Edmund simply because he was her *only* choice, but what else could she do?

The one man she had wanted to marry had given her a wonderful, perfect kiss and then vanished into the night like the rogue he was. It was the sort of thing that ruined a woman for all other men because no man would ever compare to Brock Kincade. And she'd been a fool to think he might come back for her after the disagreement between Brock and her brother had been settled but he hadn't.

Because there's something wrong with you... The thought slithered from her brain deep into her heart.

She tried to move through the crush of people near the dance floor, not that it mattered. Her card had the next three dances empty, and what few dances she did have on her card were with married men who were older and business acquaintances of her brother's. She shouldn't have come tonight, but Ashton and his fiancée, Rosalind, had wanted to spend some time enjoying Bath before the wedding.

Joanna's mother had all but given up on her finding a man to seriously court her, and she'd essentially left her alone. That meant Joanna had avoided most social engagements and instead chose to tuck herself away in the circulation room of Meyler's library—mostly to avoid Edmund. He'd learned she'd come back and was doing his best to run into her in every tea shop, every assembly room, and even on the street while she tried to ride. It was frustrating. All she wanted was to be left alone to consider her options.

It hadn't escaped her notice that she was not the only young woman using the hidden magic of books to escape the social scenes of the city. Only yesterday, she'd run into a friend from London, Lydia Hunt, at Meyler's. They had commiserated over their shared matchmaking woes. Lydia's younger sister, Portia, was a true beauty and quite full of trouble, which meant Lydia spent much of her time declining invitations from young men who were interested in her because her little sister would try to steal them away. Given that Lydia's father openly supported Portia's desire to marry before Lydia, Lydia had given up hope of a match because any man she desired would be turned toward Portia instead.

Joanna didn't have the excuse of a scheming younger sister, however. She simply wasn't *wanted* by any man except Edmund.

A crowd of young men stood around the refreshment table drinking ratafia and laughing raucously, in spite of the group of disapproving mamas who watched from a distance. One of the men glanced her way and offered a smile, but he did nothing more to encourage her. She'd never felt more invisible in her life.

All she wanted was to be loved, to share the passions of life with a man, yet none would consider her. She'd wondered from the moment her first season had passed whether the debts and scandals her father had created before his death had left her name blackened somehow. Was it possible that the past was ruining her future? What other reason could there be for men to avoid her like this?

Ashton had restored their family fortune, it was true, but as the daughter of a baron and now sister to one, she was, to be frank, at the bottom of the ladder when it came to the peerage. Most men wished to marry up, not simply acquire fortunes. And Ashton wouldn't allow the more attractive fortune hunters anywhere near her—not that many had tried. Most men seemed content enough to smile and talk with her, dance once or twice, but never anything more. Even those who showed initial interest one evening would ignore her the next as if they'd never met her.

All that remained was Edmund Lindsey, and her brother had laughed in his face when he'd expressed his interest in Joanna. Her brother's open dislike of Edmund hadn't made sense, but when she'd questioned him about it, Ashton had simply told her not to bother with Lindsey, that there would be a good man out there for her to marry someday. Yet despite her brother's callous and dismissive treatment, Edmund remained persistent.

Joanna hastily made her way to the corridor outside the assembly hall, resting a gloved hand against the wall to catch her breath. So far, she'd successfully avoided Edmund. He was here somewhere, but Bath was flooded with people this time of year, and there were hundreds in attendance tonight. It was easy to get lost in the crowd when one wanted to. When she heard voices, she ducked around the corner into a small corridor off the main rooms, afraid Edmund had found her. But it was only a pair of ladies, and their voices echoed down the hall, clearly audible to her.

"Have you seen *them*?" one of them whispered.

"Them?"

"The Kincades—those Scotsmen. The brothers of Lady Melbourne. She's marrying Lord Lennox in two days, you know. It's all very scandalous..."

Joanna sucked in a breath and waited, listening hard. Could it be...?

"Why is that so scandalous?" the other woman asked.

"Lord Lennox is one of those *rogues*, my dear, you know the *League*. But if you ask me, it's the Kincade men who are far more wicked."

"Yes...wicked *how*?" The second woman was clearly frustrated by her friend's failure to provide details.

Joanna could tell them just how wicked one of the Kincade brothers was.

He had kissed her and then ridden off into the night with his brothers and sister. Ashton had traveled all the way to Scotland to convince Rosalind he loved her. When that was resolved, Brock and his brothers had stayed in Scotland while Rosalind returned to England. They had been invited to the wedding, which was only a few days away. Had they accepted the invitation? No one had mentioned it to her if they had, of course. No one seemed to notice her at all these days. Her mother was busy fussing over Ashton and his future bride, and her other brother, Rafe, had left for London without so much as a word except a single promise that he would return for Ashton's wedding.

The ache only grew deeper in her heart. *I am alone*.

"Well, if you *must* know..." The first woman's voice then lowered to the point where Joanna could no longer hear. Cursing silently, she peered around the edge of the hall to get a better look at them. The two ladies wore turbans festooned with ostrich feathers, and as their heads bent to gossip, the feathers wavered and danced in the air. It would have been comical enough to make Joanna laugh, but she truly desired to hear what they were saying.

"No. You believe it's true? That he really...?" Again, the conversation dissolved into whispers. "And they are here tonight?" the second woman suddenly blurted out.

"Yes! In the assembly rooms. Not dancing, of course, but prowling about. All three of them are like wolves. I won't let my daughter near them."

"I should think not," her friend agreed. "Are they wife hunting?"

"Wife hunting? Those scoundrels? I doubt it. They're more likely skirt chasing. They are trouble, mark my words."

"Trouble indeed," Joanna agreed in a mutter. After Brock Kincade had stolen a kiss, she had been unable to think of any other man, let alone someone as dull as Edmund Lindsey.

Damned Scot! The despair within her was transformed into anger—anger at Brock. They hadn't seen each other since that night, and it was about time she changed that. She had quite a lot she wished to say to that wretched man. One could not go around kissing ladies in libraries at midnight and not expect them to be affected. Not a word or an apology given after—it was unconscionable.

Joanna squared her shoulders and headed back to the assembly room, determined to find Brock and give him a good telling off. That at least would unburden herself of these feelings building up inside her. Then she would only have to put up with him for a few days during the wedding festivities, and she would be free of him. She would likely never see him again, which was just fine by her.

The assembly hall was still crowded; the couples in the center were just finishing a dance. She searched the faces around her, but there were at least a hundred guests in the dance hall. She spotted her mother and Rosalind talking with friends. Ashton and Charles stood in conversation near the refreshment table. Joanna bit her lip. She felt like she belonged with neither group, and the thought only made her mood bleaker.

And then she spotted them. A trio of tall dark-haired men wearing simple buckskin breeches and waistcoats lounged against a pillar by the orchestra. Brock, Brodie, and Aiden Kincade. Infamous devils the lot of them, if the gossip she'd heard about them was correct.

She had not yet had the pleasure of meeting Brodie and Aiden, but there was no mistaking the three as brothers. All had dark hair and stormy eyes, with strong jaws seemingly carved of marble. They were handsome men who would tempt any woman to be reckless with her virtue.

I was certainly tempted. She thought this with a scowl as she stared at the trio.

Several couples moved out of Joanna's way as she strode toward the Scotsmen. But before she was halfway, she was waylaid by a short masculine form who stepped directly into her path.

"My dear Miss Lennox! What a pleasure it is to see you here tonight!" Edmund Lindsey exclaimed.

God's teeth! Joanna forced a smile on her face as she turned her attention to Edmund. He bowed his head to her, and she couldn't help but note his unfashionable hairstyle, a decade out of date, and the rather foppish style to his clothes. While his face and features were genuinely considered fine and attractive, it did nothing for his personality. His cravat was far too elaborately folded and was wilting in the heat of the room like a hothouse flower losing its bloom. He struck her as a rather pathetic creature, and Joanna suffered a twinge of guilt that she could not find it in her heart to like him.

"Mr. Lindsey," she said on a sigh. "How are you?"

"I am well, now that I've had the good fortune to run into you." He preened beneath her gaze, and she resisted the urge to roll her eyes. His open flattery, once tolerable, had become quite irritating. "I don't suppose you have any dances open?"

"Why...no. I'm so sorry." It was a lie, but she was not about to dance with him, even though he seemed to be the only man in England who wanted her. Yes, it was completely rude to lie about one's dances like that. Everyone knew a young lady ought to accept any dance offered, no matter who the man was and whether or not she liked him, but she couldn't bring herself to accept.

"Then perhaps I could fetch you a glass of ratafia?"

"Er, yes, I suppose that would be all right." It would at least give her a few minutes alone, and she could plan her escape from the hall. It would be easy enough to flag down a hackney if she could make it outside without Edmund following.

"Be right back, my dear!" Edmund bustled off, nudging his way through the crowds. Joanna sighed in relief before she located Brock once again and headed toward him and his brothers.

Brock seemed to notice her when she was within a few feet of him because he pushed off the pillar and stood straight as she came up to him. He did not bow, nor did he incline his head or provide anything other than a civil greeting. Her heart pounded against her ribs as she glared at him. By God, she was going to get an answer from him, scandal be damned.

What was the worst that could happen? Yet another empty dance card? No bouquets of flowers? No eager gentlemen upon her doorstep? She was used to such disappointments already, except for that damned Edmund. But that was a whole different problem to deal with.

He was wealthy and quite connected in society, but those qualities held little interest for her. Plenty of other women had made it quite clear they would marry him, so why couldn't he turn his affections toward one of them? There was just something about Edmund—the way he looked at her when he thought she wasn't watching—that unsettled her.

An idea occurred to her. Perhaps she could create a scandal to scare him off? By this point, it seemed to be her only option.

Better to be alone than Edmund's bride. The thought threatened to drown her with its bleak outlook. She understood that many women married for security, but she could not. The idea of marrying a man, sharing his bed, sharing in his life when she did not feel a passion for him... Her stomach rolled again, but she kept her composure.

"So you've returned?" she asked, not caring that people were already starting to turn and look her way.

"Aye, I have," Brock answered in that soft, dark voice that made her insides melt. It was a lover's voice—not that she was supposed to know such things.

"And you did not think that perhaps you ought to pay a call to my brother...or *me?*" she added, trying to hint at what he had done to her without letting her hurt and anger flare too openly. He had *kissed* her, for heaven's sake. The least he could have done was to come back to make things right between him and Ashton and...*kiss me again*.

"We came down for the wedding. And I did pay a call to your brother when we first arrived two days ago."

"You've been here *two days?*" She hated how shrill her voice sounded.

"I would have come sooner, but I canna leave my lands alone for long. There's much that needs looking after."

He didn't want her, then. Nothing about their encounter seemed to have remained in his memory. The kiss had been nothing more to him than a means to silence her so he could rescue his sister. She staggered back a step, the fresh pain from this blow being all too unexpected. Brock stepped close, catching her hand and lifting her dance card out where he could see it and the bare spaces where men's names ought to have been.

"Empty? Did you arrive late?" His eyes searched hers for answers.

She swallowed a harsh laugh. "It's *always* empty. I'm not worth a dance."

A spark of fire lit his eyes. "Not worth a dance?" The edge in his tone was unnerving, as if the words she had spoken offended him. Then he gripped her hand and dragged her out into the middle of the couples lining up for a dance. Too stunned to refuse, she got in line with the other ladies, still staring at him as he shoved his way between two gentlemen to pair with her. The music began, and they started to follow the steps, twirling, clapping, marching, but all of her focus had fallen on him and the way he never took his eyes off her. He was a wonderful dancer, which surprised her.

In the last month, she'd conjured up all sorts of silly dreams about him and what he was like. A dashing Scottish warrior, a brute, even a highwayman, but never a fine dancer. Rosalind had spoken a little to Joanna about her past and the cruel world her father had created for her and her brothers. Joanna knew that Brock had often taken beatings meant for his younger sister to protect her. In a grim world like that, how could he have learned to dance like such a gentleman? It was one mystery that she would likely never have answers to.

The dance ended, and the couples around them began to pair with new partners, but Brock stayed close to her.

"Another?" he asked.

"But... We shouldn't. People will talk..."

"Talk doesn't bother me." And it apparently didn't. His eyes never left her face, even though quite a few people now stared at them in wide-eyed shock. It was completely forbidden to dance with any man more than once. Yet she didn't find it in herself to care in that moment what rules she was ready to break for this man. His intensity and the way he didn't seem to care about anything but her made her feel wild and reckless, like when she'd been a child and had toured part of the countryside near Cornwall. She'd stood on the edge of the cliffs, feeling the wind buffet her body hard enough that she'd almost fallen to her death. The spark of fear and excitement of that moment and this were almost the same. She didn't want to stop feeling so...*alive*.

"Very well." She let him dance with her again and again, and then, when that dance was done, *again*.

By the fifth dance her feet were aching, but Joanna couldn't have cared less. Dancing with Brock had erased her black mood. She'd been smiling, laughing, not caring in the least about the attention focused upon her as each dance progressed. Only when the music stopped did she finally feel the hundreds of eyes upon her and the whispers spreading like wildfire in the crowd.

"No wonder she hasn't found a match. *Five* dances..."

"Must be his mistress..."

"Too improper, dancing with that Scotsman..."

"Her mother will be ashamed..."

Everywhere Joanna looked there was judgment and callous disregard for her feelings. What had she been thinking? Courting scandal by dancing with him? Even if this scared off Edmund Lindsey, was it truly worth it? What of the gossip that would hound her in hushed whispers wherever she went? A man like Brock wouldn't marry her. She was simply a toy for a reckless Highland lord to play with when it suited him. Just kisses in libraries at midnight and dances to stir the scandal sheets.

"Lass..." Brock whispered, holding out his hand.

She stared at him, and before she could think twice, she'd wound back one hand and slapped him hard across the face. The assembly hall fell into a silence punctuated by the violins coming to a halt when the players dragged their bows discordantly over the strings. Everyone, it seemed, was gaping at her. Brock didn't move, didn't so much as flinch, even though a soft red shade was forming on his cheek.

Oh Lord, why in heavens did I do that?

The thought made her hysterical enough that she was torn between laughing and crying. She'd just slapped Brock in front of half the *ton*. If she wasn't going to be at the top of the scandal sheets for dancing too long with him, she'd surely end up there now for striking him in public.

Joanna turned and fled. She was going to be the laughingstock of all England.

She flew down the steps to the front of the assembly hall and onto the street, clutching her reticule as she prayed her family wouldn't notice her absence. But how could they not? Everyone had been staring at her by the end of the fifth dance, and then she'd gone and slapped Brock in front of them all.

She waved at a hackney driver a dozen feet away. He

picked up his whip and gave a gentle flick to his horses and headed toward her. A breath of relief escaped her.

I can go home and forget about tonight...I hope...

Just then, someone grabbed her from behind, a hand covering her mouth. She yelped as she was raised up and shoved into the coach she had summoned.

"Oi! What are you doin'?" the driver shouted.

"Just take us to Finchley Street! I'll pay double the regular fare," the man who held her said. Joanna stilled for a brief instant as she realized that the man who'd grabbed her was Brock.

"How *dare* you?" She tried to escape, but Brock blocked her path as he climbed inside with her.

"Hold that temper, lass. I'm not going to harm you, which is more than you did for me back there," Brock snapped. His hands captured hers, pinning them to either side of her head against the cushions behind her on the seat.

"Let me go, Lord Kincade," she demanded. His handsome face was a mask of moonlight and shadows in the dim coach interior as his lips curved into a grin.

"Not just yet. You and I need to talk." The smile faded, and he looked deadly serious now. If he hadn't been holding her wrists, she would have slapped him again.

"*Talk?* You should have talked to me a month ago. But no, you left me tied up in a library and kidnapped my brother's fiancée!"

"I didna kidnap her. I was *rescuing* her," he corrected.

"Well, you might have been rescuing her, but you *left* me," she said with a growl. "You cannot go around kissing ladies like that with no consideration for their feelings. And then you convinced me to dance and you danced so wonderfully that I forgot to stop and now *everyone* is talking because you're a known skirt chaser and a rogue, and then I slapped you and it will be all over the papers tomorrow. I'm ruined, and it is entirely your fault..." She struggled to get free, fury raging through her, but she couldn't get him to let go.

"Lassie, you talk too much." That was the only warning she had before his mouth slanted over hers and the world exploded around her in delicious sinful fire for the second time in her life.

CHAPTER 3

Brock smiled against Joanna's lips as she melted against him. She was just as wonderful as he remembered. He kept her wrists pinned against the back of the coach for a moment longer until he felt her surrender to his kiss. When he released her, she curled her arms around his neck. Every time his mouth covered hers, he felt unable to get enough of her natural sweetness or the dreamy intimacy that settled around them as they embraced. His stomach flipped with boyish excitement as he pressed against her. He had his lovely English lass back in his arms where she belonged.

In the month since he'd first met her and had to abandon her to rescue his sister, he had been reliving that heated encounter in the library of Joanna's country home. He had vowed to come back for her to make her his.

The time had come at last.

He longed for a bride, one who could share his bed, make him laugh and smile with her lively talk and brilliant mind, and whose dowry would help repair his crumbling castle. Joanna was that woman. But there was a problem—her brother would kill him if he asked for her hand in marriage. They were on civil terms after the matter with Rosalind, but they could not be considered friends.

So how then to get his beautiful blonde siren away from her protective guard dog of a brother and his damned band of rogues?

An elopement, perhaps? Yes, that would do nicely. A race to Scotland. He knew the roads better than any Englishman and could travel faster, even with Joanna in tow, assuming he could convince her to marry him.

"Brock," Joanna whispered against his mouth between kisses. "You are...the most wicked man I've ever met." Her breathless accusation held no real venom, only sensual delight and surprise.

"I've not even started to kiss you properly," he said with a chuckle, brushing the backs of his fingers over her cheek.

She gazed up at him. "You haven't?" Those blue eyes, deep and mysterious as the loch by his castle back home, were so damned lovely and wide-eyed with innocence.

A bone-deep ache grew inside him whenever he looked at her. This wasn't simple lust; she filled him with a longing for things he'd dared not to dream of since he was a lad. She was a ray of sunlight, a hearty laugh, a wink and a smile all rolled together. She was everything good and pure in life, and he *wanted* her—wanted her more than he'd ever wanted anything before.

She must be mine, at any cost. It was a greedy thought, he knew, to think he could possess her when he didn't deserve such a beacon of light in his life, and once she realized she was kissing a damned devil she would hate him. Yet he couldn't bear to face that truth just yet.

His father's cruelty had destroyed so much of him that even his heart was made of stone.

"When I kiss you properly, lass, you will know." He nuzzled her throat before he pressed a slow, languid kiss above her collarbone. She sucked in a breath, struggling against his hold, but it wasn't an attempt to get free—it was an attempt to get closer.

"Where are we going?" she asked between gasps as he moved his lips back up to her throat.

"To my home, at least for now. My brothers and I are sharing a residence on Finchley Street for the duration of the festivities."

"Your...home?" Some of the drowsy lust in her voice faded. "No, we mustn't..."

This time when she fought his hold, he allowed her to pull herself free. She shrank away from him on their shared seat. "You must take me home at once."

"Joanna," he whispered. "Surely you know why I have come."

"For Rosalind's wedding," she said coldly.

"That is only one reason. The other is *you*." He reached for her, but she slapped his hand away.

"You left me alone for a month! You kissed me and left me without a word! And now you want me to believe that you're here for me? I doubt you thought of me at all before you saw me at the assembly."

The hurt in her eyes wounded him, but there was no way to make her understand. The night they had met had been dangerous, and he couldn't have done anything more than kiss her. He could not have made it back to Scotland with both Joanna and his sister. And he could not have written to her or sent word, because her brother no doubt had been watching her ever since that night.

Brock had convinced himself—or tried to—that leaving her alone was better, that she belonged with a man who could love her. But he had been a damned fool to think that he could stay away from her, though, not once he saw her again.

"Marry me," he blurted out.

Her eyes widened. "What?"

"Let me take you to Scotland, make you a proper bride."

She gazed at him, mute, trying to process his words. "But..." He could see the indecision in her eyes.

"We still have two days before the wedding. You dinna have to decide now." He opened the coach window and gave the driver her brother's address. Once the coach turned around, he sat back on the seat across from her and tried to remind himself that she needed time. Taking her into his arms for another kiss wouldn't necessarily change her mind. Women needed more than passion in their lives; they needed stability, a common ground. He could offer none of that. His past had been vastly different and far harsher than hers. But it didn't stop him from wanting her enough that it made him ache inside to think of letting her go.

When he and his brothers had arrived for the wedding, he'd hoped to see her sooner, but her damned brother had kept her safely away each time he'd tried to visit, though always making it seem coincidental. Even with their differences settled there was a cat-and-mouse game of civility between them. It had only been luck that he'd seen Ashton disappearing out of the assembly hall when Joanna had approached him to dance; otherwise, he never would have had the chance to talk to her, let alone share five dances with her. He'd expected her brother to storm in at any moment and drag her away, but he hadn't. The overprotective fool had slipped up in Brock's favor, but Brock wasn't stupid enough to believe that Ashton wouldn't figure out where his sister had gone and who had chased after her.

He knows I want her, and he's protecting her, just as I tried to protect my sister from him. Brock was never one to enjoy situations of irony, and this one made him want to punch a stone wall.

"Why do you want to marry me?" she asked after a long silence.

"Why?" he echoed, confused.

"Yes. Why? Do you love me?"

He stumbled in his response. "Well... I mean..."

"Right, you don't, because we don't even *know* each other. Marriage should be based on love, not lust."

He laughed. "Love? Lass, you are far too innocent. I've met only a few people who ever married for love, and those marriages didn't end well." His parents had married for love, but his father's greed for power had been stronger than his love, and it had broken his mother's heart. He would never forget what she'd told him only a few days before she died.

"Love, true love, fills the heart so completely that there is no room left for hate or greed. I thought I was enough for your father, but I wasn't..."

Brock didn't believe he could ever love someone that much—not because he didn't want to but because his heart had been hardened by hate and anger. It was weighed down with stones of the past. There was a darkness inside him, one that he could not banish. A man like him could never be filled with love and nothing else.

Because if he did love fully and all-consuming, whoever held his heart would make him pay dearly for it. She would crush him the way his mother had been crushed. His spirit would be broken and his will to live destroyed when he would not be loved back. Joanna was a danger to him, and she didn't even know it. She could leave Scotland, return to her family and friends in London, and leave his castle empty and his heart in pieces on the floor. No...if they married, he would have her heart and body, and she would have his body and affection, but no love. It was too dangerous.

"I won't marry you." Her soft reply stung worse than any blade sinking into his chest. He hadn't expected her to reject him.

He had been listening tonight at the assembly hall, had heard the mocking whispers that she would never find a husband, that something was wrong with her.

There was *nothing* wrong with Joanna. What was wrong was that the damned *Sassenachs* thought their women should be meek as lambs and silly as geese. Sweet Joanna was fierce, intelligent, and had her own mind, and those bloody English fools knew it.

"I'll ask you again after the wedding," he said as the coach stopped at Lord Lennox's residence.

She frowned, and the furrow between her brows made her look adorable. "I won't change my answer."

He smiled. "You might. A man can hope." He opened

the coach door and assisted her down, holding her close as he set her on her feet. She stared up at him, her blue eyes like dark pools beneath the muted light of the streetlamps. A loose curl of pale-blonde hair brushed the tops of her breasts, and he slowly stroked her silken strands back with his fingers. Her breasts rose in response as she took in a sharp breath.

"Sleep well, fair Joanna, and dream of me tonight."

She scowled. "I most certainly will not."

He cupped her chin, tilted her head back, and feathered a lingering kiss on her lips before he stepped back and climbed into the coach. "Aye, you will."

She would change her mind. Brock had two days to convince her that marrying him was something she wanted. He would be a good and loyal husband, and he would see her well cared for and well satisfied, in bed and out.

So long as I can keep her safe from my family's past.

He hadn't forgotten what Rosalind had shared with him. Their father, Montgomery Kincade, had betrayed his fellow Scotsmen by helping an English spy assassinate the leaders of a rebellion more than twenty years before. That spy was still alive, and Brock's father had threatened him with proof of their dealings being made public before he died. Rosalind had found that proof and had given it to Ashton to use against their sworn enemy. Instead, Ashton had chosen to burn it to protect her.

Brock didn't believe that was enough. He didn't trust the English, and he fully believed that the Kincade family and anyone they cared about would be in grave danger if the truth about their father ever came to light. He had to find a way to protect his family and his future bride from the bloody hands reaching through the mists of time, hoping to drag him down into darkness. But how could he stop a powerful English spy or his own countrymen if they cried out for vengeance?

I am not my father. I will not hurt Joanna. I will protect her with everything that I have.

EDMUND LINDSEY HELD THE GLASS OF RATAFIA, frowning as he searched for any sign of Joanna Lennox in the ballroom. He'd gotten used to finding her quickly in a crowd over the last few months. She was taller than most ladies, and her pale-blonde hair was like a shining beacon beneath the chandeliers.

"Lindsey, you continue to disappoint me," a cold voice said from behind him. Edmund spun to face a handsome aristocrat with dark hair and even darker eyes. The man had appeared from a shadowed corner of the ballroom, unseen by the nearby guests. Edmund glanced about, expecting to spot a door or some pathway to explain the man's sudden appearance, but there was no such place from which he could have emerged. It reminded him of just how skilled the man was and that he was not to be trifled with.

"Sir Hugo." He bowed his head at the man who had been sending him his orders for the last three months. Those orders had been clear—that he must seduce and marry Joanna Lennox. How he had found himself in that position was a matter he preferred not to dwell upon.

"I did not spend my time and resources trying to convince the eligible bachelors in the country to avoid Miss Lennox just so you could somehow drive her off."

Edmund tried to puff up his chest, taking some professional pride in his abilities. "I am on the verge of winning her over. In fact, I was about to ask her for a moment alone so I might confess to some of our shared interests—the ones you so kindly provided."

"That will be difficult, seeing as she is no longer here. She fled with that Scottish brute, Kincade. It's been three months. I was informed you had ways of winning women over, but it appears those rumors are simply that—rumors."

The verbal slight didn't go unmissed. Edmund would have thrown the ratafia in any other man's face, but not Hugo Waverly. Waverly held power far beyond what his title would suggest. If it hadn't been for the excellent funding he had received from the man, Edmund would never have taken this task on.

"Perhaps I should have picked a more aggressive man to woo her," Hugo said, then looked Edmund up and down. “Taller as well. But I thought by now she would be more desperate. I had dearly hoped to see her shadowed with self-pity as she accepted your proposal. It seems I miscalculated either her desperation or your effectiveness.”

Edmund knew better than to react to such an insult. He knew he was attractive, and while not particularly bulky in muscle, he offered pleasure to any woman in his bed. Plenty of women had learned quickly enough that what he lacked in height he made up for in other ways. Yet Joanna had not even given him the chance to show her his charms. The little chit could barely contain her open dislike of him, and it filled him with a frustration that he barely concealed in his polite manners. Such constant rejection was no good for one’s self-esteem.

“It’s clear she will not choose me,” Edmund confessed. Oddly enough, saying the words out loud came with a strange sort of relief. “Perhaps you ought to bribe the Scot?”

Waverly’s cruel mouth twisted with a venomous smile.

“I’m afraid the Scot is not for sale. But you have given me an excellent idea. I had intended for you to make her miserable as a husband, but perhaps my plans were not ambitious enough. But that man’s father and I have a history. It opens certain...possibilities.”

Edmund repressed another shudder. Now he was grateful for Miss Lennox’s rejections. Hugo’s plan no doubt would have made them both miserable, and money could compensate for only so much in life.

Whatever Waverly was planning, Edmund wanted nothing more to do with it. He preferred staying alive. Waverly had protection from the Crown, it was true, but Edmund had no such luxury. And if someone died from Waverly's games, well, Edmund might be the one to hang for it.

"Should I assume our business is concluded then?" Edmund asked quietly.

Waverly stroked his chin, his black eyes looking at something in the distance that Edmund could not see, and for a moment he feared he might have to repeat his question.

"Yes, I am done with you. My office will tender a final payment in the morning, and I will see no more of you."

Edmund couldn't agree more on the last point. He hastily retreated into the crowds, smiling at his good fortune. Another thousand pounds would be lining his pocket, and all he had done was chase Joanna Lennox into the arms of someone else. Lady Fortune was smiling upon him, at least.

He tried not to think whether or not Fortune would soon frown upon Miss Lennox.

Hugo stood at the edge of the ballroom, lurking in the shadows kindly afforded by an unlit lamp in his corner of the room. He watched the oblivious couples dance. His wife was out there tonight, no doubt dancing with some fool. He didn't care if married ladies weren't supposed to dance except with their husbands. His wife enjoyed dancing, and since he could not give her the time for a dance, not while seeing to his plans, he was content to let her have her amusement wherever she could find it.

A flash of pale-blond hair caught his attention, and he had to keep his heart from racing as he saw Ashton Lennox on the dance floor, his Scottish bride in his arms.

My prey…so close. He had to keep himself from reaching for the small blade he kept on him at all times. The dagger that he dreamed nearly every night of plunging into the hearts of every last member of the League of Rogues.

Only a few days ago they had held the key to destroying him in their hands, and yet they had chosen to burn it. He still could not reason out why. Not that it mattered. He would not stop; he would not show mercy.

I will bring you down, one by one, with a death of a thousand cuts. And one of those cuts will be Joanna Lennox.

All he had to do was let it slip to the right Highland clans that Lord Kincade's father had betrayed his countrymen, and that the Englishman who had helped him was Ashton Lennox. And he knew which clans held their grudges for generations.

They would kill Joanna, Lord Kincade, and likely

Ashton as well. Even if Ashton somehow survived Highland justice, losing his sister would destroy him. The sweet irony would be that Ashton himself had just destroyed the very evidence that might have saved her.

And no one will be the wiser that I played a part in any of it.

It was so easy to be the devil at times—so very easy.

Grab Brock and Joanna's story HERE to see how it ends! For print readers you can order the book wherever you purchase print books.

ACKNOWLEDGMENTS

This series has become one of the most important and satisfying experiences in my life. Sharing the League of Rogues with you, my darling readers, has been wonderful. I cannot thank you enough for following me and those bad boy rogues over the last five years. I wish I could name everyone who's had a hand in making this series what it has become. But if you're reading this, you're one of the people I wish most heartily to thank.

I'd also like to give a shout out to Amanda Pereira, one of my dearest friends who's been an essential member of my team over the years, editing, talking through the stories and being there for me like a sister. She also wrote the Lady Society letter from the Desperate Society Mama at the beginning of this book. I couldn't have done this without her.

I'd also like to thank my editor Noah China who got into the trenches with me on this series and helped me shape it into something amazing that I couldn't have achieved on my own. Jessica Fogleman, my talented copy-editor also deserves my undying gratitude for her ability to navigate the complex world of the League and make these books sparkle. And last, I'd love to thank Samantha Folkner for her final stages beta reading.

Thank you everyone from the bottom of my heart... and don't worry, the League is only just getting starting. The stories are far from over.

ABOUT THE AUTHOR

USA TODAY Bestselling Author Lauren Smith is an Oklahoma attorney by day, who pens adventurous and edgy romance stories by the light of her smart phone flashlight app. She knew she was destined to be a romance writer when she attempted to re-write the entire *Titanic* movie just to save Jack from drowning. Connecting with readers by writing emotionally moving, realistic and sexy romances no matter what time period is her passion. She's won multiple awards in several romance subgenres including: New England Reader's Choice Awards, Greater Detroit BookSeller's Best Awards, and a Semi-Finalist award for the Mary Wollstonecraft Shelley Award.

To connect with Lauren, visit her at:

www.laurensmithbooks.com

lauren@Laurensmithbooks.com

facebook.com/LaurenDianaSmith

twitter.com/LSmithAuthor

instagram.com/LaurenSmithbooks

amazon.com/Lauren-Smith/e/B009L54K-TC/ref=sr_tc_2_0?qid=1384012235&sr=1-2-ent

bookbub.com/authors/lauren-smith

Made in the USA
Coppell, TX
28 July 2023

19705561R00277